A GIRL,
A RACCOON,
and the
MIDNIGHT
MOON

A GIRL,
A RACCOON,
and the
MIDNIGHT
MOON

by

KAREN ROMANO YOUNG
illustrated by JESSIXA BAGLEY

chronicle books · san francisco

To my mother.—K.R.Y.

Library of Congress Cataloging-in-Publication Data available.

ISBN 978-1-4521-6952-1

Manufactured in China.

MIX
Paper from
responsible sources
FSC
www.fsc.org
FSC™ C144853

Design by Kayla Ferriera.
Typeset in Poynter.

10 9 8 7 6 5 4 3 2 1

Chronicle Books LLC
680 Second Street
San Francisco, California 94107

Chronicle Books—we see things differently.
Become part of our community at www.chroniclekids.com.

"'Heaven bless the babe,' they said.
'What queer books she must have read.'"

— "HUMORESQUE"
BY EDNA ST. VINCENT MILLAY[1]

1 From the poem "Humoresque," from *The Harp-Weaver and Other Poems* by Edna St. Vincent Millay (Harper & Brothers, 1923).

PART ONE:
THE TURNING POINT

"Had I known that you were going
I would have given you messages for her. . . ."

— "TO ONE WHO MIGHT HAVE BORNE A MESSAGE"
BY EDNA ST. VINCENT MILLAY [1]

1 From the poem "To One Who Might Have Borne a Message," from *The Harp-Weaver and Other Poems* by Edna St. Vincent Millay (Harper, 1917).

BEFORE THE SCREAM

The scream was so loud it could have been building up for a lifetime.

It had sure been brewing inside Pearl even before she woke that late August morning. It heated up as she and Mom waited for their takeout order at the Cozy Soup and Burger on Seventh Avenue. It bubbled and percolated as they walked the damp early sidewalks to the library, Mom in her heels, Pearl in her black-cloth Chinatown shoes with the buckle straps. Unaware of anything unusual, Pearl climbed the steps and leaned the cardboard tray of coffees on the curve of the wrought-iron banister while Mom found the front-door keys and pushed inside. She held the door for Pearl and they stepped into the foyer.

A cool, dark floor of speckled marble. The waxy smell of old oak. The metallic rhythmic tock of the pendulum in the brass clock on the wall behind the circulation desk. Frosted glass in diamond-shaped panes, soft light from the back hallway that led to the garden.

The library.

Mom stepped into the shadows of the stairwell and called up toward the roof. "Anybody home?"

"Hiya!" came a distant yodeling voice. Bruce Chambers, the library manager, was already up there in his office, toiling over the proposals he was making to the library board. Proposals to fix things up, bring patrons in, make ends meet, and keep the library from looking too worn out compared to the new Knickerbocker branch. Bruce knew his branch's days were numbered.

Pearl went to check the book drop, pulling the cart from under the slot. Only six books had been returned in the night. Not surprising, since not that many books went out in a day.

Pearl carried Bruce's coffee and cinnamon-swirl doughnut to him. Up the spiral stairs, past the children's room on the second floor, to the third floor and into Bruce's rat's nest of an office.

It was a tall rat's nest. The third-floor ceiling of the library was extra high, with edges that Ramón, the reference librarian, said were called dental molding because they looked like square white teeth nibbling at the tasty edges of the walls. The piles of books, papers, magazines, newspapers, journals, catalogs, and mail may as well have been the recycling heaps outside the newsstand on the corner. The highest cabinets towered higher because of the things stored on top: an empty birdcage, rolls and rolls of posters from book conferences, old stacked-up coffee cups, and—most impressive of all—the head of the Ranger Rick raccoon costume that Bruce had brought from Catskills National Park five years ago when Pearl was five, when he'd quit being a park manager and come to manage the library instead. Made of chicken wire and fleece and fake fur, Ranger Rick's head stood propped eyeless and eerie over an old metal garbage can turned upside down. Below the head, the gray fleece body hung from a cabinet door on a massive hanger, and was still long enough to wrinkle on the floor.

In the middle of all this, behind a cluttered desk, was Bruce himself. Dark brown skin, with black hair like a wire brush, big glasses, and tall enough to reach the top of the tallest pile atop the cabinet. He called himself inwardly organized, since he could always find what he was looking for in his rat's nest. Pearl called him outwardly a disaster because, well, what a mess.

She stepped through—never on—all the junk he said he was going to need "someday," placed the coffee in his hands, and wended her way to the window.

"Aren't you going to sing out with me?" Pearl said, dodging a box of discarded catalog cards.

Last year Mom had said the office smelled like a rat's nest as well as looked like one. "Once a day," she had insisted, "just once, open the window for ten seconds."

Bruce had opened the window and sung out, "*Ah, sweet mystery of life, at last I've found you!*"

"You're an idiot," Mom had said happily, squeezing his arm.

"Try it, it's great," Bruce had said to her and Pearl. The three of them had done it together, just that once. "*Ah, sweet mystery of life, at last I've found you!*" Their voices swept out over the garden, over the head of the statue down there, over the flowers at her feet, into the tall pine trees where birds and bats nested and raccoons nestled.

Pearl fell in love with the echo of their voices off the buildings. Since then, it had become part of her and Bruce's morning routine. But now he didn't pay any attention to her. He just waved his hand rapidly, distractedly, toward the window and bent his head over the papers.

So Pearl cleared her throat, looked down into the garden, and opened her mouth to sing out to the world. But when she saw what was down there, she screamed.

There had never been anything like Pearl's scream.

The scream had horror in it. It had shock. It had fear. And it had loss.

What was lost?

A head. A stone head. The stone head of the stone statue that stood in the library garden.

It was a statue of Edna St. Vincent Millay, Vincent for short (as she had referred to herself), the famous poet who used to live right around here.

Who lost her? The whole city, actually. The taxpayers of New York. They were to whom the statue belonged.

But most of all, the library had lost her. The whole library, but most of all, the Lancaster Avenue branch. The Lancaster Avenue branch, but most of all, almost-eleven-year-old Pearl Moran. That's who loved her the most.

1: THE SCREAM

Pearl's scream blasted from the third-story window at the rear of the Lancaster Avenue branch of the New York City Library and carried out over the late-summer air, over the yew hedge, up the rear wall of the white-brick apartment house that backed up to the garden, through the trash-can alley, across Clancy Street, and on.

It was a noisy neighborhood in the first place, a city neighborhood on the edge of things, with lots of people in it—people who sometimes screamed.

Babies screamed for the usual reasons.

Little kids screamed for the Mister Softee truck or if one of the big kids was pretending to be a coyote or a robber or something else scary.

Adults screamed sometimes, over a big game, or in frustration with the kids or the job or the language or just the city.

The city was enough to make anyone scream.

But among all these screams, Pearl's scream stood out. It made people stop what they were doing—picking up groceries at violet-haired Rosita's Rosebud bodega, browsing in Gully's Buck-a-Buy. Even Mr. Gulliver, Gully himself, paused, right as he was ringing up the two dozen animal-shaped erasers that Alice Patel was buying for story hour in the library's children's room. Alice was the children's librarian, six months pregnant. "That's Pearl!"

said Alice. She grabbed the erasers and ran, her sneakers pounding across Lancaster Avenue.

One girl, stuck alone in her granny's apartment above the Buck-a-Buy, hung out the window so far her black braids brushed the top of Gully's sign, but she couldn't see who was screaming. She broke her granny's rules and ran out of the apartment.

People in the shops, at Tallulah's newsstand, in the apartments on either side of the library and all along Lancaster Avenue, looked out their windows, but they couldn't see what was causing the scream. For the first time for most of them, they beelined for the library—and barged inside.

(Of course nobody knew I was there, hidden in the yew bushes.)

In his third-floor office, Bruce leaped out of his chair, grabbed Pearl by the shoulders, and looked hard into her face. "What is it? What's got you? Where does it hurt?"

Pearl didn't have any wind left. She just pointed.

"What's wrong with Pearl?" Alice came tearing up the stairs, her sari held up to her knees to give her speed, Mom hasty and loud in her high heels.

"What is it?" cried Mom.

A Sidebar About Sidebars

Say you're watching a play and the characters are all talking to each other and suddenly one turns and says something to the audience like "Watch this!" or "But he was wrong." That's an aside.

Or, say someone's telling a story and they pause the action for a second and say, "If she had only known then what she found out later." That's another example of an aside.

But in writing, how do you do an aside? Well, in parentheses, of course. (Here is a third example of an aside.)

When you put an aside on the side like this, then you call it a sidebar.

Sidebars have bylines, a line that tells you who wrote them, just like any written piece in a newspaper, magazine, or book. This one was written by

—M.A.M.

Bruce held up his hands to calm them both. "It's not Pearl. It's Vincent." He pulled Pearl back from the high narrow window so they could look out.

In the garden, the statue stood headless in the morning light.

Mom closed her eyes and sighed when she saw. "Oh, rats. Oh, Pearl," she said. "What'll we do?"

Alice thumped her fist on the windowsill so hard the glass in the panes rattled. "Those idiots!"

"Who?" said Pearl. "Who do you mean? Should we go after them?" She stood with her feet wide, fists clenched, eyes fierce, hair wild, ready for battle.

Bruce held up his hand. "It's too late now!" Then he led the mad dash back down the stairs: All of them charged down the one narrow staircase from the third floor to the second, then Mom and Alice ran down the straight back stairs and Bruce and Pearl ran down the spiral stairs to the first floor, where they were met with the entire neighborhood.

"What's wrong?" yelled Gully.

"Who's screaming?" asked Tallulah, the shuffling, stripey-haired, bright-eyed woman who ran the newsstand.

"What's going on?" asked all the neighborhood people.

"It was me," said Pearl fiercely. "Our statue's head is gone. And I'd like to know why!" She glared around with squinting eyes, suspecting them all.

2: BEHEADED

STILL AUG 28

"This way, everyone," said Mom, beckoning the crowd of curious neighbors to the garden. Pearl trailed behind, one hand on the doorframe, the other on her stomach, furious and sick. What did everybody need to come here for now, when things were bad? They didn't come when things were good.

Vincent's head was completely gone. Where it had previously been anchored, now there was nothing but a metal spindle coming out of her stone neck. Her stone body looked solemn, shortened, sad. Now her outstretched hand, usually generous or hopeful, seemed truly empty, raised palm up, as if to say, "Give it back!"

Pearl hung behind. She thought maybe she was going to throw up.

The cops pulled in, swirling their lights, their siren making hearts jump all over Lancaster Avenue, bringing more people running—including Simon Lo, the library page, showing up late to his job shelving and straightening the library's 41,134 books, sweating, swearing, his black hair in a ponytail, dismounting his bicycle elegantly. "What're the cops doing here?"

The girl who lived across the street over Gully's turned with a flounce of her sparkly, ruffled shirt and a flop of her braids, and answered. She knew who Simon was from watching him out the window of her apartment. "That library girl's gone insane," she said.

"What'd she do this time?" Simon pushed his way through the people to where Pearl stood beside the statue pedestal, shaking with fury, a hand protectively pressing Vincent's foot. He put his hand on Pearl's shoulder to get her attention. "What's going on, Pearlie?"

Pearl's eyes flashed hot at Simon. "Vincent's head," she said. He hadn't even seen!

He glanced up and gasped, then hooked his arm around Pearl's shoulders. Pearl loved him for it; even Mom hadn't thought to hug her. The tears that had been welling in her eyes started coming down her cheeks. "Why would someone hurt Vincent?"

Simon said softly, "It didn't hurt."

"Punks!" said Gully. "Teenagers! College students!" He always thought anyone under twenty was trying to steal from him.

"Who says?" said Pearl.

"You can't go accusing people just for being a certain age," said Ramón.

But the police seemed to accept Gully's suggestion just fine. "It's bound to be pranksters," one of them said.

What a disappointment the police were! Their main contribution was to stand around looking at the statue and shaking their heads, as if they didn't know where to begin. Pearl could tell they were already thinking, "Case closed," and she had to speak up.

"What makes you think it was more than one person?" she demanded of the three cops—a tall lady with dark curls, a big pink young one, and an older black man with a mustache. They looked at her like she was just a kid and didn't answer.

"Just think of it, Pearl," said Simon. "You'd have to climb up and take the head off that pole on her neck."

"That would take a lot of muscle," said Alice, who was pretty athletic herself.

"It looks like someone had trouble doing that very thing," said the mustached cop. He led the way to the side of Vincent's pedestal and pointed out a deep scrape in the polished stone.

"And here!" said the girl with the braids. There was a chip in one fold of Vincent's long skirt.

"And see here," said Pearl, glaring at the girl—who was *she*?—and not wanting to be outdone by some new kid. This was Pearl's library! She pointed out a sloping rectangular imprint in the soft sand between the paving stones.

"That's from the ladder," said Simon. The ladder always stood leaning against the back library wall, where the window-washer left it. Pearl walked over to look. In the sandy soil at the base of the wall, she saw a few small footprints, as if a miniature human with long hobbit[1] toenails had been here.

"So somebody grabbed your ladder and used it to get the head," the policewoman said. "Then they must have put it in a car and driven away. How heavy a piece of stone was it?"

"Piece of stone!" said Pearl indignantly.

Behind the yew bushes, on the far side of the dumpster, a silent, stealthy intruder pricked up his ears at the mention of stone.

"What makes you think there was a car?" Mom asked the cops. "Why not just that wheelbarrow?" The lawn-mowing men kept the yellow wheelbarrow against the wall beside the ladder.

"How could you wheel a head away without anyone seeing?" asked Pearl.

---

1 *The Hobbit* by J.R.R. Tolkien (George Allen & Unwin, 1937). Features hobbits, humanoid creatures that always go barefoot.

The police exchanged a glance and couldn't help smirking. "Head'll end up somewhere funny," the mustached man said.

"Somewhere *funny?*" Pearl burst out. She stood between them and what was left of Vincent, arms crossed over her middle.

Bruce said, "Steady, Pearl."

"She's right! It's not funny. *I* think it's scary," announced the girl from across the street. Pearl stared at her. *Why does she think anyone cares what she thinks? (Wish I had long braids like that.)* But also, Pearl was a little scared herself.

Mom stepped forward, too. "What exactly do you mean by *funny?*" Pearl knew that tone of voice and the judgment it carried; Mom might as well have been talking to someone about incurring fines.

"I just mean . . . amusing," said the mustached policeman, with a guilty little shrug. "Like, maybe the head is tucked in with the pineapples in the greenmarket."

"Or on the pitcher's mound at Yankee Stadium," said the pink one.

"Oh, I get it," snapped Pearl. "Somewhere *funny* like that!"

The cops smiled because Pearl was a bratty kid. But just a kid. "We'll do

A Sidebar About Police

When it comes to crime, police have to set priorities about what gets their attention.

Priority goes to the crime that has the biggest impact—that has the most rich or famous people, that causes the most trouble, that sets records for blood or drama.

What doesn't get priority?

Holdups at doughnut shops.

Someone's radio getting stolen.

Wild animals getting into the garbage.

Stolen heads of statues in the back gardens of old libraries that nobody visits.

But the police aren't the only ones setting priorities. People looking for stories find the kind they're looking for more easily than the kind they never considered. But some of the best stories come as surprises.

—M.A.M.

what we can," they told Mom and Bruce, and they finally got professional on their way to the police cars and examined the driveway for tire tracks, but found none except the ones from Ramón's pickup. "Think he's got a head in the back?" the pink policeman joked.

Pearl said, "Ramón wouldn't take the head! He's from the *library*."

"Just a joke, young lady," the mustached policeman said.

"Not funny," Bruce said, so Pearl didn't have to. Bruce waved the police officers away. "Keep us informed," he said to them, but it was plain that the library was on its own with its vandalism problem.

3: AFTER THE SCREAM

Mr. Gulliver was the last one to leave the garden, chuckling to himself in a not-nice way. He was a graying, balding, skinny man who always seemed to be wearing brown (even though, as Simon said, his favorite color had to be green, for money), and his expression at the moment was half laughing at someone, and half smelling something stinky.

"What's so funny, Gully?" asked Mom.

Gully laughed as if anything could happen now. "That head being stolen is probably just the start," he said.

"The start of what?" asked Pearl.

"The start of the end," said Gully, loving the attention.

"The end of *what*?"

"This business." He waved his hand toward the library. "If you can call it that."

Mom got a steely grip on Pearl's elbow. "Thank you, Mr. Gulliver," Mom said, and pushed Pearl toward Bruce to make sure she didn't say anything else. Over her shoulder, Pearl watched Gully scuttle across the street.

Pearl would have liked Gully's Buck-a-Buy if it wasn't for Gully. The store was big and bright and tacky and grungy, one of those stores that had everything cheap and junky, from pencils to hair curlers. It was a good place if you only had a buck and wanted something for it, so Gully did a decent business—but not decent enough to suit him. In Gully's opinion, a library did not attract spenders. And Gully wanted only shoppers parading up and down the street, not people who liked free books. He thought he knew what was good for America, for New York City, for Lancaster Avenue, and, apparently, for Pearl.

Bruce was staring at the statue as though it really was the end of the library, to have such a landmark vandalized. He seemed frozen until he reached for Pearl's hand. "There's more to the library than—" he began. He trailed off. "The garden's what I've always loved about this place," he said. "Other branches don't have this kind of space, this kind of artwork, and trees that shield it from observers with criminal intent. And maybe it's better if they don't. But maybe—"

"Maybe the garden came with the building!" said Mom. "Maybe the statue came with the garden! And maybe it's up to us to preserve it!" Mom was red-hot with action. "Have the newspapers been called, Bruce?"

Bruce stared at her. "No, Patricia," he said. "That actually wasn't the first thing I did when I saw we had been victimized by vandals."

Mom strode off through the back hall, her phone already to her ear. "Yes, this is Mrs. Patricia Moran, of the Lancaster Avenue branch library. I'm calling to inform you that our landmark statue of the New York poet Edna St. Vincent Millay has been vandalized. I think the *Moon* should cover the story. Yes . . . Lancaster Avenue. Yes, I'll hold."

Bruce followed her. "Trish, why do you want *them* to know?"

"Don't we get enough bad press on Lancaster Avenue?" asked Alice, coming along.

"Too true," said Bruce. "No doubt they'll write about how the library can't protect its own property, falling apart at the seams, bleeding money."

"It is not!" said Pearl, feeling more hopeful than certain. She didn't know what to make of the idea of "bad press" or the fact that Bruce and Alice seemed sure the library would get it.

"It is, though," Simon said gently. "We don't even have a gate."

Bruce tapped his fingers against his lower lip. "It *could* mean attention. Funding for better security. I'll send another email about our budget to the board. Or maybe the mayor."

"The mayor, who's never even been here?" Pearl added. She felt bad news sinking into her heart. "The mayor, who only goes to *new* libraries?" Her Honor the mayor had cut the ribbon at the opening of the new Knickerbocker branch.

"Vandalism is just going to expose us as being undervalued by the neighborhood," said Ramón.

"The mayor already knows the library is old. We don't want her to think it's risky to operate, too," said Alice.

"Old is historic," Pearl insisted. "Not risky."

"It's both," said Bruce. "So why would we want to tell the newspaper?"

Mom ignored them all: Someone at the paper had finally picked her call back up. "Yes, I'm calling to report a crime against the city," she said into the phone. "This is Mrs. Patricia Moran from the historic branch library in the old Lancaster mansion on Lancaster Avenue—with the statue of the beloved New York poet Edna St. Vincent Millay—whose head has disappeared in the night! No leads at all yet, but . . . fine!" She hung up with an expression of mixed surprise and satisfaction. "They're sending a reporter."

"Swell," said Bruce unenthusiastically.

"Wait and see," said Ramón soothingly.

The girl with the braids was still standing in the circulation area. As if she had any business poking her nose in! The girl gave a loud sniff, and that drew tenderhearted Alice's attention. Alice always reached out to any kid, even ones she'd never seen. "What's your name?"

"Francine," the girl said. "I live across the street."

"Well, I'm sure we'll find our Vincent, Francine," Alice said.

To get the attention back, Pearl said, "You're such an optimist, Alice." It was what Mom always said to Bruce when she hoped to console him, in her good moments, when she gave him a glass of wine and a kiss on the top of his head, when he came over after the library closed. Unlike the times, more frequent lately, when she'd told him his management skills needed improvement or he was going to get himself fired, and didn't ask him over after work.

Alice took Pearl's hand. "We have to try." Pearl let go of Alice's hand because Francine was watching. But then Alice asked Francine, "Coming to story hour?" and gave Pearl one of her invisible nudges, and together they went up to the children's room.

In summer Pearl always listened to Alice's story hour every morning, hanging around the edges because it was actually for little kids. Francine eyed Pearl, who stood by the window, and plopped down in a beanbag chair so she could see the pictures. The book today was *Mike Mulligan and His Steam Shovel*,[1] which ought to have been popular enough in their neighborhood, where so much was being demolished and other stuff being built. But only four little kids came, all with one mom.

On the first page of the story, Francine leaned toward Pearl and said, "A steam shovel named Mary Ann?" (As if there was something wrong with the name Mary Ann!) Then, "This is for babies." Pearl stood there steaming as much as the shovel. Picture books were for anybody! When Francine said, "Dig a

....

[1] *Mike Mulligan and His Steam Shovel* by Virginia Lee Burton (Riverside Press, 1939).

basement in just one day? That's unrealistic!" Pearl stomped out. She ignored the sad face Alice made at her. Let Francine sit there and challenge the best book ever! So much for new visitors.

Pearl went downstairs. There was more traffic in the library than usual, people traipsing through the building to get to the garden to see Vincent's sad statue with their own eyes. Pearl saw them pass and tried to pretend they didn't exist. She kept her head down and scooted into the reference room, where she tucked herself into her own personal nook, on the floor beside the globe and the shelf of atlases, which shielded her from the room. Mr. Nichols, a homeless man, not scared like lots, not scary like some, with graying brown curly hair and glasses, who came there nearly every day, sat in the chair beside the atlas shelf with the newspaper up in front of his face, eyes shut. He did this often, and Pearl knew that when he began snoring, she should jiggle his sleeve gently—not enough to wake him, but enough to make him quit snoring, because if he snored, Ramón would

A story should start at the turning point, the moment when everything changes. A scream is as good a change as any, if it means something new happens. The reason for the change can come after and add a little to the mystery, simply by being late.

Also, just because the scream changes things, that doesn't mean it's a straight path after that. There might be another big change, another turn in the road, maybe a turn that comes right after another scream. Wait and see.

—M.A.M.

have to come bump the table nearby to wake him. You weren't allowed to sleep in the library.

Pearl realized Mr. Nichols must have slept through her scream and all that came after it. He alone did not know what had happened to the library. She crept away quietly. She didn't want to have to tell anyone. That would make the theft seem more real.

Sometimes in this neighborhood, there were burglaries. Robbers got in through the windows, down from the roof, up from the fire escape, and made off with computers and TVs and phones and anything else good. You couldn't expect to ever see your stuff again. Someone had broken into Ramón's apartment at the beginning of the summer and taken his Bose sound system with the wireless headphones, and his microwave. "I don't miss the microwave much, but boy, do I miss that Bose." He was saving up for another one. What had bothered Ramón most, even more than the Bose, was the idea that somebody with criminal tendencies had been in his home. And now someone with criminal tendencies had been in the library garden.

Well, if the police weren't going to take the crime seriously, someone was going to have to, thought Pearl, even if the prospect of confronting a criminal made her stomach curl.

She wished she could be in some other situation than this. But where else would she, could she be? The library was Pearl's home.

Almost eleven years ago, she had been born here, right here, in the Lancaster Avenue branch of the New York City Library, and she had been here practically every day since.

Pearl's mother, Patricia Moran, the circulation librarian, told Pearl the true story of how she was born in the calm, book-lined, window-bright Memorial Room, coming too fast for Mom to make it to the hospital. Mom shook her finger at Pearl when she told this part, meaning: *Always in such a hurry!*

Pearl had the same light brown skin as her long-gone father (Mr. Michael Moran, whom she'd never met) and Mom's green eyes and fluffy hair (though Pearl's was brown, not red like Mom's), but mostly she was her own self. For the first few months of her life, Pearl lived in a basket that Mom carried every morning from the apartment around the corner on Beep Street. A pillow cushioned Pearl's head, and a quilt made by the old library director, Mrs. Abramo, kept her cozy. Mom tucked library books around Pearl, to transport them.

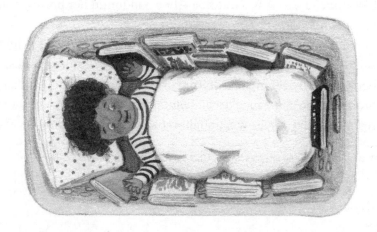

Now Pearl slept in a pull-out chair-bed with Frances the stuffed badger[2] on her pillow, Strega Nona the witch doll under her arm,[3] and a poster of the boy from the book *In the Night Kitchen*[4] on the wall. The boy, Mickey, visits a giant bakery and falls into a bottle of milk. He drinks some, then says, "I'm in the milk and the milk's in me!"

But even their cozy apartment wasn't home, it was just a place to sleep. It was just the place where Pearl and her mother went at night. Home was—would always be—the narrow, tall, three-story brick building with 41,134 books, a book elevator, two straight staircases, and one spiral staircase. It had a display case full of old-time photographs of the city, some slow computers, a giant papier-mâché giraffe made out of a folding ladder, and in the back garden, under some of the rarest pines in New York, the statue of Edna St. Vincent Millay.

Pearl felt like Mickey in the milk: She was in the books and the books were in her. The library was home, and the staff was her family.

Alice always said Pearl was born with her nose in a book. Alice had just graduated from library school when Pearl was born. Now she was the children's librarian, and had been here long enough to watch some of her first regulars bring their own kids. Since Pearl was a toddler, Alice had found her books, read to her, and helped her to read on her own.

Simon Lo, the teenage page who came when Pearl was eight, said Pearl was a bookworm that had turned into a real girl, a book butterfly. Simon had started as a volunteer when he was 13, brought moo shu pancakes and fantail shrimp from his mother's restaurant in Chinatown, bought mozzarella veggie burgers and

----

2 A character in the Frances books, starting with *Bedtime for Frances* by Russell Hoban (Harper, 1960).

3 *Strega Nona* by Tomie DePaola (Simon & Schuster, 1975).

4 *In the Night Kitchen* by Maurice Sendak (Harper & Row, 1970).

Funny Bones from the Cozy Soup and Burger, and made grilled marshmallow and peanut butter sandwiches in the toaster oven in the staff room. Pearl had never not loved Simon Lo.

Ramón Cisneros, the reference librarian, had run up both flights of stairs to bring the paramedics, who told Mom what she could already see for herself: Pearl was quick, she was healthy, and she was loud. As the reference librarian, the smartest, oldest person in the place, Ramón helped her with her homework, improved her vocabulary, and showed her old *Top Cat* cartoons on the computer—a show about a gang of ragtag city kitties. Ramón looked like a rumpled owl awake in the daytime—short and strong with black-and-gray hair like feathers.

Bruce, who had never wanted to run a library and prided himself on his management skills (despite what Mom said), not his literary ones, had started Pearl on reading reviews of children's books when she was eight. While they still had a budget to build the book collection, she'd put a check mark in the catalog next to the books she thought they should request. When the books came, Pearl got to read them first.

And Mr. Nichols, who had arrived one day last spring— "from all around," he'd said; Bruce had said, "He's some kind of professional, look at his hands"—and who spent the day behind the atlas shelf in the reference room—Mr. Nichols listened to Pearl. "I'm all ears," he'd say. He listened to every word, held the books by the edges respectfully, reading a paragraph she pointed out here and there, and tucking books she was midway through in her nook's secret hiding place under the *Historical Atlas of New York State*.[5] He never told any stories of his own, but he was happy to listen to Pearl's.

....

5 *Historical Atlas of New York State* by William P. Munger (Frank E. Richards, 1941). It's rare and out of print, like lots of wonderful books in our nation's libraries.

All these people watched over Pearl, and if anyone asked what a kid was doing behind the official-looking circulation counter or in the staff-only area along the roped-off mezzanine of the elegant reading room, one of them would answer, "That's Pearl. She's the librarian's child."

People would say, all jokey, "The librarian's child? Bet she never makes a peep!"

Bruce said drily, "Not exactly."

"Paradoxically, no," said Ramón.

"Kind of the opposite," Alice would say with a grin.

"Yeah, right," Simon said.

Mr. Nichols, if anyone ever asked him, would simply answer that Pearl had plenty to say.

Pearl's mother made up a poem about her, starting with an old rhyme:

> The shoemaker's child goes barefoot,
> The toymaker's child has no toys,
> The dentist's child has loose teeth,
> And the librarian's child makes noise.[6]

"*I do NOT,*" said Pearl in protest.

Yet Mom's poem was true enough. If someone was making a noise, it was usually Pearl. She was the one running down the steps in her flip-flops, singing in the book elevator (where grown-ups didn't fit), making squeakers with her sneakers on the wet marble floor. It was Pearl who kept spinning the summer reading roulette wheel in the children's room until Alice told her to quit. She'd play "Chopsticks"[7] on the piano in the Memorial

---

6 Lesley Keogh, then of Bethel Public Library, now of Wilton Public Library (both in Connecticut), long ago altered this old rhyme to fit her son Jack.

7 "Chopsticks" was originally named "The Celebrated Chop Waltz" by Euphemia Allen under the pseudonym Arthur de Lulli, 1877.

Room until Simon closed the lid. And once a day she'd open the window to air out Bruce's rat's nest of an office on the third floor and sing out to the stone statue in the garden:

"Ah, sweet mystery of life . . ."[8]

or

"Zip-a-dee-doo-dah! Zip-a-dee-ay . . ."[9]

or

"Hey, now! You're an all-star!"[10]

or some other song.

The last loud song—ever?—had been a scream.

And now Vincent was gone, or the most important part of her was. Pearl thought about all the mystery stories she'd ever read, and how the characters solving the mysteries had sat down and figured out all the clues they had. She guessed that was Job One.

8 "Ah, Sweet Mystery of Life" by Victor Herbert, lyrics by Rida Johnson Young, from *Naughty Marietta*, first performed in 1910.

9 "Zip-a-Dee-Doo-Dah" by Allie Wrubel, lyrics by Ray Gilbert, for the 1946 Disney movie *Song of the South*.

10 "All Star" by Smash Mouth, 1999, from the album *Astro Lounge*.

4: A VISIT FROM THE *MOON*

On the day after Vincent lost her head, Mom gave Pearl an assignment. "I ought to know this by heart," she said to Pearl as they waited to pick up the morning coffee at Cozy Soup and Burger. "But I'm going to need a refresher if I'm going to talk to the press."

"Refresher on what?"

"Vincent," said Mom. "I was wondering if you could gather up some stuff about her life. You've read it all more recently than I have. Make me some notes?"

"Why do you need *that*?"

"A reporter's coming. Don't you see, Pearl—maybe if the word gets out about the statue, if there's a story in the paper, if Vincent had a life that was . . . *meaningful* to us, our city, our library, in some way, some way that connects with people, let's hear it. Then someone'll see that head somewhere and get it back to us. We can't do very well without it."

"All it's doing now is making more people come to the library to see a headless statue," Pearl said darkly.

Mom just looked at her a second, then said, "Come to see a statue, stay to read a book?"

Pearl snorted, but Mom pointed to the stairs and tried again. "Listen, maybe they come for the crime, but they stay for Vincent. If she brings people to the library—one way or another—won't that reverse the bad luck of her head going missing? And isn't that worth a little bad press?"

(They say there's no such thing as bad press. Debatable.)

So here Pearl was, up in the mezzanine above the circulation desk, running her fingers over the titles of nonfiction books in the 800s—books with plays, songs, and poetry, according to the Dewey Decimal System, which told you, with a numbered code, where to shelve every nonfiction, factual book, and had categories as tiny and specific as soup or hedgehogs or bass guitars[1]—to find books about Vincent. Not just Pearl's favorites. She even brought down the thin book called *The Princess Marries the Page*,[2] a somewhat sappy play Vincent had written about a girl with braids like Francine's and some silly royal page boy. Pearl carried the stack down to her mother.

Mom stood at a file cabinet in the reference room, researching the statue in the library files. "I'm looking for how Vincent came to this building," she said. She sat down with Pearl and showed her what she'd found—the faded copies of three newspaper stories from the long-ago days when the statue had been sculpted and then signed over to the library. There were photographs that showed the library back then, when it had been the Lancaster family home.

"What should I work on?" Pearl asked.

"Find me the basic facts of her life," said Mom. Ramón pushed the box of old catalog cards and a little pencil toward Pearl, and she took them to her nook along with the books,

---

1 Soup—641.813 if it's not specifically vegetarian, 641.5636 if it is; hedgehogs—599.33; bass guitars—787.87193.

2 *The Princess Marries the Page: A Play in One Act* by Edna St. Vincent Millay (Harper & Brothers, 1932).

A Sidebar About Statues

Before you go thinking Pearl was crazy for screaming about Vincent's head being stolen, just hang on a minute there. Imagine you are making a statue of someone you love or admire because that someone is going to be gone sometime, and the someone is so loved that you want them never to be forgotten. If you are a realistic sculptor, not the kind who makes stuff out of other people's trash like Francine's granny, but the kind who uses stone and a chisel to show what somebody was like in their actual life, then the statue left behind should make people wonder. Because things that make you wonder sometimes make you love them.

Here came Vincent, striding along in stone, her book and pen in her hand, dreaming up stories and poems. Whatever else she did in her life, there was a statue of her that showed she was a writer.

to take notes on. She found Edna St. Vincent Millay's birth and death dates, the names of her parents and siblings, and some of her most famous works. She tried to stick to the facts, but she got caught up in the tale of Vincent's life—especially her early days in hardscrabble coastal Maine, struggling for survival and trying to make art. *Just like Jo March, that girl in Little Women,[3]* thought Pearl.

When she had delivered her notes to Mom, she went to the garden to look at poor, headless Vincent.

What was the statue of Vincent *doing,* with her hand outstretched, her expression utterly calm? It was a question of much debate. Mom always said Vincent was waiting for an idea for a new poem to drop into her hand. Bruce said she was checking for rain. Pearl had seen a baby raccoon, a kit from the nest in the pine, sit on Vincent's stone palm to eat a peanut-butter-sandwich cracker Pearl had lodged there. The raccoon knew what Pearl knew: that Vincent remembered everyone who'd ever come to the library, even the raccoons in the trees. Pearl was convinced.

....

3 *Little Women* by Louisa May Alcott (Roberts Brothers, 1868).

Later that day, she told Mr. Nichols all about Vincent's life. "Peculiar," he said, the way he always did. "But what really changes, now that she's lost her head?" Nichols asked.

Now Vincent seemed to Pearl more like a real person, someone who had been robbed of her dignity. "Nothing will change," she said stoutly. But it already had, a little.

Nichols didn't say anything. He held the evening *New York Moon*[4] newspaper closer to his face.

"You need better glasses, Mr. Nichols," Pearl told him for the hundredth time. But, with his distance vision, Nichols had glimpsed someone arriving, and unfolded the newspaper to hide behind it.

Brisk footsteps came up the stairs from the street into the foyer. The double foyer doors burst open, someone making an entrance like in old Western movies. A thin young man in a slate-gray button-down shirt, wire-framed glasses, ironed jeans, and ready-for-anything hiking boots walked quickly over and stuck his hand out toward Mom, on her stool behind the circulation counter.

What's more, Vincent used to live here, right here where Pearl lived now, back when the library was shining and well-kept and full of readers, full of people who loved her. Because why would there be a statue of Vincent unless she had lots of friends who loved her? And that—the love of friends—was part of Pearl's dream, too. The most secret part.

And now somebody had made off with Vincent's head. It was enough to make any of us weep. So chew on that thought before you judge.

—M.A.M.

---

4 A made-up newspaper.

"Jonathan Yoiks!" he said. "From the *Moon.*"

"Yikes?" whispered Pearl.

Nichols tilted the paper toward Pearl, adjusted his glasses, and said, "Yoiks, not yikes. Looks like a go-getter." He pointed to the byline on a *Moon* story about the city budget. "I'll bet this library looks like small potatoes to him." Nichols read all the papers every day: the *Moon,* the *Star*[5], and the *News*[6] (the city papers), the dailies from other cities nearby (Hackensack and Stamford and Albany), and *The Wall Street Journal*[7].

Yoiks rocked on his toes and scanned his surroundings. Pearl could tell that wherever he was, he considered it His Surroundings. She could tell he didn't see Mr. Nichols, just some faded guy reading the *Moon.* And he couldn't see Pearl, out of view on the floor. He asked briskly, as if Mom was some receptionist wasting his time, "Which way to the statue that got beheaded?"

Pearl leaped to her feet and ran across the floor. "I'll show you our statue," she said, "but only if you're *considerate* about it."

"Considerate?" he repeated.

Yoiks wasn't as cool as he thought he was. "Have you ever read any of Edna St. Vincent Millay's poems?" Pearl asked.

"I have my master's in journalism with a minor in English lit," he said.

Pearl said, "That doesn't answer my question."

"Pearl, do please show the young man to Vincent," said Mom.

"My editor may not have mentioned this, but I'm the author of the *Unique New Yorkers* column, and I'm considering—"

---

5 Another made-up newspaper.

6 There is a New York newspaper called *The New York Daily News,* but this one is meant to be made up.

7 There is a New York newspaper called *The Wall Street Journal.*

"Do people have to be grown-up to be Unique?" asked Pearl. "Because Vincent—"

Yoiks talked right over her words. "I'd appreciate it if someone knowledgeable could tell me more about the subject of the statue."

"You'll find you're in good hands," said Mom. "Pearl will escort you to the library garden."

Yoiks had no choice but to open his pad, get out his pencil, and follow Pearl.

"This is the garden?" he asked. It was little more than a backyard, with scruffy pine trees that only partly blocked the view of a dumpster and a chain-link fence. Nothing special, you could see it in Jonathan Yoiks's expression. But that just showed he'd never seen Vincent's face.

"So, somebody ordered a statue of Edna St. Vincent Millay after she died," Pearl began. "But the customer who ordered the statue didn't like how it came out. He was crazy in love with Vincent, and he said she was more beautiful than this."

Jonathan Yoiks gazed up at Vincent's empty neck. "I believe it."

"She *is so* beautiful." Pearl curled the fronts of her flip-flops under her feet. Again she noticed a small, toed paw print, drier now than the one she'd seen before. "She was, anyway."

Yoiks turned away from Vincent with a disinterested air and looked at Pearl. "So? He didn't like the statue, then what?"

"He even hired a lawyer to make the sculptor fix it," said Pearl. "But a judge told the customer and his lawyer that they didn't have a case. 'Art is art,' he said." Pearl quoted the judge, holding one finger in the air.

Yoiks said, "I think we need to shorten this conversation, my young friend. You're losing track of the point."

"Maybe you don't know how to tell a story," said Pearl.

Yoiks sniffed and sighed. "Go on," he said.

Pearl went on. "So then the customer said he'd take the statue the way it was, but the sculptor said that now he couldn't have it."

"Another lawsuit?"

"No. The sculptor had grown up on Lancaster Avenue, so she wanted the library to have it if the customer didn't love it."

"She? The sculptor was a *she*?" asked Yoiks.

"Yeah, well, even Vincent called herself by a boy's name, which was a statement even way back then."

"Wasn't *she* brave?" Yoiks walked away, looking around, tapping his pencil on his pad.

Pearl said, "She was named after the hospital that used to be here. St. Vincent's."

"Hmm, her way of embracing the neighborhood?" Just like that, Yoiks zoomed back into the library without another word to Pearl, then came out again with Mom, Bruce, Ramón, Alice, and Simon.

"A few poses, please," he said, waving them toward his camera. "Let's have a few people gathered around the pedestal." He posed Bruce at Vincent's feet, and placed Mom next to him. But when he squeezed Pearl's shoulders, she spun away.

"Come here, Pearl girl," said Bruce. "Come stand by me."

Any other time, she would have. A staff picture in the paper of her and her lovely mother and Bruce, standing next to Simon, with Alice's hand on her shoulder, Ramón on the other side? Her whole family? Normally it would have been a definite yes.

But it wasn't her whole family. "No!" said Pearl. "Not without Vincent's head."

"I'll be in the picture!" said a voice, and that girl Francine, with the braids, from across Lancaster Avenue in the apartment over Gully's store, came clopping—were those tap dancing shoes she was wearing?—up the stone path and into the picture. *Click* went the camera.

5: FICTION VS. NONFICTION

Imagine Francine getting to be in the picture for the paper!

Pearl's outrage—and fury at herself for letting it happen—was too much to bear. She gasped and ran from the garden, past the reading room, and through the circulation area, opened the book elevator, and curled herself into the bottom shelf of the book cart. She sat there fuming a while, until the feeling faded into thinking, into developing a theory that needed some information, a theory about how heavy Vincent's head was and what kind of person it would take to move it. It couldn't possibly have been whatever little animal had left those paw prints. It couldn't have been an accident. It had to have been a crime.

There was a thud and a jolt, and the book elevator began to go up. Basement-breath damp air rose up the pitch-dark elevator shaft and cooled her. The elevator hummed and buzzed, lifting her to the second floor. Simon, who had climbed the stairs to meet her, pulled the cart from the elevator into the nonfiction stacks.

"Oof, Pearl," Simon grunted. "You are one heavy volume."

Pearl tumbled out of the cart and lay on the floor in a heap. "Simon, you're pretty muscular."

He laughed an embarrassed laugh. "So?"

"Could you lift Vincent's head off her neck?"

"By myself? Maybe. But get it down a ladder and into a car? Only if I rolled it across the ground. And why would I?"

"But if someone did, don't you think rolling would make a dent?"

He thought. "The grass would be flat like a bowling ball had been rolled across it."

"I'm going to check," said Pearl, and she went barreling down the spiral stairs.

Mom and Bruce were having an intense exchange in the garden. Their grim conversations had been going on a while, but since the theft of the head, they had grown even darker, more intense, more frequent, and more secret. Now the two were circling each other on the other side of the yew bush hedge, their voices hissing back and forth. Pearl tiptoed closer to the open door to spy.

"What are you *doing* about it?" Mom's voice rose right over the hedge.

"Trish, it's not a neighborhood hub anymore. People get their news and magazines online, and only the desperate few need computers as sluggish as ours."

"Desperate? Dedicated, maybe. Dignified."

"Desperate," repeated Bruce. "And destitute."

"It's still important." Mom's fists were clenched at her sides.

"I didn't say it wasn't important to *us*. But to the city? There has to be a better reason for people to come than slow computers and wrinkled newspapers."

"Are you giving up?"

"No, I'm not giving up," said Bruce.

"At least write another proposal. Keep asking for more books. Fill out order forms. I don't know—describe the specific audiences that need the books. The board has to see you're making every effort."

"It's just busywork!" said Bruce. "I can't ask to increase the collection again now. What reason would I give? They'll just reject it again. The budget for books isn't going to come if they won't fix the building."

"So you *are* giving up?" Mom asked again. Pearl felt the question like a thump in the chest.

"Is that what you want me to do, Patricia?"

"How can you ask me that?" demanded Mom.

It was Bruce's voice that hurt Pearl's heart. She dashed out the door and interrupted, "Of course she doesn't. What would we do without you, Bruce?"

It took nerve, butting in like this. But the idea that Mom thought Bruce should resign, if he was just going to give up otherwise. No! Not on top of everything else. Mom said, "Pearl, we're talking *business*, not personal life."

"Are we?" asked Bruce.

Pearl couldn't look at their faces. She got down on her hands and knees, her head turned to one side to put her eyes at the height of the grass, scanning for the kind of path a head might make, glad in the certainty that she was a distraction.

"What now, my love?" said Bruce tenderly. "Have you lost your marbles?"

Pearl said, "Don't you think if Vincent's head got rolled across the grass, it would have made a dent?" She wondered if Mom was crying. She couldn't bear to look up to check.

But Mom said, with just a light sniff, "You think the head was rolled across the ground?"

"Well, there are no wheelbarrow tracks," said Pearl. "But look, Bruce." There were a few more of those footprints with the long claws.

"If raccoons could talk," said Bruce.

"Then we'd know it all, huh?" asked Pearl. She was sure he was the only library manager in the city who could tell raccoon prints from those of skunks and rats and opossums.

Bruce said, "If only."

"Who says they can't?" asked Mom.

That relieved Pearl. Mom was okay if she was on the subject of talking raccoons. As for Bruce, Pearl figured he'd rather talk about raccoons (like he did in his old job, and as a volunteer for a nature-watcher program called City Wildlife) than what he had to talk about to manage the library.

"If Mrs. Mallomar and her daughter Matilda could hear you, they'd be very insulted," said Mom. She pointed to the trees and put a finger to her lips to hush them.

Bruce rolled his eyes over Mom and her wacky raccoon characters.

"Next you'll be telling me we need to leave a bowl of milk for them," he said.

Pearl said, "That's baby stuff." It had been at least three years since the last time Mom had convinced her to put out milk for the raccoons, or gotten her to leave them a letter, or told her a story about their bedrooms inside the pine trees.

"That doesn't mean they wouldn't appreciate it," said Mom lightly.

Bruce snorted. "Sure," he said.

* * *

Raccoons on her mind, Pearl went back up to the second floor, to nonfiction, to the 500s—science, facts, reality; Bruce's side of the raccoon story. Five hundred ninety in the Dewey numbers, that was big books about animals. She figured *Raccoons: A Natural History*[1] would have what she was looking for: a paw print. Before she went, a weird title caught her eye. *Raccoons*

---

1 *Raccoons: A Natural History* by Samuel I. Zeveloff (Smithsonian Institution Scholarly Press, 2003).

Are the Brightest People.[2] The cover said the book was by the best-selling author of *Rascal,*[3] so she went looking for that in the 599s. It was a memoir about a real raccoon, with a picture of a raccoon that sure looked like it would have been a bright person—enough to make the author write a special book about the whole species. Pearl grabbed them both.

The prints in the book matched the prints by the statue. But what did that really mean, anyway? Pearl already knew the raccoons hung out by the statue. There was no way they could have stolen Vincent's head. Pearl sat down on the warm bricks and leaned against the base of the statue, turning her face up in the sun.

When she looked down at the books, there was a catalog card on the lap of her blue-jeans skirt, right where the shadow of Vincent's fingers fell. It had fallen out of one of the books.

On the card was written in what looked like Sharpie:

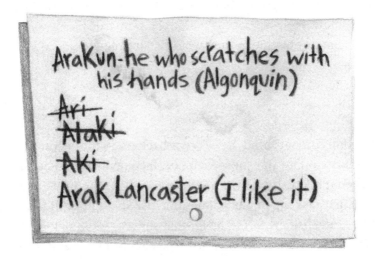

2 *Raccoons Are the Brightest People* by Sterling North (Dutton, 1966).

3 *Rascal* by Sterling North (Dutton, 1963).

Someone had been researching raccoons before Pearl. Fair enough; it was a library. But what did "Arak Lancaster" mean? Who was that? Lancaster, like the old owners of the library? The "I like it" after the cross-outs made it seem like someone was choosing names. Why that name? And who was naming someone that? There weren't any more actual Lancasters around here—were there?

Pearl climbed the stairs *again,* this time all the way to the third floor. She turned on the lights in the Memorial Room, where ghostly portraits showed the puffy faces, weird hair buns, and old-fashioned clothes of the family whose house this had been before they gave it to the city, along with the garden. Pearl walked along looking at the names: Herbert and Amalie, Walter and Margaret, William and Carol. . . . Each couple was 20 or 25 years younger than the last, passing the house down the line. They all held hands over the same little white table, which had been passed down, too, and was still sitting there now, empty, under the portrait of William and Carol, the last. All these people were Lancasters. But nobody was named Arak.

Pearl decided to put the catalog card with the names in her pocket and its puzzle in the back of her brain. She picked up *Raccoons Are the Brightest People* and tried to fit what she was reading with what she already knew about raccoons.

She realized her knowledge was a bit fuzzy. (Indeed!) She hadn't thought about the neighborhood raccoons for years. And, she realized, while she used to spend a lot of time thinking about raccoons, most of those thoughts seemed silly now. If she divided up what she knew about raccoons into non-fiction and fiction, the facts would have come from former park ranger Bruce, and the made-up tales would have come from Mom. There were raccoons around the neighborhood, said Bruce, the same as there were in any North American city. They lived in the library garden up in the trees, and they slept in the day and came out at night: nocturnal. Those were the facts.

But before Bruce had come to the library, most of what Pearl had known about raccoons came from made-up tales. When Pearl was four, Mom had taught her to put a bowl of water outside the garden door at night for the raccoons to drink and wash their food in, and sometimes a saucer of milk for a treat. Each week they set out used copies of the *Moon* for the raccoons to shred to line their nests. Mom told Pearl that the raccoons actually read the *Moon*s before they shredded them, which was why she didn't give them the *Star* or the *News,* because she didn't want them reading "that trash." Mom showing Pearl these things seemed no weirder than other parents teaching kids to fill bird feeders or to put acorns out for fairies.

"How did the raccoons learn to read?" little Pearl had asked.

"Same as you," Mom always told Pearl, even in the years after Bruce arrived, shaking his head at the fiction. "By having so many stories read to

Legends are stories that get bigger with multiple tellings. They can seem like obvious lies; for instance, Paul Bunyan having a big blue ox named Babe for a pet[4]—nonsense—and yet it's a lie you want to be true, because who wouldn't want a big blue ox for a pet? You might say it's a myth, which is less of a lie and more of a story. Whatever the reason, people like the idea, so it sticks around and gets retold as a tall tale. Sooner or later it's described as a legend, which is weird because that makes it respectable, which is a funny thing to become after all those not-truths. But really, what could be more respectable than a reading raccoon?

—M.A.M.

---

4 *Paul Bunyan: A Tall Tale Retold and Illustrated* by Steven Kellogg (William Morrow, 1984).

them." When Mom was a child she had come to this very library for story hours, and the children's librarian, someone Mom loved named Mrs. Whitney, had read books outside by Vincent's statue. "The raccoons always woke from their daytime sleeping and lay drowsy in their nests, listening to Mrs. Whitney's tales."

When Pearl was smaller, she was always peering up into the trees trying to see any raccoons at all. Bruce reminded her that in the daytime they were inside the trees, snoozing. At night Pearl slept through their activities: scouring the neighborhood for left-behind tidbits, washing their food in the bowl, drinking the milk, taking the newspapers away to read, or using shredded newsprint to fluff up their nests. But occasionally, on lucky nights, she'd see one of the little bandits in the alley at dusk.

"When they reach a certain age, young raccoons go off to seek their fortunes," Mom had told Pearl, and Bruce did agree with that, because, he said, "They are territorial. They get competitive as they near reproductive age, so only a couple of raccoons stick around any area. The rest go off to find their own place."

Mostly, Mom's stories were about the raccoons that lived near the library. "Mrs. Mallomar and her daughters, Matilda and Eilonwy, are the library raccoons," Mom always affirmed.

"Mallomar, like the cookie?"

"Yep. And Matilda is another name for the moon. Are you surprised?"

Pearl had thought maybe it was Matilda like the one in the Roald Dahl book she loved.[5] Then she thought maybe *that* Matilda had been named for the moon, too. When she asked

------

5 *Matilda* by Roald Dahl, illustrated by Quentin Blake (Jonathan Cape, 1988).

who Eilonwy was named for, Alice handed her a book with a boy and a pig on the cover.[6]

Pearl had asked once, "Where's Mr. Mallomar?"

Mom had shrugged. "He went off to seek his fortune, too, I guess."

"Like my dad?" Pearl was always trying to find out about her father.

"Just like," Mom had said. "Gone forever. Let's focus on who's here."

Pearl looked up at Bruce to see what he would say, but he was studying Mom with a little sweet smile, and he didn't say anything at all.

6 *The Book of Three* is the first of *The Chronicles of Prydain* pentalogy by Lloyd Alexander (Henry Holt, 1964–1968).

6: HEAD OF THE LIBRARY

AUG 30

The next morning, Mom sent Pearl to the newsstand. Tallulah seemed half asleep as she gave Pearl her change. "Late night?" asked Pearl.

"Late edition," said Tallulah, yawning. With the *Moon* tucked under her arm, Pearl passed Gully's store as he came out with his own paper in his hand.

"Look here!" he said. "My neighbors are in the paper!"

Pearl blurted, "*I'm* not."

Gully peered at the picture Jonathan Yoiks had taken in the garden. "Bet you don't even know who that kid is!" He pointed to Francine. He leaned closer, smelling of sweat and coffee. "Brazilian," he said, as if it was a secret. "The kid showed up after school ended. Never seen her before. Not sure she's legal. Every day all summer she's home by herself banging on things and blaring that music while her granny's out shilling her trash sculptures."

"Oh?" said Pearl. She turned away, scowling. Gully didn't go on. What did he mean by legal? Was it illegal to make too much noise? Or to be Brazilian? She almost smiled, thinking of Francine tap-dancing up there on Gully's ceiling, then remembered she didn't much like Francine, gave Gully a look, and left.

Pearl hadn't always disliked Gully. When she was younger, she had realized he held the key to candy, Magic Markers, tie-dyed bandanas, and little toy sushi imitations that had been a fad for a while at school. She went to his store a lot. But lately she had realized that the only time Gully came to the library was when he thought there was some drama going on. And she had also become aware that he kept his own collection of information, his own version of stories. Gully loved gossip.

She didn't open her copy of the *Moon* until she had crossed the street to the library.

The paper had a big headline:

LIBRARY LOSES ITS HEAD.

The story said how the library was low on money and reflected the *transient* neighborhood. Pearl laid the paper on the reference desk in front of Ramón and asked, "What does that mean?"

He spun the dictionary toward her. Pearl sighed, and turned to the *T*s. "'Transient' means impermanent, transitioning," she said. "What does *that* mean?"

"It means a lot of people coming and going," said Ramón. "It means change."

Nichols came out of the hallway bathroom, his face shining because he'd just shaved and washed and combed his hair. He did this sometimes in their bathrooms. It wasn't allowed, but who would ever want to enforce that rule? To hide the fact that they'd noticed, Ramón and Mom kept their eyes on Pearl, who said, to fill the silence, "Aren't people *supposed* to come and go in a library? What's wrong with being transient, anyway?" Then she stomped upstairs.

Bruce was sitting in his rat's nest writing something. Pearl held up a sheet of pink paper that Ramón had given her.

She said, "Look, Mr. Nichols drew this picture of Vincent. He's a good artist, don't you think? And Ramón copied a bunch

LOST HEAD

$REWARD$

INFORMATION
LANCASTER AVENUE
BRANCH
NEW YORK CITY LIBRARY

and they're going to put them up on all the trees and signs and light poles." She handed over the sign. "Ramón put up his own $100 as a reward."

But Bruce's eyes stayed on his papers and his fingers were on his phone, running up and down the calculator, tapping out numbers.

"What are you doing?" she asked.

"Telling myself a story," said Bruce.

Was he teasing her?

He seemed to realize she might think that, because he looked up and said, "I mean it. Numbers tell the story of how the library is doing. I'm trying to make your mother's circulation numbers show that we're supporting ourselves, that enough people come here and take out books to make it worth staying open—and adding a garden gate."

"But do the numbers show that?"

Bruce shook his head.

"No happy ending?"

"Why not?'

He blinked, reached out, and touched her cheek. "Because numbers don't lie. Because money talks. Because money *can* buy happiness."

"You mean business is bad, Bruce?" said Pearl. "Like Gully says?"

"I'm sorry, Pearl girl. It's just—people aren't coming in, so books aren't going out."

From outside the window came an echoing, tapping noise, as if someone was hammering on the bricks down in the garden, around Vincent's feet. Pearl felt her face tense up, but Bruce smiled.

"There's someone new now," he said. "I've got you to thank for that. You and your vocal cords."

Francine was in the garden, having broken her granny's rule about going out again, dancing in her tap shoes up and down the stone paths, in and out of the lavender plants, tossing back the dark braids that fell all the way to the waist of her shorts. When she got to the base of the statue, she jumped back. "Ooh!" she squealed. Pearl could hear her overdramatic tone from three floors up. She figured this was the noise Gully had yelled about, tap-dancing banging around in the apartment. Then Francine stuck her hand in her shorts pocket, climbed up the base of the statue, which was definitely not allowed, and pretended to put something into Vincent's outstretched hand. It was nothing, Pearl could see that from here. Francine was just doing some kind of pantomime. Now she darted away from Vincent as if her shorts were on fire. "That girl needs a doctor!" said Pearl.

Bruce said, "Aw, she's just a little kid."

"She's ten like me," retorted Pearl. It had said that right in the caption of the newspaper picture. "She's just short. Anyway, who does she think she is, just walking in here?" Pearl couldn't stand that Francine had been in the newspaper representing the library, instead of her.

She wished he'd say, "I'm all ears," so she could talk. But Bruce gave her a little pat on the shoulder.

"I've got to get this budget proposal sent out, Pearlie girlie, and it's giving me such a headache."

"It's all right, Brucie goosey," she said, started to leave, and promptly tripped over the foot of the coatrack into the hall, which toppled, walloping the tall cabinet. The raccoon costume started to slide from its hanger. The head of the raccoon rocketed toward them off its garbage can holder, its black-screen eyes dark and empty.

Suddenly Mom appeared, in time to grab the shoulders of the costume, push back the file cabinet, and manhandle the

You've got to have a library manager who runs the business of the library; figures out the budget (how much money goes to paychecks, book and materials collections, building maintenance, and so on); takes care of marketing (proving to the public that the library is a great establishment you'd want to visit); and solves whatever problems come up. That was Bruce Chambers, and he wondered lately whether he should have stuck with parks instead of books.

Then you need a circulation librarian. At Lancaster Avenue, this person was also the collection librarian, and was also Pearl's mom. Ramón was the reference librarian, who helped people find answers—which meant looking things up in books or finding magazines or using the internet or whatever. Alice was responsible for choosing all the best children's books to order, and setting up things for kids: story hours, costume parades, arts and crafts workshops. Simon was the page, who was responsible for keeping all the books on the shelves in order.

raccoon head back into place. They all teetered, then steadied themselves, staring at each other, panting.

"Sorry!" Pearl yelped.

Bruce said, "Mrs. Moran, ma'am, I thank you for saving my head."

"Did Pearl show you the *Moon?*"

Busted. With a sigh, Pearl pulled the paper out from the chair cushion and handed it over, not wanting to hear Bruce's response to the picture. Also, she recognized that when Bruce called her mother Mrs. Moran—not Patricia or Tricia or Trish—he was flirting, making up for yesterday's quarrel. This realization made Pearl itchy, and she didn't want to stay in the room with it, glad though it made her.

So she took off. Through the frosted-glass second-story floor Pearl could see the dark blue-black of Alice's head and the reddish blob of the sari she was wearing, downstairs at the circ counter, stamping date-due cards. (Alice: "Patricia, why are we still using this ancient date machine?" Bruce: "Because she doesn't trust the computer." Mom: "Do YOU trust the computer not to crash? Keep stamping, Alice.") *Clunk-bum* went the old date machine, stamping "SEP 20," three weeks from today. School would have started by then. Ugh.

Pearl was not enthusiastic about school, but at least it would make a change. It had been a long, hot, dull summer before the theft. There had been hardly any books to put away, only one story hour a day for Alice, hardly anybody coming through the door except parents needing something to do with toddlers, or the lawn mower men picking up their check, or the tired people who fell asleep with their heads on the table or behind a newspaper.

Face it: The library had been slower than ever since last November, when the brand-new Knickerbocker branch of the library opened—only thirty blocks away, in a "nicer" neighborhood with high-speed Wi-Fi in the air, solar panels on the roof, and, in the basement, not bugs and slugs, but a coffeeshop and a gift store.

And since circulation—books getting borrowed—was the number the whole library was measured by, Mom had all kinds of strategies about how to increase that number. The plan had been to build up "services," to make the library a hub of the neighborhood. Bruce counseled people on their résumés to help them get jobs, Alice's husband, Danesh, offered financial planning to help them manage their money,

This was probably the smallest number of people who could ever run one branch library, which ought to tell you something about its budget problems. I'd heard there used to be more people working here, and there used to be more patrons, too. Things had been going downhill since long before Vincent lost her head.

—M.A.M.

Ramón taught English as a Second Language, Mom scoured secondhand shops for more DVDs, and Bruce scraped together funds for more computers and faster internet. The whole idea was that if more people came to the library for more things, they'd get library cards, they'd take things out, and circulation would go up. Then support for the little neighborhood library would go up, too.

But it hadn't caught on yet. Would it? Pearl knew the situation was getting desperate—all she had to do was watch her mom and Bruce—but she tried to ignore it, the same way she tried to ignore their arguing. She was unsuccessful in both efforts. That was the trouble with her family being the library staff—when something went wrong, EVERYTHING went wrong.

Clunk-bum, said the SEP 20 stamp. *Tappety-tap,* went Francine out in the garden. Beneath Pearl in the fiction section, Simon was straightening shelves. *Shuffle-thump. Clunk-bum. Tappety-tap-tap.* They were all sounds you'd never even notice if the library wasn't so completely dead.

The stamping machine suddenly stopped. "Simon?" Alice called. "Someone's here with a clipboard. Where's Trish?"

7: A HECKUVA PLAN

A clipboard? That sounded official. Pearl slid swiftly down the spiral-staircase bannister and landed at Simon's feet.

"Shh!" he told her, and pulled her behind the *S* shelf.

"Hahaha!" came a loud laugh. Then, "That's a heckuva plan!"

"Let's see what we can do about it," said a more measured, businesslike voice.

The doors opened, and two men came into the library, one in a button-down shirt, one in a sweatshirt, both in baseball hats.

Up until then, Pearl hadn't realized that the library could be yanked out from under them, like a skateboard whipping out from somebody's clumsy feet.

After they came, she gave them names in her mind, Mr. Bull and Mr. Dozer, in self-defense: If she couldn't somehow make fun of them, she might have exploded.

"May I help you?" Mom materialized behind her desk as the men came up, defending her territory by saying, "There's a hook here for your hats." Pearl watched Mom's code work: The men took their hats off.

"Just looking," Mr. Dozer (in the button-down shirt) said dismissively, but Mr. Bull (in the sweatshirt) was smiling with one corner of his mouth, as if he thought taking off your hat inside was a silly rule that wouldn't be a problem for long. The two men stood off to one side of the desk, gazing at the ceiling and walls like Mom wasn't there.

"Square footage is great," Mr. Bull said.

"Fourteen units, affordable for families," said Mr. Dozer. "Little kitchenettes, two bedrooms. Great space!" He twirled the cap on his index finger. "Rewiring, casement windows . . . I can see it."

Pearl wanted to shout something disruptive. Mr. Bull dropped his cap right on the circ counter and got busy punching the buttons on his phone and making sketches on a little pad. "Three-quarters of a million. We could market it as housing for professionals with families. Something like that," he muttered.

"Be doing the city a big favor."

None of the rest of the words Pearl caught—"bidding . . . electrician . . . December 1 if the city goes along"—made much sense. Then it was over. The two men brushed past, calling, "Thank you, folks!" Pearl made a motion with her foot behind the men, as if to kick them out the door. Simon put a death grip on her elbow. Mom swept past and followed the men, and everyone watched through the window.

When Mom came back in, they swarmed her.

"Those guys have some nerve. They parked right on the sidewalk," Francine piped up from behind them. "They blocked the whole driveway. A fancy car, with a lion on the front. And a pickup truck with 'G.C.' on it."

Mom said, "'G.C.' means 'general contractor.' They're developers—people who figure out how to make money from land or buildings."

"Can people just decide to build something new where a library already is?" Pearl cried.

Simon said, "Those two don't care if this is a library or a log cabin."

Mom said, "They want to make it into apartments. Four two-bedrooms, four one-bedrooms, and six studio apartments."

Francine and Pearl both screeched, the first thing they'd ever done together. Mom looked worried. She smoothed the front of her skirt. "I'll tell Bruce," she said, and headed up the spiral stairs.

Francine didn't even have the politeness to leave. It was as if she thought she had the same stake in things as Simon and Pearl. The three of them stood silently, waiting for an explosion from Bruce's office above.

When it came, it wasn't from Bruce's office, but from the sky. Thunder boomed in loud startling cracks, lightning flashed, and Pearl stared at her own reflection in the glass of the front door and counted off the miles. "One elephant, two elephants, three elephants."

Francine said, "You're supposed to say, 'One, one thousand,' not 'one elephant.'"

"It doesn't matter," Simon said. "It just has to be three syllables, that's all."

"Yeah, Francine," Pearl said sarcastically. "Are you even supposed to be here? Kids are usually here with parents."

Francine said, "My parents are in Brazil. Got a problem with that? And I'm ten—same as you, right?"

"Do you have permission from your grandmother?" Pearl found herself feeling vicious. "You're short," she added.

"Pearl," said Simon. "What is your problem? Nothing that's happening is Francine's fault."

"Fine, *I'm* leaving," said Pearl. "I have things to attend to." She grabbed Ramón's huge red umbrella from the can by the door and took it out front to look for Alice, who was coming with coffee. Then she realized that copycat Francine might tag along, so she stepped into the alley, out of sight of the library, the rain tumbling around. Immediately she felt jealous that she'd left Francine alone with Simon!

Pearl couldn't think what would happen if they built apartments in the library. All of it—her mother losing her job, the rest of the staff splintering apart, her whole world shattering down like dropped dishes—could not be allowed to enter her head, and the effort of keeping it away made her dizzy.

Pearl sniffed hugely. She stepped carefully along the narrow strip of grass that bordered the building, past the dark basement windows. And then: Up against the window, in a flash of lightning, slapped a tiny scrabbling hand—a *paw*—with long claws like those prints in the garden.

The paw inside the window had creases like a person's palm. It looked like it was pointing—right at a small slip of paper on the ground. By the time Pearl looked back up at the window, the paw had disappeared, replaced by a black nose and two dark eyes. The eyes met hers, then blinked off.

She bent quickly, grabbed the paper, looked back at the window. The raccoon had disappeared.

She told herself that she hadn't really seen what she thought she'd seen. Raccoons did not live in the library basement. They

lived in the trees! And even if one did happen to be down there, why would it be pointing out a note to Pearl?

And yet the note was real. She uncrunched it and read it.

Ask Mrs. M.

No, she hadn't been seeing things. It really did have Sharpie writing on it, and it was another catalog card. Was this note written by the same person who had written the note about the mysterious Arak Lancaster? As soon as she could, she'd compare the two catalog cards side by side. Maybe they had been written by the same hand.

Or paw.

Nonsense! Pearl told herself.

But who was Mrs. M? Mom, Mrs. Moran? She flashed on Mom's fantastical raccoon stories. Mrs. Mallomar? *Oh, stop it.*

Just then, Alice came bounding through the rain in her sneakers, her wet sari plastered around her sticking-out belly, her ponytail flopping down her back, her gigantic black umbrella crooked around her upper arm. It was her day to get snacks for the four o'clock meeting, and she wouldn't let anyone do it for her, no matter how pregnant she was. A box of doughnuts in a carrier bag was looped over her lower arm; one hand balanced a coffee tray and the other held the paper coffee cups steady. Pearl wondered what Alice would say if she told her a raccoon had just sent her a note, but it looked like Alice was already dealing with enough.

"Are you supposed to run like that?" Pearl pocketed the card to think about later and took one of the trays from Alice's hands.

"Thanks, sweets," said Alice. She put a hand on her baby bump and said, "She slept through the whole thing." The staff gathered at the circ counter and Pearl passed out the coffee: light with sugar for Bruce. Milk and sugar for Mom. Cream only for Alice. None for Ramón, who made himself green tea in the staff room. And black for Nichols, out of the kindness of Alice's heart, since he couldn't pay.

It seemed clear to Pearl that Francine was dying to be part of the library. Right now, for example, she was pretending to read the dictionary. Alice gave Pearl a nudge, so Pearl said to her, "Want half a doughnut?"

"Thanks," said Francine, and they both smiled a little, but only a little.

Mom asked Francine, "Francine, right? Do you have a library card?"

Francine shook her head.

Pearl said, "Why not?"

Francine swallowed. "How much does it cost?"

"Perfectly free," said Mom.

"All you need is an address," said Pearl.

"You ought to tell the kids at school that," said Francine. "Nothing else is free. Nothing."

Before Pearl could finish thinking up a reply to that, Bruce cleared his throat and looked around the room. "Friends, thanks for meeting. I need to bring you up to date. Those men you all saw this morning have been making inquiries at the city building office about repurposing this building. And if they can get it approved for affordable housing, they may have a case."

The front door let in a roar of rain from the street, and Nichols. He was drenched. His gray-brown hair dripped in wet curls down his forehead.

Alice said, "Mr. Nichols, was that your black umbrella I saw in the foyer? *Someone* must have left it here. And you sure look as if you're missing one."

He looked back at the doorway and shook his head.

Alice rolled her eyes. "Well, take it if you want it," she said. "People treat this library like it's the Salvation Army box. Hats, scarves, umbrellas! We've got it all."

Pearl knew for a fact that Danesh had given Alice that big black umbrella to cover her giant belly. Mr. Nichols refused all gifts, and it wasn't always easy to get him to take things that might help him. Alice was babbling, trying. Pearl whisked the attention away from Mr. Nichols, awkward in his dripping clothes, and asked Bruce the question that was burning up her heart. "What would happen to the books?" she asked.

"They'd just get thrown in the dumpster," Simon interrupted horribly.

"No they wouldn't," protested Ramón. "They'd get trucked to other branches."

Nichols asked, "What's going on?"

"They want to build apartments—here," said Bruce, flapping a hand. "I don't see how."

Nichols didn't seem amazed, or even dismayed. "It's possible," he said. "Reinforce the walls, maybe. Drop in a ceiling, frame out the space. You'd fit two one-bedrooms right in the reference room alone."

Mom and Bruce exchanged a glance. It was obvious Nichols knew what he was talking about. How?

"They won't keep Vincent," Pearl said, realizing. "They'll take the rest of the statue away and pave the garden over. There's no other way to make space for parking."

"Hang on," said Mom. "It's just a proposal. Just because it could work doesn't mean it's going to happen."

But Bruce shook his head. "It's going to be easier now that the head was stolen. What's the point of a statue without a head? What's the point of a library if it can't even keep a statue safe? The city would welcome having the library taken off its hands."

Pearl's misery deepened into a sick feeling. Oh help, what embarrassment! Tears came streaming down her cheeks. Simon, sitting on the stair above her, didn't see. Francine stared curiously, then turned away to be polite. It was Bruce who looked up, jumped off the cart, and put his arms around Pearl.

Mom watched this and took a breath. "Come on now," she said. "If we're going to go down, let's go down swinging." She picked up the phone and hit speaker.

"City desk. Yoiks!" they all heard a thin, reedy man's voice say.

"Mrs. Patricia Moran, librarian, Lancaster Avenue branch." Bruce straightened and confronted Mom with a stare, but he didn't stop her this time, either. "I wanted to be sure the paper knows what's going on here today, about the possible sale and development of this historic building."

"Historic?" repeated Jonathan Yoiks. "Tell me more. Is it in the National Register of Historic Places?"

"Well, no," admitted Mom. "It was turned down because of renovations to the children's room in the 1960s. But most of the main features of the library are beautiful original elements— you know, the cast-iron balcony in the reading room, the glass floor, the spiral staircase, the mullioned windows. . . . They want to make apartments out of us, but we're not going to let them do that."

Pearl had the sense that Mom was blabbering a little bit.

There was a slight ruckus in the background at the city desk of the *Moon*. "Thanks for getting in touch, Ms. Moran," said Yoiks.

"It's *Mrs*. And may I look for a story tomorrow?" persisted Mom.

"I've got some, uh, breaking news to attend to right now, and a *Unique New Yorkers* column to file. Tell you what, you check your paper, Ms.—"

"Mrs.," said Mom. But he'd already hung up.

"Who's this week's Unique New Yorker?" asked Bruce.

"Some tightrope walker from France," said Alice. (That had been one of them.)

"A Mohawk ironworker," said Ramón. (Mohawk ironworkers had built the skyscrapers.)

"An artist who built a cat castle in Brooklyn," said Mom, rolling her eyes. They had been paying attention to the *Unique New Yorkers* column while feeling sure they didn't qualify for uniqueness in Jonathan Yoiks's eyes. It seemed that you had to be superhuman to be featured.

"What breaking news is there?" demanded Simon.

"Murder and mayhem, probably," said Ramón. "That's what sells papers."

"Maybe the president is in the city," suggested Alice.

"Maybe the United Nations is in session," said Bruce.

"Or something's on fire," said Nichols.

"Or somebody found a finger in his lunch," said Simon.

"Maybe a bank had a robbery?" asked Francine.

"*We've* had a robbery," said Pearl. She couldn't imagine a single thing happening that was more important than what was happening right here.

8: ON THE STOOP

A clacking footstep told Pearl that Francine was nearby, so she sneaked to the end of the nonfiction stacks and peered into the children's room. Francine was in the picture book section, slowly studying the spines.

"What're you looking for?" Pearl asked.

"See if she'll tell you," said Alice. "She won't tell me. She actually came in and registered for a library card this morning, took the oath and everything." She lowered her voice so only Pearl could hear. "Pearl, *this* is what we want people to do. It's what we need them to do! So what if she's not a big reader *yet*. Go easy on her."

One thing that was aggravating about this library: how everybody on the staff thought they were Pearl's parents! "Why should I?" whispered Pearl. "She's weird and annoying and she thinks she belongs here, and she thinks it's just all so dramatic and exciting that Vincent's head got stolen, and—"

"She *does* belong here," said Alice. "Anyone in the neighborhood belongs here. Besides"—she put a hand on Pearl's head—"imagine having no place else to go. Be kind." Pearl pulled away, but gently, and went and looked out at Lancaster Avenue. She wanted to be kind to Alice. But Francine? Maybe not. Not yet, anyway.

....

1 Except for the last three lines, this oath is the one that was instituted by Anne Carroll Moore, head of the Office of Work with Children, in 1911, when children were first allowed into the New York Public Library—at the Central Children's Library at 42nd Street and Fifth Avenue.

Up there above Gully's store where Francine lived, the windows were dark. But it was cozy inside the library, all the lights lit on this cloudy, still-rainy morning. Anyone would like it here.

She went closer to Francine. "Do you need help finding a book?" Pearl was very formal, like a host.

"Nope," said Francine. "I mean, no thank you." She made a little bow.

Such a weirdo.

"Why not?" asked Pearl, insulted. "Recommendations are created by the staff, with inspiration from the spirit of Edna St. Vincent Millay herself." She had made that up on the spot to impress Francine.

"I bet," Francine said with a short laugh. "No, I'll know it when I see it. I like picking stuff myself personally. And then I'll take it out with my own personal brand-new library card and take it home to my own personal house."

"You can do that with any book in the whole library," said Pearl.

"*This one* has to be the first one. But I don't know what it's called." She took a deep breath and let Pearl help, looking wary. "It's got construction equipment in it, a shovel called Mary Ann."

"*Mike Mulligan,*" said Pearl, rolling her eyes.

"*Mike Mulligan and His Steam Shovel,*" said Alice, swooping past. She bent over, holding her belly, to scan the *B* shelf.

The book wasn't there.

"Well, I just read it for story hour this week," said Alice. "Maybe one of the kids who was there took it out."

"That's where I heard it," said Francine.

"I'll put a hold on it," said Alice. But when she looked up the book, it hadn't been taken out. It was just missing. Another theft?

Francine's face fell. Alice handed her a different book by the same author—*The Little House,*[2] which also had steam shovels in it, but not one named Mary Ann.

Francine flipped through; Pearl couldn't help glancing over her shoulder from time to time. *The Little House* was beloved, too. How could you not love the little house that stayed the same while big houses took over the meadows beside it, as taller buildings took over the houses, as skyscrapers took over the buildings, and the city came to the country? And then the ending, when the little house gets yanked up and put on a truck and taken away—

Francine slammed the book shut. "Mine," she said, and hugged it.

* * *

Together Mom and Pearl sat on the front stoop of their apartment in the low evening light to play gin, listening to the city's hum-thrumming tune of horns, sirens, strollers, bikes, skateboards, feet walking, people talking, baths and beds and babies.

Billie Bilbao, the artist lady, Francine's granny, humped and lumped along the sidewalk toward them. She'd been Gully's tenant forever, so they knew her by sight. She was a modern artist who went around every evening pulling a kids' red wagon, the

2 *The Little House* by Virginia Lee Burton (Houghton Mifflin, 1942).

kind with the high wooden sides, filling it full of clattering, banging, heavy-looking stuff, some of it broken.

"Evening!" she called up. Pearl and Mom laid their cards in their laps. "My granddaughter wants to formally introduce me."

Francine came trailing up behind Billie, looking like introducing her was the last thing she wanted. "This is my granny," she said. "This is Mrs. Moran and Pearl Moran. They're the library people."

"Francine is in love with the library!" exclaimed her grandmother. "She'll be a fifth grader," Granny/Billie Bilbao said. "And we are new to each other."

"Really?" asked Mom. It was an invitation to tell more.

"Francine is living with me while her parents are out of the country."

Francine's eyes, usually so full of light, got dark like the sun had gone behind the clouds. She clearly didn't like hearing Granny talk about her parents. That made even Pearl not say anything.

"Look," said Granny, maybe to make a distraction. "A broken lampshade, knockoff Tiffany." She pointed at the wagon, indicating a stained-glass shade with yellow tulips and green leaves on a marbled plum-colored background. "And look at these fabulous springs!" They were thick metal coils. "And my favorite of the day—three spent Mylar balloons." They looked—well, like she'd pulled them out of trash cans. Pearl guessed that was the point. Granny grinned at the look on her face. "Everybody's a fool for something. Well, come on, Frank. That's enough for one night."

Frank? Francine's dark look changed to alarm at what was obviously a nickname she was not fond of.

Pearl smiled. "See ya," she said. She thought the whole scene was funny. Francine—so fancy and glittery! Covered in trash! Being called Frank! But she could see Francine was mortified, and that made her feel some sympathy, and she didn't say anything rude as Francine slumped away.

But that was enough Francine for the day, Pearl felt, so she changed the subject to something she knew would grab Mom's whole attention.

"Could a raccoon write?" she asked.

If Mom was surprised, she didn't show it. She didn't even blink. "If you can read, you can write," said Mom.

"Oh, Mom," said Pearl. "I meant, *physically* could it write."

"It? He or she, please."

"Come on. With those paw . . . fingers, you know? That's what I mean."

"Your *fingers* aren't what write," said Mom. "It's your brain that writes."

Pearl flopped backward on the stoop and looked up at the shadowy leaves and the slate-blue sky beyond them. She couldn't remember the last time Mom had read her a story. She longed to be years younger, when she was still little enough to curl up next to Mom and hear a story, when the library wasn't going anywhere and everything was perfect. "Ma?" said Pearl. "What do the raccoons that live in the garden do in the winter?"

Mom laid her gin cards in her lap. "I'd have thought you were too old for raccoon stories," she said. Pearl didn't look at her mother's face; she kept on looking at the leaves. But she invited, as her mother had taught her when she was very little, "Do tell."

"Well," Mom said, warming to the old invitation, "*You would think* that raccoons would just make a nest in the leaves, curl up in a stripey ball, and sleep the winter away."

"You would think that," said Pearl. *"But . . ."*

"But," Mom said, "our raccoons aren't just any raccoons. They know what's what."

"And what's that?"

"They know that winter is the best time to curl up with a book and *read* the cold away."

"Don't they get cold in the tree? Don't they ever go inside?" Pearl was thinking of the paw in the basement, the note that had seemed to be—but couldn't have been—could it?—from the raccoons, *Ask Mrs. M.* Wasn't that what Pearl was doing right now? Asking Mrs. M.?

"Inside where?"

"Maybe someplace out of the way, like the basement," said Pearl, feeling like she knew a secret.

"Not that I've ever observed," said Mom. "Nope, they stay in the trees, where they can keep an eye on things, patrol the rats, and stay out of the way of the coyotes, and, probably, reread those letters you wrote them."

"Oh, and they kept those?" She hardly believed it.

"How else do you think they know you?"

Yes, that's right. Pearl had left tiny notes and letters and even books she'd drawn and stapled together, tucked under the edge of the saucer of milk. Whyever had she stopped? Because of Simon, of all people. Now she knew he wouldn't have teased, but when she was in second grade, she'd thought that writing to raccoons might seem like something only little kids did.

"They grow up so fast," said Mom. "Little Matilda Mallomar and her sister Eilonwy might have children of their own now! I wonder if they do."

"Why don't you ask Mrs. Mallomar?" Pearl suggested. *Ask Mrs. M. again.* She felt her heart pick up, but she tried not to look flustered.

Mom shrugged, sighed. "She's so busy, and we're on such opposite schedules, our paths never even cross. Once I saw her when I was up in the middle of the night, coming home from work."

Here was the story Pearl had been looking for. "What's Mrs. Mallomar's job?" she asked.

"Putting out the midnight *Moon,* of course. She's the editor in chief," Mom said. "Otherwise how will the raccoons of Lancaster Avenue know who's who and what's what?"

("Who's who and what's what" is the motto of the midnight *Moon.* The midnight *Moon,* in Mom's stories, was the nighttime edition of the regular *Moon* newspaper, catering to a nocturnal readership—not like the morning and evening *Moons,* with their diurnal, night-sleeping readership.)

Pearl laughed, rolled onto her stomach, and turned over her playing cards.

"You don't believe me?" said Mom.

Pearl smiled. She saw again, in her mind's eye, the raccoon face in the basement, peering through the glass. She thought she might tell Mom about it, but—

"How do you feel about school starting?" Mom asked out of nowhere. "Are you glad Francine will be there?"

Mom meant she'd have a friend at last. Pearl didn't want to talk about friends. She blurted, "Mom, who are *your* friends?"

Mom didn't go out with people, men or women. Her only boyfriend, if you could call him that, was Bruce. Mom hadn't stayed in touch with her older brother since their parents died, when Pearl was a baby. And she didn't have the least idea where Pearl's own father was. So she'd better not keep asking Pearl about Francine!

Pearl didn't want to think about fifth grade yet. She would rather hear about Matilda and Eilonwy, babyish as it might be. There was a girl in Pearl's class—Khadija—who she'd have liked to be friends with if only Khadija wasn't friends with mean Elsa. Then she had a horrifying thought: What if Francine got to be friends with Elsa and Khadija and nobody, *nobody!* was friends with Pearl. Everybody in fifth grade was jerks! She hated that Mom had brought up the subject of school.

"Relax," said Mom. "Your shoulders are up to your ears."

Pearl dropped them and scowled down at her cards.

"Francine likes you, Pearl, that's all," her mother said.

"She does not," said Pearl.

"Oh, then it must be the books," said Mom. She stared at Pearl until Pearl had to smile. "Admit it," Mom insisted. "She likes the books *and* you."

Pearl shrugged.

"What's so weird about that?" said Mom. When Pearl didn't answer, she said, "Are you going to play your turn or not?"

Pearl drew a card and considered. Francine *liked* her? The thought had not occurred to her. Yes, Francine wanted to be where the drama was, and ever since Vincent's head had been stolen, that was the library. And because Francine was a kid, naturally she would glom onto another kid, whoever was there.

Pearl crossed her arms over her stomach, as if to guard herself from being friends with Francine. But she couldn't deny, as she questioned herself closely, that the idea of being liked gave her a warm little glow under the place on her stomach where her left thumb rested.

"You're surprised?" Mom asked.

Pearl nodded, and pulled her lips inside her mouth to stop the smile.

"Well, you shouldn't be."

9: THE FULL GAME

SEP 5

The first morning of the new school year, when Pearl stepped out her door, who should she find standing there, bouncing up onto her tippy-toes, but Francine.

"Please—walk to school with me, or else Granny's going to. She only let me come this far alone because I swore I'd walk with you, and I have to rush back and buzz her so she can look down and see I'm not walking alone, or she's going to come down and walk me, and—" She grimaced. "I don't think I'll make a good first impression if she's there." She tucked her hands into the sides of her bright new school jumper and took a deep breath.

Pearl thought about Francine's parents being all the way in Brazil so that she had to live with Granny and go to a new school. She swallowed her curiosity and tucked her thumbs under her backpack straps. "Fine," she said. "Let's go."

It was just as well not to have to walk to school alone. As they walked the eleven blocks to school, more and more students joining the sidewalk at every crossing, it was good to have someone at her side for once, although it would have been better if Francine was in the same class. She dropped Francine at another fifth-grade classroom and turned nervously toward her own.

Pearl knew she shouldn't be afraid of the girls in her room, but she was, a little. She couldn't figure out when or how they had become such good friends. It seemed like everyone had all been friends forever—but never friends with her. No one was mean to her, they mostly didn't think about her. There was no reason for them *not* to be friends with her, but there was also no reason why any extra effort should be made for Pearl when they just naturally already *were* friends with each other.

It was awful.

But whenever Pearl pushed the matter, things got even worse. She couldn't understand it, and she couldn't stand it, either. She knew there was nothing wrong with her. She was nice! She would be a good friend and not tell on anyone! She was an interesting person who knew about books and could recommend them and quote from them and even give a brief synopsis of them if someone wanted her to. But after five years of going to school with Pearl, the kids only asked her for book reviews in order to distract her or appease her or make the teachers think they were talking to her for real.

Maybe this year would be different.

At lunch, Pearl didn't see Francine at first, so she sat down at the fifth-grade table next to a new kid, a tall brown girl named Millie Perez, who had just moved to New York all the way from Miami Beach, Florida. Pearl liked the look of Millie, with her navy socks that slouched down to her ankles, tiny glassy earrings, and a long brown ponytail as straight as a broom. But Elsa Mann was sitting on the other side of Millie, and when Pearl sat down, Elsa moved farther away from Pearl and motioned to Millie.

"Why?" said Millie softly, but Pearl heard.

And she heard Elsa whisper back, "BOR-ing. Watch."

Then Elsa asked Pearl if she'd read all of Harry Potter,[1] which of course she had. "Tell us what it's about?" Elsa had invited her

---

1   The Harry Potter series began with *Harry Potter and the Philosopher's Stone* by J.K. Rowling (U.K.: Bloomsbury/U.S.: Scholastic, 1998). If you're reading in the United States, you know the first book as *Harry Potter and the Sorcerer's Stone*.

A Sidebar About Harry Potter

There is such a thing as being in the right place at the right time. There is also such a thing as being born to greatness. But most heroes aren't great just because they were born in the right place at the right time or were born to greatness. Especially female heroes. Ask Hermione.

Or ask Francine. Do you really think she didn't see Pearl in the lunchroom? When I heard this, I thought Pearl was anything but a hero.

—M.A.M.

in an insincere voice, so Pearl should have known enough to resist. Who didn't know what it was about, anyway?

Pearl asked, "You want a synopsis of all of Harry Potter?"

"Well, however much you've read," said Elsa.

Francine walked in just then, and stood scanning the room. Pearl knew she was looking for someone to sit with—looking for *her*.

"Pearl?" insisted Elsa. "Potter?"

Khadija's and Millie's eyes were on Pearl, too.

"Please?" said Elsa. "You know I could never get through a book that thick."

Pearl was shocked at the idea that Elsa hadn't read it. She looked at the other two. They glanced from Pearl to Elsa.

Elsa said, "They haven't read it either, probably. Please tell us."

"From the beginning?" Pearl ducked her head to avoid Francine's eyes.

Elsa nodded, smiling. "You're the best at"—she tried for the word Pearl had used—"synopsis-es." Millie shrugged, and smiled, too.

So Pearl caved, determined to prove Elsa wrong about her being boring. She gave a synopsis of Harry Potter so complete, passionate, and engrossing that it took every minute of lunchtime. She hardly had time to take a bite of her tuna sandwich, only it was worth it to have someone listening with intense eyes like Millie's.

But when the bell rang at the end of lunch (Pearl had told only through Book 1), Elsa turned her shoulders away from Pearl and took Millie with her.

"Where ya going?" Pearl said. She knew it was a mistake but it came popping out of her mouth. She followed them, trailing slowly. Along the way, Elsa grabbed hold of Khadija, and by the time Pearl got there, they had set up a jump rope game.

"Can I jump in?" Pearl asked.

"Game's full," said Elsa. "There are two turners and one jumper."

"I'll wait my turn," said Pearl.

"Well, none of *us* wants to wait," said Elsa, jumping. "We've got just the right number as it is."

"Sorry, Pearl," said Millie, and looked it. But she didn't argue with Elsa.

"Sorry, Pearl," said Khadija, who knew how things usually went, and usually went along.

Pearl said, "Two people can jump at once, you know."

"That's not the plan," said Elsa.

"Why?" demanded Pearl, then felt too ashamed to continue.

They didn't even glance at each other, just watched Pearl while they turned the rope, the rhythm like a heartbeat.

Pearl turned away. She took *When You Reach Me*[2] out from under her arm and sat by the wall.

But she couldn't focus on her book. Something made her think of Francine. She glanced that way, and there was Francine in a group of kids from her class, playing four square. When she

---

2 *When You Reach Me* by Rebecca Stead (Wendy Lamb Books, 2009).

saw Pearl, she smiled and waved. Pearl tried to make it look like it was her choice to be sitting by the wall with her book. Well, wasn't it? Wasn't this the reason she'd brought the book with her, just in case? She gave Francine a big cheesy smile and a thumbs-up sign, and raised her eyebrows as if to say, *You okay?* She was going to pretend she hadn't seen Francine in the lunchroom. At least Francine hadn't been there to see Elsa embarrass Pearl.

Pearl skimmed her eyes around the playground. Just about everyone here was older than her. If only fifth grade was still on the lower playground, she could have gone to the lower-grade teachers and offered to push kids on the swings or catch them on the slide. She could have brought her own jump rope and taught the little kids. She could have pretended she wasn't interested in jump rope or playing or friends anyway. And she wouldn't have to pretend she was sitting alone on purpose.

10: NOT JUST ANY NEW YORKER

SEP 8

The first stupid week of the school year was finally over when the bad news came in the form of an email from the mayor's office in Bruce's inbox. At the four o'clock meeting that afternoon, Bruce dropped the bomb of this news onto his staff.

"Listen, all," he said, and he read out the email: "'Please be advised that a real-estate developer (he meant Mr. Dozer) has entered a proposal to buy the library building from the city. At its meeting on October 2, the library board will vote on whether to consider the proposal, which involves repurposing the building for residences. The vote will take into account the library's consent (or lack thereof) and budget for the coming year. If the proposal is approved for consideration, a vote to decide between the two proposals will be put before the neighborhood in the district vote on Election Day.'

"So October 2 is the vote on the question," he concluded.

"What question?" asked Pearl.

"Whether the library building can be repurposed—given another use."

"Then what?" Pearl said, gaping.

"Of course we'll submit our new budget plan. But if the library board votes October 2 to consider the new proposal for the library building, then the neighborhood will get to weigh the apartments against the library on Election Day."

"And that could be that," said Alice. "If they vote for apartments, then no more library."

"Unless the voters think we have a better plan, a better budget," said Bruce.

"With better circulation," said Mom.

"And better neighborhood support," said Alice.

There was a frightening silence.

"They can't just do that," said Pearl. She wrapped her arms over her middle, to hold herself strong and upright.

"We'll appeal to the city to throw out Mr. Dozer's proposal, of course," said Mom.

Bruce's shoulders sagged. "Yes, Patricia, but they'll allow it anyway," he said. "Look at our circ, up only a few percent, and that's just because Vincent's head got stolen and people felt guilty walking in to see *that,* so they took out a book. No other reason. Nobody cares!"

Pearl exploded. "This is a *library*. It's *our* library. You can't just—" She held up her hands as if grabbing a big globe. "You can't just barge in here and take over and build new apartments because you don't like what's already here!"

"If you have enough money," said Simon grimly, "you can."

"But we—" Still grabbing at the air, Pearl found a phrase she'd heard somewhere. "We perform an important public service!"

Everyone smiled kindly. Mom said, "There's only so much room for services performed by the city. The city can't just *give out*. It needs to bring money *in*—or it needs buildings to be at least self-sufficient. Which ours isn't."

And there was something about this thought, this story of the way things were, something so solid, sure, real, and solemn, that all the grown-ups seemed stopped by it. They seemed ready to let the moment to fight pass right by.

Not Pearl. "This is war!" she said.

There were some exhalations that were almost little laughs. She glared around wildly.

"Well," said Bruce. "You're right that those builders have certainly thrown down the gauntlet."

"A gauntlet's a glove," explained Ramón, before anyone could ask. "It's a challenge to the status quo—the way things are."

"What's wrong with the way things are?" Pearl wailed. "This is our *home!*"

But nobody answered that. Bruce turned and went back upstairs, and Mom followed him.

Pearl thought her heart would jump out of her chest.

The others were giving her sympathetic looks, and she felt even worse, because if they were being sympathetic with *her,* they must think she couldn't handle it. "I'll be on the stoop," Pearl said sharply, making eye contact with no one, and blasted onto the bustling street full of people going home to their own status quo, not realizing how quickly a gauntlet could be thrown into it, or whatever! Pearl tore down the steps almost to the sidewalk, stopped abruptly, and stood leaning on the iron rail, feeling as if she had run a long distance but still had far to go.

Nichols came out and sat on the steps, his backpack beside him. Pearl walked up past him, then back down again, then did about seven more ups and downs before he said, "Stop."

She stopped. She said, "None of this would have happened if Vincent's head hadn't gotten stolen. That's how those bulldozer guys found out, because it was in the paper. If we could get the head back, it could get in the paper again, and then maybe people would see *that,* and know the neighborhood cares." She paused.

It was Mom who had called the paper in the first place. If she hadn't, would Mr. Bull and Mr. Dozer have had their idea to turn the library into apartments?

"Well, what are you gonna do?" said Nichols. It may have just been something people said when there wasn't anything to say, but Pearl took him seriously.

"Find the head myself!" She thought about Harry Potter, how the adults in those books were always telling the kids things were under control, but they never were, and how the kids always had to sneak around figuring things out for themselves. And Pearl didn't even have magic on her side.

"Who do you think took it?" Nichols stood up and pulled his backpack onto his shoulders.

She was silent, but her mind whirled.

Nichols said. "Work on that, Pearl. G'night."

"Bye," she said. He disappeared into the crowd. Pearl sat down. Rush-hour people tramped in and out of green-haired Rosita's Rosebud bodega and home, carrier bags over their arms. Gully's Buck-a-Buy looked busy, too. The lights were on upstairs in Francine's apartment. Things seemed calm but felt the opposite.

Pearl thought back on the head's disappearance and all the theories people had put forth about the thieves in the two weeks since then.

1. Alice had guessed idiots. (That could be anybody.)

2. Gully had accused punks, gangs, college students. (Also unspecific.)

3. The police figured it was pranksters. (But the head hadn't turned up anywhere they had suggested it might.)

4. One cop had suggested Ramón. (No way.)

5. Bruce himself thought it was criminals, robbers. (Obviously, but who?)

6. Pearl suspected the raccoons. (Too small, not strong enough. Good climbers, though.)

Pearl stopped. In Mom's stories, anyway, the raccoons saw and heard everything that happened in the garden. That's how they'd learned to read, after all, according to the stories. (Pearl couldn't believe her own crazy thoughts.) But still: Had the raccoons in the trees seen the head get stolen?

Alice, Simon, and Ramón came out just then, and trooped down the front steps to the sidewalk. Ramón backed his pickup truck out of the alley driveway and drove off. Simon threw his leg over his bicycle and whizzed away, his guitar case on his back. Alice walked to the corner to wait for Danesh to pick her up on his way home from the school where he taught. Last of all, Mom came out and said, "Ready?"

"Where's Bruce?" said Pearl.

"Writing the appeal," said Mom. "Going to battle."

Pearl and Mom walked two blocks along Lancaster Avenue, then turned left on Beep Street, and up the stoop to their tiny apartment.

Pearl picked up the mail from the floor. "Look, the *New Yorker*," she said, knowing Mom would be glad, and Mom gave a little "Hooray!" The *New Yorker*[1] was Mom's one treat to herself, and she took one evening a week to read it cover to cover, no matter how late she had to stay up to finish it.

Mom heated the skillet and melted butter. Pearl microwaved peas, got out the milk and eggs, and put English muffins in the toaster. When the eggs went sizzling into the pan, she asked, her throat opening just enough to let the words squeeze out, "Can those guys really go building all over the library if they want to?"

---

1 The *New Yorker* is an actual magazine.

"Not if the city doesn't decide to sell the property. But now they're first in line to make a bid, and the city is willing to at least look at a bid, and maybe accept it. We're surely not making the city any money. So we have to prove we're doing the city good in another way."

"But why?"

"Because the city owns the library building. But they just built a new library, so maybe they think there's a more economical use for our building. And the contractors are asking for the library board to say that the building can become residential—a place where people live."

"Will they let it?" Pearl wished Mom would say *the library,* not *the building.*

"Probably. Everything else around here is both commercial (that's businesses) and residential, so I'm sure our building can be both." Pearl thought of all the stores that had apartments on their upper floors.

"But the city is saying the library gets to counter-propose," Mom went on. "If we can make a case—if Bruce can—then they'll let the district vote on what they want the building to be."

Mom dished up the eggs and buttered the English muffins. Pearl spooned peas onto the plates and felt Mom waiting for her to ask the next question.

"When will we know if the district gets to vote?"

"October 2. You heard the email."

"October 2 is too soon!"

Mom studied Pearl as if wondering whether she could handle the truth, then announced, "It's probably been in the works since well before the Knickerbocker branch opened."

Pearl fingered the mailing label on the *New Yorker* cover, stuck and unstuck it on her hand, silently counting months. "Almost a year?" she asked. How could these plans have been going on without the library itself knowing about it? How was that allowed?

"Pearl girl, I know it feels awful and sad, but we're going to have to get our heads around it," Mom said. "Change might be coming."

Pearl folded a whole English muffin into a bundle and stuffed it all into her mouth so tight she could barely breathe. She chewed a long time and finally swallowed. "So you're just going to let the library get sold?"

"What can I do if that's the way things turn? What can anybody do? Look at poor Bruce, trying to write an appeal so the city will keep the building. Especially because there are so many physical problems with it. If the city decides it's too expensive to address them—"

"Would they give you a job at the Knickerbocker branch?" asked Pearl.

"I doubt it. They've already got a circ librarian. Maybe if they needed a new library director, but—"

"What about Bruce?"

"Who knows. He's always talking about going back to his park."

"What? Why? Wouldn't you want to go with him?"

"I'm not thinking about that, Pearl," Mom said.

It was a weird answer.

"There's a lot of staff," she went on. "I don't see how any one branch could have jobs for all four of us."

"What about Simon? What about Mr. Nichols? What about *me*? Would I have to go to a different school if we moved?"

Mom said only, "Pearl, hand me the milk." Then she leaned in so close that their noses nearly bumped. "We will survive. We can survive anything. And be sure of one thing, Pearlie. If we have to move, it won't be because *I* didn't try to stop it."

"But how? What can anybody do if Bruce's appeal doesn't work?" Pearl was sticking and unsticking the mailing label furiously now. She hadn't seen Mom do much of anything except call up the paper—*which seemed to have been the start of all our problems*, Pearl thought meanly.

But Mom snatched the mailing label away from Pearl and smacked it back on the magazine cover, right over the title. "That's it," said Mom. "*New Yorkers!*"

"What about them?" Pearl remembered something. "You mean Unique New Yorkers? Like the ones that Jonathan Yoiks wants to find?"

"Some of his Unique New Yorkers are a little too unique for my taste," said Mom. "Tightrope walkers! Cat-castle builders! I'm all for being talented, but I prefer regular neighborhood people who do unique things. Brave things."

"What kinds of things do you want neighborhood people to do?"

"We have to get the neighborhood to want to save the library. We need a marketing plan! You're the detective, Pearl—" She tapped her fingertip on her daughter's forehead. "Who was the last person to come in the door for the first time?"

Pearl thought a moment. "Francine," she said. "Is she special?" She sure hoped not.

"Absolutely right. What brought her? Books?"

"Vincent," said Pearl.

Mom nodded. "Now there was a Unique New Yorker. But for doing what? Not climbing skyscrapers, although heaven knows New York needs that, too. But for just being good at what she did every day, which was writing poems."

"Well, what do you want me to do, scream every day?"

"Francine doesn't come to hear you scream," said Mom. "She looks at books. We need to figure out how to make more Francines."

But Pearl heard something else underneath what Mom was saying about the library. She heard something that was just about Francine—and about Pearl herself. Francine had come for the scream and stayed for the books, but now she kept coming for Pearl, too.

* * *

It was out on the stoop, many rounds of gin later, when the traffic finally seemed to go quiet and Mom glanced over her shoulder.

"Oh, look!" she whispered, so quietly she was practically mouthing the words.

A large humpbacked raccoon had emerged from the shadows below the stoop of the next house and was loping along the front of their house. It skirted the stoop, then scuttled along the front edge to the shadow of the next stoop. The raccoon was surprisingly fast. Before Pearl could react, it had reached the corner and turned toward Seventh Avenue, just like any neighbor heading for the subway.

"Where do you think he's going?" Pearl asked, thinking of the paw inside the basement window of the library. Those prints had seemed to be the same size as the ones in the garden. This raccoon's paws were definitely bigger.

"*She,*" Mom told her. "Work, of course. That was Mrs. Mallomar."

"Do tell," invited Pearl. Her mouth was hanging open. It was the first time Pearl had ever seen Mrs. Mallomar—or any of Mom's raccoons—in person.

Mom studied her cards a moment, then folded the hand into

her lap and began. "Well. Mrs. Mallomar must have just put the midnight *Moon* to bed."

"*What?*"

"That's a press term. 'Putting to bed' is finishing the paper so it's ready to be printed and sold."

"What's the lead story?" Pearl asked.

"You know," said Mom, "there hasn't been much news lately, so it's been a while since the midnight *Moon* went to press with anything but gossip and personal ads. Mrs. Mallomar and her staff have been combing the neighborhood for events. Naturally they interviewed the coyotes."

Pearl laid her cards facedown on the stoop and folded her arms comfortably, settling into the story.

"There are plenty around here, and they're even more stealthy than the raccoons. Coyotes have always got their noses to the ground, like good detectives. But the coyotes didn't have any gossip. So Mrs. Mallomar went to the skunks, but they hadn't caught a whiff of anything, either."

Pearl couldn't help but laugh. Mom was a good storyteller, you couldn't argue with that.

"The opossums said Matilda was looking for a nest in the pine trees, but they had the story upside down as usual. Matilda was up in the tree trying to talk to the flying squirrels, who had been talking to the bats. And the *bats* finally revealed something interesting. You know how the library has two chimneys?"

It did. There was a fireplace in the reading room, and another in the reference room, both long-ago sealed up.

"Well, the bats had winkled their way into one of the chimneys and found it was not completely closed off. They couldn't get into the fireplaces, so they couldn't get into the library, but they had found a route to the basement."

"There are bats in the basement?"

"No, they're just scouts. They don't want to live inside any-way," said Mom. "They told the flying squirrels about a certain space behind the drainpipe on the garden wall. They'd been in there doing research. That is, eavesdropping. Typical bat behavior. The bats' editorial column this week is all about the contractors' proposal."

Pearl's head spun. "So what's Mrs. Mallomar's story about?"

"It's about the impact of new construction on raccoon habitats near the library. If the library gets turned into apartments, they'll cut down the trees for parking, and all the raccoons in those trees will be at risk. Think of all the little raccoon kits running around—that'll be dangerous for them."

"Mom," said Pearl. "Do you think the raccoons saw who took Vincent's head?"

"Hmm," was all Mom said.

"So where's Mrs. Mallomar going now?" Pearl asked. She pointed down the street in the direction the raccoon had taken. She was pretty sure telling this story was cheering Mom up, and she wanted to keep that happening.

"To take the midnight shift at the newsstand, of course," said Mom. "Just because she's put the paper to bed doesn't mean *she* goes to bed. It's the middle of the day for a raccoon! And Tallulah has to sleep sometime."

"Did you ever think Tallulah and Mrs. Mallomar could be related?" she asked her mother. "Like she's the human version of Mrs. Mallomar and Mrs. Mallomar is the raccoon version of her?"

"The question is why Mrs. Mallomar has chosen to let us see her going about her business *now*, when she never has before."

"Then how did you know her business?" Pearl asked.

"Oh, that was just—"

Pearl knew Mom wanted to say "a story." Instead she reached for Pearl's cards. "Time to put *you* to bed."

11: THE INVADER

SEP 9

At 3:17 a.m. Saturday morning, Mom's phone rang. Then: "Someone's broken into the library!" she told Pearl, whispering her awake. "The police are on their way. Bruce wants us to meet them at the library. He'll be there, too."

Police cars were pulled up right on the sidewalk in front of the building and squeezing into the tiny alley, their lights flashing against the windows. The library's alarm system was buzzing in the misty, humid city night. The police—two of the ones who had come about Vincent's head, plus two more—were at the front doors, shining big flashlights through the heavy glass. If someone had broken in, why weren't *they* in? And what had been stolen this time?

"Is it Vincent again?" yelled Pearl, running up the sidewalk. "Maybe the founders' portraits? Or the clock?"

Mom took the front steps in two leaps. The police stepped back so she could open the door with her keys, but they wouldn't let her or Pearl in until they'd gone in first to check things out. You could see their flashlights shooting light up the stairs to the floors above. After a while they returned to the first floor and opened the door for Mom, shrugging.

"False alarm, maybe," Pearl heard the policeman with the mustache say as he finally let them in. Mom flung open the door. Pearl tore into the back hall, flipped on the back hall light, and saw, through the window, no change to Vincent. When she came back, the blue uniforms were all clustered around the circulation desk.

"Maybe a raccoon set off the security system," said the puffy pink policeman.

(As if a raccoon would do that, either accidentally or on purpose.)

Pearl walked back outside. It was the deep dark middle of the night. She didn't dare go farther than the front sidewalk. Over Gully's storefront, Francine's shades were drawn and the windows were dark.

Pearl stopped and turned back toward the library. In the window at the dimmest corner of the reference room, she saw something—a face! Salt-and-pepper hair, gray shirt, and a face the color of last week's newspaper, eyes that had never looked so lonely and lost. "Mr. Nichols!"

Pearl waved at him wildly and ran back inside. A small swarm of police officers had already surrounded him, flashlights flaring, pulling him into the light of the circ area.

"Some old drunk!" a policewoman bawled over her shoulder to Mom.

"He's not drunk! Leave him alone! He was just sleeping! Get your hands off him!" Pearl stood squarely in front of them, blocking their way.

"What is he, then, if he's not drunk? Lost? Misguided? Typical."

"Not typical of *him*!"

"Pearl, I'm all right—" Nichols looked dazed, but he stood straight, trying to get her to simmer down.

"You know him?" said the red-haired officer.

"It's all right! We know him." Pearl had never been so proud of her mother. Mom took Nichols firmly by the arm as if to say she'd be in charge of him, although Pearl knew there was no taking charge of Nichols. He might move slowly, but he went where he wanted.

The cops said something about breaking and entering, but Mom cut him off. "The library won't be pressing charges."

"This is a city establishment, *miss*." "Miss" seemed to be emphasized.

"It is the *library*," said Mom. "And I am the *librarian*."

The policewoman shook her finger. "Well, if the *city* decides to press charges—"

Mom shook her own finger right back. "Oh, I'd *love* to see the city get involved with the library," she said fiercely. "Maybe we should make a report to the mayor."

Mom led the police away, distracting them from Mr. Nichols by asking their opinion about the situation of crime in the neighborhood: Was there more breaking and entering lately? Were there more robberies? Should the city update the library's antique security system, in their opinion? Would they put it in a report?

Nichols and Pearl were left at the dusky circulation desk. "I fell asleep," Nichols told her. "In the chair behind

A Sidebar About Exclamation Points

It's my opinion that you just about never need to use an exclamation point. Basically, if your writing doesn't make it clear that something is a big deal, then the exclamation point is not going to fix that. And yet!

It's not just words that make something a big deal. Even more important is something called *inflection*—the *way* something is said. That's what an exclamation point is good for: adding emotion that is *different* from what's already in the words.

Compare, for example:

"He's not drunk. Leave him alone."

Sounds kind of lazy, doesn't it?

"He's not drunk! Leave him alone!"

That's much more urgent, the way Pearl was when she said it.

the atlas, where we always sit. When I woke up, it was dark." He held his forehead in his hands, rubbing. "I tried to find my way out, but the doors were locked on the inside. Then I must have tripped the alarm somehow. All of a sudden there was a light in my face . . . sirens . . . yelling . . . noise!" He covered his ears with his hands and closed his eyes as if he was so embarrassed he wanted to shut her out. "I'm sorry!"

Pearl pulled his hands down from his ears. She hated, absolutely hated, how scared he looked. "It was Bruce's fault for locking you in," she said.

"No," said Nichols, shaking his head, trying to gather himself together.

"It's okay, Mr. Nichols," Pearl told him. "Don't worry," she added.

Bruce—finally, he was here!—elbowed his way through a small crowd of neighbors that had gathered on the street, toward Mom and the cops. "I'm the library manager," he said. "It's my fault this man was in the library."

"And now I'm on my way," Nichols said, his voice still quavering. He turned and made a little bow. "Thank you, Pearl. Thank you, Mrs. Moran." He hoisted his backpack over his shoulder and walked off into the dark. At least he hadn't been arrested.

But the night wasn't over. Gully came tearing across the street, his hair messed up from sleep, having maybe slept in his clothes. He seemed to wish he could run two ways—toward the cops, and after Nichols. He flung his arms in each direction, demanding, "You're not going to just turn a man like that loose in the neighborhood at this time of night, are you?"

None of the police moved a muscle.

Bruce put an arm around Gully's shoulders. "No harm's been done," he said.

"No harm! Lights and bells in the middle of the night! This area didn't used to welcome—"

"What?" said Bruce.

Gully shut up a second, then changed tack. "Anyway, I think the papers should know about this."

"Mr. Gulliver," Mom said through her teeth, "I think we should all go back to bed."

Gully went.

Pearl slumped down onto the front steps, her cheek against the iron railing, bone tired. The police took their time writing up their report as if the library was some huge crime scene instead of just a place where one man neglected to wake up and another forgot to check a dark corner.

Pearl's head dropped onto her chest for one minute . . . two minutes . . . a half hour. Then Mom's hand was on her shoulder.

"Come on, Pearl girl. Let's go home."

Pearl sleepwalked her way home between Mom and Bruce. She staggered to her chair-bed, kicked off her flip-flops, and rolled in. She stayed dimly awake for at least three minutes, long enough to notice that the sky was already getting a little bit light. It was long enough to notice that Bruce was still here in the apartment, in the kitchen talking to Mom, each of them calming the other one down after the scare. It was long enough to notice that they were laughing, the way they used to, when they used to talk about something else besides the library.

12: THE ROCK LADY

Pearl lay in the garden grass below Vincent's feet, still sleepy from the wild night before, her head buried in her arms, when she realized Francine was there beside her, toes clicking against the bricks.

"What are you doing, Pearl?"

"Writing a story."

"I don't see a pencil," said Francine.

"In my head," said Pearl.

"You've got a pencil in your head?"

Pearl rolled her eyes.

For several minutes Francine was so quiet Pearl thought she'd gone away until she said, "What's it about?"

These were magic words to a storyteller like Pearl. "It's about Vincent," she said, pointing up at the statue. She was sharply aware that for once an audience had come to her—usually she had to look for one.

Pearl began her story: "So. Vincent wakes up one day, a cold winter day, a cold winter day when the snow is falling, and she's freezing, hard as an ice cube. She wants to go into the library to get warm, but she can't move, since she's a statue."

"In my dance, the Rock Lady can move," said Francine.

"Your *dance*?" What was Francine talking about? "Also, Vincent is *not* called the Rock Lady."

Francine laughed. "Okay," she said. "Tell me about the Rock Lady—no, *Vincent*—before she starts moving."

Irresistible. "All right!" said Pearl. "So she starts to think about all the things she could do and see if only she wasn't frozen in place."

Francine said, "Want to make up the story together?"

If Pearl thought Francine had been listening, she was wrong. "Not if your story is about being headless," Pearl said.

"I've never known her any other way *but* headless," Francine admitted. "It's just that drama is more interesting than books. You should know, you're the one who screamed. What *book* did you ever scream about?"

"I screamed because Vincent has been here since before I was born. So she's like a member of my family. And how would you feel if one of your family members *got her head stolen*?"

Francine just said, "I think she's kind of cool, headless."

"What else do you think is cool, dead dogs and car wrecks?" Pearl felt, even as she said the words, that they were way too harsh.

It was Francine's turn to gape. "No," she said in a tiny voice, before tapping slowly away down the alley.

Too bad, Pearl thought, surprised at the drop she felt in her stomach at Francine's departure. Any audience was better than no audience.

But then Francine came flying back, her feet clattering. "He's coming! That reporter!"

And Mom and Simon appeared in the doorway with Jonathan Yoiks.

Two days ago, Pearl would have been overjoyed to see Yoiks: more publicity to help them get Vincent back. Now she thought of Mr. Bull and Mr. Dozer and how *that* publicity had turned out. What would Yoiks do with the Mr. Nichols "break-in"?

Francine was grinning up at the reporter, acting like she was ready for her close-up.

"Edna St. Vincent Millay was a Unique New Yorker," Pearl offered slyly.

Yoiks said, "That's not my angle on her." He walked around the garden taking pictures of Vincent from different sides.

(That was not what he meant by angles. He meant type of story: News? Feature? Human-interest? Profile? At the moment, Vincent didn't fit any of those. The truth was that Yoiks didn't seem to know exactly what kept drawing him back to the library. I call it journalistic instinct.)

"What did you come back here for?" Pearl finally asked.

"I came back to see my friend," Yoiks said. Francine stood taller and smiled as if she was ready for another pose. But Yoiks was nodding at Vincent.

"Is this for the paper?" Francine couldn't resist asking.

"Just for me, for now," Yoiks said with a sigh. "Until I can convince my editor it's worth covering. A human-interest story from a neighborhood like this? It would help Lancaster Avenue's image. Or even some crime leads? You

A Sidebar About Saving Other Souls (you might call it S.O.S.)

If you want to save someone, knowing what to do is half the battle, whether it's figuring out what to give a homeless person, rescuing a helpless animal, and so on. These are common skills you can learn.

But the hardest battle is noticing that there's a problem in the first place. That is another ability altogether, something that comes from the heart.

—M.A.M.

don't have any clues about the lost head yet, do you? It would be a better story if it got found someplace dire. That would make everybody happy. Good and dramatic. Headline-worthy."

Pearl squinted at him. Why was he here, if there wasn't a story good enough, dramatic enough, for his editor? She said, as if she was a television detective, "Well, they didn't use the wheelbarrow, and they didn't roll it in the grass."

"They?"

"The head robbers," she said. "The criminals."

Francine said, "The decapitators," in a way that made Yoiks chuckle.

"How much do you think a head like that might weigh?" he asked.

"As much as a bowling ball," Pearl said. "It's like a block of concrete."

(There was a strange little outraged peep from behind the bushes, but not a person there heard it except the boy who made it.)

"Here's another thought," said Yoiks. "From what I've seen of vandalism, it's about cheap thrills. Sometimes people just want to mess with your head—oops, sorry."

"What do you mean?" asked Simon, sidling over. Pearl caught his eye: Why was the reporter here, since there was nothing to report on? Why was he hanging around talking to a bunch of kids about a statue of a dead poet?

Yoiks turned to Simon. "I mean, the thrill for vandals is beheading the statue and having everybody wake up and find it gone. Once the pranksters have done that, they might just take the head and toss it somewhere nearby. If I were a vandal who'd stolen a head," Yoiks mused, "the first thing I'd do is get rid of the evidence."

Now Simon caught Pearl's eye: If the kids could solve the crime, would that be a juicy enough story for Yoiks's editor?

"Hey!" Yoiks gave a startling sort of whisper, and caught all their eyes. He cocked his head toward the garden and the pine trees. "Who's that kid?" he asked softly.

They looked to where he was pointing his chin and saw the back of a boy wearing baggy cargo shorts and a Day-Glo green shirt. The boy saw them looking and darted away, across the yard that backed up to the library garden.

"He's a spy!" Pearl said. "I've never seen him before in my life!"

"You, you think you know everybody," said Francine. "But I've seen that kid. He goes to Gully's all the time."

"Well, he's gone now," said Yoiks. "And so must I be. You all keep your eyes open and your thinking caps on." Since that was the kind of smarmy thing adults said to kids, Pearl and Francine caught each other's eyes and made faces.

"Trouble is, you don't know a good story when you hear one," said Pearl.

"Tell it to my editor," said Yoiks. "Or maybe I should say, 'Tell it to the marines!'"

"Stand up to him," said Francine. Yoiks just laughed, and left.

Simon trailed him, but not before hissing at the girls, "Leave that kid alone, you guys. If he's too shy to come to the library, don't make it worse for him."

The minute he was gone, Pearl began crawling through the yew bushes along the back of the library property. "What are you doing now?" asked Francine, tapping nervously next to the statue.

"Looking for Vincent's head, what do you think? If that boy can sneak around back there, maybe it's a good place to hide things." Pearl had to crouch to avoid clonking her head on the low branches of the pine trees. It was surprisingly dense in there.

"Is it spidery? Are there rats?" called Francine.

Pearl didn't answer, on purpose to increase the suspense. She felt as if she was in a forest.

"Pearl? Are you okay?"

"Quit worrying about me!" yelled Pearl, creeping back to the fence. An old wooden shed-shaped box came into sight. Could it be that easy? She'd open the lid, look inside, and there would be Vincent's head?

No. It was just somebody's old stuff: a flannel shirt too hot for a day like this, some other clothes, a duffel bag, and a mailing tube. She opened that: a thick roll of envelopes, letters to some woman Pearl didn't know, Berniece Hernández, Esq., in Albany, New York, which was the state capital.

"Did you find her?" Francine called from outside the bushes.

"No," said Pearl. "Just some old junk." She emerged from the trees, asking, "Why would that boy lurk around here near those smelly dumpsters?" She felt satisfied with herself about the exploration and proud to have the secret of the box to herself.

Francine suggested, "Maybe he's just shy."

"Maybe he saw you dancing," Pearl teased. "Maybe he wants you to dance some more."

Francine looked amused. She started tip-tapping on the path.

"Anyway, what's the story behind your Rock Lady dance?" Pearl asked, cursing herself for even thinking the name "Rock Lady."

Francine gave her a distrustful eye and sat down in the grass, leaning back on her hands. "Tell me your story first."

"Why?"

"Because I don't believe you can think of a really good one. You don't seem to have that much creativity to me. You just tell stories out of books."

Pearl went deadly quiet. She knew a challenge when she heard it. She thought Francine was—what had Ramón said?—throwing down the gauntlet. She leaned forward and tapped her forehead. "It's all right here," she said, as if her brain held treasure.

Francine snorted, but a man's voice said, "I'd put my money on any story of Pearl's."

"Mr. Nichols!" Pearl jumped up.

He looked the same as ever: denim jacket, clean khaki pants, one of his four T-shirts, the one with the arrowhead on it and the words ARROW NAILS. Pearl didn't know why, but part of her had expected he would look different after the alarm incident.

"I'm here to tell you that your mother is looking for you. And that I'm leaving."

"It's not closing time already, is it?" Francine sprang up from the ground. Pearl wondered what the drama was about closing time. What would that granny of hers do if she came home and found Francine not there? Anything?

"No, hon," said Nichols. "It's not even noon."

"You're not leaving *for good*, right?" asked Pearl. "That isn't what you meant? Going back where you—"

"Where I came from? No," he said. "I don't have anything back there."

"What do you have here?" Francine asked.

Pearl could have killed her. But Nichols smiled his sweetest smile. "All this!" he said, spreading his hands again. "But Pearl, your mother is not happy with me."

"She's just worried about the library's reputation," said Pearl. She'd woken up to Bruce and Mom arguing about "how this will look to the neighborhood" that morning.

"Fortunately for me, I think Mr. Bull and Mr. Dozer have the hotter story," Nichols said.

"Vincent's the hot story," said Pearl desperately, knowing she was wrong.

"Not that many people are interested in an old statue," he said carefully.

"But the statue started all this," said Francine. "Didn't she?"

"Among others," said Nichols.

"Like who?" said Francine.

"How about you?" said Nichols, to Francine. Pearl couldn't believe Francine would get all the credit, again.

"*Me?*"

"You'd never been to the library before the head went missing, right?" And with that Nichols turned and went down the driveway, his heavy, worn-out backpack over his shoulder, the umbrella under his arm.

The girls watched solemnly. Francine might not know everything about Vincent and the library, figured Pearl, but she knew that Nichols was homeless and liked him anyway. Grownups always told you not to talk to the homeless people that slept on the street. But what was so bad about not having a home?

Shouldn't everyone feel sympathetic to people who didn't have a place to live?

She could tell that Francine, too, was wondering where Nichols was on his way to, maybe asking herself where he was going to sleep, and that made Pearl warm even more toward her.

But then Francine said, "Do you think *he* stole the head?"

"What? That's stupid. Why would he?" Pearl stalked off, leaving Francine kicking at the grass.

"I don't know! Everyone seems to think the stolen head is what made me come to the library. But it wasn't. It was you, screaming."

"Drama, in other words," said Pearl with great scorn. She threw her arms around Vincent's pedestal and wondered what was going to become of them all.

"Drama? I thought someone was being killed!"

"That's not drama?"

"No, that's caring. I thought maybe you were hurt. I thought maybe you needed saving."

Pearl snapped, "And you thought *you* could save me?"

Francine looked so hurt. But she changed to mad really fast. "Save you? No, obviously. You do everything *yourself*. You could save yourself *yourself*." She wasn't even making sense. And with that she was gone, running down the driveway, her tap shoes clacking no rhythm at all.

Pearl was left behind, alone and thinking about Francine wanting to save her. *Was* it drama? She, Pearl, *had* screamed for a real reason. And Francine's reason for running to her rescue— to help—was actually quite noble. And the rest of the neighborhood? Had they had such good intentions?

Take Gully, for example. He was a neighbor. He had known her mom forever. It was natural that if something went wrong at the library, he would want to know what was up. Maybe caring was what made him want to know what happened. But drama was what had made him come and see for himself. It was Pearl's scream—the whiff of drama—that had brought him to the library the day Vincent's head got stolen. (Or was it worry that his business was going to be affected by that drama?) It was flashing lights—scary and awful to Pearl, but drama to the max for Gully—that had pulled him out of bed at three in the morning.

Pearl got an idea like a glimpse of light through a dark window. If drama had made Gully come running, what did it do for other people? Answer: It made them do things they would normally not do, for one reason or another. Like come to the library.

Pearl hadn't meant to scream, but she had created drama that once. Realizing this felt like a little jolt of power. She wondered—could she do it again? And how?

13: ALMOST FLATTENED

For the next week, the library staff reacted to the Nichols incident by being extra careful at closing time. One after another, they checked Nichols's chair behind the atlas stand, not wanting to shut him in again. From across the street, on his stool behind the register at the Buck-a-Buy, Pearl could see Gully watching, too, his curiosity or need for drama or business security unsatisfied. One night Simon had to accidentally-on-purpose crash the book cart into the atlas shelf and wake Nichols so he could leave in time for closing.

Pearl found herself considering Francine's idea that maybe Nichols had stolen Vincent's head. *No way,* Pearl told herself. What on earth would Nichols want with Vincent's head?

"At least it's not cold in September," Mom said, after he'd gone one night.

"It will be in October," said Pearl.

"Hey, the college students are back," said Alice, looking for something cheerful to say. There were always a few ragtag students who adopted the public library because it was quieter and cozier than their massive university stacks. They even took books out, which lifted circ a few more percentage points.

"Hope we're still here at midterms," said Ramón.

"You don't expect the starving students to pitch in for our miserable heating bill, do you?" asked Bruce.

"Or the spiral staircase. It's wobblier than ever," Simon observed.

"So use the straight stairs," said Pearl, who would admit nothing wrong with her library.

"If only there was more money in the world," said Ramón.

"There are so many amazing new children's books coming out," Alice said to herself. "But when's the last time a new school-age kid came in here?"

"It's the library's image," said Mom. "Teens and tweens are too cool for it. The library is for moms and toddlers and old people."

Pearl felt the burn deep in her tween heart. "And homeless people." To change the subject, she asked, "What does Mr. Nichols eat?" She'd always wondered, but never felt like she could ask. Now, post–"break-in," things felt different. She wanted Nichols to be okay.

"There's that soup kitchen in the basement of the firehouse," Mom reminded her.

"Who pays for that?" Pearl asked.

"The city," said Simon.

"Money for soup kitchens, but not libraries?" asked Pearl.

Mom gave her a frown. "Food or books, Pearl?" she asked. "Which would you choose, if you're the mayor?"

Bruce touched Pearl's shoulder. "Or police protection?"

"Or fire protection?" asked Ramón.

Pearl swallowed. How could anyone choose? "Houses," she said. "Warm, safe houses with food and books."

Alice said, "That's what they want to put in here."

"Everybody should have both," said Pearl.

"Amen to that," said Mom, and hugged her.

"Amen," they all agreed.

But to herself, as she and Mom packed their tote bags and headed home, Pearl thought: Agreeing on needing houses and books was one thing. Waking Nichols to ask him to leave at night was another. Pearl started to think about the library at night, how it just sat there empty once Bruce finally left. Why *couldn't* Nichols sleep there?

* * *

That night after dinner, while it was still light, Pearl walked to Tallulah's for the *Moon*. She had a banana and a granola bar in her pocket, and she stopped at the library to pop the snacks into the little shed-shaped box she'd found, where the old clothes and the stack of letters were. It was almost dark by the time she walked back, wondering if a certain someone would find the food she'd left.

She had just passed Gully's when she heard a thin, savage scream.

(Another scream? Yes. And another turning point, too.)

Pearl spun around. She glimpsed movement along the foundation of the library. A raccoon—a tiny one, nowhere near as big as the one she and Mom had seen from the stoop, even smaller than the one Pearl had seen in the basement. A baby?

At that moment, all of the following things happened. First, she heard a loud *ak-ak-ak* chattering, as if an animal was scolding. Second, a taxi came whizzing down Lancaster Avenue. The little raccoon was in the headlights in front of it, staring into the beam. The scream was nearer now, louder, coming from another raccoon in the alley, a larger one. It was screaming at the little one, trying to stop it.

"No!" Pearl shouted, darting into the street.

Pearl bounded into the headlight beam, scooped the wild animal into her hands, and jumped back to the sidewalk. Brakes screeched. The taxi driver gave a furious yell. "Stupid kid!" The taxi peeled out, and the traffic raced on.

Pearl was shaking. The little raccoon was going nuts in her hands, spinning and twisting and doing its own miniature version of the *ak-ak-ak* noise. The alley rang with the scolding of the bigger raccoon. Scolding *Pearl* now, she guessed, a mama worried about her baby.

Pearl let the raccoon down gently onto the sidewalk. It dashed away into the shadow of the library, and both raccoons disappeared into the darkness. Pearl stood staring after them, but by the time her eyes adjusted from the glare of the street, nothing was there.

"Got the paper?" Mom asked as Pearl came in the door.

"Right here," said Pearl. She kept the baby raccoon, the big raccoon, the taxi, the banana, and the granola bar to herself, not knowing why.

The speeding taxi and the screeching raccoon had sent her dashing into the street toward a near-death experience. Why had she done something so risky?

Drama—and caring. The magic combination.

***

Gully caught Pearl's eye as she passed his door on the way to the newsstand the next morning. He waved the paper at her, looking triumphant. Dread grew in her stomach when she saw the front-page headline: TROUBLED NEIGHBORHOOD, ELUSIVE REMEDY. Yoiks's editor had won again.

"What's *elusive*?" asked Pearl.

"Hard to find," said Ramón. "Slippery, like an eel."

"And are we *troubled*?"

"Well, he makes the neighborhood sound sad."

(In fact, Yoiks made the neighborhood sound more like it was *trouble*. You could only hope the story was part one of a multi-part series, and that the next parts would be solutions or celebrations.)

The story was about a lot of little things that Yoiks made a big deal out of. It mentioned the animal graffiti that was suddenly all over Lancaster Avenue, as if there was something bad about street art. It mentioned the mugging outside Big Foods, as if one mugging was the symptom of a disease. And it lumped together "a would-be library patron tripping the night alarm" and "vandalism of a historic statue"—as if those things were connected—under the heading of mysterious midnight creepers (as if there was something naturally bad about being out at night.) All of this made it sound as if the theft of the head and an intruder—Nichols!—and the mugging and the coyote graffiti were all one big connected crime.

When Ramón was done reading the story aloud to the staff, Pearl said, "Thanks a lot, Gully." It was obvious from several anonymous quotes that he had been a willing source for the story.

"Is there a picture?" asked Simon. There was a small photograph of Vincent looking especially pathetic and headless, and a picture of a howling dog painted on a wall. No poems. No pictures of the library or its staff.

The caption: *Lost on Lancaster Avenue: one stone head, much neighborhood pride*

"We've lost our pride? This is like the last rites," said Bruce. "Next time we make it into the paper, it will be an obituary."

Mom hugged him, right in front of all of them. It was unusual, and Pearl felt like pebbles of light were exploding in her heart. Mom said, "Look, we tried to get the media on our side, and that hasn't worked. We've just gotten lumped in with other crimes."

"Here's another way to look at that," Ramón said. "He starts by making the reader be concerned about the neighborhood. He sets up a scenario where people are looking for a way to fix it—the remedy. Maybe the first step to improving a scenario is to bring attention to it."

"Those newspaper people aren't interested in helping us save our library," said Bruce, and that made Mom walk back out of his arms.

(Bruce was wrong, anyway. Yoiks didn't like the headline any better than we did. He'd been overridden by his editor, which sometimes happens.)

Mom said, "We have to turn it around, that's all, find a way to make the library vital to the community. That's how we get the votes we need to stop the apartments."

"Vital to the community!" Bruce looked weary. "That's a tall order."

Mom said, "If we can just get more library cards into people's hands . . ."

"What people?" said Alice. "Children?"

"Teenagers?" asked Simon.

"Young women?" asked Mom, looking at Alice, thinking of mothers.

A Sidebar About Cannoli

I love words. I love being able to write exactly what I mean. Take the word "sweet." It has two meanings that are different but not so far apart.

Bruce did not know what to do after Yoiks's sad article about the neighborhood was published in the *Moon,* so he did something sweet, in one meaning, with something sweet, in the other meaning: a box of cannoli from Little Italy.

A cannoli is a crunchy pastry tube, kind of like a cookie that comes out of the oven soft, then gets rolled around a spoon handle to make a cylinder. It dries hard, then it's filled with a mixture of mascarpone cheese (a soft sugary mush) and crushed chocolate chips.

If you want to do something both-meanings-sweet for me, go to Mulberry Street and buy half a dozen cannoli, cart them back to the library, put the box in the book elevator, push *B*, and forget about it. I'll take care of the rest.

I'm breaking my own rule about advancing the plot. This sidebar doesn't. It's just an ode—a praise— to cannoli. And to bringing food to hungry people. And to sweetness. Caring. Pick your own exact word.

—M.A.M.

"How about lonely people?" asked Pearl. "Or people who need someplace to go." She was thinking of Mr. Nichols, going off alone into the dark with just that backpack. And, she had to admit this, too, that she was thinking about Francine's sad, hurt face when she'd told Pearl why she'd come to the library the first time—to help someone. To help her, Pearl. "Lonely people have more time to care, maybe," Pearl added.

PART TWO:
THE PLOT THICKENS

"Oh, if instead she'd left to me
The thing she took into the grave!
That courage, like a rock, which she
Has no more need of, and I have."

—"THE COURAGE THAT MY MOTHER HAD"[1]
BY EDNA ST. VINCENT MILLAY

1 From the poem "The courage that my mother had," from *Mine the Harvest* by
Edna St. Vincent Millay (Harper, 1954).

14: THE ROCK BOY

SEP 18

The boy in the Day-Glo green T-shirt was inside the library. He stood with his fingertips on the edge of the circulation desk. Before Mom even noticed he was there, he announced, "I found a new head for your statue."

Pearl sat up straight so fast she bumped her head against the globe, setting it spinning. "Vincent doesn't need a new head!" she yelled across the reference room, startling an old lady who was poring over pictures of tulip bulbs in a big *National Geographic*.[1]

The first thing she noticed about the boy, now that he was near, was his eyes. They were a light bright green in his pale, pale face and were almost as oddly lit as his shirt and his white-blond hair. The light didn't come from the color of his eyes, and it wasn't reflecting from

GO
CLIM
A
ROC

---

1 *National Geographic* is an actual magazine. Most of the covers have bright yellow edges.

his shirt. The light had something to do with what he was saying, or how he was saying it.

He came over to her nook behind the atlas shelf. "It's granite," he said. "There's lots of granite around here. It's native to this part of the country. So if you want to get the new head carved, I'm a good man with rocks—" Here his voice rose, all hopeful, out of a low beginning-teenage voice to a still-in-middle-school one. "And I've found the perfect piece of granite."

The front of his shirt said

GO

CLIMB

A

ROCK

The back said

YOSEMITE CLIMBING SCHOOL.

Pearl asked, "Did you go to Yosemite Climbing School?" Yosemite was a national park like the one Bruce used to work in. It was in California or somewhere.

"When I'm sixteen," the boy said, "I'm going cross-country. I'm going to buy a car and just drive until I get there."

He talked in that way of someone who was really smart about one topic and made you pay attention even if you weren't even interested. Pearl wasn't interested (in Vincent, yes; in raccoons, definitely; but granite? no), yet she couldn't help being impressed. She had never thought about what she'd do—just herself without Mom or anybody—but this boy had his plans made already.

"How old are you?" she asked.

"Fourteen." He put out a hand. "Oleg Boiko," he said. He could have added "professional rock geek," but he didn't have to. The rest of the geeks in the room had already figured him out.

"Pearl Moran. What grade are you in?" she asked, shaking his hand.

"Eighth," said Oleg. "At Lancaster Avenue."

Pearl's school. She hadn't noticed him there. "Transfer?" she asked. "From where?"

He named an elementary school, and she knew without being told that he'd fallen behind the year before. Nobody in eighth grade was already fourteen in September. Plus, Pearl's school was a magnet for messed-up middle-schoolers from other public schools. Something told her Oleg was good at science, but you had to be good at everything to be good at school.

"Would you like a library card, Oleg?" asked Mom.

"Sure," he said, coming back to the circ desk, probably because it was so obviously the right answer. Mom handed him an application and he started turning out his jeans pock-ets, scattering their contents on the circ counter: pebbles, a marble, a red bandana all scrunched up and dusty, a dirty sheet of folded pink paper (the "LOST HEAD" sign), and a dollar. "I don't have much money on me."

"Library cards are free," Mom said, and Oleg looked relieved. He started filling out the application.

"We have rock books," Pearl said, coming nearer to peer at Oleg's handwriting, which was tiny and neat, not what you'd expect from a bad student.

"Really?" Oleg's face was all light.

"Sure, in the geology section," said Simon, and the two boys went upstairs to the 551s.

"All this talk about why anybody comes to the library? *He* came out of kindness," said Ramón.

"I'm not sure we can count on kindness to bring our circulation numbers up. Kindness is a rare commodity. Anyway, you sound like you're talking about a space alien," said Mom. *"He came in kindness. I come in peace. Take me to your leader."*

Bruce shuffled quickly down the spiral staircase with a package for the library board office just as Francine's tap shoes clicked up the steps.

"No new head," Pearl was saying. "We don't want a new head."

"What, never? Just keep her headless?" asked Ramón.

"If she gets a new head, it will never look right. It could be all wrong! Plus people will stop trying to find the old head." Pearl was appalled at the catch in her voice, and struggled to control it.

"I don't know about that," said Bruce. "But payment for the sculpting of a new head is more money than I want to ask for."

"Bruce," said Mom. "If she stays headless, nobody will know who she is."

He blew out his breath. "We have to make choices!"

Pearl suddenly understood that it wasn't just money; it was also how much time you could put into any one problem, and Bruce just couldn't *do* everything. She grabbed Francine by her sparkly shirt and pulled her into the reference room. She whispered, "I've got a theory. That boy might be the thief."

Simon had left Oleg upstairs and followed them in. "Oleg Boiko?" He rolled the name across his tongue.

"Yeah. Did you see his muscles?"

Francine giggled.

Simon said, "How come you're noticing muscles lately? *I* didn't notice them."

Pearl flushed. "Simon, think! He climbs rocks. Maybe he can lift them, too. He could have lifted that head. And he was out there spying last week, from the other side of the fence."

Mom came in. She'd overheard them from behind the circ counter. "Let me get this straight," she said. "You think this boy has been staking out the library from some apartment over there, waiting for his moment to steal a *statue's head*? And he came and did it under the cover of night—"

"Yes!" Pearl liked the way Mom described it.

"Why would he do that?" called Ramón.

"Huh?" the girls said.

"It's not enough just to have a way to do it or the muscles to do it." Ramón came up and leaned against the doorframe. "Plenty of people have muscles. *Why* would that boy steal Vincent's head? What's his motive?"

Simon suggested, "Because he wanted the job of replacing it?"

Pearl had an idea, of course. "So, first he removes the head. Then he offers to replace the head. That way he gets the thrill and he gets the—"

"The reward of money!" said Francine. "When we pay him for the new head!"

"Could be," said Ramón. "All you have to do is prove he stole the old one." His owl eyes were twinkling, and Pearl could tell he was teasing them.

"Find the head in Oleg's house," said Simon, nodding mock-seriously. "Blow things wide open."

"The point is," said Mom, "the boy has a stone. And if Vincent gets a good head, we get some good publicity. We have a little ceremony. The press comes, some neighborhood folks—"

"So you're *for* it?" Pearl wailed at her mother. "But there's no way the head will look the same!"

Mom said nothing. Ramón shrugged. Simon raised his eyebrows. Only Nichols, who apparently had been awake for a while over in his chair, gave the group a sympathetic look, pushing out his lower lip and nodding sideways.

"Then it'll be a little different," he said.

15: APOLOGIES FOR MY DAUGHTER

SEP 22-23

On Friday night, Bruce came to dinner. Pearl took her veggie burger into the bedroom along with her vocabulary homework and *Pinky Pye*,[1] a good book about a cat who writes a story about solving a mystery, and who knows a thing or two about drama.

(Cats writing—that's a good one! I'd like to see a cat write Pearl a note.)

She worked, then read, then thought about raccoons solving mysteries, then eavesdropped enough to know that there were some interesting discussions about whether Alice's baby was going to come before Thanksgiving. The silences were also interesting. But then she heard Bruce say it had been Mr. Gulliver who'd told the real-estate men that the library building might be available for repurposing, and she had to clap her hands over her mouth to keep from shouting out. All along, she'd assumed that Mr. Bull and Mr. Dozer had gotten their idea from the first *Moon* story.

Her mother only said calmly, "Well, some developer would have figured it out eventually, the way things are going with

---

1 *Pinky Pye* by Eleanor Estes, illustrated by Edward Ardizzone (Harcourt, Brace & World, 1951).

developers moving into old neighborhoods all over the city."

"And kicking *out* all the old neighbors," said Bruce.

"Gully *is* one of the old neighbors," said Mom. "He ought to know better than to mess with me."

Pearl waited, but the conversation moved on to black vs. green tea at this time of night, and she didn't get to hear what her mother intended to *do* about Gully. But she thought about it until she fell asleep.

She wasn't able to do anything about it until the next morning at the library, when she casually said she was going to Gully's and slipped out. She was on the curb in front of the library, striding away, when Mom called down from the third floor, "Pearl! Wait!"

Mom emerged from the library, ran down the steps, and hurried across the street to Pearl.

"Why can't I go alone?" Pearl asked quietly. "*Gully* was the one who told those construction guys to come check out the old library!"

"Oh, Pearl!"

"I know I'm not supposed to eavesdrop, but you guys were talking so loud I couldn't *not* hear. Gully can't keep on

A Sidebar About Urban Legends

The most famous urban legend set in New York is the one about the alligators in the sewers. Like other legends (see chapter 5), it's a story that gets larger with retellings. People used to be stupider about taking animals out of their natural habitats. Rich people vacationing in Florida could buy baby alligators and take them home as pets, keep them in aquariums or even a spare bathtub.

But sometimes they'd get sick of the pets and flush them down the toilet. Sometimes the bathtub wouldn't have enough water to keep the alligators content, and they'd escape. Legend has these alligators growing to huge sizes, feeding on rats and garbage. Truth is, some alligators really did wind up in the sewer system of New York City, which is extensive. And so sometimes these sewer alligators would actually surface in the middle of the city.

All this is a long way of saying that there's a grain of truth in every story, even the most bizarre fiction.

—M.A.M.

telling stories about us! He's trying to wreck everything with his lies!" said Pearl.

"So you're going over there to accuse him? That's not the kind of drama we need." It was like Mom had been hearing all those thoughts about drama that Pearl had been having. She almost asked, "What kind *do* we need?"

But Mom said, "You can't just go confronting people, Pearl girl. That's not the way to get things done. You have to learn how to make the most impact: be diplomatic, not get yourself and the rest of the enterprise in trouble because you're mad at"—she lowered her voice and angled her head away from Gully's window—"a certain busybody neighbor. As I'm sure you heard me say last night, some developer would have had this idea soon anyway."

Pearl put a hand on her mother's arm. "So what are *you* going to do?"

"Diplomacy," said Mom. "Watch and learn." She led the way into the store.

"Good morning, Mr. Gulliver!" said Mom with false cheer.

"Maybe for you," said Gully. "It's practically lunch time!" He opened every day at 7:30, for the rush-hour traffic and the kids on their way to school. He kept to that schedule even on Saturdays.

"Gully, you're just the expert I've been needing to ask," Mom said. "Don't you think that if the library were open in the evenings, there would be more foot traffic on Lancaster Avenue?" Was this what Mom meant by diplomacy, asking an opinion where one was not needed?

Sure enough, Gully puffed up like a pigeon on a cold day. He liked being asked his opinion. "You think there'd be more foot traffic?"

"And it would be safer," said Mom. "The way things used to be." (Those were Gully's favorite words.)

"We remember," he said to Mom. He smiled down at Pearl, his voice almost gentle for once. He had been running his store since Mom was a little kid living on Seventh Avenue, and he was friendly to her because they both remembered that time. Mom was wistful about when her parents and brother lived in the neighborhood. Gully was nostalgic for the days with more white people—and not such poor ones, either. Now he said, "Safer would improve *my* marketing, that's for sure. You think I'd make money at night with all these punks and let's-call-them-newcomers around here?"

"Why not, if the library brought in customers," said Mom. "'Til nine, at least. There'd be the old hustle and bustle on the avenue."

But the moment of nostalgia had passed for Gully, and he flapped his hand at Mom. "Library was on the chopping block even before that head got stolen."

"No we're not!" said Pearl. "We're just"—she borrowed a phrase she'd heard Bruce and Mom say—"*under proposal*."

"Under *proposal* to be turned into *residences*," said Gully, pointing his finger at her rudely. "And a good idea, too. Why not just close and get out? Let them make the place into something—restaurants, a little shopping street?"

But her mother said, "What would be great is if an established local businessman like you would send a letter of support for the library to the board."

Gully looked like he'd swallowed salt, but Mom had an idea in her teeth and she wasn't going to let go of it. "Even if you *did* suggest development to Mr. Bull and Mr. Dozer—" Mom rambled right on, her eyes focused somewhere over Gully's head, as if she didn't even notice that he gulped and blinked and cleared his throat when she said it. "A local institution of learning and culture like the Lancaster Avenue branch library is an expression of this neighborhood's high *values*—and you should think about where your store fits into that." She paused. "If you want to survive the coming changes. Your building is real estate, too."

But the threat of becoming the next target for the developers was lost on Gully, who was dashing to the corner, where Nichols lingered outside the newsstand, looking at the headlines on the morning *Moon.* "Hey, paying customers only! Keep moving!"

Mom caught Pearl's arm as she charged forward in pursuit, holding her so tight it hurt. "You'll only embarrass Mr. Nichols, Pearl!" she said into her ear.

Gully came back in, punched the register's keys, and said, "Stinking bums."

"Mr. Nichols doesn't stink and he isn't a bum," said Pearl.

"He's homeless!" Gully spat out the word. "Why doesn't he get a job?"

"Why don't you give him one?" Pearl said. Mom put a hand on her shoulder.

"People like that are wrecking this area," said Gully. "It's bad for business!"

"Mr. Nichols has as much right to be here as—"

"He's our friend, Mr. Gulliver," Mom interrupted. She hoisted her purse up her shoulder and hauled Pearl out the door, adding, "My apologies for my daughter."

"*I* don't apologize!" said Pearl.

"Shush!" said Mom.

They banged out of the store. Francine was lurking in the doorway. Pearl could tell she'd heard the whole thing.

Pearl chased after her mother. "Your apologies?" she cried. "I stand up for someone, and you apologize for me?"

"Gully is our friend, too," Mom said, storming across the street. "You have to be polite to him."

"No," Pearl said. She shook her head all the way up the library steps. "Not if he's rude to Mr. Nichols and me!"

"Then you are banned from his store until you *can* be polite to him," said her mother.

Here came Francine. "I wouldn't have apologized either," she said. "But I'm hardly allowed to talk to him. He's our *landlord*." Suddenly, her eyes widened.

And then everyone's anger popped when they saw what Francine was looking at.

Francine grabbed Pearl's arm. "Those men!" she hissed. "They're back!"

(Drama. It grabbed people!)

Mr. Dozer and Mr. Bull were pulling up and parking right on the sidewalk.

Sure, maybe they had read about the lost head in the newspaper and found the library themselves, simple as that. But maybe Gully had actively sought out the real-estate guys to encourage the idea of the library as a site for repurposing. Or maybe Gully had stolen the head himself to get a story in the paper and bring somebody to the neighborhood to look at the library!

He certainly has the motive, thought Pearl. He wanted to get the library sold away, bring in new development, raise rent. And he could have beheaded Vincent—he was strong enough to lift the head. And who else would know when the library staff had locked up and gone home for the night, leaving Vincent vulnerable, just waiting to have her head stolen?

Pearl whirled back toward Gully's store. He was standing in the doorway, smiling toward the trucks, nodding.

"Pearl," said Mom warningly. "I think you girls should go—"

"Come to my place!" interrupted Francine. "We can see the library from there."

"Go there and nowhere else," ordered Mom.

What else could Pearl do? She went.

16: BECAUSE OF FRANCINE

Francine's granny's studio was a high-ceilinged, odd-smelling room with heaps of what some might call art materials and some might call dumpster debris. One corner held a stove and a sink. The collapsible card table had one chair and one stool, and there was a hot glue gun on it. Francine tapped across, and immediately there was a thumping sound from below.

"Is that Gully?" Pearl asked.

Francine nodded. "See why I have to go outside to practice?" She led Pearl through the kitchen to a tiny room that might have been a pantry once. Lit by a small, bathroom-sized window was a table covered in newspaper printed in what Pearl figured was Portuguese. Francine had hung clear plastic shoe bags from Gully's on the two walls. The shoe compartments were full of craft stuff: beads, glue, feathers, pipe cleaners, sequins, glue sticks, scissors, Popsicle sticks, gimp string, hemp string, pom-poms, googly eyes, and fluorescent Day-Glo fabric paint.

It was a place for making things, not just living.

"Cool," said Pearl. "Where'd you get all this stuff?"

"My mother, when she left for Brazil," said Francine.

"Why didn't you go?"

"It's better for me here."

That statement froze Pearl. With all the blabbing and blubbering she'd been doing about losing her *library,* here was Francine being calm, cool, even cold on the subject of her missing parents. For all her caring response to Pearl's drama, she didn't show much worry about her own.

"I wish we were in the same class at least," said Pearl.

"Me too," said Francine.

Their eyes met.

After a beat, Francine asked, "Want to glue some fish on your flip-flops like I did?"

"What?"

"Look." Francine slid her hands into two yellow flip-flops. There were plastic goldfish stuck on the thong just above where the toes would be. "I got them at Gully's." She reached into one of the shoe-bag pockets and pulled out a handful of plastic animals. "Pick something."

"Really? Cool." Pearl sifted through the pile and selected two blue-gray dolphins. She looked up to check again with Francine and said, "Thanks."

"So you're the big expert on this neighborhood, right?" Francine asked.

Pearl shrugged. Was she about to get made fun of for knowing something?

"So, tell me about it," Francine said.

"Well," said Pearl, relieved. "Since you ask: I've got a theory about Gully." And she told Francine her suspicion of Gully's garden invasion in the dark of night.

But Francine's face fell, empty of excitement about the mystery. "He better not want Granny and me to move," she said. "I just *got* here!"

Pearl got mad at herself. Why hadn't she given a second's consideration to how Francine might feel about that idea? She said, "Well, we're not going to let it happen, are we?"

"How are we going to stop it?" Francine was at the window, staring down into the street, motionless for once.

"We'll think of something." Pearl walked over and found herself staring right into the second floor of the Lancaster Avenue branch library. "Oh! Wow! Weird," she said. It was like opening the newspaper and seeing a photograph of someone you knew. "There's Simon!" He was neatening shelves.

Francine went back to her little craft spot and said, "OK, give me your shoes." Pearl kicked off her flip-flops and set them on Francine's tiny table. Francine used the glue gun to squeeze a clear blob of glue onto the center of the V of one flip-flop, then pressed one of the dolphins onto it. "Yow!" she said. "Hot."

Pearl laughed. "Let me do the other dolphin?" she asked, picking up the glue gun.

Francine stuck her bare toes into her flip-flops and did a little getting-back-at-Gully dance, dainty and precise, her soft braids swooshing. "We're not. Gonna. Let it. Happen," she chanted over the rhythmic slapping of her dancing feet.

Pearl knew Gully could hear her through his ceiling, and smiled. She pulled the trigger on the glue gun and shot a blob of glue onto her flip-flop. She stuck the dolphin on the blob and didn't burn herself, and later, on her walk back home, she could still feel the warmth.

* * *

Pearl figured if she wanted her mother to be honest, she herself was going to have to start acting more practical and less emotional. She needed information, straight. So at dinner she asked, "What were those two contractor men doing back today?"

"Funny you should ask." Mom laughed a bitter laugh, and pulled out a business card. "Mr. Dozer suggested we go on a little tour, and he wrote down these sights we should see."

"Who's 'we'? Me?" Mr. Dozer wanted *her* to go on a tour with Mom?

"Well, Bruce refuses. I thought you might want to," said Mom. "One building that used to be a school, now it's apartments. The other was a bathhouse, now it's a restaurant downstairs with a gym upstairs."

"That sounds weird," said Pearl. "I don't even know what a bathhouse is."

"Exactly," said Mom. "Do you want to find out?"

"Do I have to?"

"Of course not. I think we can assume these men are good at repurposing. They're just trying to get us to feel better about letting go of our 'real estate.'" And Mom crumpled the business card and tossed it in the trash.

After dinner, the buzzer sounded. Pearl dashed to the door to push the button. "Who is it?"

"It's Francine. Can you walk and get ice cream?"

"Go," said Mom right away. "I'll give you money for both of you."

"Sure, okay." Did Pearl seem that desperate for Francine's friendship? Did Mom feel sorry for Francine? Or did Mom want time alone?

"Where do you like to go for ice cream?" she asked Francine, down on the street. "Do you have a favorite place yet?"

"Whatever," Francine cut her off. "Just come on." She hurried Pearl along in silence, and when they'd turned the corner, she grabbed Pearl's elbow and pulled her across the street and along one of the darkening streets of food factories and warehouses.

"I don't know any ice cream place this way," said Pearl. The buildings on this block were empty of people, the businesses inside them closed at night. "Where are we going?"

Francine said, hushed as if she thought someone might hear them, "I followed Mr. Nichols. I found where he sleeps."

Pearl halted. "Where?" She knew, she absolutely knew that Nichols wouldn't want them to know where he slept, and would be appalled if they actually *saw* him sleeping somewhere.

"It's okay," Francine said. "He won't see us. We'll stay at a distance. I just want to show you." Pearl was still frozen, so Francine tugged at her. "I know you worry about him." She dragged Pearl along and then stopped abruptly on a darkening north-south avenue that the setting sun didn't even sneak around the corner of. They were so far west that the river couldn't have been far off. "All right, just spy around the corner," said Francine. "You'll see a loading dock."

A Sidebar About Homelessness

Reasons Why People Become Homeless (a partial list):

1. "The rent is too damn high." (You've heard of the Democratic, Republican, and Independent parties? Well, there's a political party in New York named this: The Rent Is Too Damn High.)

2. The salary is too low, or nonexistent. (You don't think every human with a job can afford a place to live in New York City, do you?)

3. The urge to roam.

4. Can't deal with life very well. I refer to addiction or mental illness or just a lack of coping ability.

Maybe you can think of some others.

Reasons Why Animals Become Homeless in New York

1. Pets get abandoned. This is why not everybody thinks dependence on humans is a good idea for animals.

That's it. Only pets become homeless. Wild animals, on the other hand, can always make a home. They know where to look, and they know how to cope. That's just one reason why they deserve respect from people who are always calling them vermin and calling in the exterminators.

—M.A.M.

Pearl peeked and saw a blocky platform like a stage. On it, all she could see were lumpy forms. This was a place where homeless people slept, shielding themselves from the eyes of passersby with cardboard or shopping carts or, rarely, a tent. There was even someone lying down behind a big black umbrella that was tilted on its side like a wheel.

"He's the one with the umbrella," said Francine.

"How do you know?" With a sinking feeling, Pearl recognized the umbrella as Alice's.

"I told you. I followed him. Followed him by going ahead of him." She told Pearl how she had walked half a block ahead of Nichols, keeping the distance just long enough for him to not notice her.

Smart.

"When he stopped, I hid down the block behind some stairs, and I saw him open up that big umbrella and settle down."

"Did he have any dinner?" Pearl asked.

Francine just looked at her. "I couldn't see what he did behind the umbrella."

Pearl thought about the banana and granola bar she'd put in the shed-shaped box—it was for him, she admitted to herself now, since she was pretty sure she recognized the flannel shirt she had found in the box. But what could a banana or a granola bar do, *really*? She felt helpless, useless. She didn't know what to say.

But neither girl knew what to do for Nichols. Pearl didn't want to look at his sleeping place anymore. They leaned on the wall of the corner building in silence.

Finally Francine said, "They have the best pistachio at BGI on Sixth."

Pearl said, "My mom gave me money."

"Then come on."

"Oh!" Pearl stopped. "But we could give the ice cream money to Mr. Nichols."

Francine said, "But then he'd know we know where he is."

"Oh."

They were mostly silent as they walked, except for little comments like "Let's go, we can still make it" as the crossing light gave its countdown, or "This way." Francine got strawberry cookie dough with rainbow sprinkles in a cake cone, and Pearl got pistachio in a sugar cone with crushed peanuts, and when they were finished, the last best triangle bites of cone consumed, "I'll walk you back," said Pearl. "You already came and got me."

"Okay," Francine said. "Thanks." Then, seeming nervous for the first time Pearl had ever seen, she asked, "Are you glad or mad I showed you Mr. Nichols?"

"Glad," said Pearl. "I guess we might as well know."

17: A MESSAGE TO MRS. MALLOMAR

Pearl told Simon how she had gotten in a fight with Gully, and asked, "Why do you think Gully wants the library gone?"

Simon had a look on his face like he smelled a rat, and the rat was Gully. "Look, it's a question of money," he said. "Your mom explained it to me."

"My *mom*?"

"Gully's not just a storekeeper; he's a landlord. He lives there and works there, but he also owns that building. So it's not just that he thinks he'll have more customers if the library turns into apartments; he thinks the value of the street will go up, which would mean he can charge more rent. Don't you think he'd love to kick all the grannies out and get some fancy young *professional* couple in there to pay big rent?" Simon had a way of flinging his hands around when he got irritated; he was doing it now.

"Well, what fancy professional couple wants to live above a lousy, junky store?" sputtered furious Pearl. That apartment was Francine's!

"No problem," said Simon. "If the tone of the neighborhood got raised, he'd rent the store out to some chain furniture store and retire to rake in the bucks."

This only helped confirm Pearl's theory. "Do you think *Gully* took the statue?"

"With those little bandy arms?" said Simon. "No muscles on him!"

Pearl giggled. "Maybe he paid someone else to do it."

Simon looked into her face with sympathy and shrugged. "I don't think he needed to have the head stolen. The real-estate vultures were already circling, as your mom said. If it wasn't Mr. Bull and Mr. Dozer, it was bound to be somebody else. It's a beautiful property."

"It's not a beautiful *property!*" Pearl exclaimed. "It's a beautiful *library!*"

"It *is*," said Simon, in a way that told her he didn't know if the library would always be beautiful, or would always be a library. He put his hand on her head as if to wiggle it around, but then went back to work.

"If I could just find the head . . . ," Pearl said.

"Your mom thinks Oleg's new head will get us another story in the paper—a hopeful one."

"Sure, well, wouldn't finding the old head do the same thing?"

"If only the raccoons could talk," said Simon.

Pearl laughed. "Then we could charge admission."

She got into the book elevator and sat there alone so she could think in the dark, cool peace. Was she crazy, thinking Gully might have taken Vincent's head? Was she crazy, thinking a raccoon had left her a note? In a situation like this, she'd heard Mom tell Bruce enough times, it was vital to think creatively, outside the box.

Speaking of boxes . . . hmm. Pearl thought of the shed-shaped box in the yew hedge—and of who came and got the stuff out and when. She knew now that it was Mr. Nichols, and she guessed he came at night. So maybe he'd seen Gully take the head, and that was why Gully distrusted him.

Or maybe he'd taken the head himself, and *that* was why Gully distrusted *him*?

And as for the raccoons writing notes, she figured she'd just heard too many of Mom's stories, so her imagination was overactive. It was Mom herself who had told Pearl she needed to face reality.

Reality was—what, exactly?

Reality was raccoons not writing.

Reality was granola bars not making up for not having your own kitchen.

Reality was an umbrella keeping people's eyes off you, but not keeping out the cold.

Reality was the real-estate market.

Reality was not enough books circulating, because of not enough library patrons coming in the door, because not enough people were readers.

"Pearl!" Simon yanked open the book elevator door. "Quit"—he peered in, stared at her face—"moping or hiding or whatever you're doing."

"I'm facing reality," said Pearl.

"Do you have to do it in the book elevator?" He gave her his hand and pulled her out. "It's your day to do the coffee run. Better get going."

* * *

Pearl trudged off to Cozy Soup and Burger, pausing at the newsstand on the way back for the evening *Moon*. Tallulah seemed even more grumbly and sleepy than usual. "Yes, the delivery's late! One second, one second!"

Pearl hitched her cardboard coffee tray onto the ledge, thinking she should just come back later if the paper wasn't even there.

But then Tallulah turned and smiled as though it was a relief to see her. "Pearl, you live on Beep Street, don't you? Think you could carry a message for me?"

She pulled a sheet of paper from her order book and wrote on it in pencil. Pearl heard her mumble as she wrote: "What *I'm* supposed to do about night staff being late, I'd like to know." Tallulah folded the sheet and tucked it and a newspaper between Pearl's thumb and the side of the coffee tray. "Twenty-two-and-a-half Beep Street," she said. "Don't buzz—you'll wake up the resident. Just put it in the lower mail slot. That's all."

So instead of heading back to the library, Pearl made an overburdened dash for Beep Street. Hmm, which one was 22½? Her own house was number 8. How had she lived her whole life without realizing there were half numbers on their street?

Number 22 was a metal-gated door with a stoop like most on their street, this one festooned with twisted wisteria branches and veiled in ivy, with one mail slot that just said 22.

Where was 22½? She didn't see a door that went with that number, only a tiny slot on Number 22's front wall, the length of Pearl's little finger, with a small full moon above it. You'd have to roll the *Moon* to fit it into this mail slot, and letters could only be a quarter of the size of a postcard.

Tallulah's note was folded absurdly small and tight, but Pearl couldn't resist peeking at it.

This collection of names set Pearl's heart racing.

This note represented two possibilities.

One, Mom had been telling stories about raccoons that she'd named after a bunch of *people* who also knew Tallulah and to whom Tallulah was sending this note. *I don't think so,* thought Pearl. As far as she knew, Mom didn't know any other Matildas.

Two, Tallulah's note was for the same raccoons Mom's stories were about. *Yeah, sure, uh-huh,* thought Pearl. Why would Tallulah write a note to any raccoons, never mind Mom's?

Mrs. M. Mrs. M., who lived at 22½ Beep Street. She was the big lumbering raccoon who'd walked by Mom and Pearl, and she was due at the newsstand at twelve. Twelve *midnight.*

And *Matilda?* Pearl knew that one, all right: Mrs. Mallomar's daughter, whose name was another word for the moon.

Mary Ann? She must have been the bigger raccoon of the two that had been in the alley, the one screeching at Pearl to put the little one down, because *Arak?* That name she'd seen in the raccoon book, needing to be kept *out of trouble* like that little raccoon she'd saved, when *Mary Ann* couldn't keep him off the street?

Pearl knew she was supposed to think that Mom's stories were just stories. Not real. Despite all those stories about the editor in chief of the midnight *Moon* and her daughter, it was Mom who'd told Pearl to face reality.

And yet, as Pearl stood there facing it, she realized she knew more than Mom, because she knew Mary Ann and Arak. They were part of the neighborhood's reality. Which was: raccoons.

* * *

For the rest of the afternoon and evening, Pearl was unusually quiet, so quiet that by the time they'd gotten through the four o'clock staff meeting, closing, homework, supper, and bath time, Mom asked Pearl if she was feeling all right.

"Yeah, why?" said Pearl, blankly-on-purpose.

Mom felt her forehead and shrugged. "No reason," she said, looking into Pearl's eyes. Pearl shrugged back.

She went to bed at her normal time, and told herself to go to sleep, but she lay there looking up at her *In the Night Kitchen* poster until Mom finished in the bathroom and got into bed herself. When Pearl was a little kid, she had been intrigued by what happened at night while she was sleeping. She knew, of course, that adults stayed up later, their lights on, doing things. You couldn't live in New York City without developing an awareness that someone, somewhere was always up and about.

And yet she was also familiar with the sleeping faces of buildings and businesses: shades down, metal gates unrolled, shutters shut, and, at Tallulah's newsstand, the absence of Tallulah. The only time Pearl went to the newsstand after dark was Saturday night, when you could get the Sunday paper early, so then you could just stay in your pajamas and be cozy on Sunday. Every other night the rest of the week, Tallulah closed up and turned off the lights by nine.

So what about the midnight *Moon*?

Pearl jerked awake. The kitchen clock showed 11:51. Almost 12!

Was anyone in the newsstand now?

Pearl had to see for herself. She padded across to the apartment door. Mom was snoring in her bedroom. Pearl could join a band of robbers herself, she was so sneaky. She pulled on Mom's black hoodie and stuck one flip-flop in the apartment door, tiptoed down the stairs, and wedged the other in the building door. Then she was fast, so fast. She ran barefoot on a New York City sidewalk! She headed along Beep Street, across Lancaster Avenue to Seventh Avenue, and stopped just short of the corner. Around that corner was the subway entrance, with the newsstand beside it.

A glow of light showed it was open, but not at the normal window that even Mom had to reach up to. This was a door with a window cut in it, right at Pearl's knees. The perfect height for a raccoon, she realized.

She felt the rumble of a subway train coming underground; after a few moments, the sound and vibration stopped, then started, then diminished. There was a hustle and bustle as people emerged up the steps and made their way down the street. Nobody paused at the newsstand, and nobody saw Pearl, crouched silently on a stoop. *Any minute now,* she thought, *my theory will be proven—or not.*

And just then, she heard it and froze. It sounded as if someone was dragging a coat so long that it swooshed along the ground. And there it was: a raccoon. It was the same one she'd seen with Mom, all right: Mrs. Mallomar. The swooshing noise was her fat striped tail brushing the pavement. Could she see Pearl? Could she smell her? (Pearl realized she really didn't know that much about wild animals.)

The raccoon swept past and crossed the street to the newsstand, hurrying along on all fours, making that *ak-ak-ak* squawk Pearl now realized was raccoon talk. She went into the little door in the newsstand—it *was* a raccoon door, Pearl realized, with happiness that she'd guessed right. Then Tallulah came out the regular side door, reached up and pulled a newspaper from a clip, rolled it into a tube and stuck it under her arm, and passed by Pearl as she headed along Lancaster Avenue. In the little low window, Pearl could see the black, intelligent gleam of Mrs. Mallomar's eyes as she gazed out from amid the clotheslined fringes of *Moons,* the bags of almonds and sunflower seeds that might have appealed just as well to raccoons as to humans, the multicolored magazines and wrapped candy.

Pearl backed away, smiling. She trotted home, keeping to the shadows of the small trees along the street, tiptoeing down the sidewalk, and let herself in, removing the flip-flops wedged in the doors. Surprisingly quickly, she found herself sitting on her chair-bed, where she belonged, sleepy but wired. Had any of this really happened? Yes. Sure. Right?

Her mother turned over in her sleep and called out, "Pearl?"

"Just going to the bathroom." Pearl made her voice drowsy. She went into the bathroom, flushed the toilet, and went back to bed. And then she had a sort of argument with herself in which she went over everything that had just happened as if she was explaining it to someone extremely logical, like, say, Ramón. Or mean Elsa at school. She had to give just the evidence, no fantasy.

First: She had dropped a note in a mail slot, a note about someone named Mrs. M showing up for work at the newsstand at midnight.

Then: A raccoon had gone inside the newsstand and taken up position at a smaller, raccoon-sized door.

Then: Tallulah had left the newsstand, as if she was getting off work. Like someone else had taken over the shift.

Pearl lay back in her chair-bed and stared up at her poster. Strange things did happen in New York at night. Pearl had just seen proof. But who was to say reading raccoons were any stranger than people doing math worksheets or getting choco tacos from the Mister Softee truck or sleeping behind umbrellas or riding in tunnels under the street at all hours of the night? Every one of those things would sound like fiction if you didn't know they were true. Pearl could feel herself teetering on the brink between believing her eyes and sticking to the facts.

Raccoons reading papers, raccoons writing papers, raccoons selling papers.

And with that, Pearl chose to believe it was true. It wasn't just the New York City night that made it true. It was the fact that when New Yorkers needed something, they made it happen, no matter what. New Yorkers needed to move around the city at all hours, so trains ran underground all night. New Yorkers needed bread in the morning, so there were bakers baking it all night. New Yorkers—nocturnal New Yorkers, but New Yorkers, nonetheless—needed the news, so there were raccoons writing it, and printing it, and selling it—and Pearl had just seen proof, if she needed any.

Why should she need any? Hadn't her own mother told her about these very neighborhood raccoons her whole life?

Pearl brushed her feet together and some sidewalk dust rubbed off, proof of her midnight expedition. She'd always believed her mother's stories were made-up. But now it turned out that she had been wrong and Mom had been right. A raccoon really had gone to work selling the midnight *Moon,* after reading a note that Pearl had delivered with her own hand. Pearl decided it with a bang: She had seen what she thought she'd seen.

A Sidebar About Bread

Maurice Sendak (who wrote and illustrated *In the Night Kitchen*) wrote about the mysterious quality of bread. As he wrote, bread is made in the dark of the night, a time when kids know that anything can happen. Not only is bread not there at dusk and there at dawn, it is made by people who do what human children cannot: get up in the middle of the night and stay awake until dawn. Kids wake up at dawn, and by that time, the magic is complete; the bread is baked.

There's another mystery about bread, in how it rises to its beautiful crusty roundness. There's a potion, a fermented soup of grain or fruit that has a chemical reaction with the water, salt, and flour of the batter. That reaction bubbles up; it makes the bread's size change. Bakers save a bit of the potion, feeding it to the next batch of bread. They pass it down like stories, from one loaf to the next, and when they move to a new location, they carry their potion in special jars, keeping it safe for the following generation.

—M.A.M.

18: LIBRARY CARDS, FREE

SEP 26

WHAT DO YOU NEED TO GET A LIBRARY CARD?
LOVE OF READING!

"Not very sexy," said Alice over Patricia's shoulder, peeking at her screen. "You'll have to do better than that, Trish."

Pearl said, "Loving reading isn't even the point. The point is you don't need to have an ID. Or money. Just an address."

Mom said, "The point is, it's a free country. If you want to read, you can."

Francine said, "How about just: 'Library cards, free.'"

"Got it," said Mom, hitting *print*. "I'm putting a sign on the door."

"I'll hang it up for you," said Pearl. She was itching to get away from everyone, to take off around the building and down the basement stairs where the raccoon—but no, Francine just *had* to come with her to hold up the sign while Pearl taped it.

Francine said in a hurried, excited whisper, "I've got an idea for a dance to make more schoolkids come, not just babies. You're not going to like it, though, Pearl."

A dance? Pearl had no time for dances. She was piecing together a story in her head, a story with drama and mystery and potential.

"It's got the Rock Lady in it," Francine said as they came back inside. "The *headless* Rock Lady."

A Sidebar About Mothers

In societies where fathers stick around during the gestation of children and help rear them, sometimes you get a division of labor and responsibilities that is purely biological. The females, who are biologically responsible for pregnancy and nursing, stay close to home and children, while males go out to find or hunt food for their families.

In societies where fathers mate with the mothers and then disappear right away, the mothers are responsible for everything. My grandmother says it's better this way—less messy and less scratching and snarling. The mother relies on her own resources, for better or worse, and the children grow up to reflect her strengths, as well as her weaknesses.

There is never just one influence on a child, not among raccoons, oh no: You get the full benefit of grandmothers and aunts as well as your mother. Lucky for me, my grandmother's house is nearby and my aunt's tree even nearer. Even luckier, my aunt is literate and ambitious, even if that makes for certain bratty cousins who put on airs. Luckiest of all, I'm my grandmother's favorite granddaughter.

"She might not be headless much longer," announced Ramón. "Oleg Boiko has found stone carvers."

"What? You mean he can't carve it himself?"

(Pearl was getting tired of Oleg being such a hero.)

Francine said, "Who on earth can carve a head out of stone?"

(She truly was impressed. So was Ramón. So was Pearl, really; she was just jealous.)

"A sculptor," said Ramón. "Right here in New York City, we have a cathedral under construction, with a team of stone carvers. Can you believe it?"

"And they're going to carve the head?"

"Your mother is drafting a letter to them right now."

Pearl did not know what to think about this. She couldn't imagine Vincent wearing some new head. She couldn't stand to envision what it would look like. But what she was impressed with was how much Oleg knew about his one thing—rocks!—and how he was using it.

He was a geek, too, and everyone liked him.

(To Pearl, this was enlightening.)

Mom and Ramón were already talking excitedly about what kind of a ceremony they might have to introduce a replacement head, and how Mom could write a press release to get the media to cover it—good press, positive press, the library striding boldly into the future as the centerpiece of Lancaster Avenue, an event they could announce to the board before their October 2 vote to make sure it knew the library intended to fight for its right to be a library, not apartments.

Pearl couldn't argue with this, but that afternoon, she couldn't stop feeling crabby about the new head. She trudged up the straight stairs and pulled some picture books for Alice to consider for a story hour, just to remind herself which kid was key around here.

But Alice was babbling about an idea for a Rock Lady costume Francine could make, "since she was so good with her hands," and it was too much for Pearl to take. Pearl took advantage of their annoying excitement and escaped back down the spiral stairs. When she heard Mom carrying on about the "new head night" and Ramón suggesting calling it "a gala . . . a fête . . . an extravaganza!"— she knew they were too distracted to worry about where *she* was. So she opened the basement door and ventured down the worn wooden steps.

My grandmother's writing holds our society together, informs and inspires us. But the story I'm telling has the power to save us from the loss of our most precious resource: our castle, our hearth, our library.

My mother's weakness is a longing for her own history, not *ours*. If only my own mother was not so hell-bent on recapturing the magic of a certain two nights of her life. Like Cinderella, she met her prince not once, but twice. My brother and I, each only kits with no littermates, are together the offspring of the same union. And my mother is always looking for my father. She has a dream of getting out of the city and taking my brother and me with her to live with our father—her Prince Charming, the one who got away.

But I have a different dream. I intend to be more than ready to stand on my own. When it comes to writing, I'm a geek, like my grandmother, I guess. It's Grandmallomar—Grandmar for short—who taught me to read, and is nagging me now to teach my brother, before he gets away, too. Someone else can be her mother's daughter. I'm saving the world, one paragraph at a time.

—M.A.M.

Now, understand: Pearl was a brave, fierce girl, but she wasn't used to darkness. She was a city girl, and the city was always blinking and shining, so places where the darkness was unbroken were few. Even Pearl, who had nerve enough to sneak onto the street at night, avoided such places. She couldn't help being fascinated by darkness, of course: Like any city kid, she had gone through a phase of riding in the front car of the subway so she could peer into the blackness beyond the headlight's beam. She had been at summer concerts in Central Park; she'd gone out after sunset. But even there, there were headlights and fireflies.

And she finally let it in: She was afraid.

Pearl didn't want to admit to herself that she was afraid of what might be in the ancient, dirt-floored, low-ceilinged, absolutely unlit, pitch-dark basement of her very own library.

But now, there was something at stake. Now there were raccoons who might have news to share, raccoons who Bruce thought lived in the trees overlooking the garden and the statue, raccoons who were the only ones who might know what happened in the garden the night Vincent's head was stolen. Raccoons who could write. What else they could do, a bunch of them together, was beyond Pearl's understanding right now. For all she knew, in this overdramatic moment, *they* could be the thieves of Vincent's head. Maybe the head was down here right now!

(Did she think she could slip in, find the head, not wake the sleeping raccoons, get back upstairs, and arrive, triumphant, to restore Vincent to her former glory?)

The door snapped shut on some kind of spring behind her. She pushed away all thoughts of cobwebs, silverfish, rats, and corners you couldn't see into. *I'm still in the library, still in the library, still in the library,* she told herself with every step she descended. The only light came from the cloudy window that looked onto the driveway, Pearl's own flashlight, and the glowing EXIT sign at the top of the stairs. It smelled like dirt. *Still in the library.* And when she stepped through the doorway at the foot of the stairs, she shouted inside her head, *I'm still in the library!*

Something down here was holding its breath along with Pearl. She heard it rustle, and she thought: They really are here. I wasn't making it up.

"Hey," she whispered in a singsong low voice. "It's only Pearl. You know me. I won't hurt you. I just need your help."

There was a small scuffle and muffled chattering.

The flashlight's weak beam picked up the gleam of two shining eyes, then two more. She raised the beam slightly and saw two black-masked, white-whiskered faces. The tiny one was the raccoon kit she'd scooped out of the street, she was sure of it.

Pearl crouched down and put out her hand. The little one stepped forward, gathered its nerve, and skittered out of the reach of the larger one, who tried to stop it. The little one reached out a paw and touched Pearl's finger, then ran back to the other one.

"I want to find out if you know where Vincent's head is. Who took it? How do I get it back? Because maybe if we know then we can convince people that the library's worth saving."

The larger raccoon grabbed hold of the smaller one and they both disappeared into the darkness. What was back there, some kind of hole or tunnel or nest or burrow? Nothing else happened. The head didn't roll into view; the raccoons didn't suddenly speak. The books said—and Mom's stories said—that raccoons nested in hollow trees or shallow holes in the ground. But in the city, why shouldn't they nest inside, too, their nests lined with shredded *Moon,* especially with winter coming on?

What was I expecting? Pearl stood there feeling hugely stupid. It made perfect sense for raccoons to be in the basement.

That didn't mean they wanted to help her, or even that they knew who she was.

Pearl emerged from the basement, peeking through the glass window of the door first to make sure the hallway was empty.

"Where were *you*?" said Simon when she got to the circulation desk.

"Nowhere," said Pearl. She stared at his head. He'd done something to his black hair—the ends were dyed red and orange. "Have you gone insane?"

"That seems to be the general opinion," Simon said. "It's for my band. If we're going to stand out, *I* need to stand out."

"You already do," said Pearl, then quickly asked, "What's your band called now?"

"We're still working on it," said Simon. "What do you think it should be?"

He was always doing this—talking about the band without giving its name. He'd tell her what songs they practiced, what he wanted to play next, but all he did when she asked the band's name was tell her to suggest one.

Now she said, "The Masked Band-Its."

"Like bandits, like raccoons?" he asked, cocking an eyebrow at her.

"Yes," she said.

"Sounds too criminal," said Simon. "So what *were* you doing in the basement, Pearl?"

"Don't say anything, Simon, promise? I'm looking for . . . what was that headline? A something remedy?"

"An elusive remedy," said Simon.

"There's your band name," said Pearl.

19: IN THE GARDEN

The next day after school, Pearl led Francine on a search of all the alleys leading off Lancaster Avenue. She told Francine they were looking for Vincent's head, but actually Pearl was looking for something else: She noted the raccoon footprints in the dirt around trees and along garden edges. What were their trails, their routines? And when did they leave their homes—on Beep Street or in the basement or up the trees—and when did they come home?

For all Pearl knew, Mrs. Mallomar was the only aspect of her mother's stories that was in any way real. The raccoons in the basement could just be trash pandas—Bruce's phrase—who had just happened to be at the window next to that wet note in the grass. Pearl wanted to get to the bottom of the raccoon stories once and for all. If she could do that, maybe next she could figure out how to ask them if they'd seen who stole Vincent's head.

Francine clicked along behind Pearl in her tap shoes, doing her Rock Lady dance in her head, her hand out like Vincent's, reaching toward Pearl. "I want—" Francine moaned. *Clicka-clacka.* "I want something from you!"

She wanted Pearl to ask what the Rock Lady wanted, but Pearl's focus was on her own goal.

"Where are your goldfish flip-flops?" Pearl asked in annoyance.

"Where are your dolphin flip-flops?" asked Francine.

"They're too noisy," Pearl said pointedly.

Francine shrugged. "Let's go back to the garden," she said. "My taps sound better on the bricks."

"I don't want that Oleg spying on us," Pearl said. But she hadn't seen any tracks for a few blocks, so they turned back.

Francine rolled her eyes. "I'm sure he's too busy with his rock-hunting."

On the bricks around Vincent's sad form, Francine performed a strange dance to music that played only in her head. "Rock Lady," Francine said to herself, but loudly, so Pearl could hear. "If only Pearl would let me show her the Rock Lady dance!"

"Pearl won't," said Pearl. "Pearl has other ideas."

"None as good!" said Francine.

Pearl shinnied up a tree, peering higher in hope of spotting a nest. From there she saw—what was that? A white card rested in Vincent's palm, folded small so it wouldn't blow off, and tucked into the crack so it couldn't be seen from the ground.

She scrambled back down the tree and up the statue.

Come down again, the note said in demanding, thick Sharpie letters.

Pearl knew exactly who it was from and where she had to go.

She left Francine to her dancing and sprinted toward the basement—and ran into Nichols coming out of the bathroom and into the back hall, wearing that dark green flannel shirt from the box.

Oh! Right in the middle of everything! She would go "down again" to the library basement. But this collision called for a momentary detour. She matched Nichols's pace back to their spot by the atlas.

"You're sort of nocturnal, aren't you?" Pearl asked him. "Like a raccoon?"

"What about raccoons, now?" He leaned back in his chair, waiting for her to feed him some nonfiction.

"Did you know," she began, channeling Mom, "that there's a whole bunch of raccoons who read the paper every night and they live right around here?"

"Peculiar!" mused Nichols, just like always. He seemed unsurprised, unimpressed, with a similar air to the one Mom had when she told her stories: not as if anything had been made up. As if everybody knew, and Pearl was the one who was just figuring things out.

Pearl matched his casual tone. "So. They have a sort of city alongside our city," she said. "They mostly sleep in the daytime, like you," she added.

"Why do you keep bringing me into it?"

"You're out in the nighttime," said Pearl. He nodded. "And you sleep in the day. Nocturnal, the same as them."

"Who are these raccoons?" he asked.

"They're journalists. There's a night edition of the *Moon* that's for raccoons, and Mrs. Mallomar is the editor. I'm just learning about the rest of them—her daughter, Matilda, and Matilda's kids, Mary Ann and Arak."

Nichols had to smile. "Reading raccoons? Publishing their own newspaper? What kind of news would they have?"

"That's what I'm trying to find out," said Pearl. "I'm trying to find out how good their reporters are at digging up news."

"Well, when you get some answers from them, you come and tell me what you learn," Nichols said. His glasses were on his nose, the paper open in his hands. He looked a little sleepy. He smelled outside-ish, the way you'd smell if you'd slept in Central Park all night and hadn't had a chance to change all your clothes.

Pearl looked at his flannel shirt and thought about where it had come from. "Mr. Nichols, would you just tell me—don't be embarrassed—" His gray eyes peered over the glasses at her. He was very still. "Are you comfortable enough at night?"

He smiled. "Comfortable enough for now."

She wanted to ask him a lot of things, including some questions about raccoons, but none of them seemed important against the idea of him—not only raccoons—out in the dark.

* * *

That night, homework done, Pearl lay on the pale green plaid quilt on her chair-bed, hanging her knees over the side, her toes grazing the floor, thinking about school, thinking about Nichols, and waiting. She waited for the moment she knew would come.

Then it did: Mom called from the bathroom. "Pearl? I'm going to henna my hair, let it rest, and take a shower, okay? Get the phone if it rings."

Pearl calculated: shower, five minutes. Henna, five minutes. Letting the henna "rest" while sitting on the closed lid of the toilet reading the *New Yorker,* half an hour. Shower, ten minutes. Plenty of time. The opportunity was now.

She was out the doors like a shot, flip-flops wedged, pounding down the sidewalk to the beat of a blasting car radio, barging past a flow of people getting off the bus. The library loomed up before her, its front windows dark. It was dark in the alley, and it only got darker as she entered the garden, a note folded tight and clutched in her fist.

Tonight was a test—a test of the raccoons, and a test of Mr. Nichols. None of them knew what she was up to, but they soon would. Pearl wanted to know if Nichols spent nights in the garden sometimes.

The library's side and back lights were out except for the ones in Bruce's office that were left on at night to give the impression that someone was up there working. Pearl pulled the cheapo flashlight from her pocket and shone its weak beam along the garden path. If she hadn't already known the place like the back of her hand, she'd have fallen on her face at least twice.

Finally, the weak beam of Pearl's flashlight showed the wood of the box. She slid some snacks and the note into the box and let the lid down stealthily. She would have tiptoed out of there if only a spiderweb hadn't fallen right across her forehead, and she went crashing out of the bushes.

"Who's there?" came a deep voice.

20: IN THE
GARDEN AT NIGHT

Pearl dived behind the pedestal of the statue and shined her little light into the dark. "Mr. Nichols," she said. "It's me."

Silence. Then, "Pearl?"

"Of course!"

"What are you doing here, Pearl girl?"

She told an elaborate tale so he wouldn't know she'd been looking for him. "Just checking on . . . Vincent, because Francine and I were making up scary stories, and she wants to make hers into a dance, and I'll write mine down and then she'll translate it and tell it in Portuguese, so we can tell Vincent's story in two languages, plus dance, the universal language, not just English, since so many people speak so many languages around here— like Danesh speaks Hindi and Ramón speaks Spanish and Oleg said he speaks Ukrainian. So I thought I would see if coming here at night would give me a clue about her missing head. Because if I could find it, then I'd be a hero—and we wouldn't have to do any of that new stuff, and things could just go back to the way they were."

"Things never do," said Nichols from the dark. "Besides, maybe the new stuff will be good. And who says you're not a hero?"

But Pearl felt she hadn't done anything to be a hero, and she wanted to quite badly.

"Is this your sleeping place?" Pearl said, unable to keep herself from asking. She wanted so very much for Francine to be wrong about who slept behind the umbrella on the loading dock.

"I don't want to answer that." He gave her his hand, and pulled her out from behind the statue. "I don't want you to know that," he said. He was looking up at the back of the library. "Pearl, where does your mother think you are?"

"In bed."

"Then I'm walking you back," he said. "But first I want to show you something."

Avoiding the rectangles of light from Bruce's window, Nichols tiptoed to the door that led from the garden and into the back hall. Across the hall, a low light glowed from the reading room. "Here," said Nichols. He cupped his hands so Pearl could step into them and gave her a boost. "Quiet," he whispered. "Don't let them hear you."

Pearl shaded her eyes with her hands pressing lightly on the old glass of the reading room door, and saw three small spots of pale-blue light—desk lamps along the narrow length of the reading table. Who was in there? Three raccoons with books open before them: The largest had a thick red book; the middle-sized one with a chapter book (Pearl could see it was *Bud, Not Buddy*[1]); and the littlest one with *Mike Mulligan and His Steam Shovel,* not a huge picture book, but still way too big for him—the very book that had been missing from the children's room for weeks. Pearl herself, the librarian's child, could not help being impressed that such a young raccoon could read independently. But, of course, Arak lived in the library, too.

---

1 *Bud, Not Buddy* by Christopher Paul Curtis (Delacorte, 1999).

Nichols shifted; Pearl stepped down silently.

"I knew it!" she said.

"You're not surprised?" asked Nichols.

"I guess not!" she said, only partly a lie. She did a little skip and added, "Mrs. Mallomar has her own newspaper."

"As you said," Mr. Nichols answered. "But that's *Matilda* and her two children in there. Mrs. Mallomar's daughter and grandchildren."

"They're the ones who live in the basement," Pearl said. "That's why they can read. That little one is Arak. I saved him from getting hit by a car!"

(As if that wasn't heroic!)

She was beaming. She folded her arms across her stomach, holding on to her elbows as if her arms might rise up and she might fly away. She tried very hard to stay on the ground, but she almost could have flown.

"Be careful who you tell," said Nichols. "People might think you're bonkers. Now come on." He led her down the alley.

(Could it be heroic if nobody knew?)

The sidewalk under the pinkish streetlights was glowing. A train must have just come through the subway station: A swarm of people trooped toward them along the sidewalk. Automatically,

A Sidebar About Brothers

Start simple if you want to try to tell your brother anything. There will be a certain amount of resistance, and it's usually better to show instead of tell. Keep in mind that if you try to tell your brother to do anything, he is likely to do the opposite. For instance, if you want him to leave you alone, he will tag along. If you want him to live his own life, he will hang on you like he's stuck there. If you want him to be an individual, he will copy you until you're ready to kill him.

Use this brother tendency to achieve your goals. How? Act all bossy like you want him to follow you around, stick by your side, and do what you say. What do you think he's going to do? Finally leave you alone!

—M.A.M.

without a thought, Pearl reached over and took Nichols's hand. Nichols barely reacted; he held her hand calmly, firmly. Neither of them made a sound, but a silent sigh passed between them as the pedestrians went around.

But then Nichols's grip tightened. Pearl recognized Gully coming along and realized Nichols was squeezing her hand because he was afraid of Gully.

And what did Gully think of seeing Pearl, the used-to-be-adorable-but-lately-kind-of-obnoxious librarian's child, and Nichols, the nuisance homeless bum, out walking hand in hand at nearly ten o'clock at night? He merely let out a sharp breath of surprise and filed away what he'd seen for future use.

Pearl wanted to giggle. What if Gully knew there were raccoons reading in the reading room, right now while he was plodding along the sidewalk as if there was no magic in the world whatsoever?

Nichols swung Pearl around the corner of Beep Street to her building. She wanted to ask him a thousand things, but she just opened the door and picked up her flip-flop. Nichols put his fingers to his lips. She waved and climbed the stairs.

A damp, showery, soapy, clean-mother smell met her at the apartment door, but Mom was still in her room. The stove clock said 9:58. Pearl had been out 28 minutes, but it seemed like hours. It was unbelievable what a sneaky person could get away with.

"Mom?" called Pearl. "Do you want tea?"

"Sure," answered Mom.

Pearl turned on the kettle. She hit the shower, got into her pajamas, and returned to the kitchen in time to pour the hot water into two mugs. She took Mom her tea and got into bed with her own, finally free to think about this amazing thing she had just seen—a fantasy become fact.

Reading raccoons who could also write. Writing raccoons who could publish their own newspaper. Raccoons who strolled to the corner newsstand to get the midnight edition. Pearl laughed to herself. Who would ever believe it? Did Mom know that it was really so, and not just an urban legend, that it had more than a grain of truth?

Nichols knew.

Pearl set her mug on the floor and snuggled on her side in bed, her back to the window. She reached under her pillow for the catalog card and read it in the light from the streetlamp outside:

Come down again.

She would, tomorrow. After all, she had to get *Mike Mulligan* back for Francine.

21: A FAVOR
FROM A FRIEND

SEP 29

A chilly morning told Pearl it had been a cold night. Half awake, she was glad to think of the little raccoon family in the library, cozy and warm. But then had Nichols slept in the garden, in the cold? After walking her home, had he gone back where she had found him?

Pearl's shoulders sagged. She was disgusted with herself. The whole point of her nighttime trip last night was to confirm where Nichols slept, but all she'd thought about was the magic of the scene in the reading room.

She could fix it now. "Mom?" she called. "We have to leave a little early this morning, okay?"

"Fine, put the kettle on, and—"

"Mom, can you make tea at work?" Before Mom could respond, she added, "I'm drinking milk right now." She opened the refrigerator, knowing Mom could hear. "And I'm getting out a yogurt and a granola bar, okay?"

"Pearl, I've got errands to run before—"

"No, Ma, this is important. You've got to come." Pearl was sure that Mom was going to argue. She thought of the man in question, of how he listened, of how he helped her figure out things about the raccoons, of how he kept on coming to the library each morning, of how he kept on walking off into the darkness each night. What could *she* do for *him*?

Mom opened the bathroom door with her mascara in her hand, her eyebrows raised.

"I want to show you where I saw Mr. Nichols sleeping one time," Pearl said.

"Pearl, that's his business," said Mom.

"Just come."

Mom looked reluctant, embarrassed, but she followed Pearl to the shadowy street near the river. A tent was pitched on the loading dock, and a couple of cardboard boxes could be seen there, too. But no umbrellas. No Nichols.

"At least sometimes," said Pearl, "he comes here, and sleeps behind Alice's giant umbrella."

Mom sighed.

"And then I'm also pretty sure he stays in a sleeping bag in the library garden," Pearl said. "I think that might be where he slept when he first got here, because he hid some clothes in the box in the garden, but he didn't sleep there for a while after the so-called break-in." She paused and looked at Mom pointedly. "If *I* was an adult with an apartment of my own, I'd invite Mr. Nichols to stay with me."

Mom said, "Oh, Pearl. He wouldn't come. I know that for a fact."

Pearl thought about what that meant. She knew Mom cared about Nichols. But she hadn't considered that Mom might have already offered to help him. "You asked him?" What else had Mom done that she hadn't told Pearl about? "Why are you only telling me this now?" she demanded.

Mom put her hand on Pearl's shoulder. "Because it seems like you understand better now?" she suggested. "Because you're looking for solutions, too? Because the complexity of the situation is not lost on you?"

Pearl thought about those words, deciphering them. "There are things I don't get about him," she said.

Mom smiled, sighed. "Yes," she said. "That's what I mean. Knowing what you don't know is a big part of growing up."

"Aren't you going to explain to me the stuff I don't understand?"

"There *is* nothing to explain. That's the thing."

Pearl rubbed at her face. "I don't know what you're talking about!" she said stormily.

"What I mean is we're equals on this one, Pearl. We're together in only knowing part of what matters when it comes to Mr. Christopher Nichols."

"Christopher?"

"That's his name. You didn't know?"

"I never thought about him having a first name."

"Well," said Mom. "*Now* we're equals."

* * *

Second things second. If only school wasn't a factor in her life—but it was! She had no choice but to head down the library basement steps well before opening, even if eight in the morning was most certainly too late to wake a raccoon up.

She tiptoed into the gloom behind the stairs, turned on the flashlight to avoid stepping on anybody, and rudely shined its beam right into the bigger raccoon's face. The little kit squeaked and turned his face away, sticking his head under an old piece of carpet that formed part of their nest.

"Sorry, Arak," she said. He stuck his head out and met her eyes for a beat, then hid himself again. The other raccoon—Mary Ann—reached up a paw and pushed the flashlight aside.

"I saw you in the reading room," Pearl whispered.

Mary Ann shook her whiskers and glared. Was this an answer? It sure looked like a "no," but maybe it was just a random raccoon gesture.

"Can you talk?" whispered Pearl. Mary Ann shook her head again.

"Can you write?" Pearl pulled out her Sharpie and some catalog cards and laid them on the floor. Easily, as if she'd done it a million times, the raccoon curved the claws of her right front paw around the pen. Her grip looked awkward, but the writing came steady and even and quick. It was the same writing as on the two notes—*Ask Mrs. M.* and *Come down again*—but not the Arak Lancaster writing from the raccoon book.

We speak, but it's usually just phrases like "Come on" or "Let's go" or "Hurry up."

"Those all mean the same thing," said Pearl. It was an automatic response, but she could scarcely suppress her amazement. She tried to stop beaming. She was trying to hide that she was astonished that a raccoon could communicate at all—never mind with other raccoons, but with *humans*. Never mind communicate, but *write*!

Exactly

wrote the raccoon.

"Raccoon talk seems like the seagulls in *Finding Nemo*[1]," said Pearl. "They say 'Mine! Mine!' but people think they're just screeching. Your talk sounds like *ak-ak-ak* to me."

....

1 *Finding Nemo*, Disney/Pixar movie, 2003.

We're better than that. It's not all just squabbling.

The raccoon fell silent, her pen poised. Her sentences even had proper capitalization and punctuation, Pearl noticed.

"I'm Pearl Amalie Moran," she said. The raccoon nodded. "What's your name?"

You haven't guessed?

"Actually, maybe I have—Mary Ann Mallomar." She finished saying it just as Mary Ann finished writing it. "Yes!"

Mary Ann Mallomar

There was a satisfied silence between them. Then Pearl said, "My initials are P.A.M. Yours are M.A.M."

Mary Ann nodded. She wrote:

P.A.M. and M.A.M.

"You're a poet and you know it," said Pearl. "Like Vincent."

Vincent. She was the reason Pearl was here—to find Vincent's head, to save the library—but she knew she needed to go slowly, not demand everything at once. And still she was trying to calm down about the fact that she was holding a discussion with a wild animal. So she made conversation. "There's a lot of squabbling in my house, too," said Pearl, trying to pretend this was all normal. "My mother and I don't see eye to eye on everything, such as cleaning standards."

Mary Ann's little white teeth showed for a moment.

My mother gets mad at Arak for making a mess.

"My mother's the messy one," said Pearl. "She gets all the control stuff out of her system at the library, Bruce says."

Does she control you?

"She tries," said Pearl. "But I have my own plans."

Like what?

Pearl had thought maybe she could teach the raccoons to talk or do tricks, once she had found out from them who had taken Vincent's head. Now she found herself wondering if Mary Ann was smarter than she was.

"An investigation. And a marketing campaign, I think."

She had pulled that phrase "marketing campaign" out of the back of her head.

To save the library?

Pearl nodded. Yes, that was it—saving the library by marketing it. Not to Mr. Bull or Mr. Dozer, either! No, to people who wanted to keep it the way it always had been.

Mary Ann wrote one of the first things she had ever learned to read, a slogan that used to be on an old billboard over Lancaster Avenue.

Just do it.

"I don't know where to start."

My grandmother told me about selling papers. The first thing is to let people know the paper's there. Then you have to make them want it.

"Your grandmother, Mrs. Mallomar?"
Mary Ann nodded.
Just then they heard Mom calling out for Pearl.
Mary Ann put down the Sharpie. She held up her paw.
Pearl held up her hand, too.

A Sidebar About My Cousin Eloise

My cousin Eloise wants to beat me at everything.

She is snotty to me and tells me to get my head out of the books. I tell her, "Knowledge is power." She tells me to pay attention to the real world and maybe I'll see some surprising, even disturbing things.

Eloise lives in the tree right above Vincent. She claims she knows who took Vincent's head, but she won't tell me who. She says the criminal's true identity would surprise and disturb me.

"So if knowledge is power," says Eloise, "then I beat you, brains and all."

—M.A.M.

Pearl thought, *This probably isn't real.*

Just in case it wasn't, she stood still and said, "Did you see who took the statue's head?"

The raccoon shook her head. But she took two steps toward Pearl.

"Pearl!" Mom yelled from above. "School!"

Pearl thought, *Well, that is real, Mom upstairs. So it must be real downstairs, too.* She crouched low, looked into Mary Ann's deep, dark eyes, and said, "If we could find the head again, it would be a big deal. It might bring people back to the library." She took a deep breath. "Will you—will you ask around and see if your family knows anything?"

Mary Ann bobbed her head once. Then she stepped back into the shadowy corner of the basement.

Pearl crept up the stairs. She dashed through the foyer, grabbing her backpack from the floor in front of the circ counter along the way.

"I'm walking to school with Francine!" Pearl bellowed to her mother, and was gone.

22: CHARISMA

Pearl ran across the street and buzzed Francine. As she stood on the sidewalk waiting, she didn't care about Gully watching out his window, didn't care about anything. *I had a conversation with a raccoon*, she thought, and laughed to herself. *I have a friend who's a raccoon. How bizarre!* And this raccoon friend was going to help Pearl find Vincent's head.

"What's up with you?" said Francine, coming out. Pearl was practically bouncing up and down.

"Nothing," said Pearl, and giggled to herself.

Francine was not in any such giddy mood. As they walked along, she said, "I looked out my window last night, and you'll never guess who I saw walking down the street. Mr. Gulliver himself."

"So? I hope you threw a flip-flop at his head."

"*And*," whispered Francine. "I saw *you*. You and Mr. Nichols. Holding hands and walking down the street."

Pearl wished a crack would open in the sidewalk and swallow her up. But she confided, "Mr. Nichols was in the garden last night. I think he sometimes sleeps there, so I was checking to see if that was true." Francine gaped, but Pearl rushed on, "He didn't have anywhere to sleep, and if Gully thinks he's trespassing on library property, he'll get him sent to a shelter. You heard what he said that time we were in the store: He wants Mr. Nichols and all the other homeless people out of the neighborhood.

So you can't tell anybody you saw us, Francine, you just can't, not if you're my friend."

She felt exhausted, and they weren't even at school yet. "Can't you see? Holding his hand showed Gully Mr. Nichols wasn't trespassing."

She wanted to say, "I've been talking to raccoons." But a harsh, prickly mood was coming from Francine, and Pearl felt compelled to smooth it. So instead she said, "I showed my mom the loading dock, too." She searched her imagination for some appropriate words. "You did a good thing, showing me. Maybe something good will happen for Mr. Nichols now. Maybe we can do something good, I mean."

"Oh," said Francine. Then, "Okay."

The silence fell again. Had Pearl been too formal? Did Francine think she was being weird? Or crazy for walking around at night hand in hand with Nichols? She searched her imagination again, this time for a peace offering, and brought up a subject she knew Francine wanted to talk about. "What's the scariest story you know? I mean fictional, not nonfiction. Not real life."

"The Rock Lady dance," said Francine.

"I said *story*," said Pearl. Then she worried that she was being a book geek again. "You *like* being scared by stories, right?'

Francine nodded, a little embarrassed.

"Then I need you to help me make the story about Vincent even more dramatic. I know you've been working on that Rock Lady thing." Just like that, Pearl let go of her ownership of Vincent, forcing her chin up, even if it strained her neck. If Mary Ann could help, maybe so could Francine.

Francine tapped her toes, even though she only had her school shoes on, and smiled at last. "After ignoring all my ideas, *now* you want me to act out the Rock Lady dance? What for?"

"You said you came to the library because you were scared by my scream, right?"

Francine nodded.

"We're going to scare more people into coming to the library."

Francine smiled, and wiggled her eyebrows.

* * *

All day, Pearl kept reminding herself of the morning conversation with Mary Ann, checking in to see if it still felt real. It didn't, but it was. And she kept thinking about Mary Ann's idea for a marketing campaign to save the library, and all of Francine's Rock Lady ideas that maybe weren't so crazy after all. Pearl wasn't sure what would make adults come to the library, but she knew she ought to be smart enough to figure out kids.

At school Pearl was all eyes, silently observing everything that went on around her. Since the first day of school, Elsa hadn't asked Pearl to give any more story summaries for Millie or anyone else—none of the girls had even spoken to her.

Pearl still didn't understand why they excluded her. It made her leery of trying to tell them *any* story, really. But the plan she was devising with Francine's inspiration could only have a story at the center. And dimly, in her heart, Pearl knew that the problem wasn't the story (after all, Harry Potter had taken over the world; it wasn't *his* fault those girls wouldn't let Pearl jump rope with them); no, the problem was her.

Pearl was afraid that any story she told would suffer from *her* being the one to tell it.

(She was going to need Francine's help after all.)

At recess Pearl sat alone, holding up her book, pretending to be examining some illustration, while actually peering around the playground. Games of four square that always had four

players already. Three-girl jump rope that she wasn't allowed to join. And the boys playing H-O-R-S-E or just shooting baskets. In that group was Oleg Boiko.

Now Pearl observed Oleg over the edge of her book. New to the school, a dropout from somewhere else, *he* didn't seem to have any trouble making friends. He hooted and shot and leaped with the rest of the eighth graders as if he had known them all his life.

On the way home, Pearl mentioned this, and Francine said that Oleg Boiko had *charisma*. "Granny says it's a quality you have to have if you're going to be a good performer, like if you're going to be a tap dancer."

Pearl could see what charisma meant: an odd green shirt and a lit-up expression, and then you were allowed to join H-O-R-S-E games. But also, she figured, while Oleg was playing H-O-R-S-E, he would have to be talking about basketball, because that's what H-O-R-S-E is, so he wasn't necessarily talking about rocks the whole time. That gave her a sort of clue to life. People didn't mind you being geeky if they already liked you for yourself.

"Did Granny say *you* have charisma?" asked Pearl. "Because I think you do, and it's nothing to do with the tap dancing."

"Personally, I think I could light up any stage as the Rock Lady."

Pearl hoped Francine's confidence could carry them both. "Are you coming over? Are we going to work on this dance or not?"

"The *dance*? The story? You know what it is? It's a performance," said Francine. "And a performance needs more people."

Pearl's heart sank: She didn't dare ask anyone else! Well, wait, maybe one: "Let's go ask . . . Oleg," said Pearl.

Francine was astonished. "But he's an eighth grader," she said.

"So he is."

A Sidebar About Reading

Sometimes reading comes gradually. Sometimes it comes like a smack upside the head. For my grandmother, it happened the second way.

Before she moved to 22½ Beep Street, she lived in the library basement where we live now. One night, my grandmother and her friends scared off a swarm of rats that had stolen a box from a carton behind orange-haired Rosita's Rosebud bodega and dragged it to the foot of the statue in the garden. The attraction was a soft cookie, a dense dome of fluffy, succulent marshmallow, covered in dark chocolate as light and brittle as an eggshell, and meltingly delectable.

The *M*s were the key to her reading. As she said the name "Mallomars"[1] over and over to herself, she studied the letters. Two humps meant "mmmmmm." Two vertical lines said "ullllll." An *A* was an open mouth. After a certain amount of repetition,

....

1 Mallomars are cookies that have been around since 1913, mostly in New York. Think graham cracker cookie plus marshmallow plus a thin, crisp, delectable outer coating of dark chocolate—which is why you can only get them September to March. Otherwise they melt. That's just one reason they're precious.

"And he's . . . popular."

"So he is," said Pearl again.

Francine whispered, "So he might not want to have anything to do with—"

Pearl interrupted. "SO?"

Francine shut up, so Pearl shut up and waited, too. But she couldn't ever shut up for long. She let go of her pride and said, "So come on." Two people with charisma plus one without it (her)? *Fine.* They walked around the corner to Clancy Street and rang the bell to Oleg's apartment.

Oleg looked out a second-floor window and called, "The buzzer doesn't work."

"Come over to the library!" Francine yelled up. "We'll be in the back, by the statue!" She ran away giggling. Pearl, feeling gawky and over-serious, trudged back to the library behind her.

The girls stood in the garden and watched the driveway until they heard a noise behind them and turned to see Oleg balance for a moment on the brim of the library's dumpster and jump between two trees to land gymnastically on the grass.

"Hello," said Pearl, acting as though everyone entered the garden this way. She took charge of the situation before

Francine had a chance. "Okay, look. We've got this plan for school, and we need you to help us spread the news about the library."

"About how it's getting made into apartments?" said Oleg.

"If you spread *that* news," warned Pearl, "then you'll never get to help with Vincent's new head."

Oleg's face fell; he sure wanted to be a hero. "Yoiks doesn't think the statue matters," he admitted. "But the librarian does."

"My mother?"

"She's your mom?" Oleg focused on Pearl. "Oh yeah, I can see it. Same intense eyes. Anyway, she's working on an idea to tell people who—Vincent, you call her?—was. She's thinking about trying to get sponsors—you know, 'buy an ear' or something like that."

"People are going to buy one of Vincent's ears?" Pearl said, hearing panic come into her own voice. From the way Oleg was eyeing her, she knew she needed to settle down.

She was relieved when he smiled and answered. "Sure, like buying a brick outside Citi Field. It helps the Mets. Or, my cousin's school in Pennsylvania, they put money on a square of their

R and *S* also released their sounds to her. She learned the sounds of the rest of the letters by studying every word that had the letters she already knew.

Her first name was a raccoon word: Mrzx. Now she became the first raccoon to claim a last name like the ones humans use—in fact, a human word: Mallomar. My mother, Matilda, came along soon after, and then her sister, Eilonwy. I'm my mother's daughter, named after her favorite steam shovel, a book Vincent sent my mother in which a basement plays an important role. I am the one who found the nonfiction book that gave my brother his name, in the course of doing research about what humans think of raccoons.

Both Mrs. Mallomar's children were taught to read, but not all embraced this human-style learning. Even Aunt Eilonwy, a reader who lives in the tree above Vincent, had a rebel—her daughter, my cousin, Eloise. Eloise the exotic, who wants to see the world. Eloise the illiterate, who barely knows the words she'd need to find her way across town on the subway.

—M.A.M.

football field, and somebody lets a cow on the field, and the square where it lets one go—"

"What?" shrieked Francine.

"True," said Oleg, grinning. "It's called a cow-patty raffle."

"So people buy an ear, or an eyeball, or her skirt—and the head gets paid for." Pearl was trying to understand. "Peculiar."

"Your mom thought of *that*?" asked Francine.

"And," continued Pearl, working Mom's plan into her own, "people might especially want to buy parts of something that's haunted."

"Haunted? The statue or the library?" asked Oleg.

"Both!" said Francine.

"And that's what we need you for," said Pearl to Oleg. "Here's the plan: I'm writing the scary story. Francine's going to turn it into a performance."

"What am I supposed to do?" Oleg asked.

"You're the plant," said Francine, as if she were bestowing an honor.

Oleg looked blank. "I'm a geologist," he said. "At least let me be a rock."

He was funny. They laughed.

"She means you're going to be in the audience. Planted there. Your job is to help people believe it," said Pearl. "It's easy. All you have to do is believe it yourself. After the performance, you ask kids, 'Have you heard about the library? I heard it's haunted.'"

"I hardly know anybody at this school yet," said Oleg.

"What? You're friends with everybody on the basketball court," said Pearl.

"It's just basketball," said Oleg. Pearl was surprised to see he looked uncertain.

"You'll be fine," said Francine."Look at the entrance you just made here." She gestured to the dumpster. "You're a born performer."

"We're like reporters." Pearl nodded at Francine. "*We're* the ones who have to make the story real."

"Make it *true*," corrected Francine. "And scary."

"But without the audience, we're nothing," said Pearl. "They have to be able to envision what we're seeing."

"That's where *you* come in," Francine said to Oleg. "You act scared. You tell them what *they* should be scared of."

"Why should they believe me?"

Pearl said, inspired, "Because it's real to *you*."

He looked into her eyes and nodded. "It's official," he said. "I'm a plant."

23: WATCHERS

Later that afternoon, a kerfuffle in the circ area struck Pearl's ears, a clamor of loud excited voices. Bruce was there, and Mom, and Oleg. As Pearl came in the back, Nichols came in the front. Bruce spread out his arms to them both, beaming.

"A head! A head! My kingdom for a head!" Bruce announced.

"What are you talking about?"

Oleg glowed. He said, "The stonemason I found—at the Cathedral of St. John the Divine. Your mom wrote her a letter, and I took it to her. And I showed her that photographer's photographs in the paper, and she said yes! She agreed to carve Vincent a new head."

Mom said, "I'm going to send Jonathan Yoiks a note," and turned away.

Pearl barely heard her. She was demanding of Oleg, "Who's going to pay for *that*?"

"Pearl," said Bruce. "Cool it. Oleg's being a big help." He shook his head at her and went up the stairs.

Feeling scolded, Pearl turned and went out to the garden.

But Oleg followed. "Wait, but Pearl! The stonemason is going to do it for free!"

"What? Why would she?"

"Nobody's about to let her carve anything's head at the cathedral," said Oleg. "She's an apprentice. So she'll do it for free for the chance."

Again Pearl said, "Why?"

"Look, it'll be in the paper, right?" Oleg went on. "So it will be good for her, and good for the library. Isn't that the theory?"

"Yes," said Pearl slowly. "That's the theory." She still couldn't stand the thought of a new Vincent.

"You know that picture on the 'lost head' poster?" Oleg asked. "That's the original Vincent, right? Should I send that to the stonemason to copy?"

"She'll never get it right," said Pearl.

Oleg stopped moving as suddenly as if she'd hit him. Then he looked away and stepped onto the bricks edging Vincent's pedestal and ran his fingers over the smooth, warm granite. Pearl felt sorry all of a sudden. Oleg cared about Vincent, too, even if it was for different reasons.

"You really think a new head is a good idea?" asked Pearl.

"She's doing it for nothing," Oleg said again. It seemed to really matter to him that Pearl was on his side. "It's not just for fame or money. She wants the *experience* of replicating the head."

"I'm worried Vincent will never look the same," said Pearl. But she found it impossible not to like how much Oleg liked the statue, even if it was just a piece of stone.

Hang on a second. Her eyes narrowed. Could he—*could* he?—have planned it this way? "Was it you?" she asked. "Did *you* steal the head, so you could get to replace it?" For a moment it was as if Pearl's whole brain stood on its tiptoes, stretching, reaching.

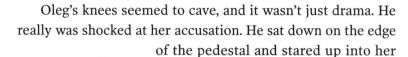

Oleg's knees seemed to cave, and it wasn't just drama. He really was shocked at her accusation. He sat down on the edge of the pedestal and stared up into her face, devastated.

"Of course not," he said.

She believed it. Oleg was too sincere, too real. Real was real. She decided to trust herself on this one—which meant trusting Oleg.

"Sorry," she whispered. She would have liked to reach out, but was too shy to take his hand. But *he* put his hand up to *her,* and she had to pull him up. He didn't just stand, he leaped to his feet.

"You've got superpowers," he said, and flexed his own bicep at her. "Woo!"

He was nice, and she was mortified. "I didn't mean to call you a thief," she said again.

"Okay if you did," he said. "But I'm not like that."

"I know," she said. He waved as he walked away. Yes. She believed him.

* * *

But these were slippery times in Pearl's mind. Whether Vincent got a new head or got her old head back, the question of the criminal tendencies would not go away. Who had taken it, and why? And now—even now, when some new people were coming to the library thanks to the *Moon*, was there still someone out there who wanted to do Vincent harm?

"Mr. Nichols?" Pearl slid in alongside the atlas, wedging herself between the shelf and the corner. There was something she had to know, even if it brought up the whole question of his sleeping place again.

"Yup?" His eyes were half closed.

"What do you think about Vincent getting a new head?"

"Seems like progress," said Nichols. He folded the *Moon* over his chest.

"Mr. Nichols," she whispered, "were you sleeping in the garden the night her head was stolen?"

His eyes opened all the way. He said, "Yes."

"Why didn't you tell me?" Pearl's mind whirled. "Do you know who took it?"

He nodded.

Her voice was hardly audible. "Do you know where the head is now?"

He shook his head.

"Will you tell *me* who took it?"

He shook his head again.

She exploded, "WHY NOT?"

Mom called from the circ counter, "Pearl!"

Nichols opened the paper and hid his face.

"Why not?" Pearl whispered hotly. She thought she might cry.

"It was dark," he murmured. "I can't be sure. So don't ask anymore." In a more normal voice, he added gently, "I don't want to have to lie to you." He put down the paper and bent in her direction, but she pulled away, her back pressing against the atlas shelf.

"How could you just let somebody do something that hurts the library?" asked Pearl.

"The library has worse things wrong with it than the missing head of a statue," said Mr. Nichols.

"Like what?" Pearl's voice was rising again.

Nichols held up his hands. "Even if everything was the way it should be and circulation was up and the library had zillion-speed internet and it was a great neighborhood, there would still be the question of this building here."

"What do you mean?" she whispered.

"There's a building code in this city," Nichols said. He touched the fingertips of his hands together, thumb to thumb, pinky to pinky. "A building code is a set of rules for safe buildings. This library is in violation all over the place: the glass floors, the iron railings, the fire escapes, the width of the doors." He stopped, his clear gray eyes looking firmly into Pearl's. "Not to mention the wild animals."

"Are we supposed to fix all those things?" It sounded to Pearl like just about everything in the library was in violation.

"Yup. And that takes money."

"Well, the city has money."

"Not much money. And that bad publicity you've been hearing about, from the head being stolen, that's the kind of thing that makes the city nervous to spend money." He closed his eyes as if he was done talking and wasn't going to say any more.

"But that's not the whole story," Pearl protested. "We're not just some . . . village of criminals!"

Nichols opened his eyes. He sat forward and took her hands. "I know it breaks your heart. And you're not the only one who feels that way. But I'm here to tell you that even when the bottom falls out of something, you can keep going."

If you want to feel really depressed about your prospects of fixing something, listen to a friend when he tells you he's been there before and gotten through it—and have that person be a lonely man with no job or home. It did not exactly fill Pearl with confidence. But it did not make her want to give up!

Nichols leaned back in his chair, waiting. Then he exhaled softly and said, without looking at Pearl, in a very soft voice, "Just do your best." He opened his eyes a slit and said, deeper, "And think more about the raccoons!"

"What do you mean by that?"

"Use what you know." He put his fingers to his lips. He lifted the paper up again. He was done talking.

What did that mean? Use what you know? The raccoons? Was he trying to say the raccoons had stolen the head after all? Pearl was done with this theory. It was impossible.

Pearl went behind the circ counter and leaned her head on her mother's back, between her shoulders. "Mom," she murmured. "Mom, Mr. Nichols says he knows who took Vincent's head."

"Does he know where the head *is*?"

"No."

Pearl didn't expect Mom to leap into the air and yell, "*Gadzooks!*" but she didn't expect her to just stand there calmly stamping cards for books due three weeks ahead, OCT 21. Halloween, one month away, was the date Mom and Alice had named for the new-head ceremony. It would be a neighborhood party. Or maybe nobody would come but Yoiks, to document the library's doom. *Clunk-bump.* She didn't see how Mom could keep her cool.

A Sidebar About Publicity

Some people think any publicity is good publicity, whether what's being said about you is good or bad. They think the point is to get somebody thinking about you, to let them know you exist.

It's what somebody does once they start thinking about you that's more concerning.

—M.A.M.

"No, but Mom, if you could get Mr. Nichols to tell us, we could grab that person and make them . . ."

"Pearl. Do you really think Mr. Nichols wants to report anything to the police?"

"Oh. No," Pearl realized. "That would make more trouble for him." This stopped her completely.

"We've got a new head coming now, and that means good press," said Mom. *Clunk-bump. Clunk-bump. Clunk-bump.* "Ramón is working on improving internet service. You and I are working on circulation—and Francine, too. Alice and Simon and I are working on a couple things for the Halloween new-head ceremony. And Bruce—bless Bruce—he is still running the numbers and applying for grants like a crazy man. For all I know, there's some magic glue out there that can stick all these pieces together. You know what I told you, Pearl girl. We're not going to look back on this time and regret anything we *didn't* do that *could* have made a difference. Let's keep doing everything we can."

24: COYOTES

SEP 30

Pearl left a note on the bottom basement step for Mary Ann. She had written it out carefully, sitting in her nook, revised it, and copied it over by hand, not wanting anyone to see it on a screen or in the printer. Even if it wasn't addressed to the editor of a newspaper, it was her best effort at a persuasive letter to a city reporter.

(Yoiks wasn't the only one covering this neighborhood.)

After this, she climbed the ladder to the mezzanine of the reading room, where the public was not allowed to go. It had long been closed off for being rickety. She scooted under the railing close to the end of the alphabet, where the stacks were full of *Time* magazine and *U.S. News and World Report* and *Utne Reader*.[1] Then, inside her head, she walked through the story she had been writing, putting in more than one of Francine's cuckoo ideas, enough to make her a contributor, but certainly not a coauthor: Vincent waking sweetly that summer morning, discovering that her head is missing, screaming with devastation, and setting off to walk through the neighborhood, demanding its return, pledging books in exchange. Until she got her head, she would hunt down everyone in the neighborhood individually, promising the exact right story for every single one of them—if only

_____

1 These are all real publications.

they'd come to the library and pay homage to her by ... making an offering? Bowing down and dancing around her pedestal? Or just taking out some books, and raising circulation, and making the library look good?

Pearl thought the rest of her story over for what must have been the nineteenth time. It pleased her. It was kind of over the top with the drama. Pearl thought kids would like it. It was good and horrifying.

Simon came down the back hall with Jonathan Yoiks. "Oh. Beautiful!" Yoiks was saying.

Pearl watched him take a number of pictures of the reading room's pretty iron vines, the old-fashioned sliding ladder, the afternoon light coming on dusty beams through the garden windows. She knew Yoiks didn't know she was up here.

Simon told Yoiks, "May as well photograph it while you can."

"Exactly," said Yoiks. "What's left of old New York." He glanced around the stacks. "Do you know about Jacob Riis and his photographs? One of the first activist journalists, helped get policies changed regarding child labor."

"What did he photograph?" asked Simon.

"People. The way they really lived. A side of New York that most of the people who could afford a newspaper never knew existed."

Simon brightened. "You mean your paper's looking for real-life stories? You've come to the right place. Publicity would really help the library right now. And if you can get it in the paper before the library board votes about letting builders propose putting apartments here, destroying, you know, a cultural paradise, that would be great."

Yoiks sighed. "That's not exactly the type of story I'm looking to do," he said. "My editor is looking for—"

"Dramatic breaking news," Pearl called down from above.

"Uh, yes, and if I'm the one to deliver it—"

"If you are, so what?" asked Simon.

Yoiks's eyes bugged a little. "Well, then I might—"

"I mean, sure, if you're lucky a fire truck might crash into a cop car and you'll be there on the scene to take a picture with your phone," said Simon. "Congratulations. I could do that, too. So could anybody. Or you could do what this Jacob Riis guy did."

"Jacob Riis documented poverty," said Yoiks. "He showed the conditions people were living in, and when people saw his photographs, they were shocked at the human condition."

"Exactly," said Simon. "So he documented the way things were . . . which meant he was on hand while they changed. Not just at the sad end or the scary beginning."

"You could do that here," said Pearl. "Show what things are like *normally* on Lancaster Avenue, instead of writing stories about awful things that happen one time only."

"Exactly," said Simon. "Call it human-interest." (That again!)

Yoiks looked thoughtful. "Well, this sure is a side of New York most people don't think exists anymore," he said. "No one wants to come down here."

"Down here? What if you already live 'down here'?" said Simon.

"Yeah, what if 'this' is *your* side of New York?" said Pearl.

Yoiks winced. "I'm sorry, kiddos. I don't mean it like that. It *is* called *down*town."

"That isn't what you meant," Pearl said. "You meant people don't want to come down *in life*. You meant that we're in a part of the city people are scared of."

Below her, she saw Mom in the doorway, listening.

"Do *you* think it's scary?" Yoiks stood back and peered up at the mezzanine and Pearl.

"I do NOT," Pearl said stubbornly. But she remembered last spring, when she'd gone to visit the new Knickerbocker branch library with Mom—how clean and shiny it was, with all those computers, nothing old or crumbling about it. It didn't smell of old wood; it smelled more of new paint than books, but it was still, well, she had to say it—*nice*. But jealous? Her? Hardly. After all, the Knickerbocker surely didn't have raccoons in the basement.

"This is where we live," said Simon defensively. "What are we supposed to do about it?"

"I'm sorry," said Yoiks. "I like this library, too."

Pearl piped up. "But you don't like the neighborhood?"

"No," said Yoiks bluntly. "But I know the story is important. That's why I'm here now. I want the library to be remembered."

There was a silence in which Pearl realized what he was up against—the same thing the library had been up against—before she screamed, and after, too. If there was anything Pearl could understand, it was the need for good stories. And once people expected them, well, you had to deliver.

"Work on it," she said.

"How?" he asked.

"You're the reporter!" she responded.

Before he could get annoyed, Mom said, "And if you can get your story in the paper the day the library board votes, October 2, that would be great. The board is voting on whether to take the building proposal seriously. It needs to see enough value in the library to at least send the decision about how to use the building to the district vote."

A Sidebar About Persuasion

Persuasion is the art of convincing someone that they want to do what you want them to do. I present Pearl's letter as a case study concerning the power of the pen, the power of the public schools (where, I presume, she learned to write such a letter), and the power of persuasion.

Dear Mary Ann, (Why not *Miss Mallomar?* Because we were past such formalities.)

Since you are a library resident and the local expert on raccoons, (Establishes the reason for writing to this person, and a little flattery can't hurt.) I would like to ask you to give me your opinion about a story I am working on. (Establishes the goal of letter.)

It is not very long, and won't take you much time. I can leave it on the step like this and you can return it at your convenience. (Makes an offer that seems easy.)

"'Whether to take the building proposal seriously,'" repeated Yoiks. "And that depends on—"

"On whether the board thinks our branch is valued by the neighborhood," said Mom. "On whether the building would be worth more sold as real estate."

"Horrors," said Yoiks. For the first time, Pearl smiled at him. "I mean it," he told her. But she could already see that. He turned back to Mom. "Do you think they'll accept the proposal?"

"I do," said Mom. "They have to. It's just good business."

"Then what?"

"Then we'll have a very short time period to win neighborhood support and make everyone here want to vote for the library over apartments."

"Listen, here's my plan," said Simon hurriedly. "We're going to have a rock concert."

"When?" Yoiks said.

"Halloween," Simon said. "If we can get people to come to the garden, if they like the library well enough, maybe that will convince the neighbors to vote for it."

"Hey, Francine and I have a Halloween plan, too," Pearl said.

But just then Yoiks's cell phone rang. "Yoiks," he said into it. He listened a moment, then said, "Got it." He said to the library people, "Gotta dash." Yoiks pointed up at Pearl and said, "I want you to tell me more. Later." Then he was gone, Mom following in his wake.

Typical.

Pearl let her feet dangle over the edge of the mezzanine and looked down at Simon. If growing up, for Pearl, was a river, with grown-ups on one shore and, on the other, little kids with no worries about real life and real problems, then Simon was a rock in the middle of the stream, a safe landing spot where she could check whether her little-kid ideas could work with grown-ups, or if they would get ignored or laughed at. But lately Simon seemed different, quieter, busy inside his head, older, more worried. Was this what happened when you were a teenager?

How long ago was it that he'd brought her almond cookies and sat on the floor of the children's room to read her picture books, the two of them giggling until Alice lost patience?

When Pearl was younger, she had always thought she was Simon's best

It concerns local characters and settings, and I hope you will find it interesting. (Makes the proposal seem personally appealing to the addressee.)

With this story, we just might save the Lancaster Avenue branch of the New York City Library. (Raises the stakes. Makes the reader feel like part of something grand. Aims for the heart.)

You will want to be a part of it. (Call to action.)

Yours truly,

Pearl A. Moran

—M.A.M.

friend. Since she had been Simon's best friend here, she'd thought then, she must be his best friend everywhere.

Now she realized this idea was one of those little-kid ideas, something she'd thought of when she didn't realize the world existed outside the library. Now she knew Simon had secrets. Lately she felt on the outside of things with him.

But he was still her rock. She wanted to believe that.

Pearl folded a card-catalog card into a paper airplane and flew it down toward Simon's fiery head. He looked up. His eyes had dark circles under them. "You look like a raccoon," she said, and immediately thought it was a dumb way to open the subject. "What's the matter with your eyes?" she asked. "Didn't you sleep last night?"

Simon shook his head and mimed playing a guitar.

"All night?"

"It felt like it," he said. "I had to. I have to get better or I won't get into Berklee." That was the music school in Boston that he wanted to go to. He put both his hands on his head and rubbed his hair, hard. Then he kept his hands up there and didn't say anything for a minute.

Poor Simon! She was glad she had something to distract him with. "Speaking of raccoons," she continued, "have you ever thought about the raccoons around here? How, uh, *tame* they are?"

"If by tame you mean well-adapted . . . I guess they'd have to be to survive the mean streets." He was clearly still mad about the way Jonathan Yoiks had described their neighborhood.

"Do you"—she flipped through some verbs in her mind: Think? Believe? Know?—"*realize* they can read?"

"Reading raccoons? That would be a good one." Simon wasn't put off by Pearl's goofy raccoon suggestion, but his mind was already moving on. "Pearl, remember when you said the band-its? Is that because they look like bandits? Or because a bunch of them is called a band?"

"Hmm. I don't know what a bunch of them is called."

(I could have told her. And I would tell her when she asked: A bunch of raccoons is called a mask. Or a gaze. And if you don't think that's beautiful, you mustn't be a lover of words— or raccoons.)

"Well, a bunch of coyotes is called a band," said Simon.

"Coyotes? Bruce says there are actual wild coyotes around here, but they're too smart to ever let you see them. *Ow-oo!*" Her howling didn't make Simon laugh.

"Why do you ask?" Pearl said.

But Simon wouldn't answer and seemed distracted. He didn't seem to have heard her about the raccoons, either.

25: THE SCHOOL PLAN

On Saturday afternoon, Pearl wanted to work on her story, but got distracted imagining Khadija and Elsa and Millie responding to the performance. Try though she might to focus on the other 779 kids in the school, she couldn't stop picturing their faces, hearing their voices sneering, thinking she was stupid, or geeky, or ridiculous. She couldn't get those girls out of her head no matter how much she said to herself, Just do it. Just do it. Just do it.

Suddenly, she thought, *why do they matter so much?* She had Francine, and she was a friend, wasn't she?

Pearl also sort of had Oleg. He was coming over to work on the plan with them on Sunday, in preparation for Monday at school. And he was an eighth grader! So what if he was just doing it because he wanted the library to use his replacement head on their statue?

And she had Nichols. Sure, he was a grown man, even further away from her age than Oleg, but he had shown her the reading raccoons. He believed in them, and he believed in her. That made him a real friend, no matter how old he was.

And then there was Mary Ann. Pearl really did have a friend who was a raccoon named Mary Ann.

And that was enough to ease her nervousness about her story and the performance. Pearl slipped down the basement steps and woke up Mary Ann for the second time that week.

Nocturnal, wrote Mary Ann.

Pearl winced. "Sorry," she said, but was too excited to be sorry for long. "I need *Mike Mulligan*. And in return I want to tell you my story. Did you read my letter? Will you be my practice audience?"

Mary Ann wrote, What makes you think we have Mike Mulligan?

"I saw it, thief!" said Pearl. She was a bit shocked at herself, acting like Mary Ann was just any human, talking to her like that.

But Mary Ann was *laughing*, showing her little teeth.

"Please," said Pearl. "You'll get input on the story, too. You'll get to be an editor, like your grandmother."

Mary Ann wasn't writing anything, but maybe that was because she had been awakened from a sound sleep and she wasn't used to a human talking to her directly, making demands and offering deals.

"You'll get to help make kids come to the library, if the story's good enough," continued Pearl. "I'm trying to do what you said. You know—just do it."

Mary Ann seemed to be considering the plan.

"I need someone impartial," Pearl went on. "Francine and Oleg are too close to the story to be impartial. And at school, nobody likes me because nobody cares about books as much as I do." Something about talking to a raccoon allowed her to admit this truth out loud for the first time.

When you do something other people don't do, they think you think you're special.

"Is it my fault I've read more books than any other fifth grader in the whole city?"

Listen to yourself.

Just then, there was a moaning sound, and a bigger raccoon loomed out of the gloom.

Finally! Wait until Pearl told Mom she had actually met Matilda, the daughter of Mrs. Mallomar.

Pearl stared as the older raccoon leaned close to her daughter and whispered, *ak-ak-ak*ing. Then she heaved a sigh, like Mom sometimes in the middle of the night, and went off—back to bed, presumably.

Pearl whispered, "What did your mother just say?"

She said to take the editing job.

"Yes!" said Pearl.

When do we start?

"Today," said Pearl.

I'm going back to sleep.

"It'll be here when you wake up."

Pearl worked on her story until closing, and well after Mom and Bruce had locked the front door, and while they sat hunched over the circulation numbers. She typed on Ramón's computer until she didn't know what more to write.

Of course it wasn't all going to make it into the performance, but it gave the performance *background*. The foreground—what the audience would see—Pearl filled with suspenseful silence, shocking sounds, and ghostly visions. For herself, she wrote the background, the back-and-forth between her and Oleg, punctuated by bizarre moves from Francine.

And then she sneaked down the basement stairs and left it on the bottom step for Mary Ann: three printed sheets, double-sided, triple-spaced to allow room for edits, as Mary Ann had instructed her.

* * *

Sunday morning it seemed like fall had arrived at last: bright, cold, sunny, windy. Pearl put on jeans and socks and the cool secondhand clogs Mom had bought her at Housing Works the week before. She clopped as she and Mom walked to the library, then took the clogs off in the back hall and went down the basement stairs in her sock feet.

There was her story manuscript, folded in half the long way on the second stair from the top. Ecstatic, Pearl snatched it and ran up the stairs two at a time, put her clogs back on, and took a couple experimental skipping steps across the foyer toward her nook.

"Don't tell me *you're* taking up tap dance," said Mom.

Pearl snorted and settled down behind the atlas. Her papers were now covered with notes and cross-outs and arrows from Mary Ann. Pearl worked on the story all morning, scrawling changes, adding ominous asides, posing questions that she'd let her audience answer in their own imaginations, and getting rid of boring stuff that led nowhere.

At noon, Pearl went up to the nonfiction stacks in the children's room, peering at the photographs and other illustrations in biographies of real people who had fought the way things were—civil rights fighters in the South, girls and women in other countries fighting laws that kept them from going to school, LGBTQ people right here in New York City. She studied the signs people held and the slogans on the signs and the names of the groups that were marching.

There was a loud emotional sigh, and Pearl looked up to see Alice looking grouchy, her hand on her stomach. Then she came and lay right down in the aisle and groaned.

Pearl was greatly alarmed. "Are you all right?"

Alice just laughed. "I'm seven months pregnant," she said. "I feel like a cow swimming through rice."

Pearl looked at the mountain that was Alice, lying there. She patted Alice's hand and said, "Want me to read to you?" She read a line from one of the open books: "'You must be the change you want to see in the world.'"

Alice said, "Free spa treatments and chocolate for all pregnant women. That's the change I want to see."

Chocolate made Pearl think of Halloween, and costumes made her think of a parade Alice had always wanted to have. "What's your idea for that children's book costume parade?" she asked. "We could add that to Halloween, too!"

Alice groaned some more. "Who's going to organize that mess?" she asked. "Not me."

"Think of some good costumes," said Pearl. "That's all you'd need to do."

"Easy peasy," said Alice. "The playing-card gardeners from *Alice in Wonderland*[2]—just cardboard and string. A mouse with

---

1 This common quote is often attributed to Mahatma Gandhi, who actually said, "As a man changes his own nature, so does the attitude of the world change towards him. . . . We need not wait to see what others do."

2 Actually: *Alice's Adventures in Wonderland* by Lewis Carroll (Macmillan, 1865).

mouse ears and a giant cookie made of poster board for *If You Give a Mouse a Cookie*.[3] Harriet the Spy[4] with glasses and a notebook and a flashlight."

Pearl wrote things down in her own notebook. Halloween was the second part of the plan. But they had to get through tomorrow before she could focus on the Halloween part.

Tomorrow was the big day, the day of the plan at school.

They had their last rehearsal that afternoon, the whole team nervous. Francine had come early, and Pearl got worried Oleg would blow them off, so she made Francine walk over to Clancy Street to get him. She felt somehow that he was the key to convincing people at their school to see her differently. Maybe it was because he was a boy, or because his grades weren't that good but he still liked the library, or because he was athletic and strong. Whatever it was, his allegiance would make Pearl look different to the kids at school.

The moment Pearl heard Oleg's footsteps pounding up the steps and saw the smile he had for everyone, including her, she felt herself smiling back. And for the rest of the day, it was almost like she really did have charisma. Their act went off well every time they ran it through.

It was only later that the jitters returned: Would "well" be good enough? That evening, after their practice, Pearl climbed into bed with her manuscript, fighting a nauseated feeling in her stomach at the thought of executing the plan. Well, the fact was, time was up. Whatever she had now was what they'd go with tomorrow. Again she saw Elsa's eyes, and Millie's. But then she thought, *at least it won't be just me they'll be looking at.*

....

3 *If You Give a Mouse a Cookie* by Laura Numeroff (HarperCollins, 1985).

4 *Harriet the Spy* by Louise Fitzhugh (Harper & Row, 1964).

There were three of them. And, looking down at her manuscript, with Mary Ann's edits written on it, she thought: no, four.

She read the story over and over until she knew it backward and frontward by heart. Then she turned off the light. For a while she tried to keep her fingers crossed, to put a good-luck spell on herself for the morning. But falling asleep, she knew her fingers would come uncrossed, and there was nothing she could do about it.

26: THE HAUNTING OF LANCASTER AVENUE

OCT 2

School that Monday morning felt frighteningly normal. When something strange is going to happen and you're the one who's going to cause it, you feel weird and wary inside. Pearl knew she was going to have to pull some kind of magic trick to make the kind of change she wanted to see. *But first, settle down,* she told herself. Just follow the plan.

She went and buzzed Francine, and when they got to the corner, Oleg was there waiting for them. Some kids were coming from the other way. *Go time!*

Francine led off: "It might not be haunted the way it is in our story, but *somebody's* haunting it in their own way."

It was part of the plan for each of them to say exactly *that*, at various points along the route to school—loudly, so everybody in earshot would hear them, making everybody who heard wonder *what* was haunted. Then they'd move on to the next spot, stand there as if they were waiting for somebody, letting the school traffic pass until there was a new set of kids nearby, then they'd say it again.

Pearl hooked her thumbs in her backpack straps and held down the blowing sides of her vest with her elbows. Besides her nerves about the plan, she found herself slightly embarrassed at

A Sidebar About Home

I may be two years old, but I'm more mature than Pearl. And Eloise, who is three, is more mature than me. Eloise is mature enough to want to leave home.

"But it's also a matter of sophistication," Eloise explained to me snootily, more than once. "There are better places than this, Miss M.A.M."

"Travel all you want," I told her. "But when you decide you want to come home, wouldn't it be great if you still had a home to go to?"

"What makes you think I'd want to come back?"

I gasped. "Anything could happen out there in the world. What would you do if you didn't have anywhere, and you needed it?"

I'll never know what thought flitted through Eloise's small mind, but she paused and looked nervous. I didn't hesitate: "You've got to tell me, once and for all, who took Vincent's head. Otherwise we could lose the library!"

"Why do you suddenly want to know about that statue so much?" said Eloise.

being with Oleg, an eighth grader. In the school's pale yellow uniform instead of his customary Day-Glo, he seemed oddly formal. His sleeves were rolled to the elbow; he wasn't one of the kids who could afford short-sleeved shirts as well as the required long ones.

"Hey, Rock Boy!" A big round-faced boy clapped Oleg on the shoulder.

Pearl recognized him as an older student from her school. "What's your name?" she asked the boy.

"Jaime," he said, surprised at her boldness.

"This is Pearl," said Francine, not to be outdone. "And I'm Francine."

"Oh, yeah?" Jaime recovered his poise. "And this is Rock Boy, with rocks in his head, who used to live on South Street. Where you living now?"

"Clancy." Oleg grinned in a silly way. They all kept walking toward school. This wasn't the way Pearl had thought it would go, just talking to one person this way. But she didn't know how to fix it. "I've been at Lancaster Avenue since the start of school. I'm just walking a different way today."

"You repeating?" Jaime asked.

Oleg just smiled and shrugged and said, "I homeschooled all spring and summer. More time for field study."

"Rocks!" Jaime hit himself in the head. He was being funny, Pearl realized, not mean. He liked Oleg.

She cut right in with her act, even though this wasn't part of the plan. *Whatever works.* "The most incredible things have been happening on Lancaster Avenue, actually."

"Oh, really?" Jaime said, rolling his eyes.

"Magical things," said Francine, chiming in.

Oleg's turn. "That library's haunted, you know," he said, flat as that.

"What library?"

"The Lancaster Avenue library," said Oleg.

"It is," Pearl said nonchalantly. "Haunted."

Jaime plainly thought they were bonkers. "There's no such thing as ghosts." Now they were at the school gate. The first bell was already ringing, and Francine hustled away to her classroom—her teacher was stricter than Pearl's about sitting down before the bell—while Oleg went ahead toward the eighth-grade rooms. But Jaime was still right beside Pearl. He said, "So, are you and Rock Boy, like, going out?"

What? "It really is haunted," Pearl said, ignoring his question. "But I don't

"Well, I've been curious all along."

Eloise leaned in suspiciously, and made an accusation. "You don't care what happens to me. You just want to know so you can break a real news story."

"Well, news is the family business," I said. "If only you'd care about that."

Eloise tapped her toenails on the tree, *rat-a-tat*. (She's growing them long for the country, she says.) "I have nothing at all to say about it," she said, and disappeared into her nest.

"You'd better hope they don't build a parking lot here and tear down your trees!" I called after her brutally. "Then where will you make your home?"

"Haven't you heard, Mary Ann?" Eloise shouted. "There are plenty of trees in the world!"

—M.A.M.

have time to tell you about it now." She took off toward the school door. "Don't tell anybody about the haunting!" she yelled back to him down the hall, with sudden inspiration.

He shook his head. He thought she was bonkers, but who cared, he had heard her, which meant he was thinking about the library. It filled her with a bubble of hope that did not pop, because her nervous mind just couldn't come up with a downside.

Despite her nerves—she knew she'd remember nothing in class all morning—Pearl felt lighter, elated, excited: Everything had gone just right so far. But the hard part was still three hours ahead: recess.

* * *

Francine stood in the schoolyard, just inside the invisible line between upper school and lower school, in Vincent's pose. Her left hand extended, open, waiting. One foot forward. And now she did the bravest thing of all: She closed her eyes.

The closed eyes really made her look made of stone. They were not squeezed shut, just smoothly closed, and she wasn't smiling. She had Vincent's serene, still look on her face. *She's good,* thought Pearl, and worried whether she herself could meet Francine's acting standards. Then she thought of what Alice had told them: Be matter-of-fact, just tell it. Truth reeled people in—especially dramatic truth. Think of a headline, Alice had said—not the *Moon,* but the *News* and the *Star,* trashy rags that baited people with drama that might be real.

Pearl sped toward Francine across the playground. She had to scare all the kids on the playground with just words, that was her job. Pearl's heart was jumping around inside her chest, but she thought of the library and the worse horror of losing it. *Come alive,* she told herself. *Tell it to the hardest person, and then everyone else will feel easier.*

So she grabbed the nearest person—Millie—by the elbow and said, "Look! It's the Rock Lady!" Her voice trembled with nerves, but that was the perfect touch. Millie's eyes widened, and Pearl leaned across her to Khadija and Elsa. The three hardest people. She didn't let herself think; she just told it. "See?" she insisted. She pointed a wavering finger at Francine, standing there with her eyes shut. "She's standing like that library statue, you know? That headless one. I think she wants something." She knew Elsa would come along if she played Millie right. And if she got Elsa, well, then Khadija would follow.

The girls looked at each other for a second, like, *Is she for real?* And if Pearl didn't get this right, Elsa could wreck the whole thing on her own.

Pearl almost threw up, she felt so anxious. *It's not really me they're turning away from, it's the story.* In one part of herself, she knew this was a lie; she used the story to get past the fear. "Come help me," she said, making her voice as desperate as she actually felt, and reached for Millie's arm again. This time, Millie came. And so Pearl and Millie and Elsa and Khadija advanced toward frozen, eerie Francine.

Heads turned as they crept past people. Pearl stopped a few feet from Francine and held the others back with one hand. "Wait!" She circled behind Francine, who hardly seemed to be breathing. She spotted Oleg across the yard, near Jaime. He started toward them and—yes!—Jaime and some boys trailed along with him. *Let it catch on,* Pearl prayed.

Francine opened her eyes but still did not seem to see, staring as though a spell had been cast over her. Some girls from seventh grade gathered.

"What's with *her*?" Millie asked Pearl, giggling.

Oleg arrived then, just in time for Pearl to roll her eyes at him and say loudly, "Francine's at it again."

"Oh, no," said Oleg, as rehearsed.

"She's at what?" said Jaime, bumbling into the circle. "Hey, kid! Snap out of it!"

Francine turned slightly toward Jaime, but her expression didn't change. Her eyes glassy, she reached her hand toward something invisible straight in front of her. Jaime giggled nervously and waved his hand in front of Francine's eyes. She didn't blink.

"She's possessed," Pearl informed them all. More kids gathered. Oleg walked around Francine, examining her, then shook his head.

"Possessed by what?" asked Khadija, rolling her eyes.

"The ghost of her lost brain," said Elsa, trying to steal the spotlight. Everybody laughed uncertainly, but Francine never changed, and Oleg and Pearl stayed serious.

"Nope, it's Vincent again," Oleg said, as though confiding to Pearl.

Pearl nodded solemnly. "Same as it was all summer," she told the group. A few more kids came over now.

"Who's Vincent?"

"A statue," said Pearl.

"A poor, headless statue," Oleg added.

"What statue?"

"At the Lancaster Avenue library," said Pearl.

"Where's that at?" someone asked.

"Lancaster Avenue, stupid," someone else answered.

Khadija asked, "Are you trying to say it's haunted or something?"

Oleg and Pearl stopped, hearing the cue they'd planned. They looked at each other over Francine's head, forcing themselves to look worried and sad despite the triumph. "I'd say so, wouldn't you?" said Pearl. "At least, she's under a spell."

"Probably, yeah," said Oleg regretfully.

"Just tell us, already. Who's Vincent?" asked Elsa.

"Vincent is powerful," Pearl said, not exactly answering.

"And angry," said Oleg.

"I guess you'd be angry too," Pearl said thoughtfully, musingly. "If you'd been beheaded." *Boom!*

"Beheaded!" came the group response.

"Who's Vincent?" Millie called out, her face full of excitement.

"You really want to know?"

"Sure," said Millie.

Pearl told. Only she didn't just reel off the plot, the way she had when she'd retold Harry Potter. She told it as if it had never been told before. She made it scary. She made it a story.

"Vincent—sweet, brilliant Edna St. Vincent Millay, world-renowned poet, beautiful romantic—becomes tired of being encased in stone, alone in the garden, as imprisoned as a princess in a tower."

To her delight, everyone leaned in. Pearl realized that although she had stopped writing her story to rehearse yesterday, the story had gone on developing in the back of her head all night and even now, as she saw it acted out before her, as she spun it in hushed tones to the crowd that had built into a thick circle around them.

"People who work at the library or in the neighborhood are constantly inspired to read a certain book or learn a certain fact—and all these people understand that it's Vincent who's inspiring them. She wants people to come to her garden," Pearl's story went on, "so she sends out messages to convince them: poems, stories, plays, songs. Nobody understands how she's sending the messages, but they receive them anyway. That's how people get ideas to read what they read. That's why people love Vincent. That's why people have always loved Vincent, for years—decades."

"And then the disaster happens." Pearl let her voice slow here. "My mother and I are coming to work one summer morning, and we sense a disturbance in the garden. When suddenly—" Pearl paused. She cleared her throat. And then she let out a silent scream, making it clear from her facial expression just how anguished she had been. "I discover the remains of our beheaded beloved statue."

How magnificently Pearl whispered of their entrance to the garden, the horrible discovery of Vincent's headlessness, and the continuing heartache and fears of the unsolved mystery. She wasn't acting at all. "Now Vincent wants her head back. At least we *think* that's what she wants. She's holding out her hand for something, but we can't figure out what." She hadn't made up the next part yet, but she let the moment stretch out as if she *did* know.

"Have you tried money?"

"Candy?"

"A pretzel?"

"How about a beer?" They laughed themselves silly about that one.

Pearl waited patiently. "It's serious," she said when they stopped. "It's starting to affect others, like Francine.

"Francine used to—" Pearl acted choked up. What did she have to lose? "She used to be normal." Pearl hid her face in her hands. "Now we're afraid. We're so afraid. If other people come near the statue . . ." Then what? She didn't know herself, but again, she didn't need to. People teetered on the edge of their own imaginings of what came next.

(That meant the story was working.)

"You mean—" said Khadija.

"Ooh. It'll rub off?" asked Millie.

Pearl said, "The trouble is . . . don't you see? Would *you* want to be turned to stone? The spell could strike *other people*. And if the thief comes back, they could lose *their* heads, too."

27: MORE DRAMA

The upper schoolers started coming to the library that very afternoon. Jaime barged in first, with Oleg and two other eighth graders trailing him.

"Where's this statue?" Jaime demanded.

Ramón startled at his desk. Nichols peered over the top of his paper. Mom paused in the stamping of date-due cards three weeks in advance: OCT 23.

Pearl leaped up. "I'll show you," she said. "But you have to have a library card to come in here."

Mom slid her eyes toward Pearl.

"I don't have any money." Jaime reached into his navy-blue uniform pants pockets.

"It's free," sang Pearl. "Just fill out this card. All you need is your address."

Jaime grabbed one, and the other boys followed their leader and started filling out applications of their own.

"Cool," said Simon, showing up for his afternoon shift, looking like all this was normal. "You can check books out once you've taken the oath and signed the register."

"Oath? Register?" asked Jaime. "For books?"

"It's a library, yo," Simon said, trying to impress the younger boys.

"All right, bro," Jaime said. Pearl figured he saw through Simon, but he did it with a grin, the way he did everything.

Simon stayed serious. He stood rigidly by the circ counter and held up his hand. "When I write my name in this book . . ." He paused.

"When I write my name in this book . . . ," Jaime repeated, still smiling, his hand high, and his friends followed suit.

When the oath was finished, Simon turned it into a high five. Then he made the boys put their names in the register book, which they each did with a flourish, as if they were signing autographs. Pearl acted barely patient through it all, then flapped her hand toward the back hall. "The garden is that way." She sighed as though weary of all the difficulties a headless statue could bring to a library. "Try to stay out of trouble!"

That was Francine's cue to appear in the doorway to the garden, where they could see her—but where Mom wouldn't, Pearl hoped, notice her from the desk just yet. Mom was already suspicious about the whole thing.

Just then, Millie burst through the foyer, pulling Khadija by the arm, with Elsa slinking along behind.

Yes! "Come!" Pearl said grandly. "This way!"

"Without a *library card*?" thundered Mom. She swooped down behind Millie and her friends and propelled them back to the circ desk. Pearl stood jiggling her knees, nervously waiting in the doorway for the girls so that Mom wouldn't feel the need to escort them. Finally they were done. "Back here," said Pearl, now feeling shy. Walking backwards, she drew them through the hallway to the garden door. Francine stood just outside the door, with a spellbound sort of stare on her face.

To Pearl's relief, the girls laughed and went out the door.

Francine led the kids across the garden to Vincent as though she was being pulled there by a magnetic field. And Pearl, who found herself tongue-tied at school, got carried along by her own story, narrating as if Vincent really was sending her inspiration. (And who says she wasn't?)

"See, the statue draws Francine near," Pearl said to the kids huddled at the foot of the pedestal. "Vincent was a poet," she said. "But now . . ."

"Now her head is gone," said Oleg, jumping from the fence to the dumpster to the yard in two bounds.

"Gone where?" Francine grabbed Oleg by both arms and stared tearfully into his face.

"Nobody knows," said Jaime solemnly.

Finally, thought Pearl. Once kids started spreading the story themselves, Pearl would know it was really working.

"She wants it back!" Francine said.

"She wants more than that. She wants—" Pearl waited, knowing there would be suggestions.

"Blood?" asked Elsa.

"People," said Francine, in the tone of someone crossing a desert, desperate for water.

"What, to eat?" asked Elsa. She mockingly reached a hand toward Francine.

"Stupid, she can't eat," Jaime told Elsa. "She's got no head."

"So what does she want people for?" asked Khadija.

"To share her sorrow over her lost head," added Francine in a hushed voice. "To love what she loves—the building, the books." She put a comforting hand on Vincent's foot. Elsa laughed, just one "ha," but Millie and Khadija reached out and touched Vincent's foot, too. Pearl wondered what they were feeling.

"What can we do?" whispered Millie.

"Bring more company!" Francine was so emotional that she couldn't meet anyone's eyes.

Pearl got inspired. "She wants to know that you're receiving her messages."

"How do we do that?" asked Jaime.

"Check out a book," said Oleg, taking the words right out of Pearl's mouth.

"A book?" Elsa reacted as though Oleg had asked for an offering of spiders. "*That's* all she wants, a lousy book?" She tossed her head back, flipping around her hundreds of tiny braids. She was flirting with Oleg, Pearl realized. Well, whatever it took!

"Vincent loves stories," said Pearl. "She wasn't just a poet. She was an actor and a playwright, too. She wants *people* to have stories. If people take out books, she calms down. She can live with—being dead." Pearl let the word "dead" come down with a thud, and Khadija stifled a shudder.

Thank goodness Mom, Simon, Alice, and Bruce were in the doorway now, and Pearl could move things along.

"Library cards?" she whispered frantically to Mom.

A Sidebar About Vermin

Look it up: "Vermin" means wild animals that are troublemakers because they cause harm or carry disease.

Of course, nobody asks the so-called wild animals what *they* think is harmful.

"Varmint" is more than just another way to say "vermin." It's what people say when they want to add intention—mischievous intention—to the definition above. But it has another definition besides wild animals. "Varmint" can also apply to mischievous, troublemaking children.

—M.A.M.

"Right here!" Mom held up a card. "Ludmila Perez?"

Millie stepped forward and took her card. She didn't put it away, just held it in her hand. Ceremoniously, the other kids stood in a semicircle, took the oath, and watched while Mom distributed cards to them as if they were medals.

"Do you guys want to get books now?" asked Oleg.

"Young adult is on the second floor. The books are just to the right of the candy up there," Alice said, winking. As they all dashed off, she said, "Come for the ghosts, stay for the candy."

Pearl led the girls up the spiral stairs.

"There may be ghost books," Elsa told her, "but there's no such thing as ghosts."

Pearl ran a finger along a shelf. "I think it's a matter of what you're open to," she said, daring herself to sound as spooky as Francine. Elsa stuck her tongue out. But she took down a book.

"What about miniatures?" asked Khadija. "Do you have books with dollhouses in them?"

"What about robots?" asked Millie.

For once in her life, Pearl had to choose between people to talk to. She pointed Khadija toward the craft books, and told Elsa to check the 130s. Then she led the way to the 629s, where the robots were.

That afternoon, it was a struggle for Pearl to stay nonchalant as the five new library patrons walked down the steps, mouths full of Starburst, library books under their arms along with their school bags. She wanted to hug her team, but Francine was in the garden, tapping in slow motion, trying to stay in character until the kids were gone, and Oleg had disappeared somewhere, maybe trailing Simon around. So she trotted briskly up the spiral stairs into the children's room, bounced across the floor to the windows, and, seeing the kids walking away in the distance, leaped into the air, then came down to earth and hugged Alice.

"You've done good, Pearlie," said Alice. "I just hope the board votes that construction proposal down tonight and makes it all worthwhile."

It was not like Alice to want to burst Pearl's balloon, so this was a reality check. Pearl was newly aware of the very real possibility that the library board could, that very afternoon, burst a whole bunch of balloons. And if that wasn't enough, here came Bruce, brandishing the evening *Moon* high above his head and calling, "Publicity! Free publicity! Just in time for the board meeting! Go, team!" He made a deep bow and presented the paper to Mom.

With a crack and a swoosh, Mom opened the paper and read them the

story of how the stonemason at the cathedral had agreed to carve Vincent a new head. When she finished, she added, "Good."

"Good what?" Pearl asked.

"Good about Yoiks," said Mom. "Keep him coming. I want him to cover our new-head Halloween party. That'll help."

"It's going to be all but too late," said Bruce.

Mom resumed stamping date-due cards.

"Not if the Rock Lady story keeps on working," said Pearl. "And it will."

PART THREE: RISING ACTION

"I'll keep a little tavern
Below the high hill's crest,
Wherein all grey-eyed people
May sit them down and rest.
There shall be plates a-plenty,
And mugs to melt the chill
Of all the grey-eyed people
Who happen up the hill.
There sound will sleep the traveller
And dream his journey's end,
But I will rouse at midnight
The falling fire to tend.
Aye, 'tis a curious fancy —
But all the good I know
Was taught me out of two grey eyes
A long time ago."

—"TAVERN"
BY EDNA ST. VINCENT MILLAY[1]

---

1 The poem "Tavern," from *Renascence and Other Poems* by Edna St. Vincent Millay (Harper, 1917).

28: THE RACCOON INVASION

OCT 2

But the day wasn't over. Late that afternoon, the sun setting, a troop of people headed up the front steps of the library. More patrons so soon?

But no. It was Gully, with Mr. Bull and Mr. Dozer, and a woman in a red uniform with an *X* on her pocket and on her cap. In the driveway was a red van to match, with a logo that said X Marks the Spot X-terminator.

"What's the trouble?" Ramón asked. "Roaches? Rats?"

"Here, I understand the problem is raccoons," said the exterminator. "That right?"

Gully, Mr. Bull, and Mr. Dozer nodded. "I've already got one in the Havahart trap from the garden this morning."

"Trap?" cried Pearl.

"It's a harmless trap," Mr. Bull told her.

Mr. Dozer chuckled. "As long as you don't mind being in it," he said.

"Anyone would mind being in a trap," said Francine, bewildered.

"Better than being dead," said Gully.

Mom got a grip on Pearl's elbow before she could say anything else. "On whose instructions?" Mom demanded of the exterminator. "This is still city property."

Mr. Bull made a little speech: "Well, Mr. Gully here had mentioned the other day that there was something of a pest situation in the neighborhood, and if our firm is going to be investing in a property here, it's important to know beforehand what measures will need to be taken."

Mr. Dozer summed things up: "It's my prerogative as a contractor with a bid on city property."

"A bid not yet accepted?" Mr. Nichols said, from behind the morning *Moon*.

Mr. Dozer gave him an appraising look. "The vote's tonight," he said.

"We're all aware of that," said Mom.

"Let me see the raccoon!" demanded Pearl.

"Yes, we need to see it," said Mom.

The exterminator demurred. "I can't be exposing children to potentially harmful wild animals, ma'am."

"The wild animal is the one that was harmed!" said Pearl.

Mom leaned toward the exterminator. "If you're going to bill the city, someone here is going to have to sign off on the invoice. That means someone is going to need proof that you

actually removed an animal. That means someone has to see the raccoon."

Mr. Dozer didn't say anything, which told Pearl that Mom must be right. Ramón said, "Just open the back of the van and give us a quick peek."

The exterminator wouldn't let Pearl near, but she finally let Mom and Ramón follow her around to the back of the van. "What are you going to do with her?" Pearl heard Mom ask in a shaky voice. Pearl's heart was in her throat.

"Relocate her, ma'am," said the exterminator. "Somewhere more hospitable to a wild raccoon than the garden of a public library."

"But if we take responsibility for her?" Mom began.

"Take responsibility? Like a pet?" The exterminator sounded skeptical. "Ma'am, this is a wild animal. At best, it's a pest. Now, it's stressful for a raccoon to be in a trap in a van like this. If you're concerned about its welfare, you'll let me take it where it's going."

Afterward Pearl told herself Mom never would have let the raccoon go if she didn't think Bruce could get her back. However it happened, though, it happened: The exterminator climbed in behind the wheel and drove away.

It was impossible to misunderstand the crumpled expression on Mom's face and the way she hunched forward as the van left, clenching her fists at her sides. Pearl grabbed her arm.

"Who was it?"

Mom looked into her eyes and said, "Eloise." Then, "Get Bruce." Pearl ran for the stairs.

"Who's Eloise?" Francine, of course, was on her tail.

"She's a raccoon!" whispered Pearl to Francine. Then she said, "Will you tell Bruce to come?" Francine nodded, and rushed up the stairs while Pearl went down.

The basement was silent. There was nothing to be gained in waking the raccoons. Pearl left a note: *Eloise has been taken away in a Havahart trap.*

(Imagine someone laying a trap for one of your family members—even your least-favorite one—and hauling them away somewhere you can't find them.)

Pearl couldn't imagine this; she only had one real family member, and if Mom was kidnapped, at least she could call the police and get them on the case. The idea that Eloise could be just *taken* was even worse than Vincent's head being stolen.

When Francine came dashing back down with Bruce, Pearl could see that Mom was barely holding back tears of stress—an hour's worth (this hour, when Eloise was taken), a day's worth (this day, when the board vote was taking place, Bruce's proposals up against Mr. Bull's, both of them vying for the same "piece of property"), a career's worth (where would she go, she and Pearl?).

Gully was still standing there defending his right to call an exterminator. He said the library was public and neglected, and overrun by raccoons. "I've been hearing stories for years. What right do they have? And you know

A Sidebar About Havahart Traps

What they are—helpful—is not as important as what they're not—hurtful.

They are *not* the kind of traps with sharp metal jaws that snap and break your legs and paws and toes.

They are *not* designed to let you get away, but that's better than hurting you so much, you'd chew off your own foot to escape them.

They are also *not* designed to kill you by slow bleeding to death or starving.

They *are* designed so you follow the bait inside and get shut in. It's scary, like being locked in a closet, but the idea is that a person checks the trap regularly enough so you don't dry out or starve to death. Then they take you to another location that is supposedly safer for animals.

The Havahart trap is supposed to be a nice, humane solution to the problem of vermin. But that, of course, is only the human perspective.

—M.A.M.

the kind of trouble they can cause," he said. "Not just for you. For the neighborhood."

"What trouble were they causing?" Bruce demanded. Mom didn't mention any of the raccoons by name, and she had Pearl's wrist gripped tightly in her hand. Pearl knew Mom didn't trust her to speak.

The phone rang, and Mom lunged for it. "Lancaster Avenue branch library," she said. Bruce and Pearl saw the news in her eyes.

"Thumbs-up to the apartment proposal," said Mom.

Bruce sighed hugely.

"That means?" said Francine.

"It means the district votes on Election Day," said Bruce.

Mom said, "It means the city's giving everyone a choice about how to use this gorgeous building. You, me, Gully—we all get equal say now."

Ramón added, "Library or housing? The people will decide."

You could practically count "one elephant" between the things people were saying, as if every sentence was a thunderclap.

"Let's get out of here, Pearl," said Francine. Francine tugged her arm, and surprisingly, Pearl went. Pearl would never know what had been on her face, only that for the first time *leaving* the library saved her, thanks to Francine.

Released as though a bubble had popped, the girls scattered through the foyer, down the stoop, and along the street toward the subway, but stopped there.

Nichols was standing at the newsstand, having whisked himself out of the library in avoidance of Gully. Pearl gave him the board vote results and stood in silence, panting. Hot and sweaty from running, she felt frozen nevertheless, as if she was holding off the emotion of the day behind some cold wall. Nichols asked only, "Raccoons okay?"

"Mom says Bruce is going to see to it that they are," said Pearl. Bruce the hero, Bruce the hardworking, Bruce the wise. Pearl's mind rattled back and forth between the freedom of the neighborhood and the pull of the library and Mary Ann.

The afternoon's papers hung from the clips at the top of the stand, along with the evening *Moon*. Francine read the headlines aloud:

Moon headline:

MAYOR CONSIDERS
RAISING BRIDGE TOLLS

Daily News headline:

BALANCE BUDGET ON
BRIDGE-CROSSERS' BACKS?

Star headline:

RESIDENTS RESPOND TO RACCOON RISK

Pearl froze in horror. "*What* raccoon risk?" she asked indignantly. "How about the risk of our library being replaced by housing?"

Tallulah met her eyes and pulled out her own copy of yesterday's *Star*. It was already folded open to the vermin invasion article. "Coyotes, raccoons, rats. All the nocturnals," she said. "This is going to be a big story around here."

"What time does the midnight *Moon* arrive?" said Pearl, her voice catching on the lump in her throat. "I bet it's going to say RACCOONS ARE AT RISK."

"Huh?" said Tallulah. Her face, turned away from the others, had a deep frown that told Pearl she shouldn't have mentioned that.

"I didn't know there was a midnight *Moon*," Francine said.

"Learn something new every day," said Pearl lightly. She inwardly cursed herself for exposing a secret. Of course Francine didn't know. Only people who knew about the reading raccoons knew about the midnight *Moon*.

"It has a limited readership," said Nichols, who knew.

"A limited *highly educated* readership," said Tallulah, who knew, too. They were trying to keep the secret safe.

"Who reads a newspaper that comes out in the middle of the night?" Francine asked.

Pearl made her hands loop around her eyes like spectacles. "Reading raccoons!" she added.

Francine asked, "Who would write a newspaper for raccoons?"

"*Reporter* raccoons," said Pearl. "Duh." *Want it to seem real? Act like it's real*, she thought.

Tallulah leaned over the ledge of the newsstand. "Even the coyotes have a right to their own side of the story."

Francine looked skeptical. "You think I'm stupid or something?" she asked them. "What's all this about?"

Pearl rushed off to the library, hoping to arrive there alone. Of course, Francine charged along with her, keeping up. "Tell me!" she said. And, hardly knowing what she was saying, Pearl gave it to her straight: the whole story about the reading raccoons.

When she was done and they were almost there, and she was about to dart off to the basement, Francine got in front of her. "I've gotta go!" Pearl said.

Francine held up the palm of her left hand as if she was Vincent, and said, "You're going to have to put that in our performance, too, Pearl. That's amazing."

"It's true!" said Pearl.

Francine laughed. "Of course it is!"

Pearl didn't know what to say. Did she want Francine to believe the story was real—or just to think she was a genius storyteller?

Francine said confidently, "Everybody's going to want to come to the library even more when they hear this new part about the reading raccoons."

So Pearl left it at that. Fiction or nonfiction, how much did it matter if it was a good story? She looked up at the brick face of the library building and knew Francine was right about how other people would react.

"We're going to have to work fast," Pearl said. "Faster than that exterminator. Faster than Mr. Bull and Mr. Dozer. Faster than Gully!"

* * *

Pearl couldn't get down the basement stairs fast enough.

Mary Ann was awake, wide awake and waiting, pacing between the book elevator and the stairs. She had already written a message for Pearl.

Find out where they took Eloise!

"We're trying," said Pearl, seriously, formally. And then stupidly, "I thought you didn't get along with Eloise?"

She's my cousin!

"I don't have a cousin," said Pearl, causing Mary Ann to make a gesture with her whole body that could only be interpreted as *SO??* "I mean, I'm sorry," she whispered.

Then Mary Ann grabbed the pen again and wrote so hard, her paw shook with the effort.

Somebody else might be next. And . . .

Mary Ann was savvy, Pearl knew, so she wasn't worried about getting trapped herself. Mary Ann must be worried about little Arak.

Once they go, they usually don't come back.

Had other raccoons been trapped before? Pearl reached out a finger, and for the first time touched Mary Ann, on the back of her paw. It was soft but bristly.

Stupid Eloise! Why couldn't she have learned to read and write? Then she could send us word.

Pearl had barely gotten through reading when Mary Ann snatched the catalog card away, crunched it into a ball as if it was the stupidest thing she'd ever written, and pulled out another one.

She must have gotten trapped on purpose.

With that, Mary Ann shredded the card into a pile of confetti and threw it wildly from the stair, dashed through it like snow, and disappeared into her nest.

Pearl heard a snuffling noise. She waited, listened, realized what it was. Pearl had heard a cat yowl, a dog whimper. Now she was hearing a raccoon cry.

Everything that happened to the library happened worse for the raccoons. Suddenly, Pearl felt the futility of the Rock Lady act. What could a ghost story and a few measly kids do that was more powerful than money and new buildings and a whole city?

"Mary Ann!" she called. "Where's your mom? Where's Arak?"

Suddenly, Mary Ann came rushing back out. She snatched a card and scrawled one message, shoved it toward Pearl, and disappeared.

> Someone who can write has to go after Eloise. She's the only one who knows what happened to Vincent's head.

Pearl gasped.

Mary Ann knew how important it was for Vincent to get her head back—to prevent future crimes, or so the library could be a solid institution for the neighborhood and not a crumbling one, or maybe because Vincent's power actually did channel magic to the raccoons and taught them how to read. No matter what, Mary Ann knew that if Vincent's head came back, the whole city would see the library in a new light. She was telling Pearl the truth—Eloise knew who the thief was!—as her last attempt to help. Pearl sprinted upstairs.

"Bruce! We have to go after Eloise!"

"The raccoon in the trap?" Bruce seemed irritated at the distraction. "She's supposed to be relocated to an open space area."

"She's the one who knows where Vincent's head is!"

"The *raccoon* knows?" asked Bruce.

"Yes!" What was wrong with Bruce? He had heard all these stories for as long as she had. Where did he stand on the fiction/nonfiction aspect of them? She realized what it meant that he stood with science—he didn't believe Mom's stories were real. "I just want to get Vincent's head back," Pearl said.

"Why?" Bruce looked loony, half angry, and double-confused, staring at Pearl, glancing at Mom—who had more to lose than Pearl.

Something strange and magical combined inside Pearl's mind. She thought of Tallulah saying the raccoon invasion would be a big story. She relived the narration she'd given on the playground to accompany Francine's performance, and the drama in the garden around Vincent's statue. She recalled the stories Mom had told of Mrs. Mallomar, and considered the one she was writing herself, with the help of Mary Ann. She thought about Francine and Tallulah and Nichols and Gully and the exterminator and Mary Ann and poor, trapped, kidnapped Eloise.

"Bruce, Eloise is a Mallomar," Pearl explained. "She is one of the youngest members of the family of smart raccoons who has been living in the library for generations, reading and writing. Eloise can barely read and can't write at all, but she's the one who saw the head get stolen. That means she has the information that will return the library to the community as a pillar of light and goodness. This is why it's important that we get Eloise back, for ourselves and for her family!"

Bruce looked at Pearl steadily, not as if he believed what she was saying, but as if he believed that *she* believed it. He said, "I never heard of raccoons like Mrs. Mallomar until I met your mother. City Wildlife's goal is to teach people ways to live alongside animals they normally think of as nuisances: raccoons, skunks, pigeons, opossums, coyotes. As a ranger, I was the reason a lot of people *quit* putting out poison, or feeding their cats outside, or shooting pigeons with BB guns. But the raccoons—" Bruce walked to the sealed-up fireplace. "Raccoons are just one more nail in the coffin for this library. I don't know where those kits are going to go if the library building gets repurposed. We're not going to be able to rescue them if we can't rescue ourselves."

"Maybe the reading raccoons will rescue *us*," Mom said.

Bruce was shaking his head, but Pearl started to pace, from the desk to the window, the only narrow, clear path in the rat's-nest office. "Reading raccoons to the rescue . . . save a raccoon and save the library . . ." She did little circles around Bruce's piles, making a breeze. She looked crazy. She *felt* crazy. But there had to be a way to use the raccoons to save the library—to save the library *because* of the raccoons.

Bruce sat down and picked up the scandalous *Star* tabloid. "Let's say the reading raccoons *were* real, Pearl. How would you get anybody to believe it?"

He was asking her seriously, she knew, meeting his deep brown eyes behind his big glasses.

"Okay, so maybe nobody's going to believe it's true," she began. She felt the way Mom must have felt all those years.

Mom said, "But they will all *wish* it was true."

Pearl realized, "They will never find out if it really *is* true."

"Why not?" said Bruce and Mom at the same time.

"Because it could be true. Because they will want it to be true. Because . . . because *we* will act like it is! Because we *know* it is!" She looked at them: Bruce, his paintbrush hair, his gangly elbows leaning on his gangly knees; Mom, small and upright, on her toes in her high heels. "And in the meantime, we're going to make them love raccoons and protect the raccoons all at once."

"How?"

"Mary Ann—my raccoon friend at the paper—can help me write their story. Everybody will think it's me telling raccoon stories and pretending they're factual, but they'll let themselves believe it's really raccoons."

"And why would they let themselves believe that?" Bruce was kind. He was trying to be kind, anyway. He thought he needed to be kind because Pearl was crazy. But she knew what she knew.

"Because! It's like Disneyland, or Santa Claus, or shooting stars. It's more funny and fun and easy to believe that raccoons at a library can read. Yes!" Pearl thumped her hand on Bruce's desk. "They'll be our mascots. If you join the library, you'll become a Reading Raccoon of Lancaster Avenue! And that will make people not want to X-terminate the real ones. And it'll all be drama and good press and it'll make people think about our library in a good way."

"It is true that humans are exceptionally good at convincing themselves to believe in things they *want* to be true," said Bruce.

Pearl's heart lifted. Did he approve?

"We just need one more answer." Bruce said, his eyes bright. "What do raccoons eat?"

What did that matter? "Okay, what *do* they eat?" said Pearl.

"They use the profits from the newspaper to buy food at the raccoon grocery store."

Pearl paused and squinted at him. "Where's the raccoon grocery store?"

"Oh, stop it," said Mom.

"Is it real, or am I making it up?" asked Bruce.

Mom smiled. Bruce smiled, too. "Ha! You're doing it," Mom said.

"Anyone can do it, if the story's good enough," said Pearl.

29: RELOCATION

Later that night, Mom's phone rang. "It's Bruce!" she called to Pearl.

Into the phone, she said, "So she's alive? And healthy?"

"Where is she?" whispered Pearl.

Mom went on listening to Bruce, watching Pearl's face. "And she was released?"

"*Where?*" said Pearl.

"What?" Mom asked the phone. "How many did you say they caught? Six."

"Where?! Who else?"

Mom waved a hand to hush Pearl. "All right, that's all we can ask for." She hung up.

"I have to write the Mallomars right away," Pearl said. "Where's Eloise?"

"The raccoons?" Mom said. "You're really going to write to them?" There it was, right there: the dividing line between what Mom knew and didn't know. Hadn't Mom been the one who'd made Pearl write notes to the raccoons when she was younger? Didn't she realize that the raccoons could read them?

"I'll write them a note," said Pearl, as simply as if she was talking about writing a note to Ramón or Bruce or Francine. Straightforwardly, directly—that was the only way to convey

A Sidebar About Storage

"Rats once ruled the basements," Grandmar often reminds me. After the bats found their way into the library basement, it was rats that chewed an old pipe hole into an entrance, loosening the brownstone enough for Grandmar and her children to dig out more. But rats can be "bought." The rats traded with my ancestors: The raccoons got the basement, if the rats got first-picking rights on the trash from blue-haired Rosita's Rosebud bodega. The agreement has stood ever since.

Since then, our family has resolved to raise literate kits. My family was brought up on sandwich scraps, apple cores, and stories. We pass them down voice to ear, raccoon to raccoon, a secret from humans, stored only in our memories. But now, for the sake of Pearl, I'm putting it into words.

Words are something humans invented. Words are storage for stories that are passed in boxes called books, paw to paw, hand to hand. Think of Vincent with her hand out, a story that's there for everybody, but also just for you. Think of Pearl with her manuscript

that something magical was real. "And we can take it to the library tonight and take it down to the basement. Or, if you don't even want to go into the library I could go in the alley and hold the note up to the window and knock. Although I don't know if Mary Ann's got a flashlight. Oh, or I could just go to Mrs. Mallomar's house. It's right down our street; Tallulah told me where. Or we could wait a little while until Mrs. Mallomar goes to the newsstand to sell the papers, you know, after the delivery goes in and Tallulah puts the papers up, just give it to her when she goes by."

She didn't know why she was babbling until she realized that Mom wasn't responding at all. Mom was listening without speaking, the green of her eyes as bright as a go-light. Mom had been the one who told Pearl that Mrs. Mallomar worked at the newsstand, long before Pearl had seen it with her own eyes. Now she was letting Pearl tell the story.

"Mom, where's Eloise?" Pearl demanded.

"That's the trouble."

"What?" said Pearl darkly.

"The X-terminator trapped half a dozen raccoons last night around the city. She didn't know there was anything special about ours. The last time anyone noticed which one Eloise was, it was me in the driveway."

"Didn't they bring them all to the same place?"

Mom shook her head.

Pearl felt cold all over. "Then where did they take them?"

Mom looked very tired. "They sprinkled them all over Manhattan," she said. "From Battery Park to Inwood. From Riverside to Carl Schurz Park."

"So Eloise could be in any park in the city."

Mom nodded sadly.

Pearl was losing patience. "Okay, so, I have to go! Now! So I can tell them!"

Mom was studying Pearl, trying to read her like a book in a made-up language. She took Pearl's hands and held them firmly. "Pearl. Well . . . Mrs. Mallomar's not home, anyway." She laughed lightly and looked off to one side. She did not wait for Pearl to say, "Do tell." She just went on, "She's got Tallulah taking her shift while she spends the night with her daughters and the little kits, at the library. I'm not going to disturb them with this news. Tomorrow is soon enough."

in her hand, getting ready to perform it for a bunch of kids who could love it or hate it. Think of me, writing a history for the whole city to see. A city that thinks of raccoons as invaders. Or vermin. And the only way they just might listen is with words—our tools.

Words are all we have. So it's up to me.

Pearl says raccoons who can read are like magic, a word she likes. She says we'll be embraced. She says we should do what we can to help the library. She says the story I'm writing could help. I'm choosing to believe her.

I'm crossing my claws that Pearl's right, that my words can keep our home from getting torn apart. If nothing else, reporting on my family's reading, putting it into words, may be our last hope of being remembered. Because I remember another billboard that hung at the subway station when I was learning to read: NO GUTS, NO GLORY. Maybe it ought to be "NO GUTS, NO STORY."

—M.A.M.

Pearl tried to place Mom's tone, and she thought she recognized the vague way that parents explained things to children when they weren't telling the truth. Mom was looking at Pearl as if Pearl had told her she was going off to hunt for an alligator she had seen in the subway. It made Pearl feel jangly, off-balance, like she was walking a narrow curb.

"If the library closed, you'd get another job, right?"

There was a beat.

"Yes, eventually," said Mom. "I mean, I'd find *something* somewhere. There might be a job open in the system, but I could also look into college libraries, or even school libraries."

"And the library raccoons—"

"They might be better off if they were *all* just relocated," said Mom.

"Without books?"

Mom met her eyes. "It's how they were meant to be," she said, and added, "That's what Bruce says."

"But they've adapted to city life—that's what Bruce told *me*," said Pearl.

"Did he?" Mom laughed a weird light laugh.

"But, Mom," said Pearl. "You and I are on the same page. The reading raccoons are real."

Just like that.

"Real enough for me," said Mom. "But not for Bruce."

"Bruce would be the first one to tell you how smart raccoons are," protested Pearl. She thought of how Sterling North, the author of the memoir about his pet raccoon, Rascal, had turned to nonfiction to learn more about Rascal's relatives.

* * *

Mary Ann's back had a hump in it, like all raccoons'. It wasn't her fault it made her look hunched, grumpy, and hostile.

Quit assuming raccoons are stupid.

"Sorry!" said Pearl. "And anyway, they're not all as smart as you, are they?" If they were, they'd take over the city.

They haven't all had the good fortune of being born in a library.

Pearl had to laugh. "Hey, both of us were born here!" she said. "But what about Eloise . . ." She hesitated, trying to read the raccoon's deep black eyes, her expression like Batman's, peering out from behind the mask that kept him secret.

We have a plan. The library isn't big enough for all the reading raccoons we want there to be. We want many more raccoons to become readers.

"So do I," said Pearl. "And Mom, and Francine."

There was a silence. Mary Ann raised a paw palm up and wiggled her claws. It was her way of saying "Do tell."

Pearl smiled. Well, there was no benefit in trying to sugarcoat things. "It's a new version of the story."

What's it about?

"It's got reading raccoons in it."

Mary Ann looked around as if she wondered whether anyone had heard.

They won't believe it.

"They have to."

Mary Ann shrugged.

What Pearl said next sounded, even to her own ears, like a speech: "If they don't believe it, then they might not save the building. And then where will you and your family live?"

Mary Ann's small eyes deepened even further. Then the raccoon reached for more catalog cards and dipped her head to write.

poison

traps

cages

It was as though Pearl saw those things through Mary Ann's eyes.

And another thing:

relocation

Pearl said, "I understand. I know it's scary. But do you really think relocation is just as bad as being killed? If they move you somewhere else, you could teach the raccoons there to read. Besides, listen! Bruce says they're not allowed to transport animals outside the borough they're found in. So you guys are stuck in Manhattan. But there are really nice park wildernesses up on the north end."

Mary Ann took another card.

the river

And she made a choking, glugging sound, and sank to the floor. She meant they drowned the raccoons instead of taking them to the wilds of the parks.

"Oh, no!" said Pearl. "This is what we have to do, then. I've got to make my story as real as nonfiction. So real it's practically unbelievable, like some of those things you can't believe are true

until some spokesperson for science comes along and tells you. The key is going to be an outside expert."

Who?

"You."

Pearl hadn't realized raccoons had eyebrows until Mary Ann's shot up.

"It's going to be the reporting assignment of your life, Mary Ann. Not just for raccoons. Not just for the library. For all of New York."

30: DO TELL

OCT 4-5

In the playground at school there was a new favorite game, just in time for the eerie Halloween season. It was called Rock Lady, of course, and it was based on Francine's performance. Francine stood, eyes glazed, hand stretched out, and dared kids to touch her hand, until after some secret number of touches, she came to life and chased them, screaming.

Pearl wasn't sure what she should do to keep new kids coming to the library, but then, of all people, *Elsa* picked up on the drama of Francine's game and started performing it herself. Pearl shouldn't have been surprised—playing Rock Lady was a great way to get attention, and there was nothing Elsa loved more. Good. Let the outgoing, popular kids build up the game while the creative force (Pearl told herself that's what she was) turned her energies to marketing raccoons.

* * *

On the way home from school the next afternoon, Pearl told Francine, "I've been working on a new part of the story."

Francine nodded. "What's it about?"

Pearl felt encouraged. "It connects Vincent with the raccoons."

There was a number of kids trundling along with them on their way home from school, including Oleg and Jaime, but Pearl ignored them, talking quietly, intently to Francine.

"So," Pearl said, "say Vincent is a neighborhood lady who is up a lot in the middle of the night writing poems. She's friends with some neighborhood cats, and leaves milk out for them. One night when she's sad, she finds raccoons diving into the cats' milk, and that makes her laugh."

Jaime butted in. "We've got a big raccoon living right under our steps."

"So?" said Pearl, and waved him away.

"Keep going, Pearl," said Francine.

"She keeps leaving milk out for the raccoons, so pretty soon they aren't afraid of her anymore. Also, she stands in her garden and reads them poems. She looks a lot like the statue in the garden when she does this." Pearl struck Vincent's pose, head up, hand out.

"So how does this connect to the raccoons?"

"Well, she tosses all her lousy poems in the garbage, and later the raccoons will find them. They already know what the poems say, but now they figure out how to write those sounds down."

"So that story is how they learned how to read?"

"Yep," said Pearl.

"It's a good story," said Francine.

"Is it?" said Pearl. But she already knew it was.

"Add it in," said Francine.

* * *

"Take a look," said Ms. Judge, the school principal. She spread a pile of drawings across her desk in front of Pearl, Francine, and Oleg.

"Pretty creative," said Oleg. In one drawing, a man carrying a gray head was running away from a gray headless creature. Blood and gore were pouring out of the bottom of the head.

Francine put her finger on a drawing of a tank running over the Rock Lady. "Seems kind of extreme," she said.

"Someone has been scaring the pants off the first graders with a story about a woman made of rock." Ms. Judge was wearing the long gray sweater she always wore at school, and she held her hand out in a demanding way. "She stands waiting for some kind of an offering, and if the right thing isn't offered, she chases you."

So Pearl told her a new piece of the story about the stories coming out from Vincent's hand and moving through the air, like invisible flying books that materialized into the hands of kids who came to the library. "And yes, she's got her hand out because of that, and some people say she wants something, and if only she could walk, we'd know—"

"If she could *walk*?" said Ms. Judge.

"We made a kind of ghosty story about her," said Francine.

"*A kind of ghosty story?*" Ms. Judge was smiling.

"She didn't used to be ghosty!" Pearl protested. And she told about how the head had been stolen, the police were called, the "lost head" signs posted, the newspaper articles printed, the photos taken, the rock expert and the stonemason consulted.

"So all this comes together in this story you're telling on my playground?" Ms. Judge asked.

"Performance," Francine said automatically. "Story plus dance," she explained.

Oleg had waited for his moment, and now he took it. "The point is to build interest in the library," he said, sounding dignified. "It has taken some hits lately and we are trying to save it by bringing in more people."

"Patrons," said Pearl.

"Isn't this the building that's going to be turned into housing?" Ms. Judge asked gently.

Pearl sat up straighter. "Not if I can help it."

Oleg said, "Her mother's the librarian, you know."

Francine added, "Pearl practically lives there. And I live right across the street."

Oleg said, "And I live right in back."

"But there've been other troubles at that library," Ms. Judge said. "Didn't some homeless man break in just last month? Haven't there been some problems with wild animals?" She shook her head. "This neighborhood sure isn't what it used to be."

Pearl blasted off. "It's a good neighborhood, and a good library, and a good statue. I'm sick of hearing all this other stuff! There's more—"

"Then why are you helping to perpetuate this 'other stuff'? Why are you telling ghost stories about your lovely statue of a poet?"

"To make people come to the library," Pearl said. "Because if the library doesn't get enough votes from the neighborhood on Election Day, it's going to be made into apartments. I'll do anything to stop that. So this is all leading up to Halloween, when we're having a new-head ceremony for the statue right before Election Day."

"You should come," said Francine. "Since we started telling the Rock Lady stories, we've given out fifty new library cards to kids."

"Really? Because of ghost stories?"

"Yes," said Pearl. "Circulation is up, and it's not just children's."

Ms. Judge had started off seeming like she disapproved. But now her head was cocked to one side. She said, "Here's how it looks to me: If your library shuts down, the neighborhood looks worse, and that reflects badly on the school. We don't want that, do we?"

"Definitely not," said Oleg. "A school should stand for the whole neighborhood."

Pearl hadn't thought of this.

Ms. Judge made a motion as though she was dusting off her knees. "I suppose theater in the service of saving a library—to reflect well on our school—is a worthy effort. They should both stand for the neighborhood. Would you be willing to do your performance for the whole school?"

"Yes!" said Pearl. "Then everyone in the school can come on Halloween. We want the mayor to come with her whole city board."

"I'll write Her Honor a letter," said Ms. Judge. "Education, reading, literacy, art, kids—yes, those are things a mayor should care about."

"Does she?" asked Oleg.

The principal smiled. "Let's find out."

A Sidebar About Mascots

Here in New York, our team mascots aren't furry animals. We have things: Jets and Nets, and specific kinds of humans: Giants, Yankees, Rangers, Knickerbockers (it refers to the Dutch settlers of New York City). We have one guy with a baseball for a head, Mr. Met. All of these make the teams of humans seem more heroic, inspiring their fans' imaginations.

Many other teams have animals: lions, tigers, bears, bulls, birds (cardinals, blue jays, ravens). These mascots seem less inspiring, but they create togetherness—kind of a club feeling.

So Pearl picked an action to go with her animal. This made a mascot that was far more interesting, something that made the neighbors feel heroic, inspired, and together.

—M.A.M.

31: DOWN THE BASEMENT STAIRS

OCT 6-9

With the raccoons, it was time for nonfiction.

Pearl wrote a note about her plan to Mary Ann, but it made Mary Ann afraid, to think of seeing her family history written down.

It could lead to more raccoons being trapped.

"No," said Pearl. "It'll make people see why raccoons *shouldn't* be trapped."

It's putting too much attention on the raccoons. And what if

Mary Ann wrote something, then scribbled the sentence out.

What if

"What if we don't do anything?" said Pearl.

They both knew the answer to that: The ball was already rolling, and it might as well have been a wrecking ball. The raccoons had a bad reputation, thanks to the *Star* and thanks to Gully—and having enough raccoons around to trap six of them had hurt the neighborhood's reputation, and the library's, which could mean a "no" vote in November, which could mean no more library.

Pearl was determined to fight back, to show that the raccoons were not just good, but great and exceptional, and so was the neighborhood, and so was the library. She wasn't the only one getting into the fray. The news that the neighborhood people would be the ones to choose between apartments and the library had sent the whole staff into a fever of scheming, each in his or her own way.

Simon and his still-nameless band took on extra rehearsals in preparation for the concert at the new-head ceremony. Alice put up announcements on the library website and on local bulletin boards about the Halloween book-character parade.

And tonight, Pearl was left to do her homework after hours at the reference room desk while Mom sat in Bruce's office working on math formulas: numbers of new library cards times new families, or the cost of new books divided by people taking them out, or the electric bill as a ratio of number of people using the library per hour . . . Oh, the problems could give a rocket scientist a headache! Right now Mom questioned whether the library could come out looking like a decent business, at the exact same time as Bruce insisted it was a symbol of the city's heart. Pearl thought they both were right, she didn't understand either of their positions fully, and the whole thing made her want to cry from worry. When she told them her own ideas, they only seemed to half listen. It was too easy to imagine everything falling apart.

Pearl listened to the grumbling tone of Mom's and Bruce's argument from the foot of the stairs, then went to the basement to check in with Mary Ann. Mary Ann's *What if* card was still on the stairs—

—with Mrs. Mallomar hunched over it, as if she'd been waiting for Pearl. She tapped a claw on Mary Ann's words, asking for an explanation.

Pearl sat down on the step like it was nothing to get called out by the editor in chief of the midnight *Moon,* but she was more nervous than she had been when she'd had to go to Ms. Judge's office.

"Mrs. Mallomar," she said, "I just want to tell people a story about the reading raccoons, about the reading and the writing and the midnight *Moon* and everything. I think that would make them love the library and want to save it."

Mrs. Mallomar made a low sound, and Mary Ann came out of the nest and sat like a cat, her paws beneath her, nervous, too, about what a big step this would be, outing the reading raccoons.

Pearl announced, "My idea is, if Mary Ann wrote it, it would sound more real. She's the reporter, *and* she's a reading raccoon."

Did a signal pass between grandmother and granddaughter? Mary Ann reached for the pen.

Letting people know we even exist is a risk.
You never know what they'll do once they know
you're there.

Pearl couldn't decide for them. They all sat there, waiting each other out.

Mary Ann flipped the card over and wrote. Mrs. Mallomar watched what she wrote and made no move to change anything.

You want to share a byline?

Mary Ann's eyes were on Pearl's.

Byline? "You mean you would write with *me?*" Pearl asked. "We could be"—she tried out a new word—"coauthors?"

She exhaled. So did the raccoons. Mary Ann's teeth showed in a smile. Pearl felt the lift of excitement and a tug of friendship. She pushed aside her nervousness about being called crazy.

"Nobody's going to believe it anyway," she said, "They'll think I wrote it all by myself and made up a raccoon coauthor. Same as nobody believes raccoons really write the midnight *Moon*."

The raccoons looked at each other and shrugged. It didn't matter. The effect would be huge because people wanted to believe incredible stories.

It was decided.

"The raccoons will be heroes for once, not vermin," said Pearl. "We're going to save the library together."

* * *

Darkness came earlier now, which meant raccoons were awake earlier. On this particular raccoon morning (in human life, it was afternoon), Mary Ann was the first one up.

As kids were leaving the library, warm from running around the statue, carrying books they'd taken out with their new cards, Mary Ann was reading Pearl's contribution to the raccoon exposé, chewing on her Sharpie until she bit through the plastic barrel and got a mouth full of black ink.

She'd have to swipe another one. But it didn't matter. She wasn't going to make too many edits to this story. She could see it had come from the heart, and thanks to her, Mary Ann herself, the contributing reporter, the factual pieces were mostly in place: the way Mrs. Mallomar had figured out how to read, the date the first midnight *Moon* had been published, the number of readers it had. Facts like that seemed to give the fantasy-fiction parts some solid nonfiction legs to stand on.

Sure, there was always a tweak or two that could be made to improve the pacing or heighten the drama—a cliffhanger here, a plot twist there—but Mary Ann was confident that she and Pearl could whip it into shape by October 13, the day of the school performance.

What Mary Ann felt less sure about was that the story could put her family in danger. This story was not just a baited hook to lure people into the library. It was a campaign to make them feel proud of what was already here. It was a campaign to save the library for the sake of the building, for the sake of the books, and for the sake of the reading raccoons. But it also called attention to the raccoons—which might very well not be a good thing for them.

Mary Ann worried that this attention might make them a target of people who didn't think raccoons were any better than vermin. If people realized the legend was *actually* true, what would happen to the *actual* reading raccoons?

This kind of thinking could give anybody a headache.

Here was what Mary Ann's family was doing this evening: Mrs. Mallomar was putting the midnight *Moon* to bed. Mary Ann's mother, Matilda, was still asleep in the nest. She would be getting up soon to do a stint at the printer with Tallulah, then a shift at the newsstand. Mary Ann would stay here with little Arak, teaching him his letters and working on her next assignment for the paper. "Resolutions Worth a Mention," she thought she'd title it, a sort of countdown to Halloween and the announcement of the raccoons' resolutions for the next spring.

Nothing whatever had been heard from Eloise.

The more Mary Ann thought about where Eloise was and what she was doing and how she was living, the more she realized that she, Mary Ann, did not have a clue about how to live in the country, or even just some big park, and neither did her mother or grandmother or Arak. And the more Mary Ann talked with Pearl, the more she realized that the end of their residence in the library was possibly extremely near—as near as Election Day. All this could be over with the swing of a wrecking ball, and then what? The Mallomars could die out there in the country. They were city folk.

(But there wasn't room to share any of these irrational fears. And Pearl had enough to worry about without adding raccoon fears to her human ones.)

Pearl's plan to take the reading raccoons public might turn out to be a disaster, but it might also be the raccoons' best chance. The sooner the word got out about reading raccoons, the sooner people would want to save them, and the library. Mary Ann decided to believe this: That the people—the neighbors—would want to help the raccoons *and* the library. Both.

With what was left of the ink in the Sharpie, she wrote a somewhat drippy message above Pearl's story:

OK! Print it!

* * *

At the staff meeting, Pearl told everyone the next new part of her story. Ramón was there, and Alice, her hand over her stomach, and Bruce and Simon, and Francine, who had her tap shoes on but somehow stayed quiet, not drawing attention to herself. Nichols was in earshot in the reference room. (I was in earshot three-quarters of the way up the basement stairs.)

"You know that we have a morning *Moon* and an evening *Moon*. Well, there is also a newspaper for nocturnal—uh, creatures—called the midnight *Moon*. And it's published by someone nocturnal, a grandmother raccoon named Mrs. Mallomar."

No guffaws of laughter, no smirking.

She went on. "Raccoons can read, of course. The ones on Lancaster Avenue can, that is. Because where do you think Mrs. Mallomar got her name from? Of course it was from the cookies.

Like kids reading the cereal box!" She told them about how Mrs. M. had first seen a Mallomar box, and how she'd learned to connect letters with sounds.

"And how do you think they learned to write?" Pearl explained about Vincent—before she was a statue, and the neighborhood cats and the milk and the reading out loud and the tossed-away lousy poems. "Because, well, you know how raccoons are so good with their hands—uh, paws? They can actually write."

Mom smiled; Bruce rolled his eyes.

"So, thanks to real Vincent and some of her lousy poems, and thanks to Mallomar packages, they could read. And because of the book Vincent carried in her arm, they got inspired to try to read the *books*. They started with the easy readers, and moved on to the chapter books, and then, sure enough, they could read everything. They've passed the tradition down, and even the youngest of them is learning his letters as we speak."

Bruce and Alice both had their mouths slightly hanging open.

"How did our raccoons learn to read?" said Pearl. "Because our neighborhood is special. It could only happen here. And that's why our mascot should be Reading Raccoons. The library's mascot—and the neighborhood's."

She stopped. She felt shaky. It was the first time she'd tried to tell this part aloud, and even though Mary Ann had written up the nonfiction part on paper, it sounded different coming out as speech, with the fate of the whole library depending on it.

It was Simon who reacted first. "Wow, Pearl," he said, and for a terrible, terrible second, she thought he was going to laugh at her, that they were all going to laugh at her, that they didn't believe in her plan and wouldn't let her tell her story, that they just wanted her to stop and give up. But no. Simon threw his

arms around her so suddenly and completely that she stumbled backward. "That's working," he said. "They'll buy that. That'll work." Simon, lanky and cool and elegant with his fiery hair, his black T-shirt that said NERD. She felt her face grow hot with pride.

"Okay, I'm going to get the coffee. Come on, Francine," she said, suddenly needing to race away from all of them. "Who wants what?"

"Since when do you need an order?" Alice said.

Pearl was already out the door and halfway down the steps, but she stopped and turned back. Her whole library family was standing at the circ counter under the big clock, and they were all still looking at her.

Bruce said, "We'll give it a try, Pearl. No regrets—that's my motto. If it doesn't work, you'll have given it your all. We'll know you did, and so will the raccoons."

Was it going to be good enough for the library?

But then Ramón gave her a fist pump from behind Bruce's shoulder.

"Here's to the raccoons, for giving you so much to work with," said Mom, who had told her the stories in the first place.

"We believe in you, Pearl," said reliable Alice.

Mr. Nichols, who had shown her the real reading raccoons, said, "I'd buy it."

That word again. "You'd buy it?" Pearl repeated. "Is that the same as believing it?"

"Better," said Ramón. "It's like you've made a deal."

"Of course it's a deal!" yelled Francine as she ran to catch up with Pearl on the steps.

It was in this moment that Pearl realized she needed Francine, relied on her, and knew she *could* rely on her, the scrawny little weirdo-neglected kid that she was.

They got to Cozy Soup and Burger.

"What do you want?" Pearl asked Francine as they opened the door. "I'm putting it on the tab. You're part of the library now."

* * *

Monday morning Pearl and Francine planned to walk to school together like always, but Pearl buzzed Francine's door half an hour before schedule. Into the intercom she called, "Can you hurry? Something's come up."

While Francine was clattering down the stairs, Pearl stood peering through the metal grate that kept Gully's store safe from robbers while it was closed. Francine came and gazed at the cheap stuff inside, too.

"What are you looking at?"

Pearl pointed into Gully's window. "We need to make the neighborhood into raccoons, too."

"You're going to make me into a raccoon?" said Oleg, coming up behind them.

Oleg was Pearl's chance to test her new part of the story, to start building it into the performance. "This neighborhood is known for extra-smart raccoons. Didn't you know that?"

"No." Scientific Oleg looked skeptical.

"They're self-educated, actually. They descend from the legendary Mrs. Mallomar. And you know what makes them special?"

"What?" asked Francine eagerly, as if she hadn't already heard the story.

She's such a good performer, Pearl thought.

"They're reading raccoons," Pearl said.

"They can read?" asked Oleg.

"Sure," said Pearl. "Suspend your disbelief." It was something Alice told her readers to do when they read fantasy.

"Suspend it?"

"Yeah, the same way you do if you read *In Search of Sasquatch*[1] even though you know there's no such thing as Bigfoot. Or believe in a flying Snitch when you know there's no such thing as Quidditch. Just buy it. You, any human, can be a Reading Raccoon—you can read and write and have library cards and support the Lancaster Avenue branch library! Believe me."

And it seemed like he did.

At school, Pearl looked around, thinking about the kids and how they'd respond to the Reading Raccoons. As she pondered her story, she had the feeling she sometimes had when she read certain books where kids did things she couldn't do—actions with outcomes that just wouldn't happen in real life. Things that seemed too magic, too convenient, too unrealistic: magically bumping into someone who was *just the person you were looking for!* Magically looking out the window just in time to see *a giant going by!* Magically being the one with *exactly the magical powers the situation called for, without having done a single thing but be born!* That sort of stuff had occasionally made her want to throw a book at the wall. If her own story, now, was in a book, would she believe it? Ha! This worried her more than it would have worried another kid, anyone else not born in a library.

Maybe in a book she could save the library, but in real life?

* * *

Later that night, Pearl tucked herself into the book elevator, asked Simon to push 3, and ascended to pay Bruce a visit. He was redoing the budget he would present at the library board meeting tomorrow night. He had been redoing the budget for weeks. It had been the reason for debates, fights, canceled plans,

---

1 *In Search of Sasquatch* by Kelly Milner Halls (HMH Books for Young Readers, 2011).

gray hairs, and wrinkles, and the excuse for extra coffee, extra doughnuts, extra hours, extra worry, and extra privacy.

But now Pearl had questions.

She sprang out of the book elevator. "What would magically fix the budget?" she asked.

"Magically?" said Bruce, distracted but not grumping. "If the whole world held a lottery and our library won it."

"Seriously?" Pearl asked.

He nodded. "Miss Moran, what is the actual purpose of this visit?"

Pearl pointed to the top of the file cabinet, to the raccoon head that sat up there. She knew there would be power in actually *being* a raccoon. And here was the costume, right here, but Bruce was standing in her way.

When she had first seen the costume five years ago, Pearl had told him he should rename it Mrs. Mallomar. But Bruce would not make jokes about the costume. He was 6 feet 3 inches, and his raccoon costume had been made to fit him. At his old job at the national park, he used to put it on and walk around talking about wildlife to kids. He never wore it anymore, but was fiercely protective about it.

Now he said, "What about it?"

"Can I wear it?" she asked.

"You cannot."

"Why?" she wailed. "I need it for school!" School was where she was going to try out the newest part of the story, the part where Vincent would invite the first raccoon who moved into the library basement to read an actual book.

"It's a sentimental costume," said Bruce. "It's very dear to me."

"Am *I* not very dear to you?"

He smiled into her eyes. "You *are*. But I wouldn't want it to get dirty, and it would."

A Sidebar About Fathers

"Where did you come from, baby dear? Out of the everywhere into the here."[1] Presumably, you know how babies get made. But to be sure we're on the same page, the father produces a lot of sperm, and one of them might be lucky enough to fertilize the mother's egg. The egg stays inside the mother and develops into a kit, or a kid, depending on your species—all with nothing more needed from the father.

A kid without a dad around might seem to be 100 percent influenced by his or her mother, but that's not the truth of things. Science says 50 percent is the father, and it shows up in all kinds of ways—like size, strength, voice, sense of humor, eyes, facial expressions. And in other ways, too, ways that only your mama would recognize.

Sometimes you can simply assume these things. Other times you know for sure.

But the other thing about absent fathers is that whoever's *near* you tends to have an influence that's just as profound—whether you're a human or a raccoon. In

---

1 From the poem "Baby," from *A Victorian Anthology*, by George Macdonald, edited by Edmund Clarence Stedman (Riverside Press, 1895).

She began a rebuttal, but he held up his finger. "Besides, you're not tall enough for it. It was made for me. It would trip you up and the eyes would fall out of position and you'd be blind and it would make you fall and get hurt, and that would be catastrophic. And the costume would be ruined."

For a moment Pearl was silent. Then, "That's kind of dramatic. Did you ever think of being an actor?"

"I've had enough careers," said Bruce. "Anyway, if I go back to the parks I'm going to need that raccoon costume. It has to stay mint."

"I don't believe you're going back to the parks," said Pearl. She refused to, in fact. "What would you do without us? What would we do without you?"

Bruce got up from his chair and walked to the window and stood looking down at poor, lovely old Vincent. Pearl couldn't see his eyes because the light was behind him when he turned his back to the window.

"Pearlie girl, don't you know—you're getting taller, have you noticed? Like a sprout. I bet you've grown two inches since school started."

She had to admit, "I went up a shoe size."

"Right, and you know what's next? College!"

Her shoulders drooped and she threw her head back and gazed at the ceiling. Then she said, "And I'm tall enough to see over the top of the atlas, even while I'm sitting down. So maybe it *will* fit me now."

"Be small for a while longer," Bruce said, his voice husky all of a sudden. "Stay innocent. Be the librarian's child while there's still a library to be the child in."

Pearl couldn't help hugging him. "I'm going to ask again, you know," she said into Bruce's ear. "I'll wear you down."

"Ask a thousand times," said Bruce. "And a thousand times I will say no. Nothing's going to change about that."

She couldn't help stepping away and slumping into a chair. "Everything changes," she said. "Isn't that what you all keep telling me?" She slithered out of the chair and onto the floor. She crawled across it on hands and knees, difficult in a long uniform skirt. On her way past the coatrack, she whipped up the tail of the raccoon costume so it swung and swooshed. In the doorway, she hopped to her feet and was gone.

the end you might conclude that actually having a father around doesn't matter as much as having *somebody.*

Pearl's somebody was Bruce. And he was talking about leaving. So she worked extra hard to make him mad. How else could she show him how much she cared? How much could she find out how much *he* cared?

—M.A.M.

32: ROCK STARS

OCT 11

Three third-grade kids were checking out books when Oleg burst in to say that the rock had arrived. When the kids saw Pearl and Francine go out the garden door, they followed.

Ramón's pickup truck was backed into the driveway, and the tailgate was down. The stone rested in the bed of the truck.

"We're taking it to the stone carver," Oleg said to the gathering staff. "But I wanted Pearl to see it first."

Oleg was right about the stone, Pearl saw. It *was* head-shaped. Oleg stood next to the truck as proudly as if he had invented rocks himself, and Simon and his band friend Joey—who'd gone along to help with the rock—looked almost as pleased with themselves. Ramón, his hand on the tailgate of the truck, had an air of outdoors and adventure. Pearl was jealous. They could have asked her to go, too.

Nichols came out the back door. "Where'd it come from?" he asked Oleg.

"Out Brickyard way. In the Catskill mountains."

Nichols put his hands in his pockets. "Brickyard. What a swimming hole that is. Can you still walk behind the waterfall on dry days?"

The boys said yes.

"How do *you* know?" Pearl asked Nichols.

A Sidebar About Jonathan Yoiks

It used to be that Mr. Jonathan Yoiks had two jobs: One, he considered art—his *Unique New Yorker* column, which allowed him to write about the kinds of brilliant creative artist weirdo geeks he would have liked to be if only he didn't have to pay the rent. The other, he considered good for paying the rent—reporting on the events of the city, plain and simple, for better or worse. And it was often worse, because the kind of stories his editor liked the best were the kind Yoiks told himself were battles between good and evil. Except that it was the evil his editor really liked the best. Crime paid, because it made good copy, and good copy sold papers.

Yoiks was jealous of the brilliant creative artist weirdos because they couldn't help being their geek selves, who somehow still managed to pay the rent. He couldn't see how they did it until he saw the stone that Oleg brought home from the Catskills. Then it hit him hard. Not the stone (it was big enough to crush him), but the idea of this object brought in from the wild that so obviously looked as if should be shaped into a woman's head. Not just any woman. Vincent. He'd seen only photographs of her and her statue. And he didn't know anything about stone carving, though he was going to find out.

"I used to go out there when I was in college." He leaned both arms on the truck, his eyes seeing something far away. "I remember one day after my history exam. It was at least ninety-five degrees, and I'd sweltered through the whole test. After it was over, we drove out to Brickyard and jumped right in. Nothing like it."

"You went to college?" said Simon quietly.

"To the university up there," Nichols answered.

The little kids pulled on Oleg's pockets. "Was that rock a donkey before it was here?" a girl asked. She had her favorite picture book under her arm: *Sylvester and the Magic Pebble.*[1]

"You mean like Sylvester the donkey?" Pearl asked.

"Who?" said Francine, and Pearl and the girl began to tell the story about the donkey who finds a magic wishing pebble and accidentally turns himself into a rock so that nobody knows he is there.

"The Rock Lady is a better story," sniffed Francine, and Pearl, although she disagreed, bowed.

"Thanks for the call," Jonathan Yoiks said, striding up. Bruce had called

---

1 *Sylvester and the Magic Pebble* by William Steig (Windmill Books, 1969).

him about the arrival of the stone. "I sure wish I could give the library more coverage."

"Actually, you were a bit of a shark at first, when it came to this library—more interested when there was something a little, shall we say, *dark* going on." Bruce was standing tall, being cool, looking down his nose at Yoiks.

Yoiks shrugged. "There's more light than dark on Lancaster Avenue since I met you. If only I were a millionaire, I'd start my own paper."

"'If only I were myself again,'" quoted Nichols, saying what Sylvester the donkey said when he was the rock. Nichols was walking away, looking sad.

Pearl moved to get in front of him, and made him look at her. "What *were* you?"

"An architect. An artist who designs buildings." He stared off toward the pines.

Mom came up behind them and put her hands on Pearl's shoulders. "What are you all talking about so seriously?"

Nichols didn't turn to look at Mom. "Safety," he said.

Pearl thought, *No, we weren't.*

What was inescapable to him was the destiny of that stone to be what it had to be.

The stone carver who'd said yes for free because she just had to be the one to carve Vincent into the stone—who was she, if not Unique?

So when Yoiks finally found the story and the Unique New Yorker he wanted to write about, he finally quit worrying so much about paying the rent—and just turned into what he was meant to be: someone who wrote about brilliant creative artist weirdos because that's what he was a geek for.

—M.A.M.

P.S. You may wonder how I know. Let's just say reporters all face the struggle over what makes good copy. So naturally I had my beady little eyes on Jonathan Yoiks.

33: REAL LIFE

The evening *Moon* held a picture of Vincent with Oleg standing beneath her, along with his uncarved rock, and the caption:

Library statue gets taken for granite by Clancy Street boy.

Pearl sat at the circ desk and stared at the photograph, unable to believe there was *another* picture of the library in the paper with a kid who wasn't her. She would have to do something about that, but in the meantime she was just irritated.

"This doesn't even make sense!" she said to Mom. "We didn't take her for granted. We love her!"

"It's a pun, Pearl."

"It's a cheap pun!" snapped Pearl. "It makes people think Oleg stole the head." Pearl hated to admit it, but Vincent *was* pretty creepy-looking in the photo.

Mom took the newspaper up to Bruce, ready to say good night, then stayed up there long after a quiet gloom had settled over the empty lower floors. Pearl opened the basement door and heard nothing; the raccoons must have already woken up and gone out.

She rode the book elevator upstairs to spy, and pushed the elevator door open slightly to hear Mom relating Pearl's conversation with Nichols and Yoiks.

"Does Nichols think the library isn't safe?"

Bruce's answer reached Pearl's ears clearly. "He might be right. How are we going to tell Pearl that the library board is researching the apartment proposal before the district vote?"

Pearl didn't know exactly what that meant, but it sounded good for the apartment proposal and bad for the library.

"If the paper would just quit publishing the downside of every-thing . . ." Bruce groaned. "Yoiks has been saying he's writing a story about Vincent, but that's never what gets in the paper!"

(Even the best writers still get cut.)

Instead of joining the conversation, Pearl scooted into the Memorial Room, which used to be a place for writing work-shops, speeches, ceremonies, and recitals. Did anybody even know it was here anymore? The founders looked down at her from their frames, dull and dusty above the cold fireplace. She sat on the windowsill. She could see all the way south to her school, and all the way north to the intersection with Eighth Ave-nue, where buildings were lower and the houses were smaller and even scruffier than here.

If only they could pick up the building, garden and all, and put it somewhere else, relocate it someplace where people *wanted* a pretty building and good books and raccoons and a statue with a story. It would be the happy ending *The Little House* got.

But look! Pearl pondered the situation. The head had been stolen; that was true. But now they were getting a new head made, and they were

going to have a celebration for it. And Simon and his band would play music at the celebration. Pearl knew if a few cool teenagers did something, others who wanted to be cool might follow.

And more kids from the middle school and elementary schools might come on account of Pearl's stories and Francine's dances and the Rock Lady game and the Reading Raccoons. More people were getting library cards every day, so circulation had to be going up again, it just had to.

Pearl had to admit that all this wouldn't be happening if Vincent's head hadn't been stolen. The first story, about the theft, wouldn't have gone in the *Moon*. That might not have attracted the attention of Mr. Bull and Mr. Dozer. Bruce and Mom might not have found out there was an alternate plan for the library in time to request a district vote. Other library branches had been shut down without so much as a warning to their management.

If Vincent's head hadn't been stolen, Pearl might never have gone creeping around looking for it in the dark back bushes of the garden, and wouldn't have found Nichols's things. She wouldn't have gotten to be such good friends with him, and he might not have had any reason to show her Matilda, Mary Ann, and Arak in the reading room after hours. She might never have met Mary Ann or learned about Mrs. Mallomar and the midnight *Moon*. . . .

Bring back the head, and where would they all be? Pearl turned back time to spring, when Bruce used to come for dinner without fighting. Pearl thought of Bruce and Mom's stony summer silences. Now, in the stressful autumn, at least they were talking.

And above all else, if Vincent's head hadn't been stolen, Pearl wouldn't have screamed, and that meant Francine might never have come to the library. Pearl's only friends might still be the library staff. Pearl wouldn't have made her first friend her own age.

Pearl left the Memorial Room. Mom must have gone downstairs, because there were no more voices. Pearl went into Bruce's office and stood stroking the back of the raccoon costume.

"Pearl girl," he said, and if he noticed her touching his costume, he didn't mention it.

"Hi," said Pearl. "Can I use the phone?"

She called the *Moon*. When she got Jonathan Yoiks's voice mail, she thought, *Just as well—even better*. She left him a message: "Mr. Yoiks, this is Pearl Moran of the Lancaster Avenue branch library. Raised here. Born here. And ready to volunteer to be the subject of your next *Unique New Yorkers* profile."

A Sidebar About Magic

Magic is a trick.

(If you're wondering how I know this, well, raccoons have been to plenty of birthday parties, lurking in the high weeds of backyards and parks, watching the magician, waiting for the wonderful leftovers: cake, pizza, lemonade, Tootsie Rolls. Have you ever seen a raccoon eat a Tootsie Roll? It is not a pretty sight, but they are delectable.)

Magic looks like it's real, but it doesn't behave by the rules of reality. You can't reach into an empty hat and pull out a rabbit. The trick succeeds by confusing you. The magician drapes a shiny scarf over the hat and while you're watching that, he lets the rabbit out of a secret compartment in the table. What you see is what you *think* you get, but that's only because you looked away at the crucial moment. The trick seems real—and you want it to be real—so you believe it.

When you put fantasy into a story, it's like a magic trick: You have to make everything around it as real as possible. And you also have to make people want it to be real—want it to be real so much they could cry.

—M.A.M.

34: WHAT VINCENT WANTED

OCT 13

School performance day. Pearl was past worrying about what anyone at her school might think. If that vote on Election Day didn't go the library's way, why would any of her schoolmates matter? Pearl would lose her library home, move out of her apartment, change schools, and never see any of them again. So she did her best to keep a lid on her nerves. It would have been easier if Bruce would just let her use his raccoon costume, but since he wouldn't, Pearl concentrated on putting the audience's focus completely on Francine.

Every night after closing that week, they had worked on the Rock Lady costume in the garden. Alice had made Francine put on a raincoat and draped one of her old silverish saris over her, folding it and pleating it to look like Vincent's dress, and sewed it into place. Then, while Francine stood in the driveway in Vincent's pose, they'd finished the "dress" with quick-drying varnish until the sari fabric practically stood up on its own. Oleg and Pearl did that part while Alice fed Francine a milkshake from the Cozy Soup and Burger through a straw as a reward for not moving. When they were done, Ramón had taken heavy clippers and cut the sari down the back, and Pearl and Oleg pulled the costume open just wide enough for Alice to help Francine slip out through the crack.

Then Oleg added a mess of coal dust that Pearl had brought from the basement, sand from the driveway, and glitter from Francine's supplies, so that the gray material seemed to stiffen into stone, with everything stuck on the varnish. Now, on Friday, the whole thing was rock-hard and looked as heavy as the Statue of Liberty.

All the school stretched out before Pearl as she stood on the stage. Before her, the smallest kindergarteners sat in the front, and the looming eighth graders were crammed together at the rear. Everyone else was in between. Pearl deliberately avoided looking closely at her fifth-grade class, but nonetheless she knew exactly where Millie and Khadija were sitting, and how Elsa was glowering in the bored way she always had. *Forget them,* Pearl told herself desperately.

She took a deep breath and began. "Ladies and gentlemen," she said, keeping her voice small and quavery on purpose. "Boys and girls, I come here as a representative of the Lancaster Avenue branch of the New York City Library to ask for your help. Have you heard about our statue?"

Pearl poured on the drama, letting her voice rise, picturing it like colored smoke. "So. Some of you know about our statue of Edna St. Vincent Millay. A beloved poet, silent. A death not forgotten. A person remembered. A statue, sending stories out through the air."

Here she paused, and stood looking out, meeting eyes—Alice had told her to plan ahead on whose eyes to meet because an audience can tell when a real connection was being made. Millie looked at her seriously, fascinated; Oleg smiled in a welcoming way.

"Who here has heard in his or her lifetime a truly wonderful story, has had it told to them or read to them? A story that has come their way at exactly the right time, so right that you read it over and over again, play through it in your mind as you walk or eat or fall asleep, a book that you hand to someone else and say, 'Drop everything and read this'?"

She saw Elsa and Khadija look at each other and shrug. She thrust them out of her mind.

"Do any of you know what part the statue of Edna St. Vincent Millay and the library that guards her plays in sending those stories out to you? Do any of you know that her stories are so powerful that they connect not only with people, but with the *animals* in the neighborhood?"

Pearl saw some rolled eyes among the upper graders. But she stormed ahead. "Imagine that you're an animal and you overhear stories about animals, like the ones in the Little Bear[1] books, like *The Cat in the Hat.*[2] Imagine such a magical environment where words and pictures swirl in the air! Is it any surprise that we have raccoons here who can *read*?" She paused and let that sink in. "It's true. The Lancaster Avenue neighborhood has a special magic. The Lancaster Avenue branch library has raccoons who *learned to read at the foot of the poet's statue.* The statue's hand

---

1 The first of the Little Bear books by Elsa Homelund Minarik, *Little Bear*, was published in 1957 by Harper & Row, with illustrations by Maurice Sendak.

2 *The Cat in the Hat* by Theodor Geisel (writing under the pen name Dr. Seuss) (Random House, 1957).

stretched out to the raccoons, inspiring them with stories. It wasn't long before the raccoons could read whole pages, chapters, books."

Some of the younger kids looked at each other with their mouths open. Some of the older kids looked a bit bug-eyed.

The raccoons had started as just a seed of an idea, but Pearl had gradually built it up, including the part about the lousy poems, and the Mallomar box, and the book in Vincent's hand somehow making people think a book was a good thing to have. The raccoons had grown into a fully bloomed part of her story. On the stage, in front of all those people, Francine moved, bending and reaching as Vincent would, offering stories to the little raccoons around her feet.

Pearl had her audience. And she knew that the best way to hold them was with drama. She built up to her great moment.

"That's how it was, until that night . . . that fateful night . . . that infamous night, when someone took from our statue poet that which should never have been taken—"

Pearl whirled and pushed Francine in front of her. Alice's stiff sari rose to a slender neck-shaped stump, making Francine look headless.

"Her head," Pearl finished.

The whole school gasped.

"Ew," said several fourth graders.

"And now," said Pearl, "now Vincent's hand is still stretched out, but she is not giving anymore. Now there is something she wants."

Here Francine lifted her arm and reached her hand, palm up, toward the children. She moved her legs stiffly to step forward, as though she was breaking out of a stone shell for the first time in years. The kindergarteners in front scooted their

A Sidebar About Timelines

Being more mature doesn't just come from age. It comes from experience. Pearl was innocent. She simply didn't believe that the library could close and the raccoons would have to move away to a place where they might quit reading. She hadn't seen enough bad things happen to realize that they could. That's innocence.

Not all the traps are Havaharts.

Not all the reading raccoons find writing jobs.

And none of them has had the job of telling an enormous secret to the sharp, snapping, sometimes vengeful group of humans that make up New York City.

But even if, unlike Pearl, I know that many humans aren't great, I happen to know some really good ones: Bruce Chambers. Christopher Nichols. Ms. Judge. Tallulah. Pearl Moran. They each made me want to have hope, to tell the truth, to help Pearl build her story.

I'd done the research Pearl wanted. I'd interviewed Grandmar and Mama Matilda and Tallulah. And Grandmar had brought me statistics from the midnight *Moon*'s printer: our own circulation numbers, broken down by the species of our readers—all nocturnals, of course: raccoons, rats, coyotes. I'd also learned that it was rare for any non-raccoons to be writers, because of the dexterity issue.

bottoms backward. A nervous ripple grew, and the hubbub spread to the back of the room.

"What does she want?" Pearl intoned. The kids' eyes were on Francine. "A cupcake? A latte? A phone?" Francine reached her hand out as though it had a life of its own and she couldn't control it. "She can't speak. She can't shake her head. She can only keep her hand out, asking, begging, pleading. . . ."

A child in the front row let out a scream as Francine's hand swooped near.

"Enough!" said Pearl, and Francine slumped like a puppet, her palm still raised and open.

Ms. Judge stepped into the dumbstruck silence and asked, "What does the statue want?"

It was a beautiful moment.

"I know what she wants," Pearl said in a hushed voice. Then she evoked visions she had never seen for herself but had imagined plenty. "She wants to see people climbing up the library stairs, the way the raccoons do in the middle of the night. She wants to see them reading the daily editions of the *Moon* the way the raccoons read the midnight *Moon*. She wants to see them with"—and here she recited the words she'd cooked up last night while lying in bed—"their nose in a book and a book in their paws, turning the pages with their toes and their claws. She wants you all to be readers . . . like our very own Lancaster Avenue Reading Raccoons!"

The room burst into applause.

Ms. Judge stepped onto the stage and summoned all the authority and chaos-quelling power only a principal can command.

"People!" she said, her voice deeper than usual.

She was as moved by their performance as everyone else, Pearl realized with pride.

"I have an announcement to make. I want everyone in this auditorium to visit the library and find their very own personal stories. Real or magical. Fiction or nonfiction. Join the Reading Raccoons!"

"And—" Francine stepped to center stage and raised her arms, waving them in a giant flourish to grab everyone's attention.

"Library cards are free!" Pearl exclaimed. "Absolutely free! All you need is an address where you can get mail sent. Find the book the Rock Lady

I'd done all this, believed in our dramatic story despite my maturity, even though raccoons like being invisible, beautiful though we are. We show ourselves on our own terms.

When Pearl and I saw each other last, I wrote:

You want everyone calling themselves Reading Raccoons!

Pearl said, "So? It's just so they'll think reading is cool."

I don't think I want the eyes of the world upon us.

She said, "What do you think will happen?"

What if they take me into a laboratory and operate on my brain?

Pearl put her hands over her face and shook. She rocked. She reeled. I leaned over and nudged her elbow with my whole head, hard. She looked up.

Are you LAUGHING?

"Silly," she said. "I don't think you need to worry about that."

I must have just sat there with my jaw hanging open.

"Go on and write the best story you can," Pearl insisted. She wiped the jolly off her face and bent toward me, serious now. "They're New Yorkers. They've seen it all. But they'll never believe us. Not in a million years."

—M.A.M.

has personally chosen for you. When you take out a book, you'll get a ticket to the Halloween Howl!"

Oleg slipped up the side stairs of the stage and escorted Francine down to the floor.

Now Francine ran around the auditorium in a slow-motion way that was both gruesome and graceful, Pearl and Oleg at her heels, yelling, "Watch out!" and "Come back!" and making as much commotion as possible. They did a full lap, and then the three of them dashed from the room, leaving the children screaming and cheering behind them.

35: HUNDREDS, MAYBE THOUSANDS

OCT 14

On Saturday morning, Pearl was busy working on an invitation, an announcement, and a sign when Mom called her to the phone.

"Jonathan Yoiks wants you to be a Unique little New Yorker?"

"Little?" repeated Pearl.

"Go with it," said Mom. She unmuted the phone and handed it over.

"Hello?" said Pearl.

"Pearl," said Yoiks. "Were you really born *in* the library?"

"Of course," said Pearl.

After she made an appointment for her interview, she swiped Ramón's staple gun and printed out the photo of Vincent's empty neck.

CALLING ALL READING RACCOONS
HAVE YOU SEEN MY HEAD?
I'll get a head on Halloween—will it be YOURS?
See for yourself:
HALLOWEEN HOWL!
Admission: One library card
See the re-heading!
Donations will support the library.

While posting the signs in every store window on Lancaster Avenue and Seventh Avenue, mailing them to the mayor and the library board, and slipping them under every door along the length of Clancy Street and Beep Street, Pearl thought about the old head. She knew that against everything else that was going on, it shouldn't matter where the old head was. What good would it do to get it back? None, that's what. The new head would actually bring more attention to the library, and that was a good outcome. But she couldn't stop considering that:

Nichols knew who took it.

Mary Ann's cousin Eloise knew who took it.

Which meant that whoever had information just might have four legs, a face like a bandit, and eyes that saw well in the dark. So Pearl posted a few signs at knee level, too. And she was sure to fold one up tiny and push it into the mail slot behind the ivy at 22½ Beep Street.

* * *

"Pearl," said Yoiks. "Give me a hand with this equipment, will you?"

He loaded Pearl with his tripod and a circle-shaped thing in a round bag and his backpack, and followed her up the straight stairs all the way to the Memorial Room. Then he photographed her there, looking out the window onto Lancaster Avenue. He took some other artistic-looking pictures of her sitting halfway down from the top of the spiral stairs.

He had to wait while a herd of kids from her school descended the straight stairs to take out books at the circulation desk. Pearl smiled to see them, and told Yoiks about the performance that had led them here.

"Good," said Yoiks, "but they make the spiral staircase vibrate, and I want a good, clear shot." He wandered across the mezzanine's glass floor into the reading room, where he took more arty shots, annoyingly not all with Pearl in them.

"They're not going to knock it down *tomorrow,* you know," said Pearl.

"Pearl—I want to say two things." He looked at her through his lens. "One. You should keep doing anything you can think of to save the library."

"I am," said Pearl. Hadn't he heard?

"Right," said Yoiks. "Well, that leads me to number two. You shouldn't expect to have much effect."

"Huh?" said Pearl. "Great! Well, thanks for the advice. That really helps." She turned away from Yoiks and looked out the window. Here came some more kids from her school. *Ha.*

Yoiks said, "Come on, Pearl. You've already done a lot. Tell me the whole story about Vincent that got all these kids in here to get library cards." She thought he was just being nice to her. But then he was hitting record on his little recorder.

Pearl swallowed and gave it her best shot. She drew herself up as tall and straight as Vincent and mimed the book in Vincent's right arm, looked down at it, and lifted her left hand toward Yoiks. In her darkest, lowest, most mysterious voice, she said, "Vincent lifts up her hand and she's so powerful that she makes cracks appear in the sidewalk, and wind blows out from the cracks, and books fly up into the sky, their pages flapping like wings. Vincent knows the exact book that is exactly right for each person at the exact time. They go flying out—" She paused to find better words. "Soaring, magnificently swirling and circling to find their readers . . ."

"Is this some kind of fairy tale?" He sounded like he couldn't tell if she was being serious.

"Vincent is real. You've seen her! This is what she does. If you've ever thought, 'Hey, I should read that book'—that was

Vincent, inspiring you to read exactly the right book that you need at that exact moment." Pearl really did believe this. "The books fly around the neighborhood, and they find the person who should read them next. All 41,134 of them."

Yoiks was taking notes now. He repeated, "Forty-one thousand . . . one hundred what?"

"Thirty-four." She sized him up. Was he going to print this, or was he just being a good audience, as usual? Or was it, possibly, maybe, it was an actually good story told by, dare she say it, a *charismatic* teller? She went on, full of hope. "But they don't all go to people. Some of them fly into the trees, into hidey-holes in the backs of buildings. You know who those ones go to? Raccoons. And what are raccoons going to do with the books?" Pearl felt her story taking over her whole body, her whole soul, like she was at the top of a roller coaster about to plunge downward.

"Make nests with them?"

"Don't be ridiculous," scoffed Pearl. "The raccoons of Lancaster Avenue can *read*." She said it with all the snottiness she could muster, as if any fool knew that.

Yoiks peered up from his pad, looked at her through his owlish glasses, and said, "Reading raccoons?"

"Yeah, the raccoons around here are special. Everybody near our library reads and writes—people and raccoons. To lose our library would be the worst kind of tragedy for all of us readers."

"You're making this up." He didn't sound sure either way. But his skepticism was weakening, and his belief was strengthening.

(Or maybe it was his awareness of how skeptical his editor would be that was losing, and his conviction about what he thought was important that was winning.)

"Oh, does it seem magical?" she asked, as if it was just occurring to her. "I can't help that."

He was silent. He met her eyes with a curious, cautious, "Is this kid all right?" expression.

"Yes, Mr. Yoiks, I'm completely serious." Pearl pointed at Vincent. She held her head high, looked Yoiks right in the eye, and said, "The raccoons are *not* magical, though they might seem to be. The Lancaster Avenue branch library simply taught raccoons to read. And you heard it here first."

* * *

All weekend, the new wave of kids from Lancaster Avenue Public School kept washing up at the library to sign up for cards and get books.

"Thanks to us, they all want to see Vincent," said Francine, and Pearl couldn't argue.

"The kids all call her Vinny," said Oleg.

"I'm *never* calling her that," said Pearl.

"But it's great," said Simon. "People want books now. They're not coming just to see her head."

"Good thing," said Francine, and Pearl laughed.

* * *

The last place Pearl expected to find herself was in Gully's store, after everything he'd done, but some things had to be faced if you were going to move forward in this life. Maybe Mom was right: Diplomacy was required.

Or money. She laid on the counter the yellow baseball cap Francine had bought the day before. "I have a business proposal, Mr. Gulliver," she said. "What kind of price can you get me on these?"

He turned to his computer to look it up.

Pearl added, "We'll need a lot of black eye masks, too, like these Halloween ones." She picked one up from a box on the counter—Gully loved the impulse buys for Halloween—and positioned it above the bill of the yellow cap to show him what she meant: the eye mask on the hat, making raccoon eyes. "We'll take care of the gluing-on part."

"How many do you want?" asked Gully. "Price goes down with quantity."

"If all goes well?" said Pearl. "Hundreds, maybe thousands."

Gully lifted the cap and put it on Pearl's head, studying it. "Looks like one of those so-called masked bandits that gets into my garbage cans."

Pearl made herself laugh. "Reading Raccoons," she said. "The library's new mascot."

A Sidebar About Bulk Sales

The more caps Pearl bought from Gully, the cheaper they would be. The caps were a way to do two things:

Get people on the same team with each other.

Get people on the same team with the library.

If she couldn't sell them, she'd be stuck paying for the caps herself. If she couldn't sell them, it meant people were too separated; they wouldn't come together for the sake of the neighborhood, or the library.

—M.A.M.

* * *

Pearl sat on the basement steps and told Mary Ann about the idea for the caps—and what Gully had said about raccoons.

You see what people are like. They believe in the "raccoon invasion."

"This is why we need to publish our piece as soon as possible!"

"Pearl!" Mom's voice came shouting from above. "Are you down there?"

"Yes, coming," called Pearl. She ran up.

Mom was peering at her.

"It's a good place to write, that's all," said Pearl.

"Who's writing what?" asked Mom.

"Mary Ann and I," said Pearl. "We're telling our story."

Mom looked as if Pearl had told her she'd sprouted wings and taken off from the roof. She could see Mom thought she was being strictly fictional.

"It may be strange," she told her mother. "But it's also the truth."

Then Mom laid two massive envelopes across the desk, addressed to:

CIRCULATION LIBRARIAN
LANCASTER AVENUE BRANCH,
NEW YORK CITY LIBRARY

"Hey, they're from Ms. Judge!" said Pearl.

Mom opened one envelope. "Good grief," she said. "She's got applications from three hundred and sixteen students requesting library cards." She grinned at Pearl. "Better print out some more tickets to the Howl."

36: INVITATIONS

It all depended on the district vote on Election Day, November 7. The whole neighborhood would vote on whether the library should stay or go—whether it would keep loaning out books or become apartments that would bring Gully more regular shoppers than he had now. NOV 7, said the return stamp now. By that date, the library's fate would be decided. There would be nowhere for the returns to return.

Today was a warm October afternoon, borrowed from late summer. Every day that week, over her school uniform, Pearl had worn the heavy sweatshirt Bruce had given her for her birthday that said THE BOOK WAS BETTER. But now it was warm enough that Pearl took her sweatshirt off. She dropped two granola bars and an apple into the little shed box, along with one of her Halloween posters.

Then she saw a movement under a yew bush.

"What are you doing out here in the middle of the day, Arak?" Pearl asked. "You're going to be in so much trouble."

The little kit walked right up to Pearl (very brave!), and put a front paw on the knee of her jeans. Inside the other paw was a rolled-up catalog card with Mary Ann's writing on it.

Mama is gone.

"Matilda? Where?" said Pearl.

Arak couldn't read very well yet. Did he know his mama was gone? He made a scrabbling, scrappy, squawking sound. Mary Ann must have been desperate for Pearl to know, to send her little brother back here alone to wait for Pearl to get home from school, in what was practically the middle of the night for him. Pearl wanted to scoop him up, cuddle him, protect him, but—

There was a noise from the alleyway, a cantankerous cackling. Here came Mrs. Mallomar, with Mary Ann behind her.

At the sight of Mrs. Mallomar, Arak dashed across the garden path and disappeared into a dark shadowy space under the drainpipe at record speed. Mary Ann and Mrs. Mallomar sat back on their haunches in the grass.

"Matilda's gone?" Pearl said to Mary Ann.

Mary Ann was making a motion with her paws—curling them, then spreading them forward, like she was rolling something. Arak re-emerged from the basement, bringing a rolled-up newspaper to Mrs. Mallomar. Then Mrs. Mallomar, the editor in chief of the midnight *Moon,* came toward Pearl and pushed the newspaper at her.

"For me?" asked Pearl. But the big raccoon just moved off, loping down the driveway, keeping close to the base of the library, until she was out of sight.

Pearl examined the paper.

MOON MARKETER FOLLOWS NIECE
ON FACT-FINDING JOURNEY

Pearl read:

Matilda Mallomar, assistant marketing director of this paper, is taking a leave of absence, as she has targeted the possible location of her niece, Eloise, relocated two weeks ago. Apart from the obvious objective of assuring Eloise's well-being, Ms. Mallomar has hoped to gather clues about a local theft. Eloise's mother,

Eilonwy Wanderer, commented, "Eloise loves an adventure, but that's no reason to leave her brothers and sisters without a babysitter. I'd go myself if I weren't so tied to the whole kaboodle of kits." Ms. Mallomar hastened to add that her niece is not a reader, and therefore unlikely to find her own way back to the Lancaster Avenue neighborhood. Needless to say, this is a situation that lends new weight to the paper's campaign to increase raccoon literacy.

Pearl glanced up to catch Mary Ann's eye, but instead saw her friend's tail disappear into the dark space beside the drainpipe.

The story was impeccably written as always, but what was so important about it that they'd left her to read it on her own?

And then she got to the end of the story. After the last line was a small paw-written message.

page 27

On page 27 was an editorial circled in Sharpie.

NEUTRALIZING THE NEGATIVE

The attitude toward the raccoon race around Lancaster Avenue—and certain other areas of the city—has lately become negative. This has already resulted in one of our dearest members taking a journey to an unknown destination. This disappearance has in turn caused another member to pursue her, with the outcome unknown at this writing.

This brave citizen inspires us all, and reminds us of the importance of educating the illiterate raccoons in new areas of the city and helping create harmony—as well as self-sufficiency. The relocation of an illiterate young raccoon drives home the point that city raccoons must assimilate to the city—a city that is built on words.

Let there be an end to traps. Let us, instead, tell our story, and use our story to bring new attention—a new identity, maybe even tourism—to our neighborhood. Let everyone come to join the Reading Raccoons, and stay for the beautiful library, for the statue of Edna St. Vincent Millay, for the magic of stories chosen just for you.

—Mrs. Mallomar, Editor in Chief

Pearl read the editorial aloud twice, thinking back to what Mary Ann had said long ago about the raccoons having their own plan. Was it happening now? Were the raccoons leaving the library to go teach other city raccoons how to read?

It was right here, in black letters stamped on white paper, right here in Pearl's lap: The raccoons were not willing to give up their literacy. Instead they wanted to preserve it by spreading it far and wide. Here, on Lancaster Avenue, they were willing to stick their necks out: They were making the statement that they were real reading raccoons, and asking their readers to help them get the word out. They did this for the sake of their family, and the sake of their stories—the two things were connected. Without reading, they wouldn't be the Mallomars.

Pearl knew that fighting for their literacy, fighting for staying at the library, was dangerous for them. You didn't have to look any farther than across the street to see how it could backfire, with Gully getting people like the X-terminator hired, and Mr. Bull and Mr. Dozer making the place unfriendly to wild animals. People had thought of animals as ignorant and illiterate—and therefore not worthy of respect—for a long time, and it would take some doing, and some proof, to make anyone change their thinking.

* * *

Pearl left the garden and went back into the library, which was bustling more than usual for a darkening October afternoon. The children's room was full of children for once, and the room was not the least bit restful or quiet. Pearl couldn't help feeling proud. This festive noise was her doing! But what was about to happen next—a raccoon campaign that was supposed to look like it was just a big marketing campaign but was actually real life—had her jangling with worry.

"Oh, Pearl!" said Alice. "Did you hear Danesh's great idea for my costume for the Halloween parade? I'm going to be Humpty Dumpty."[1]

Pearl started laughing, thinking of the very pregnant Alice, quite egglike so close to her due date.

"Where's the parade going to be?" Khadija asked.

Khadija was here?

"Khadija?" said Pearl. A returning patron! And someone from her class!

"In the library garden," said Alice. "Around and around the statue and down the street if we have big-enough attendance, and who knows where after that. What's your costume?"

---

1 Humpty Dumpty is a character in an English nursery rhyme, usually handed down orally, but first appearing in print around 1800. He also appears in *Through the Looking-Glass, and What Alice Found There* by Lewis Carroll (Macmillan, 1872), the sequel to *Alice's Adventures in Wonderland*.

Francine came tapping over like it was no big deal that Khadija, a totally normal, totally cool girl from school, was choosing to hang out in the library.

"I could be *Madeline*[2]," said Khadija, thinking it over. "My sister has a blue coat. I could get a hat from the thrift store, and Gully's has ribbon. It was my favorite book when I lived in Paris."

Francine said, "I can help you attach the ribbon to the hat." She added, "You lived in Paris?"

"Thanks." Khadija flipped back her shining dark hair as if Paris wasn't any big deal. "Not everyone in Paris goes to school in two straight lines."

That was a reference to *Madeline*! Pearl grinned, and told Francine, "Khadija moved here in third grade."

Khadija looked surprised that Pearl would remember. She smiled at Pearl.

Then Elsa appeared, too. "Khadija," she said, "come help me get Millie out of the books about machines. She's having a total geek attack."

Khadija flapped her hand. "Let her," she said.

"Geek attack about what?" said Pearl.

"Her STEM special interest topic," said Elsa. "Naturally she's doing *T* for tech." She said it as if she expected them to roll their eyes about Millie. But Pearl was just curious. What kinds of machines would Millie want to read about?

"What's your costume, Pearl?" Khadija asked, turning away from Elsa.

"I haven't decided yet," said Pearl. It was kind of a lie.

"I bet I know what you're wearing," Khadija told Francine.

"You bet," said Francine. "Rock Lady is going to be the best costume there."

---

2 *Madeline* by Ludwig Bemelmans (Simon & Schuster, 1939).

Khadija smirked as if she liked a challenge. "We'll see!" she said. And she gave a little salute and went off with Elsa.

Pearl let Francine tag along with the other girls and sneaked off to the book elevator, sending herself to the third floor. Time to investigate her own costume idea.

The lights were off in Bruce's office. The room felt gloomy, gray.

Feeling sneaky for being there when Bruce was out, Pearl shoved a pile of stuff out of his easy chair and curled up there, gazed tiredly at the teeth of the molding that edged the ceiling, and met the veiled, vacant eyes of the raccoon head on top of the file cabinet.

The raccoon costume was hung up like always, with the head on top of the filing cabinet like a moose head on the wall of a hunting lodge. The first time she'd seen it, when she was five and Bruce came, she had taken one look at its empty eyes and its masked-bandit face and given a little shiver. When Bruce, who didn't even know her yet, had said, "That's not to be touched," he hadn't had to tell Pearl twice.

Now suddenly everything was different. Now suddenly she felt bigger. Now suddenly she wanted to take another look.

Just then, Bruce appeared at the door. "What are you thinking, Pearl girl?"

"I was thinking that if I don't go into library science, I could fall back on acting."

"What have you ever acted in?" Bruce asked. She thought that he, too, had come upstairs seeking solitude.

"I acted on the auditorium stage," she said. "It's me who sets the mood, you know, so that Francine seems super scary." She got up, creeping toward Bruce. "I'm good. You should see me. I can tell a story."

"I know you can, Pearlie," he said. "I've heard it! Now—"

"So, can I—" She arched her eyebrows, pointing behind him at the raccoon body on its hanger in the corner.

"My costume?" Gone was Bruce's casual attitude. "No way, Pearl! You've got to stop asking this. You don't understand. What you're asking, it's like asking a general to borrow his uniform. Ranger Rick himself gave me the A-okay to wear this. "

"Well, take off the bandana and it's just a regular raccoon. And then it's a Reading Raccoon!"

"No can do, Pearlie. If you want a costume, I can help you make one," he offered.

She didn't get a chance to argue. Suddenly, Mom was shrieking Bruce's name from downstairs, and a rabble of voices—Ramón's, Simon's, Alice's—added to the chaos.

"Get down here!"

"Where's Pearl?"

"Take the straight stairs!"

"The spiral staircase! It's falling apart!"

37: THE WORST CASE

OCT 17-18

Too many had climbed up; too many had come down. Now there was an actual crack in the iron that held the spiral stairs in place. Ramón was quick to rope off the top and bottom of the staircase with lengths of line, and Pearl was dispatched to Gully's to buy CAUTION tape.

"Problem across the street?" Gully asked, eyes glittering.

"Nothing we can't fix," said Pearl, knowing it was a lie.

Upon her return, she saw that Bruce had taken action. Two-by-four pieces of wood, hammered in an *X*, kept everyone from going up the spiral stairs and blocked them from entering the glass-floored area from the reading room to nonfiction.

"To be safe—and legal—you'd better shut off the whole reading room," Nichols said, his face grave.

Of course Jonathan Yoiks chose that day to return the books about Vincent.

"What happened here?" he asked.

Next came Gully—*he couldn't resist that CAUTION tape tip-off*, Pearl thought—and he was soon followed by Mr. Bull and Mr. Dozer. It was as if the crack in the stairs was a disturbance in some force that brought onlookers to the scene of a potential crisis, and builders to a crumbling place that needed their particular steel and concrete.

Pearl felt as though her heart was barely beating. Still and shocked, she forced herself to go and stand by the reference desk, so she wouldn't miss anything. Nichols was nearby in his chair with the paper held up in front of his face.

Yoiks had his writing pad out. "Surely," he said, "if there's someone in the city who can shape a rock into a head, there's someone who can fix a cast-iron staircase."

"Not to code," said Mr. Bull—and Mr. Nichols, at the same moment. They looked at each other.

"Wasn't it to code before?" asked Yoiks.

"Well, it would have been grandfathered in," said Mr. Dozer. "Old stuff that's still in decent condition can stay until it fails. But once it fails? It has to be repaired to code—but there's no code for cast iron and glass."

"What does that mean?" whispered Pearl.

Nichols said in a low voice, "It means you wouldn't get approval for building something out of those materials today, so sometimes you can't rebuild it at all."

Yoiks nodded, as if grateful for the interpretation. "So what are the library's options? Is this going to speed things up?" he asked carefully. Pearl knew what he meant: "How bad is this for the library?"

Mr. Dozer said, "There'll have to be an inspection, and when there is, the city's going to have something to say."

"What are they going to say?" Pearl couldn't stop herself from piping up.

"They're going to condemn the building, hon," said Mr. Dozer.

Condemn it? If the building was condemned, they wouldn't be able to stop the construction people from turning it into whatever they wanted, Pearl knew. They could knock it down, wrecking ball and everything, if they wanted. A condemned building was unsafe for everyone around it.

The silence among the adults was awful. It was the silence of adults waiting for harsh reality to hit a child.

"No," said Pearl. She wasn't yelling it. She wasn't saying it angrily. She was refusing.

"No, we can't allow that."

There was a little frustrated sigh of adults realizing that a child was not about to accept reality. Mr. Dozer went out the door; Pearl wasn't his problem.

"Coming up with more drama's not going to help, Pearl," said Bruce.

Nobody else said anything. Everyone was looking at her. She knew she was meant to feel insulted, but she didn't. She just said, "Well, what are we going to do?"

Then they all glanced back and forth among themselves. All this time, since the spiral staircase had cracked, Mom had stood watchful and silent, holding back her reaction, not offering her opinion about the questions raised by the journalist and the builders and the head librarian and the reference librarian and the page and the patron (Nichols).

But when her own daughter, the librarian's child, asked, Mom spoke.

"We'll do anything we can, Pearl," she said. "We'll do *everything* we can.

A Sidebar About Truth

You might as well tell kids what's going on. They'll find out anyway.

—M.A.M.

And then we'll see what happens. And then, when we have to, we'll move on."

"Move on?" shouted Pearl. "Move on where?"

"It'll be okay, Pearl," said Nichols.

Bruce, across the room, said softly, "Come on, Pearl."

Nobody else said anything. This time they didn't even look at each other. They looked at their feet or over their shoulders or across the room.

"*I'm* not moving on," Pearl announced. "There's got to be a way to fix it. There's got to be a way to get it 'to code.'" She thought of the raccoons in the basement and what could happen to them, and it gave her even more fighting energy. "Grown-ups give up too easy! I'm not going to! This whole neighborhood's at stake—everyone who lives here! The school and the stores and the apartments and the raccoons and everything else." She stood there panting, teary.

"Nothing is permanent, Pearl," Jonathan Yoiks said softly.

Pearl couldn't let herself hear that. It was as if darkness fell around her as she ran for the foyer, crashed through the front doors, and blasted down the steps.

It was the first time in Pearl's life that she had run *from* the library.

* * *

Pearl was not there on Thursday morning when the city inspector arrived. She was not there to follow him past circulation and into the reading room, to watch his face as he examined the deterioration of the spiral staircase and the fracturing of its supports, then the rest of the bookcases, mezzanine floor, and balcony rails. She was not there to hear him laugh a weary laugh as he ran a hand over the roses embossed on the iron bookcase ends and railings and saw flecks of rust fall through the morning beams of light. She was not there to hear Alice sniff as she watched from the children's room doorway through the 800s to the mezzanine. She was not there when he filled out the form, slid it into a plastic sleeve, and posted it on the front door. But she couldn't avoid it forever. It was firmly up when Pearl came home from school.

And CONDEMNED was on it.

But.

"It's only the reading room," said Simon. "And the spiral staircase, of course." In short, anything with cast iron. And it counted the glass floor of the mezzanine that had long since been roped off from the public out of common sense—and was now officially closed.

It meant that the library could be open as long as the entrances to the spiral stairs from below and the mezzanine from above stayed off-limits.

"It's one more strike against us," said Simon.

"One more item on the budget," said Bruce.

And Pearl knew, without needing Ramón or anyone else to spell it out for her: one more nail in the coffin.

The condemned notice was an unthinkable, unspeakable change. Pearl let out a roar. She flung herself toward the back hall, crashed through the garden door, and slammed out.

Everything in the garden waited silent and unresponsive around her. The pines and yews stood there dark and evergreen, and Vincent just stood there with her empty neck, her empty hand.

The sun went down behind Oleg's apartment building, and the garden turned cold and dark. Nobody came looking for Pearl—not Francine, not Nichols, not Simon, not even Mom or Ramón or Alice or Bruce. She sat alone with her back against the only remotely warm place at the stone base of Vincent's pedestal, the grass under her bottom cool and dampening, the

lights going on in the apartment windows, the trees darkening from green to blue to black as the evening grew.

Pearl sat with her fingers laced through fading grass and lavender on either side, combing through the fronds, crumbling the old blossoms. It felt as though her fingers were the only things holding her to Earth.

She didn't know how much time had passed when she suddenly noticed movement, something small coming toward her through the grass. Mary Ann.

Pearl felt in her pocket for a pen and found a Sharpie, but couldn't find anything to write on. Mary Ann shook her head, a motion that seemed to say, *That's all right.* She sat like a cat, forepaws set neatly together, rounded back in a hump, tail curled around herself, on the chilly rocks beside Pearl. The two of them waited there together.

Waiting for what? Pearl asked herself. She didn't have an answer.

When at last Mary Ann rose and trundled toward the back of the library, Pearl stood up, too. She was stiff and cold. Mom was standing at the back door looking out for her.

Mom pulled Pearl in. "You okay?"

"Yeah," said Pearl. It was a lie, of course, told by a child to comfort her mother.

38: THE DAMAGED DEN

OCT 21-22

It got warm that weekend, sunny and beautiful, maybe the last gasp of summer. As Pearl walked through her neighborhood that weekend, she considered her neighbors, all the people going to school, to work, to home, to the store. She looked at all of them—the old ones, the young ones, the in-between ones. She heard the different languages and laughing and crying and whining and arguing and screaming and yelling and singing, and she thought, *What would happen if every single one of these people came to the library and took out a book? If Vincent really could point each person to the one perfect book, would they be hooked for good?* She got so lost in thought that she passed her usual turn off toward Beep Street and wound up at the other end, and found herself walking the way she usually didn't, past the house she now knew was Mrs. Mallomar's.

There was the little mail slot, easier to see now that the early-autumn cold had destroyed some of the ivy. Pearl examined the garden. It was full of kitschy-cute pastel plastic fairies, little tables and chairs, and a sun-bleached resin frog holding a washed-out pastel sign that said

DON'T PISS OFF THE FAIRIES.

Smart: Mrs. Mallomar really lived here, but her front yard was made of things designed to make it look like imaginary creatures lived here instead, like whoever resided at 22 Beep Street was a bit of an eccentric. It was a ruse—a perfect way to fool regular people into never dreaming that anyone actually inhabited 22½, much less a raccoon.

That gave Pearl an idea that was so fantastic, she couldn't stop grinning. She left, giggling down the street.

* * *

The lights were on in Francine's windows, and here came Granny, pulling her wagon. *What luck!* thought Pearl, and she marched right up to her.

"I have a problem," Pearl said. "And I think you're the right person for the job."

Granny snorted. "Thank you, but I've got plenty of jobs."

"I'll do the work," said Pearl.

"Help me do this work first," said Granny. Together they carried the full wagon into the building and up the stairs, Francine opened the inner door, and they rolled the wagon into Granny's studio, which was also her and Francine's bedroom.

Talk about a rat's nest! Things were sorted into stacks and shelves and tables: discarded

A Sidebar About Dumpsters

They have high metal sides and they can be lethal.

They can have great stuff inside with the potential to change your life, or your art.

Don't get into one if you don't have a plan for how to get out— unless you're trying to create some drama, because that's what you'll get.

This sidebar is dedicated to the fine work of artists everywhere, and also to my brother, Arak L. Mallomar.

—M.A.M.

lampshades, lamps that didn't go with them, chair legs, baby doll legs, balls, toys, tree branches, tiles, broken mirrors, ruined books, a hose, plastic flowers, chunks of concrete, curtains, wire, on and on. Beyond them were some of Granny's sculptures, posts with objects sticking out every which way as if pointing the direction in some kind of trash paradise.

"It's a different world, isn't it?" said Granny.

"This is just what I was hoping for," said Pearl. "I need to make clues to a raccoon world. Nobody can know but us. Here's what I want to do . . ."

Granny's eyes sparkled. Francine stepped closer, her tap shoes clicking.

* * *

Saturday's midnight *Moon* featured the following article and request:

READING RACCOONS TO BE
ROUTED BY DAMAGE TO DEN

A crack appeared in the spiral staircase of the Lancaster Avenue branch of the New York City Library, headquarters to the dynasty of reading raccoons who write, edit, and publish this special midnight edition of the *Moon*. It is the opinion of one reporter for this edition that the fate of the dynastic den rests on the shoulders of the human occupants of the library. There is one person— one person with two assistants—with the potential to inspire the neighborhood and the city to come to the aid and support of the library. We reading raccoons recognize the power of being a special, elite, intellectually superior population, and for the first time, we realize that this power is more important than the power of invisibility.

Recently, this paper has become aware of the theatrical gifts of certain human children, and so it announces an open call to our own kaboodle of kits. The parents of raccoons with charisma (or who have ever wanted a moment in the moonlight) should reply to—

—M.A.M.

* * *

Mary Ann was kept incredibly busy, to the point where she and Pearl worried she might be overwhelmed by responsibility. Her to-do list included:

- Write Rax Rex, short for Raccoon Recommendations, a new column of books to read. (How I like a catchy column name!) The first list included such gems as *The Kissing Hand*,[1] *Treehouse Chronicles*,[2] and even *Nuts to You*,[3] which was about those other tree-dwellers, the squirrels, whose own reading abilities were sadly lacking.
- Cover her beat—writing her regular pieces for the paper, reporting on neighborhood developments.
- Give Pearl editorial input on the even more expanded and even more dramatized story for the Halloween Howl.
- Audition young performers for their own Great Masking performance. (As is often the case in the arts, it's all about who you know.)

---

1 *The Kissing Hand* by Audrey Penn, illustrated by Ruth E. Harper and Nancy M. Leak (Children's Welfare League of America, 1993).

2 *Treehouse Chronicles: One Man's Dream of Life Aloft* by S. Peter Lewis and T.B.R. Walsh (TMC Books, 2008).

3 *Nuts to You,* by Lynne Rae Perkins (Greenwillow, 2014).

39: THE READING RACCOONS

OCT 22-23

A Sidebar About Uniforms

Uniforms make everyone look the same.

If people all look alike, you can't be singled out, so you're less likely to get hurt. Uniforms give you something to wear that isn't your own, so people can't judge you by your own clothes. Fur, for a raccoon, is its own uniform. As far as humans are concerned, we all look the same.

This doesn't mean that there is not occasionally an item of clothing that I would like to have; for example, Tallulah's soft velvet hat with sewn-on sequins, the color of a raspberry. There's nothing I would like more. Or so I thought until I saw the Reading Raccoon caps.

They are a kind of uniform, but different. They are not so much like the school uniform, clothes that smooth out the differences in privilege between students. The Reading Raccoon caps made everyone who wore them *part* of something—part of a neighborhood known for readers. Now that humans wanted to wear those caps, somehow we—the humans and the raccoons together—we were all on the same team.

"All these kids here getting reading 'rex' from the 'rax' are going to make it very bad public relations for the mayor to recommend against the library," said Alice to Mr. Bull and Mr. Dozer.

Like everyone in the library, Alice had been reading the copies of the midnight *Moon* that the raccoons left in the reading room each night. Now Alice did a very simple thing—she scanned each Rax Rex column and sent it two places:

1. To Jonathan Yoiks, via email, and

2. To the school, via a printout delivered by Pearl, for Ms. Judge to copy and hand out.

Pearl's mom made a plan to borrow copies of the recommended books from other branches in order to have extras on their shelves to meet the new demand, and Danesh, Alice's husband, promised to drive around and pick up the books.

Alice was tired just thinking about everything. It was a month from her due date, and she'd had it with being pregnant, had it with the tension of not knowing what was going to happen with the library building, the neighborhood, her job.

"You make us sound like vultures," Mr. Dozer told Alice.

"*Aren't* you vultures?" asked Alice.

"What do you know about vultures?" asked Mr. Bull.

"They hang around where something is going to die and they eat it—sometimes even before it's dead," Pearl said.

"What if there weren't vultures?" asked Mr. Bull. "We'd all be knee-deep in corpses."

"This library is not a corpse!" said Mom.

"Neither are the buildings we repurpose," said Mr. Dozer.

Simon entered then, carrying a big box.

"Package for you, Pearl!" said Mom. The return address on the box was Gully's Buck-a-Buy.

Pearl took a deep breath and pulled the tape off the box. A case of yellow

At first, when Pearl started this whole campaign, I was afraid people would come looking for us. Instead, this strange thing started to happen: People started to consider themselves *one of us.*

One afternoon, there was a small package on the basement stairs: three miniature yellow caps—small, medium, and large— with ear holes cut out. You might think they were from Pearl. You might think they were from Francine or her granny. You'd be wrong.

They were from Khadija. "I don't know if I believe you about your little raccoon friends," she told Pearl. "I just couldn't resist making miniature hats."

As for me, I couldn't resist wearing one.

—M.A.M.

baseball caps, and beneath it, a box containing twelve dozen black Halloween eye masks.

"What're those for?" asked Simon.

Without a glance at Mr. Bull and Mr. Dozer, Pearl said, "They're to save the spiral stairs."

* * *

Later last night in Granny's studio, after they'd finished their construction of the raccoon world, Francine and Pearl had moved on to their next project: the baseball caps. They'd argued about what to write across the bill of the cap. Francine wanted the whole thing spelled out, but I'M A READING RACCOON was too much to write legibly, and READING wasn't much of a message. They settled on:

"What if they don't know what it means?" Francine said.

"Then they'll ask," said Pearl. "And I'll say, 'The two *R*s stand for Reading Raccoons.'"

Francine said, "And they'll say, 'What are Reading Raccoons?'"

"And then we'll tell them," said Pearl.

That was the plan. Even Gully was in on it. And by the end of the night, they'd made more than a hundred Reading Raccoon caps.

They wore the hats to school. When kids said, "Where'd you get the cool hat?" Pearl and her friends just said, "Gully's Buck-a-Buy." He was selling them on special for $2—the only thing in his store that cost more than a buck.

"Twice-a-buck, twice-the-luck," said Gully to the kids who shopped for caps. For the moment, he wasn't anybody's enemy.

Soon enough, kids in the other grades were after them, too. Even Ms. Judge herself asked for one, and Pearl made hers a special pale pink, so she would stand out from the crowd. After a few days, Bruce told Mom she was going to have to relax the "no hats in the library" rule or they'd have to buy some more coatracks.

Meanwhile, Mom, Alice, and Ramón were churning out library cards to meet the demand of Ms. Judge's giant pile of applications. Pearl's plan was working: As kids stopped by with their parents to get their library cards, sign the register, and take the oath, they couldn't help buying a cap across the street.

When Jonathan Yoiks heard that profits from the caps were going to support fixing the spiral staircase, he bought two. He put one on his head and carried the second one out the front door, down the driveway, and into the garden, then took a run up to the statue and hooked the cap over Vincent's beckoning left hand. The bright yellow cap hung there like an autumn leaf on a tree, the bandit mask glimmering on top. The effect was oddly festive.

It was all a strange double scenario.

In the best case, the library was bustling, full, getting ready for a party.

In the worst case, the party would be a last gasp.

40: MR. GULLIVER AND MR. NICHOLS

After school, Gully beckoned to Pearl and Francine, who were in a hurry to get to the library. They stopped mid-jog and went into the store.

"Running makes people look guilty," he commented.

"You think everybody's guilty," said Pearl. For a moment they stared each other down.

But then Gully pulled a bright blue Reading Raccoon hat from under the counter. "Looky here. Anonymous donor. Actually—your homeless friend. Came in with an old credit card I never thought would work and bought a gross of caps. Wanted to make sure anybody who wanted a hat got one."

"Don't call him gross!"

"No, a gross is a quantity. A gross means a hundred forty-four caps," said Gully. "Mysterious guy, your friend. He had a job like that, you know." Gully tilted his head toward the library.

"Like what?"

"Contractor, construction, architecture like Mr. Dozer. Not that he was much good at it."

That just sounded like trouble, Gully trying to create drama where there was none. Pearl's neck got hot. But also—she couldn't help being interested. Mr. Nichols *had* mentioned that he'd been an architect. Had Gully uncovered the story of the mysterious Mr. Nichols?

"Don't know, do you?" He jerked his chin toward the truck. "I thought librarians were supposed to be the smart ones. But nobody over there picked up on the facts about that guy. He got a surprise when I mentioned it to him, let me tell you!"

"Thanks about the hats," said Pearl stiffly.

What was the story? She couldn't ask. She couldn't afford to alienate Gully, not now that he was her hat supplier! Francine placed a handful of tiny plastic pumpkins on the counter, the kind Alice had been using as prizes for kindergarten readers. Pearl knew she was trying to make peace, that she could see Pearl was about to go up in smoke.

"Curious, aren't you?" Gully said.

"No!" Francine said. She grabbed Pearl by the wrist and hauled her out the door.

"Thank you for shopping at the Buck-a-Buy," Gully called after them. "Ask your old pal about his bird building."

"*Will* you?" Francine asked Pearl, as soon as the door closed behind them.

"I'd better ask him alone," said Pearl. Francine nodded and waved before turning to go upstairs to her own door.

* * *

But Nichols wasn't in his usual spot. Pearl went to the reference desk. She asked Ramón extremely quietly, "Would you do a search for something online?"

"Is it a secret?" Ramón clicked his computer awake. "What are your search terms?" he asked formally.

"Nichols. Birds. Building. Architect." She could have done it herself. No, actually, she couldn't have. She needed Ramón with her now.

When the page finally loaded, he said, "Oh," as if he'd gotten bad news.

"What?" She skimmed the words on the screen.

"A wing collapsed," said Ramón.

"A bird wing?"

Ramón read some more. He said, "Uh . . . The William T. Quayle Birdcraft Museum, Hudson Cliffs, New York. Somewhere upstate. A whole wing. A whole section of the museum. Four years ago, Pearlie."

A building collapse was front-page news. It had even been on the front page of the *Moon,* even though the building was a smallish one far away. But they hadn't known Nichols then.

"'Construction weakness,'" Ramón read in a whisper. His eyes were grave. "Dreadful."

Pearl read, "'Seven dead, plus fifty-nine irreplaceable endangered bird specimens destroyed.'"

Ramón put his finger on the name of the construction company. "'The company head, Christopher Nichols, could not be reached for comment.'"

"This must be what Gully was talking about," said Pearl. "What does it mean?"

Ramón held his thoughts for a moment, then answered, "'No comment' often means someone doesn't want to talk to the press. In this case it looks like he may have been responsible for some kind of error in construction." Then he clicked again and said, "Yep."

"What?"

Three months later, there was a tiny, inch-long follow-up story in the *Moon* about how the Birdcraft Museum had been demolished because of fears of "structural weakness." And then Ramón pointed something out: "'The search continues for the head of Nichols Construction, missing since the accident and presumed dead.'" He added, "I think the search probably still continues."

Pearl hit the escape key to make the computer go back to the library's home page. "Do you mean they're still looking for him?"

"Could be," said Ramón.

"What should I do?"

"Tell your mother."

Mom understood the importance immediately. She and Pearl went up to the third-floor office and dialed Jonathan Yoiks. Pearl took the phone from Mom, and Mom let her.

"Hello, this is Pearl Moran."

"Pearl! How's the library?"

Pearl imitated Mom's "everything's dandy" voice. "Are you coming to our celebration on Halloween?"

"What's better than a re-heading on Halloween?" He sounded suspiciously cheerful.

She said, "When is my *Unique New Yorker* profile coming out?"

"Oh, Pearl." He didn't bother being gentle. "I think it's doubtful that it will."

"Why not?" She was appalled at how small her voice sounded.

"Well—*Unique New Yorker* typically has an adult readership—"

"*So?*" demanded Pearl. Mom put a hand on her arm. "You don't think adults are interested in libraries?"

"It's just that most of your interview consisted of a not-exactly-realistic story."

"Predictable!" said Pearl.

"My editor says our readership—" Yoiks began. He stopped. He cleared his throat. He started over. *"Pearl,"* he said pointedly. "How nice to hear from you. Is the head there yet? Will you do me a favor and let me know when it comes?"

"It's coming on Halloween," said Pearl.

"Well, I hope that helps lift your spirits," said Yoiks.

(But he didn't know what could possibly lift his own, after the rejection of his heartfelt story.)

Then Pearl asked him to look into another building with structural problems: the William T. Quayle Birdcraft Museum in Hudson Cliffs, New York. "Ramón says you have one of those newspaper-searching tools," she said. "We're trying to find out what happens when a condemned building gets, um, *repurposed*."

"Let me do a brief search and send you a few links."

"See you Halloween—wear your best book costume!" said Pearl.

They hung up.

"Do you think he'll find out anything else about Mr. Nichols?" asked Pearl.

"Anything like what?" said Bruce, now in the doorway.

"Anything like, maybe he was responsible for a building collapsing," said Mom.

"Gully told me," said Pearl.

Then Bruce said something very rude about Gully, something you could never print in a family newspaper.

"Bruce!" said Mom.

"Well!" said Bruce.

A Sidebar About Profanity

It looks worse in text than it sounds in speech. And it seems to release the same emotion I release through growling.

—M.A.M.

41: HEADLESS

OCT 27-29

Bruce finished some projects that week. He dropped the first—in a big yellow envelope—onto the kitchen table one night. Dinner was on the stove: homemade chicken soup, but Bruce claimed he wasn't hungry.

"Read it after I go," he said. "Don't open it until I'm down the stairs, up the street, down the subway, and across town."

"Not like you're worried about what she'll think or anything," said Pearl. "So dramatic!"

"Don't let the door hit you on the way out," said Mom.

He blew her a kiss and was gone.

Mom tore the end off the envelope. Pearl pulled her chair close and they turned their attention to Bruce's papers. He'd made a plan, some detailed sketches, and a wish list for the library. On the list were new wiring, new internet, and a new burglar alarm, plus the alarmed gate for the garden, and everything else he could think of that would be needed to bring the library up to code and into the 21st century. The spiral staircase would be restored; so would the iron roses on the bookshelves in the reading room. The children's room would have a new extra door that was four feet tall, for the littlest kids. The Memorial Room would be turned into a young adult section with a 1950s diner motif, plus a little event stage for poetry readings, he said, though Pearl thought Francine and Simon would say karaoke.

"He's not going to be able to make it look more profitable than Mr. Bull and Mr. Dozer's plans for new housing," Mom said.

"Nobody could," said Pearl. "It's like the Disney World of libraries."

Mom quoted a book: "'If only, if only,' the woodpecker sighed."[1]

"Well, I'm proud of him," said Pearl. "He's telling us his own version of how he wants things to be."

Mom snorted. "That's the trouble. It's just for us. It's a love letter. He doesn't ever intend to submit it. Not that they'd ever fund it."

"It's perfect," said Pearl, uncertain why she felt uncertain.

"It would never happen."

"Why shouldn't it?" demanded Pearl.

"The library board would never take this seriously," Mom sniffed. "They'd think Bruce was making fun of them." She stood up and went into her room and closed the door. Then she called, "It's a *fantasy* library!"

"Come out," said Pearl. When nothing else happened, she went into the bathroom, brushed her teeth, and got in bed. What would the library board think when they heard about Reading Raccoons? What if everybody thought *she*, Pearl, was in a fantasy land? What if they thought she was just a liar? Mom came out of her room and sat in her pajamas on the floor, leaning against the side of Pearl's chair-bed, her back to Pearl.

Pearl laid her open book, one by Philip Pullman,[2] facedown across her stomach and touched Mom's hair.

---

1 From *Holes* by Louis Sachar (Farrar, Straus & Giroux, 1999).

2 *The Golden Compass* by Philip Pullman was first published in the U.K. as *Northern Lights* (Scholastic, 1995).

Mom reached up and grabbed Pearl's hand. "Nobody could care more," she said. She explained that Bruce had also written a regular budget, in addition to this pie-in-the-sky budget. "Nobody could write a better one. But nobody could beat the housing plan financially. We just don't have the numbers. And the city does need more affordable housing."

"Is it going to be affordable enough for us to move into when you lose your job?" asked Pearl.

Mom had to laugh. "Hell, no," she said. And then she started crying right in front of Pearl. She put her hands over her face, dropped her face to her knees, and all of a sudden was sobbing.

At first Pearl felt like this was happening on TV, as if this was something that had nothing to do with her. But it was true, it was real, it was really her brave mother crying on the floor. She started crying herself, but stopped right away, because both of them crying would have been too much.

Instead, she tried to do what Mom would have done if it was *her* crying.

She climbed out of her chair-bed, went to the stove, and put on the tea kettle. She put two pieces of bread in the toaster and pushed the button down. When it popped, she used a butter knife to scrape the too-hard refrigerated butter onto the toast in little curls, and when they melted, she spread them. She set the plate of toast on the table next to Mom.

But Mom didn't even notice. She knocked the plate with her elbow, and the toast fell to the floor.

"Oh," she said, looking up. "Sorry, but—Pearl, what if it's just not going to work out for us? Not with Bruce or the library?"

Pearl picked up the toast and flung it into the trash. Mom blew her nose, tossed her tissue toward the trash, and missed. "You're the mom," Pearl said. "What *do* we do?"

Mom didn't answer. She went on sitting there. So Pearl went into Mom's room and closed the door.

After a few minutes, Mom knocked on the door, her cheeks very pink. "Enough of this moping!"

Pearl said what she had been thinking to herself while she'd waited. "You can take us out of the library, Mom, but you can't take the library out of us."

"You're right, of course." Mom said. "Let's get out of here, Pearl girl. Let's go get ourselves an ice cream."

"But I already brushed my teeth! I'm already in my pajamas!"

"You're the kid," said Mom. "Quit acting so responsible."

When they had their cones and were walking back home, Mom said, "I wonder what Mary Ann thinks about relocating. Have you asked her?"

"Of course," said Pearl.

(She hadn't, not yet. But now she would.)

"Mary Ann thinks Eloise might be gone for good," said Pearl. "And you know what that means."

"Oh, Pearl!" said Mom. "My point," she added after a few moments, during which they walked through the chilly evening, licking cones that melted slowly, "is that we may be in for a new adventure, and that it will be okay."

"How?"

"I have some money saved. And I've been with the system long enough that if I lose my job, they'll pay me a severance—some money to cover the gap between this job and the next."

"The next job?"

"I can be a library director wherever they need one," said Mom. "River to river. Borough to borough. Coast to coast, if need be. Everybody needs books. So don't worry about that emotional display you just observed."

"It's okay, Mom." Pearl finished her ice cream gravely. There was nothing else to say.

* * *

So instead, she asked Mary Ann.

"Haven't you ever wished you lived in the country like a wild raccoon?"

Mary Ann waited, her eyes half shut, which gave her a snotty expression.

"You don't want to be a wild raccoon?"

Mary Ann couldn't trouble herself to write anything. She crossed her paws and looked dainty.

"You *are* a wild raccoon? A wild *city* raccoon?"

That was better, but Mary Ann was still stiff and silent and too cool to write anything to Pearl or even change her expression.

Pearl looked closer. "You're insulted?" she asked.

Mary Ann raised her chin higher.

"You're *scared*," said Pearl. "You've never lived in the country."

Mary Ann's eyes closed just for the briefest moment, and Pearl knew she was right.

"You know," Pearl said softly. "I've been to the country."

A Sidebar About Projects

When things are really bad sometimes, you just have to try to make them better. Just keep going, keep working on it, and try not to get too wacky, even if it seems like you might be wacky for trying.

If you were hoping for something deeper, well, that's all I've got.

(Kindly refer to page 297, my to-do list.)

—M.A.M.

Mary Ann looked curious.

"Bruce loves it, so once he took Mom and me camping upstate. In a tent and everything, out there in the fresh air." She paused, waiting for Mary Ann to get it. "That's right, *fresh air*. I practically had a coughing fit. In fact, I *threw* a fit. I was not a fan of mosquitoes and sleeping on the ground. And Mom must not have loved it either because it didn't happen twice."

Mary Ann raised an eyebrow.

"I mean," Pearl went on, "what would life be like without hot subway breath belching up the stairs?"

Mary Ann made a movement like a chuckle.

"Without people throwing lit fireworks into dumpsters?"

Mary Ann mimed a response to an earthquake.

"So you don't have to think you're the world's only city mouse."

More shock. "Who are you calling a mouse?" Mary Ann seemed to say.

They sat together laughing, their shoulders shaking. "I guess we'd both survive," said Pearl at last.

* * *

"Look what I've done for you, Pearl," said Bruce, and he dropped a bag on the reference room table where she was doing her math homework. The bag was heavy, packed with a wool overcoat, scarf, and boots: Bruce's winter wear.

"What is this stuff?"

He was making a big deal out of it, said he was giving Pearl a piece of heritage from his hometown, Sleepy Hollow.[3] "Have you heard of the Headless Horseman?"

....

3 This refers to *The Legend of Sleepy Hollow* by Washington Irving (published in *The Sketchbook of Geoffrey Crayon, Gentleman*, 1820). The story is fiction, but Sleepy Hollow is a nonfiction town.

He took the clothes out and assembled them on Pearl. The scarf went over the top of her head, and the coat buttoned up around it. The only way to see was to peer out between two buttons on the coat. It was hot and clumsy.

"No way," said Pearl. In a fury, she tugged off the coat without unbuttoning it and threw it over a chair. "I don't care if it *is* a book-character Halloween parade. I'm not going as the Headless Horseman. I don't want to be a headless anything. I want to be the Reading Raccoon. Head and all."

"Well, you don't get everything you want," Bruce said, surprisingly affronted. He held up his big right hand. "End of discussion."

* * *

Pearl would have loved a disco ball in the Memorial Room and a karaoke stage and a mini door just for kids. But she couldn't do those things, or any of the things on Bruce's pie-in-the-sky fairy-tale plan. Luckily, she had a project of her own.

Pearl sneaked Francine's hot-glue gun into the Memorial Room and glued Reading Raccoon caps on the glass of the founders' portraits. Then she made Simon help her carry them downstairs and hang them behind the circ desk, where they could remind new patrons of the library's illustrious past and inspire them with a promise of its bright and *long* future. And she invited Khadija to the library, thinking of her love of dollhouses, and showed her the special raccoon entrance outside that she and Francine had cobbled together.

Pearl had used some bathroom tiles to make the raccoon path. Granny had cut a piece of old awning into a raccoon-sized awning to make the entrance fancy. All by herself, Francine had sawed a mostly rectangular door from an old board she found in a demolition dumpster. On a shingle, Pearl had carefully inscribed HEADQUARTERS: READING RACCOONS, along with a small arrow scavenged from some knocked-down street sign.

Khadija knelt over it, charmed. "Is it real?" she asked. "The raccoons really use a door?"

"Don't be ridiculous," said Elsa, because of course she and Millie had come, too.

But Millie said, "Wait, aren't raccoons nocturnal? So how will they find the entrance in the dark?"

Before Pearl could say anything, Khadija said eagerly, "I could make a pretend street lamp. I'd just need an old coat hanger or some pipe and a—hmm—"

Millie said, "Find some pipe we can bend, and I'll wire it so it really lights."

Pearl straightened up. "You can do that?" she asked Millie.

"My mom builds robots," said Millie. "She'll help if I have trouble."

In a flash, Millie and Khadija dashed off to Granny's with Francine to look for something they could use.

Pearl was shy, wondering what to say to Elsa. But Elsa spoke first.

"I'm not sure if you're just the world's biggest liar," she began, "or—" She was on her knees peering into Pearl's raccoon doorway.

Pearl felt how everything could fall apart if Elsa decided she was nothing but a liar. "OR WHAT?" she said.

Elsa stared at Pearl as if she truly thought she was crazy. "Or some kind of genius, that's what I was going to say, geez, take it easy."

Pearl huffed. For a second, her fear of Elsa felt enormous. A big gold leaf came flying out of the trees and whapped her right on the side of the head as if someone had flung it. It stuck against her cheek, pressed there by the wind.

Elsa laughed. In a nice way. "I'm coming to your party," she said. "I'm going to be Harriet the Spy. Have you read that book?"

"Of *course* I have," said Pearl. "What do you think, I was born yesterday?"

"Actually," said Elsa. "That pregnant librarian who gave me *Harriet* said you were born *here*."

"Yeah," said Pearl. She wasn't sure if she should say more. She wished the others would hurry up and get back.

"That's lucky," said Elsa.

"Really?"

"Don't you think so?"

"Yes," said Pearl. "Yes, I think I am lucky. Or at least unique." Elsa smiled.

The other girls came back. They worked for another two hours—until there was an actual raccoon entrance with electric light. Because it was drizzling, they did their construction in the Memorial Room, inadvertently making it into a workshop. It was as good a use as any for that big empty space that was just waiting to be filled by whatever activity each of them got into.

Look at Millie, with her decent wiring skills. That was geeky. Here was Khadija, the dollhouse geek who knew how to envision how things would be made in a miniature world. Here was Francine, the truest friend of all (that's what she was, Pearl realized) her geeky tap shoes on her feet. Here was Pearl herself, practically eleven and she couldn't stop thinking about communicating with raccoons! Now she was a geek about books *and* woodland creatures. And Elsa—well, what was she a geek about? *Friends, maybe*, thought Pearl. Maybe Elsa was a friend geek. There she was, roped into holding things while everyone glued and wired and dug and painted. The others were talking, and Francine was singing and tapping the whole time she did anything, as usual, but Elsa had grown quiet in this group of geeks. Maybe for once she was afraid of saying the wrong thing—because then she might find herself alone.

"Elsa?" said Pearl. "What's *your* favorite animal?"

"I don't have one," said Elsa. But she didn't say it meanly, she said it like she'd never thought about it before, and was glad to be asked. Then she said, "A dolphin?"

Maybe it was a start.

42: HOLIDAY MOOD

OCT 30

Mary Ann wrote,

Are you nervous, Pearl?

Pearl lied and said no, but Mary Ann surely knew better.

So much depended on Halloween, and on Election Day the week after, that if Pearl was sane, she *had* to be nervous, and so did Mary Ann. Nobody talked about what they really were scared about: the library, the library, the library. Pearl built a mental wall inside her head and focused her worry about smaller things on this side of the wall. The raccoon costume, for one thing, and how she could get ahold of it, and what the evening would be like if she had to wear that crummy Headless Horseman getup.

The Halloween Howl, for another thing. Would there be enough people there to impress the mayor? Would the mayor even come?

When Yoiks appeared in the garden, where Pearl and her mother were carving pumpkins, Pearl forced herself to push away her nervousness. She needed this reporter, with his thin frame, his wire glasses, his notebook, his boots, his intense frown. So she didn't confront him about not putting a column about her in the paper yet.

"You're going to cover the Howl, right?" she demanded, handing him a free ticket.

(The fact was, all the tickets were free, although in exchange for attendance. Not a bad marketing ploy in itself.)

"We need the press," Pearl said, to encourage Yoiks. Let *him* bring up the *Unique New Yorker* piece.

But he didn't. He flopped on the library's back step as though he'd been stabbed through the heart. "If only I could do everything on my personal agenda! First things first, Pearl. Christopher Nichols. Nichols Construction. A builder whose building fell down. Now, why is a certain young girl interested in him?"

"She's not the only one interested," said Mom. "He's a regular here, but we haven't seen him in three or four days."

Pearl knew exactly how long. "Five," she said. Since Gully had told her he had something on Mr. Nichols, he'd disappeared into thin air. He wasn't in the garden, and neither was his stuff, other than the wad of papers she wondered about but didn't touch. He wasn't on the loading dock behind the umbrella, and the umbrella wasn't there, either.

Yoiks tipped his head to one side, then went on. "This Christopher, or do you call him Chris?"

"Mr. Nichols," Pearl said.

"Is he the same guy who broke in?"

"He got *locked* in," said Pearl. She dug out some slime from inside her pumpkin while Yoiks said nothing, but Pearl could feel him regrouping.

"So, what do you know about the William E. Quayle Birdcraft Museum case?" Yoiks said.

Case? That made it sound like there was a crime involved. Pearl sucked in her breath. "Okay, if it's something bad about him

An Anonymous Sidebar

Anonymous is a word some people use instead of their name, because they don't want the credit (or blame) for what they write or draw or do.

Anonymous nouns—alligators, teenage punks, homeless—are scary in their namelessness.

Anonymous verbs—reading, gentrifying, governing—are flat and seem like phenomenons, not just actions.

Pearl and I, we prefer individuals to stand for anonymous things:

Not just anyone governing, but the actual mayor, known as Her Honor.

Not just some some fancy chain furniture store like Eastern Pine, but Gully's Buck-a-Buy.

Not just books, but *The Jumbies*[1] or *El Deafo*.[2]

Not homeless people in general, but Mr. Christopher Nichols in particular.

Not teenage punks, but Simon Lo.

As for alligators, well, we don't know any particular alligators. I don't mind if they just stay anonymous.

Signed, the not-anonymous . . .

—M.A.M.

---

1 *The Jumbies* by Tracey Baptiste (Algonquin, 2016).

2 *El Deafo* by Cece Bell (Harry N. Abrams, 2014).

that you're working up to telling us, I'd rather not know. I changed my mind. I'd rather not have *anyone* know." She dug harder in the pumpkin with her spoon.

"Let's listen, Pearl," said Mom. "Was there a court decision?"

"It sounds like you folks are on his side," said Yoiks gently. "So am I. So, after the Birdcraft Museum's disastrous collapse"—he read from his notebook—"'it was never determined whether a design problem or an error of communication doomed the construction. The court ruled there was no clearcut decision assigning responsibility.'"

Pearl thought hard. "Nobody was responsible?" she said.

"Right, and that's good," said Yoiks. "And it's lucky for Mr. Nichols, because Nichols Construction would have had to appear in court if there was a possibility that they were to blame. And then Mr. Nichols would be in trouble for not showing up."

Mom said, "I guess he thought it was his fault, and he ran. I suppose he'd rather disappear than have his name associated with a building that fell down."

"Then why wouldn't he lie about his name?" asked Pearl.

"Well, who knows it, other than you folks?"

Gully knew, that was who. Pearl understood, suddenly, the risk Mr. Nichols had taken by buying those hats, giving away his true identity to someone who might do bad things with the knowledge. "So he's innocent. The people dying wasn't his fault. Thank you for finding that out."

Yoiks put his hand on her shoulder. "I know that. You know that. Does *he* know that?"

Mom said, "If Mr. Nichols was guilty of some criminal act, then he would know it by now. He wouldn't be sticking around here."

"How would he know it?" Pearl asked.

Yoiks said, "Newspapers! Every time I see him, he's got his face in one."

Pearl couldn't help being impressed at Yoiks's observation skills. "Then why is he still—"

"Hiding? Homeless?" Yoiks said.

"Maybe he just feels bad about it anyway," said Pearl.

"Maybe he doesn't know how to make a new start," said Mom.

All Pearl could think about was that if the library closed, Mr. Nichols would spend every day out in the cold. Which was where he was now. Wherever he was.

PART FOUR:
THE PLOT TWISTS

*"The courage that my mother had
Went with her, and is with her still;
Rock from New England quarried;
Now granite in a granite hill."*

—"THE COURAGE THAT MY MOTHER HAD"
BY EDNA ST. VINCENT MILLAY[1]

---

1 From the poem "The courage that my mother had," from *Mine the Harvest* by Edna St. Vincent Millay (Harper, 1954).

43: BEHIND THE MASK

OCT 31 (SEVEN DAYS TO ELECTION DAY)

It was four in the afternoon on October 31. The portable stage Ms. Judge had lent the library stood beside the statue. Already people had brought jack-o'-lanterns, enough to line the side of the driveway and the paths through the garden to Vincent. Pearl looked down at them from Bruce's office and felt optimistic.

Bruce did not.

"Pearl," he began carefully, "I don't want you to be disappointed. A party like this might make for higher circ, and it might even get us enough donations to buy a couple of computer terminals, but it won't change anything unless the library was already the heart and soul of the neighborhood."

"It's supposed to help people see what they'd be missing if they let the library close," said Pearl. "So they will vote for it."

It was as if he hadn't heard her. "I've just spoken with the mayor's office. She's appearing at some fundraiser for the fire department, and she's running late. I doubt she's even coming."

Since it was the first Pearl had heard that Her Honor was even considering coming, this seemed like decent news. "How will you know if she's not?"

"If she doesn't come," said Bruce. "Then I'll know."

He seemed dejected, so Pearl pulled him to the window. "Look at all the pumpkins." The jack-o'-lanterns, even unlit, seemed to pump out their own orange energy into the green, dusky garden. More people were arriving as they watched—kids and grown-ups carrying pumpkins and placing them in a line along the sidewalk, more and more.

"That's a lot of jack-o'-lanterns," was all Bruce said.

And now here came Gully, carrying a big cardboard box. From the way he was walking you could tell he was pleased with what he was about to do. *Uh-oh.*

"Ew, what's he up to?" asked Pearl.

Then Ramón emerged behind Gully, beaming. Gully set the box on the ground, gesturing to Ramón, who lifted a jack-o'-lantern and held it up so Gully could put something inside.

"Oh, it's candles!" said Pearl. "Little candles for the jack-o'-lanterns."

"Oh," Bruce said. "Well, that's generous of him. I thought Gully hoped the library would go down in flames."

That reminded Pearl how much she missed Nichols—still absent.

"You could be generous, too, Bruce Goose," she said. "The raccoon costume . . . ?"

"Not a chance, Pearlie girlie. I'm going to need that when—"

When? Not *if?* So Bruce was already counting on having to leave, having to go back to being a park ranger? Pearl talked right over the end of his sentence, so she wouldn't have to hear it.

"I used to wish you were my father," she said all at once, before she lost her nerve.

"Not anymore?" he said. He blinked and turned his face away. "I see."

Pearl leaned on the doorjamb, feeling weak. She had meant for what she said to make Bruce feel good, because she thought he was feeling bad. But all he had heard was that she *didn't* wish he was her father anymore. She wanted to hear him say that he wished she was his daughter, that he wasn't leaving. She was scared of what it meant that he didn't. After a moment, she said, "I'm sorry, Brucie, but I really need the raccoon costume."

Unfortunately right then Mom appeared from the hallway. How long had she been there?

"Pearl, go downstairs," she said. "I've asked you not to nag Bruce about that costume."

"Fine!" said Pearl. She picked up the bag with the awful Headless Horseman costume. But she didn't move. She stood glaring at both of them, but nothing she could think of seemed worth saying. She wanted them to fix things.

She went pounding down the stairs to the children's room.

"Pearl, where's your costume?" asked Alice.

"Right here," Pearl lied. She flapped past Alice, dropped the bag on the floor, and hurried to the front window to see what all the honking was about. A white van had pulled up. The honking got louder as Simon, Joey, and three teen girls opened the doors and jumped out. They all wore black shirts with a full moon and a dog on the back. A howling dog.

"Alice! Do you know what that is?"

Alice went over to the window, her hands cradling her belly.

"Simon's nameless band?" said Alice.

"Look at the shirts!" said Pearl. Simon's nameless band was nameless no more—and they even had swag with their names on it! She called up to Mom and Bruce, "Lo's Coyotes are here!" They all ran outside.

The five band members stood in the driveway, holding guitars, drumsticks, a violin in its case.

"Lo's Coyotes," said Joey. "He's Lo. Simon Lo."

"Get it?" said Simon, grinning. "The *band* of coyotes."

"So you finally chose a name!" said Bruce.

"And Pearl's our emcee," said Simon.

"What's an emcee?" said Pearl.

"It's what she's been doing for weeks, isn't it, Bruce? Prepping audiences, telling 'em tales. Francine's the illustrator, the performer. Pearl's the storyteller, she's got the words to deliver."

"But they're coming about *Vincent*," protested Pearl. "They're coming for the costume contest, and the raccoons. They're coming for Lo's Coyotes. Not for me!" And yet Pearl felt her confidence gathering together under her heart so that she stood taller, like a building, wanting to do whatever was needed.

"Pearl, you're the reason they care about any of those things in the first place. You can talk anybody into loving this place."

"But what do I have to *do*?" said Pearl.

"Emcee means Master of Ceremonies," said Bruce. "It's what you've been working up to all this time, Pearlie." He took her by the shoulders and spoke softly, just to her. "Go ahead and tell your story, Pearl. Put in all the pieces you've experimented with, and all the ones you've been working on for so long. Make it the best telling ever." He raised his voice, looking around. "And get Francine in that Rock Lady costume to do her bit." Even louder, "And if I'm not back in time, you guys need to get onstage without me." He nodded to Lo's Coyotes.

"Where are you going?"

"I'm doing what *you* told *me* to do. I'm going to get that mayor and bring her back here!" He strode off through the alley and turned in the direction of the subway.

Pearl's knees felt weak. At the same time, something had lit inside her, like a jack-o'-lantern with a candle that had just met its match.

"Simon, why does it have to be me?" He just looked at her for a second, his mouth in a firm line. Then he towed her over to Oleg, who was setting up an apple-biting game with Alice.

Simon said, "Tell Pearl what you told me. Tell her about the kids in the audience at school."

Oleg pointed a finger at Pearl. "You—it's you who scared them. Yeah, Francine freaked them out, but you were the one who scared them and made them want to come and see." He waved his hand at the library, at Vincent. "You made them feel like it would be cool to come. Like they were invited."

Pearl puffed out her cheeks. Hadn't she practiced and worked precisely for this moment? She told the nervous part of herself to shut up and got ready to scrape the sky.

Mom butted in. "Simon, get those microphones set up. Pearl, throw that costume on, and come back down here in it, pronto."

Pearl squeezed the Headless Horseman bag and made a decision, but not the one Mom thought. "I'm going," she told Mom.

"Our little Pearl, the Master of Ceremonies," said Alice, rotund in her Humpty costume. "Perfect." And she huffed as though at least one thing was in order. Mom put an arm around Alice's egg-costumed shoulders and walked her down the driveway, past the glowing jack-o'-lanterns.

Pearl went into the library, but she didn't go upstairs to get ready. She went downstairs to the basement. Mary Ann and Arak were wide awake, bright-eyed and bushy-tailed.

"It's a go," Pearl said. "Will you be ready?"

Together the raccoons gave her thumbs-ups, their teeth showing.

"Haven't seen Mr. Nichols, have you?"

Mary Ann shook her head.

Pearl charged back up the stairs and emerged into the hallway.

"Pearl! Are you going to get ready or not?" It was Oleg.

"Right this minute," she promised. "What about you?" He was just wearing jeans and a black T-shirt. "You don't look like someone who is about to present the library with a new head."

"Oh, I'm ready." Oleg whipped a Day-Glo rag out of his back pocket and pulled it over his head. In glow-in-the-dark letters, it said ROCK STAR.

"Where'd you get that?" Pearl said in admiration.

"Francine helped me make it," he said. "Now go!" He turned and walked away, too.

Pearl stood there alone.

Okay! she thought.

She threw the Headless Horseman bag into the yew bushes, and made a dash for the library door. The place was mobbed. A crowd of people blocked the foyer, waving library cards as they approached. Ramón was manning the back hallway, selling beautiful prints of Yoiks's ghostly headless Vincent portrait. A steady stream of people flowed from the front door through the back hall. Pearl dodged them all, sprinted upstairs before anyone had time to notice her.

She passed the eerie second floor, with the caution tape crossing the reading room entrance, a plastic sheet covering the doorway. Bruce's office was dark, but Pearl didn't need to turn on the lights. By now the entire neighborhood was there, all of Lancaster Avenue, and a bunch of people from neighborhoods beyond. Babies in frontpacks, toddlers in backpacks, teenagers in packs, grown-ups in pairs. Loads of little kids in costume were straining at their parents' hands or running amok, even climbing the statue. She scanned the crowd for Nichols. Would he really miss this? How could he?

Other than Nichols's absence, it was great: Elsa was Harriet the Spy. Someone was a pig, maybe Wilbur from *Charlotte's Web*.[1] A little kid in a stocking hat was Peter from *The Snowy*

----

1 *Charlotte's Web* by E. B. White, illustrated by Garth Williams (Harper & Row, 1952).

Day.[2] There was a robot with blinking lights on top of some familiar-looking sloppy socks: Millie? It figured she would know how to wire that—even if Pearl wasn't sure which robot book it was from! Khadija was dressed as the Queen of Hearts from *Alice in Wonderland*, that was pretty cool. Some kids were even acting out the Rock Lady thing, chasing each other up and down the paths. Pearl couldn't believe she'd somehow convinced all these kids—the same ones who couldn't spare a moment to think about her at school—to be here, doing this, for *books*. It was some version of a dream come true.

Pearl took a moment to think what Bruce would do if he knew what she was about to do. She decided things couldn't get any worse than they already were. She couldn't take any more moments. Now was the one that counted.

The raccoon costume was even heavier than it looked, and the second she undid the hook at the neck, it fell from the hanger with a rip of opening Velcro. Pearl pointed the toes of her sneakers and maneuvered them through the legs of the costume, hoisting the torso up around her waist. It was way too big for her, just as Bruce had said. She tried to tuck some of the leg material inside her sneakers, and settled for rolling them under at the ankles. Then she hefted the furry shoulders up over her own and hooked the costume at the neck.

Pearl's stomach was doing funny things, but there was no time to get out of the costume now. She thought of one of the first things Mary Ann had ever told her. *Just do it.* The slogan didn't say anything about waiting until the moment was just right and getting into huge trouble if you miscalculated.

No guts, no story, thought Pearl. It was time for the final step: the head.

---

2 *The Snowy Day* by Ezra Jack Keats (Viking, 1962).

A Sidebar About Surprise

You go along and along and you think you know what to expect—a sort of rule of routine that comes with having been in one place a long time. And then, whammo, something comes out of the blue and you do one of three things:

1. Freeze
2. Leap into action
3. Zigzag

Pearl did all three.

—M.A.M.

She pulled a step stool over to the tall cabinet and began to climb up.

She reached the top step and lifted the hollow raccoon head off the upside-down metal garbage can that supported it. The head was bulky, heavy, high—hard to lift off the can.

Come on, muscles! She tugged harder on the head. Just one more careful pull—

The raccoon's head loosened suddenly, and Pearl fell backward off the step stool and landed in a sliding pile of books and magazines. She gripped the head tight with one hand, her eyes squeezed shut in horror. She wouldn't drop the head, she couldn't, and she didn't. She anticipated the clanging, bashing fall of the garbage can, but it didn't come.

"PEARL!" Francine hollered from far away at the foot of the stairs.

Pearl pulled the raccoon head over her own head.

"Coming!" she yelled, her voice muffled inside the head. She stood still for a moment and ran through her story in her mind. She thought of Vincent, sending out power from her hand to make the books fly into the air, the stories raining down, their characters coming to life in the kids wearing costumes down below, the raccoons who had taught themselves how to read—and herself, a beautiful, fat, furry, striped, masked Reading Raccoon.

Bruce had been right about the mask being hard to see through. Pearl peered around the room: books strewn everywhere, budget plans, book posters. And there, on the file cabinet, sitting where the raccoon head had been, was not the metal garbage can—but Vincent's stone head.

44: FOUND

Pearl screamed.

She screamed just as loud as she had when she first saw the head was missing.

But this was a different scream, a very different scream.

For one thing, nobody heard it. Why?

One, she had the raccoon head over her face.

Two, Bruce's window was closed.

Three, everybody outside was making so much noise, they wouldn't have heard her even if the window was open.

And, four: Pearl cut her scream short. She choked on it. *Because the raccoon head had been hiding Vincent's head.* So someone must have put it there. Who? And when? And why oh why?

The thought of it ripped through Pearl's imagination.

All the old ideas about the crime—college student, neighborhood punk, homeless man—seemed innocent, funny, so much better than this: the possibility that Bruce, her Bruce, Mom's Bruce, *their Bruce*, had left his office one night when he was working late and made his way to the garden in the dark. What could he have been thinking when he pulled the stone head off the spindle? How could he have done this?

Then again, who else was here in the dark at night? Who else had the strength to carry the head? And who else would

Nichols work so hard to protect—because Bruce had been so kind and protective of him?

"Pearl?" That insistent yell came from Francine, stuck waiting at the bottom of the stairs.

Pearl went thundering down the stairs, clutching the rail, half blind and half dazed. What was she going to do? Who was she going to tell? Francine? Alice? Mom?

Francine said, "That's you, Pearl, right? Hey, you got the costume!"

"You bet," said Pearl. Her voice inside the raccoon's head sounded echoey, shaky.

"Check it out, Pearl!" That voice was Oleg's. She turned her head, saw his blond hair through an eyehole, saw a brand-new stone head in his arms. "Vincent's here!" Oleg was quivering, thrilled and proud.

"Come on!" Francine said. "Everyone's out there waiting for us." She put a stony grip on Pearl's furry elbow and hauled her across the back hall. Pearl was in danger of tripping over her own furry tail. Francine said, "The mayor's not here and Bruce is not here, but Simon says you've got to get up there *now* and do whatever you're going to do or people might start leaving. Rock Lady, then the costume parade, and then the band's going to play."

Where was Mom? Pearl's stomach quaked. Her face inside the costume head was sweaty from the thousand crazy feelings running through her.

But Francine was already pushing open the garden door, walking like a statue barely coming to life. The change of pace caught everyone's attention. People laughed and gasped and stood aside. Little kids pointed and screeched. Pearl held on to Francine's hand and pulled her through the crowd.

At the edge of the circle of space around Vincent's pedestal, Simon handed Pearl a microphone. "Just push this button," he said.

Pearl goggled at Simon through the eyeholes of the raccoon head and bellowed in his ear, through the raccoon's mouth, "Simon! I have to tell you—"

Francine whacked Pearl on the elbow. "Turn that mike on and *start!*"

The round cut-out raccoon eyes didn't let Pearl see peripherally, so she had to turn her whole head to see all the people. There were an awful lot of them.

She carefully lifted her baggy, furry legs to step onstage. And accidentally, suddenly, Pearl felt herself push the button.

She began the way she always began: "So. Once there was a poet."

She had been telling herself pieces of this story about Vincent for so long, she didn't quite know where all the rises and falls were, but she never had any problem starting off. This time, Pearl made the starting point in her story a blackout.

"Imagine: The power is out, and there is no television, no radio, no internet," she intoned. "The people of the city have become desperate for stories, for news, for poems, for songs, for words that aren't their own, to give them new ideas and new pictures in their heads. Vincent, the famous poet of New York, reaches out her hand, points a finger, and all along Lancaster Avenue, a different kind of power takes hold."

Francine stood to one side, leaning forward as though cradling a book. Gradually, the audience shifted their focus to her, while keeping an eye on Pearl, too.

Pearl intoned, "She wants—"

She turned to Francine, who stretched out a wavering hand.

"She wants—" Pearl said more urgently. Now everyone's eyes turned to Francine. Her glimmering raised palm begged insistently toward the crowd, refusing to be ignored.

"What does she want?" said Oleg on cue, and others took up the cry.

"What does she want?" the audience called. "What does she want? What? Does? She? Want?"

This was Oleg's big moment. He strutted along, the crowd dividing to let him pass, then pressing in again quickly to see the new stone head he was carrying. Simon and Mom appeared and helped Oleg lift the head, and the other band members came forward to help them raise it higher. The teenagers climbed up the pedestal and lifted the head into place. The crowd clapped and cheered.

"In the blackout darkness, Vincent rained down stories," Pearl continued.

She felt light inside her heavy costume. The drama in her voice seemed to come from a deep, thrilled place it had never come from before.

"The stories were heard by the raccoons first. They were closest to the statue, and felt its energy. After all, they had learned to read from Vincent's own

A Sidebar About New York City

My grandmother once told me that New York had layers—layers of people, layers of animals. You couldn't tell just by looking what layers somebody had, how unique they were. And nobody was only one layer. You might be a homeless girl who worked in a kitchen by day and danced ballet with a hip-hop boy in the subway at three in the morning, or a well-fed fat cat who still preferred hunting rats at night, or a princely long-locked man with a fuzzy-headed daughter who spent afternoons at a climbing wall. New Yorkers are really like that.

But the other thing I've learned about New York is that sometimes the layers disappear, stop mattering, and for no reason at all—or *every* reason—everyone seems the same.

—M.A.M.

poems. They had moved into the library building for shelter, and expanded their literacy to our whole library."

Some faces looked sort of blank, some skeptical, others seemed rapt. Pearl carried on.

"Before long, Vincent the person was gone, and her statue took her place—here in this very garden. Here under these trees, where the raccoons made their homes. It was Vincent who brought them to the library, as she brings the human Reading Raccoons of Lancaster Avenue here tonight."

The crowd cheered.

"And now Vincent has come to life again through this dancer"—Francine, the stone statue, made a slow, heavy twirl—"and through this rock hound and his stone carver friend"—Oleg pulled a young woman into the light, earning a rousing cheer, and together they took a bow—"and through this rock band"—Lo's Coyotes struck a chord.

Pearl finished: "Today Vincent is once more turning the library into a place of refuge—only this time, it's a literal as well as literary shelter for people who need stories. Nocturnal animals with a newspaper of their own, reaching out with nighttime news. Daytime people needing information, education, or entertainment. Raccoon kits—and human kids!—learning to read and falling in love with books. Who are they? Who? Who?"

"Reading Raccoons!" Simon roared. Francine, now standing on the amp, pumped her fist.

"Human and animal, they want stories!" Pearl called.

"Reading Raccoons!" the crowd called back.

"They want to know what the new head looks like," said Pearl, "to see if it's really Vincent, and her family of . . . "

"Reading Raccoons!"

"They're getting library cards because they're part of the library now, just like the . . . ," invited Pearl.

"Reading Raccoons!"

"They're reading books and getting educated!"

"Reading Raccoons!"

"They're smart and getting smarter!"

"Reading Raccoons!"

Pearl recited the rhyme she'd made up:

> "Their nose in a book
> and a book in their paws,
> turning the pages
> with their toes and their claws."

"Are you here?" yelled Oleg.

The crowd roared. "Yeah! We're here!"

Then Pearl began a new chant. "Reading Raccoons are here!" A roar went up across the garden. Pearl pumped both paws in the air. "Reading Raccoons are here! Reading Raccoons!" The audience chanted with her, and she felt the power of them lifting her. Simon pulled a big book—in fact it was the New York State atlas—and put it into Pearl's hands.

Pearl stood tall, stretching her arms out toward the library, and held up the atlas, flapping the covers above her head as if the book was a bird. It was a signal to Mary Ann and her relatives in the trees.

Just then, there was a rolling sound, a flutter of flapping paper, and a series of gentle *whoomps* as the strung-up, scrolled-up props, made of cardboard painted to look like book covers, filled with old pages from the *Moon,* bounced down on strings from the treetops. The big books flapped above the crowd. "The books opened their covers like wings and flew! And out of them came stories." Pearl extended a hand toward the audience. "Book characters! Let's march!"

Shouting, laughing, chattering, the kids ran toward her. With one paw, Pearl grabbed the hand of a girl in a mermaid costume—and with the other, she lifted the microphone and held it steady.

"And now," she said, "introducing the pride of Lancaster Avenue. Lo's Coyotes!"

The band sprang forward from the shelter of the amps. Simon took the mic. "One, two, three, four!" he cried, and the music blasted out.

Everyone in the costume contest—and quite a few who weren't—formed a long conga line to dance to Lo's Coyotes' jolly Halloween music.

Here was pink-haired Rosita from the Rosebud bodega, Tallulah, Khadija, Elsa, and Millie, and Jaime and his little brothers, plus Gully himself. And who was that little lady on his arm? Francine's granny! Humpty Dumpty Alice and Mad-Hatter Danesh joined the conga line. Last of all marched Francine, dancing better than anyone else, and certainly louder.

"You're a tap-dancing Rock Lady!" yelled Pearl.

"You bet!"

The last person in the parade approached the stage. She was a tall, thin, dark-skinned woman in a beautiful suit, with a jack-o'-lantern in her hand. Even looking through the raccoon head's crooked eyes, Pearl could not mistake who she was.

Pearl bounded onto the stage and thrust herself into the band and grabbed the mic. "Ladies and gentlemen! The Lancaster Avenue library's biggest fan! Her Honor, the mayor of New York City!"

45: THE MAYOR

HALLOWEEN, CONTINUED

The first thing the mayor did was bestow an honor onto the new Vincent's head: a yellow baseball cap with the black mask of the Reading Raccoon. The mayor plopped a cap on Her own Honorable head to match.

When she took the microphone from Pearl, everybody leaned forward to see what her words about their library would be.

But into the hush, before the mayor could speak, came a horrible noise—a squawking and a scrabbling.

Ramón said, "It's coming from the dumpster!" Oleg quickly went to it and lifted the lid. Pearl pushed through the crowd.

A kaboodle of little kits scrabbled at the bottom of the dumpster, acting desperately unable to get enough traction to climb out. Pearl looked around for a box.

"Simon," she said, "your guitar case."

Simon nodded, and Oleg grabbed the guitar case, jumped into the dumpster, and squatted down.

The audience mumbled, excited. What was going on?

Bold little Arak ducked into the guitar case, and the others followed. Then Oleg zipped it closed and lifted it—with a rabble of rattling raccoons writhing inside—guiding it into Pearl's arms.

Well, this was unexpected (to everybody but Pearl). The crowd stepped back, opening a path for Pearl, in her raccoon

costume, to walk to the fancy little raccoon doorway she and her friends had made around the hole at the base of the wall. Then she squatted and unzipped the top of the guitar bag to make an opening. Everyone craned and peered and peeked to see what was going on.

The first raccoon to peek out was Arak. The crowd leaned in to get their first glimpse of whatever was coming out of the bag.

A raccoon! At the sight of Arak's little face, the crowd erupted into *awws*. Then someone said, "Shhhhhh!" and the crowd shushed itself, in love with the little raccoon and desperate not to scare him.

Arak goggled at the many human feet around him. He put his left paw forward, then raised the right one toward the sign above the raccoon entrance. On the sign were *R*s, like on the caps the humans wore.

Arak made a growling sound, *RRR*.

"He can read the sign!" said a little girl, and other small children near her echoed her words. The people murmured in astonishment.

Arak seemed not to notice them. Next came an *A* as in *ak*, then two *C*s, then an ending like the *Moon*'s. *Oon*. There was only one word that looked that way, and it was the best-looking word in the world to Arak. *Raccoon.* He knew what that meant, and he puffed out his chest a little and marched proudly down the path and right into the Reading Raccoon entrance like a prince entering a ballroom.

The crowd went wild.

One by one, the other kits emerged from the guitar case and made their way through the doorway, the crowd giggling and murmuring with delight.

With that, the mayor, all but forgotten, picked up the microphone again.

She praised the artistic jack-o'-lanterns. She praised the children in their creative costumes. She praised the Reading Raccoons.

"What a neighborhood!" said the mayor.

Big cheer!

"What a community!"

"*Olé!*"

"What a library!"

"Hooray!"

Then Her Honor led the biggest cheer of all for Vincent and her new head. "Hip-hip-hooray!" she whooped, and everyone joined in.

Stepping off the stage at last, Pearl slid behind the statue to see things from Vincent's point of view. Pearl knew she had done her job. She'd kept the party going, raised a chant for the library, told her story, celebrated her hero, saved the raccoons to the best of her ability. Whatever happened to the library now, she'd done her best.

She tugged off the raccoon head as she made her way to one side of the garden. Out of the spotlight now, she could see the audience, and Mom. There she was, thankfully beaming at

Pearl with pride instead of anger about the costume, but also looking around for someone. For Bruce?

Suddenly, Pearl's happiness was knocked down, and she sagged as if she had been taken out at the knees. She remembered: Bruce had stolen the head. What did any of it matter—the library closing, her and Mom moving away, the raccoons and Nichols cast aside—if Bruce was the sort of person who would steal his own statue's head?

"Pearl! Pearl!" It was Bruce. "Where are you?" Then he spotted her in the crowd and made a beeline for her.

She put the head back on to hide, but he picked her up anyway, costume and all, and spun her around so hard, the fur tail flopped wildly.

"Put me down, Bruce! Put me down!"

He bounced her onto the grass, whooping. "Did you hear?" he said. "The mayor gave an interview to Jonathan Yoiks. She's recommending the city keep us open as a *library*. Not apartments!"

"What? We're not condemned anymore?"

"Oh, we're still condemned. Things have to be fixed. And maybe they will be."

A Sidebar About News

The tool that reading raccoons rely on to spread our news is an old-fashioned printing press, courtesy of Tallulah. We help her newsstand stay in business, and she helps us print our news.

What's news to raccoons? Just what you'd think: warnings about poisoning campaigns; maps of relocations; reports on coyotes, rats, and other true vermin; outdoor music festivals and street fairs (raccoons love those); and personal ads. Romance is important for raccoons, same as for anyone else.

Not all raccoons are library patrons. Not all raccoons know Kwame Alexander's books[1] as well as Edna St. Vincent Millay's poetry. In fact, most raccoons like gossip, not literature. They like to stay on top of who's tearing down and who's building up. They need to know about rat poison so they can warn the rats, so that the rats will stay allies, not enemies.

It's okay. There's no need to be a snob. Remember the layers. City or country, library or tree, literature or gossip: We reading raccoons all share one story.

—M.A.M.

....

1   Such as *The Crossover* by Kwame Alexander (HMH Books for Young Readers, 2014).

"You mean they might approve your Disney World library?"

Bruce laughed. "Not likely. We'll be lucky if the new budget is enough to fix the stairway. And we'll definitely lose personnel."

How could Bruce be happy about that? Pearl was amazed that he wasn't yelling at her about the raccoon costume. But she had things to yell at him for, too, and now suspicion rose anew: The personnel he was happy to lose was *himself.* He was leaving them. But why would she want him to stay anyway, since—

She grabbed Bruce and pulled his face next to hers. "You took Vincent's head," she said. "You took it and hid it under your raccoon head and let everyone think it was stolen."

"*What?*" Bruce tried to straighten, but she held his arm and raged on.

"I stole your costume, and I shouldn't have, but you weren't going to let me use it any other way, and now I know why."

"Why would I do that, Pearl?" He sounded hurt—beyond hurt. She wanted to believe him, but what else could she believe?

With no peripheral vision, Pearl didn't see Mom come up beside her. But she heard her when she spoke. Quietly, calmly, almost peacefully.

"It wasn't Bruce, Pearl."

"Then who?"

"It was me who hid the head."

"You?"

Mom?

Mom?

46: THE HEAD ROBBER

HALLOWEEN GOES ON

Words came pouring out of Mom. "I'm the one who took Vincent's head and hid it under the costume head. Bruce didn't know anything about it. If you're going to be upset, be upset with me. I had a good reason, Pearl. Can you please take off that head so I can see your face?"

And as soon as Pearl did, she was surrounded.

"Here she is!" Francine cried, rustling up in the Rock Lady costume, happy and glittery.

"Hey, Pearl!" Oleg's face glowed, so proud was he to have found the stone, found the stonemason, broken the bad spell over the library and the garden and Vincent herself, and had his head hoorayed over by the mayor of New York City—Her own Honorable self!

"Pearl, you were great!" That was Millie, with Khadija and Elsa beside her.

"You were the star!" Simon seemed joyful: Not only was Pearl a success, but so was he—and Lo's Coyotes.

Pearl stood in the middle of her amazing friends. How could she tell them what had happened to Vincent? What would happen if they knew about Mom's theft?

She couldn't bear to look at her mother.

So she focused her energy on her friends. She acted. "You guys were the stars," she said. "You were a great Rock Lady," she told Francine. "The new head looks spectacular," she told Oleg. To Millie, Khadija, and Elsa, she said, "Thank you for building the raccoon door. It was a hit!" To Simon, she said, "You Coyotes can really rock."

Pearl stayed with her friends, letting them float her away, avoiding Mom. Pearl's fury kept her from letting Mom into her thoughts, but she could feel Mom near, knew Mom's worried eyes were on her. Pearl didn't want to hear whatever Mom had to say about Vincent. She had never wanted to hear anything less in her life!

Jonathan Yoiks elbowed his way into the group, clutching his camera.

Bruce lifted his chin toward the reporter. "What are you covering tonight?"

"The mayor pushing the library on Election Day, what else? It's breaking news, after all."

"We'll still have to do work on the place," said Ramón. "It won't just be the reading room that has to be brought up to code, but the whole basement beneath it." Pearl wondered what Mary Ann would think of that. As for this winter, she hoped the chimneys—or the trees—would be okay for such adaptable raccoons.

Pearl asked him, "What will you write?"

Yoiks tapped his chin. "How the public libraries of the city contribute to their neighborhoods and should have higher budgets, especially ones with legends about reading raccoons."

"It's not a legend, it's real," said Pearl.

"All the best legends are," Yoiks said. "By the way, your principal mentioned something to me about raccoon reading recommendations?"

"Rax Rex!" said Pearl.

"Think we could publish them in the *Moon*?" he asked. He slung his camera bag over his shoulder.

"You shouldn't promise to publish things if you're not going to," said Pearl.

"Oh, Pearl," Yoiks said softly. "You ought to know by now that people don't always get to decide what happens, even if they feel like they know what's best. My boss—"

Pearl didn't want to hear about any more decisions being made by people in authority. "A raccoon writes Rax Rex," she said. "Isn't that unique?"

Yoiks smiled and bobbed his eyebrows at her. "Well, *some* good reader writes them. Ta-ta!"

* * *

The night was winding down at last. Alice and Danesh had finished blowing out the jack-o'-lanterns and were walking up to the back door when Ramón nearly collided with them, holding out a white catalog card for them to read:

"Who wrote that?" said at least five voices.

"Vincent," said Francine.

"Mary Ann," said Mom.

A Sidebar About Ethics

I may be "just a raccoon," but I've been taught to think for myself, and one of the things to think about is doing the right thing. That's what "ethics" is supposed to be.

Good ethics means you'll do the right thing even in a bad situation.

But what if you do a bad thing—say, steal a statue's head—for a good reason? That's where ethics gets confusing.

Feel free, have a debate. Take a stand on whichever side you choose: for Mom stealing the head, which created drama and got press and brought more people to the library? Or for her not stealing it and the library being condemned and repurposed as apartments for just a few humans?

I know where I'll be standing.

—M.A.M.

"No," said Pearl. "Mary Ann doesn't write in all capitals. That's Mr. Nichols."

They looked at each other in dismay. Pearl was right. Nichols still had not been seen all evening, and look, here was his note, just as the library had found out who he really was. Now that the truth could finally be told about Nichols Construction, Nichols himself was gone.

Pearl stood still. Her heart went out to Mr. Nichols, wherever he was now, her dear friend who held so many secrets—his own as well as hers. Had he left this note on purpose tonight, when he knew he could be lost in the crowd? She wondered if and when Yoiks's article about Mr. Nichols's innocence would appear, and hoped it would be right away, before he had a chance to get so far away that the *Moon* wouldn't be his local paper anymore.

Like the sudden blart of a voice through a microphone, a realization blasted into Pearl's head. Mr. Nichols had known all along that Mom had taken Vincent's head.

And he had kept the secret from Pearl!

But she wasn't angry at him for that; he'd kept something from her that he knew would have upset her very much. That, she realized, was caring. She cared about him right back; if only she'd been able to do something to help him.

Oleg picked up his boulder-sized pumpkin to take home.

"Oleg!" said Pearl. "You're the man!" He took a bow again and disappeared.

Pearl's classmates had already left. That left Francine standing there. "And you," Pearl began, then was overcome with shyness.

"I'm the stone woman?" Francine suggested, laughing.

"Well, you're definitely covered in stone," said Pearl. Francine had at last been extricated from the Rock Lady costume, and seemed much reduced—tiny with her braids all frazzled, and her whole self covered in silver-gray dust. Francine was looking down at herself and brushing at some of the silvery coating, and that made it possible for Pearl to say, "You're the hero of the library."

Francine grinned, and shrugged, and said, "But *I'm* not the head Reading Raccoon."

And now Pearl found herself alone in the back hall. She stood there biting her finger hard to stop the tears from coming. She became aware how quiet things were. It was the kind of quiet she had once been used to in this building: the quiet of a few librarians, a page, a book elevator creaking slowly upward, and a lot of books. She had so often been the only noise here. Now lately she'd only been here with other people. Things had changed. She was not just the librarian's child anymore. She was Pearl. And that was good.

"Pearl?" Simon came into the light from the circ counter with his backpack on, his bike lock around his neck. "We did a good job. *Everything's* good. As much as we could hope for."

"Yeah," said Pearl. "I guess so."

She thought back on the evening, on the day, on the weeks and months of trying and thinking and planning that had come before. They all had tried to do something, every one of them.

Only Mom was a real live criminal, the kind that people had associated with this neighborhood all along. The idiot punk vandal head robber was—her mom!

Pearl bit her finger again but couldn't stop the tears from coming out.

Simon gently shook her shoulders and hugged her. "It's going to be okay now, don't you see?"

She nodded and tried to stop crying. Simon hugged her again. "Pearl, you're a knockout actor and storyteller. I don't know what's wrong, but so long as you're you, you're going to be okay. It's going to be okay."

"Simon," Pearl said. "You're a knockout coyote. And a rock star." She bolted the front door behind him and watched him unlock his bike from the rack and ride off down Lancaster Avenue.

"Pearl? You down there?" It was Bruce, calling from upstairs.

"Yeah?"

"Get up here, I need a hand."

Pearl climbed the stairs. She knew what she was going to find: Vincent's head sitting on top of his file cabinet.

47: WHO'S MISSING NOW?

HALLOWEEN FINALLY ENDS

Bruce waited in the doorway of his office, leaning a hand on each side of the doorjamb. Behind him, of course, sat Vincent's old head.

Pearl tried to push him out of the way. "Where's Mom? What did she do with the new head?"

"Huh?" Bruce dropped his hands to his hips.

"The new head. When's *that* going to be the victim of some crime?"

Bruce said softly, "I don't think your mother is taking any more heads anywhere, Pearl girl. The new head is still outside on the statue."

Pearl put her hands on her hips and said, "Well, I wouldn't be surprised."

She saw his throat move as he swallowed hard.

"But Pearl," he said. "You thought it was me, didn't you? Hiding it there in plain sight in my office?"

Pearl's eyes filled. Could you cry from anger?

She asked, "How could you not know Vincent was there all along? Did you and Mom have that plan together? Is that why you didn't want to lend me your costume?"

"No. No to all that. Your mom acted alone." Bruce gave her a minute to absorb the information, and to consider its implications. He didn't sound angry, just defeated.

Pearl leaned on the windowsill and looked down onto Lancaster Avenue.

"Pearl, do you have any idea why your mother did it?"

Pearl sighed deeply. She didn't want to think about this.

"I know two reasons: because she loves you, Pearl, and because she loves the library. It isn't what you think."

He walked to the file cabinet. With his big hands he picked up the heavy stone head and gently lowered it to his desk chair. He cushioned it in some old *Moon* pages, and said softly, "Think back to summer. Think back to spring. Think back to nobody coming, no circ, to the Knickerbocker library opening, and no new budget, to an inevitable slow death for this library, which your mother loves before everything else in the world, other than you."

Pearl scrunched her body small and climbed into the book elevator. Bruce lifted the statue's old head and set it on her lap. It was a very tight fit in the old elevator.

"Okay?" said Bruce. He bent his knees and squatted down to look into Pearl's eyes, grasping her hand. "Pearl—I'm leaving the library."

At this point, she was not surprised. She'd known this was coming. It was just the first of the rest of the bad things that were coming.

"Where?" She held the head in her hands, heavy as her heart.

"Back to the parks. But not up north—to New York City parks. I'm going to work for City Wildlife. And I have *you* to thank for that. You and these here Reading Raccoons."

"You're still leaving."

"I'm leaving the library. Budget reorganization," said Bruce. "Somebody on the staff has got to go. I may as well be the weak link, so I wrote myself out. Your mother is the strong one. This library is her passion. She's the rightful manager."

Pearl kicked out rudely, wanting Bruce to let go of her, but he held on tight.

"Pearl, I'll be here for her, and for you. I'm not going anywhere, not really."

He let the door close. It was pitch-dark in the book elevator. Pearl had never ridden in it at night, when there was no light coming in from the top of the shaft. And she had never ridden it with her arms and legs around the head of her beloved statue, Vincent, a wonderful neighborhood storyteller who was herself responsible for the magic that had led Mrs. Mallomar to begin reading. Weird: Pearl had never touched Vincent's head before, but her cold, smooth brow felt like something she had always known—like the library around her, and like the city around that, everything divided into fiction and nonfiction, but somehow not divided at all.

When the elevator door opened on the first floor, Bruce had run down the stairs, and he and Mom were looking in. He reached for the head, and Pearl lifted it into his arms.

"Oof," he said. "Tricia, couldn't you have found some way to save the library that wouldn't give me a hernia?"

Mom said, "Next time I'll make *you* disappear."

Pearl heard something new in their voices. Bruce was leaving the library, but he and Mom were staying together—that's what he'd told her. Maybe the library would be OK, too. For once in Pearl's life, she couldn't think of anything to say. Mom reached into the book elevator and gave Pearl her hand.

"Now, come here, Pearl, and listen to my confession."

Pearl jumped out of the elevator and pulled away. "I don't want to hear any confession."

Bruce carried the head away, to the back door and the wheelbarrow waiting there.

Mom followed Bruce, turning back to Pearl, insisting, "Come *here*." She shifted the newspapers away from the back of Vincent's head. "Look," she said.

Pearl gasped. The back of Vincent's head was cracked from top to bottom.

"A tree branch came crashing down," Mom said. "We'd removed the branch the day before, and it wasn't until the morning that I saw the crack clearly. So I had Mr. Nichols help me get it down. If it had fallen on someone—kid or raccoon—this head would have done some serious damage."

"Why didn't you tell me?"

"I was going to. Of course. But I knew your heart would be broken. I knew the city would never come up with funds to repair a statue! But before I could tell you, you saw it yourself. And that scream drew people in, and—"

"And she made me call the paper," said Bruce. "Once we got the press, people started raising questions about the building. And paying attention to us for the first time, you'll remember."

"You could have told us what was going on!" Pearl bellowed.

"There was no time to tell you. At first, I just didn't speak up. But you screamed, and everyone came running, and the drama went down like dominoes—just a little push on the first one, and that one knocked over the next."

"It sure did," said Bruce. "Pearl, I really didn't know, either."

Pearl believed him now. And Mom had gotten quiet as Pearl was getting loud.

"I just didn't say anything," she said in a guilty near-whisper. "I had to see what would happen. And at first it wasn't a big lie."

"Well, eventually it was!" said Pearl.

"But look what happened because of it." The glance they exchanged held months of—what? Trouble. Worry, sadness, work. Changes. And now, possibly, triumphs. Almost triumphs.

They gently rolled the statue in the wheelbarrow toward the pedestal so it could be found there in the morning as if, out of some new resolution made by some criminal, thief, punk, or vermin on Halloween night, the head had been returned as stealthily as it had been removed in the first place.

"Was I wrong?" asked Mom. "Doesn't it seem like Vincent was trying to help us? Maybe giving us a story, the way your story says she does? Look how *you* made the story into something that could give the library new life!"

What could Pearl say? She examined Vincent's sad old broken head as it sat in the wheelbarrow, ran her fingers along the crack, along the tendrils of her wavy hair, along her blank stone eyes and her nose and her lips.

"Poor Vincent," she said.

"Look at the new head," said Bruce. "She's gorgeous."

Pearl had to admit—the stonemason had done a good job of copying the head from the photographs.

"What are we going to do with the old head?" said Pearl.

"Memorial Room?" Bruce suggested.

"We'll have to see what happens with the district vote," said Mom. "There may be a need to come up with some kind of alibi."

"What's an alibi?" said Pearl.

Too bad Ramón was nowhere around. Mom shrugged. "A story."

Bruce put his arms around both of them.

Mom said, "Pearl, will you ever forgive me?"

Over Bruce's shoulder Pearl saw Vincent's head in the wheelbarrow, not stolen and lost.

"I guess" was all she said.

* * *

Later that night, Pearl descended the basement steps with a battery-lit jack-o'-lantern under her arm for illumination, some moo shu pancakes from the giant platter Simon's mother had sent in the van, and two books: *Guess What?*[1] and *Heckedy Peg*[2]— gifts for the raccoons' Great Masking celebration at midnight.

"*Psst!*" she said as she pushed open the door into the basement.

Mrs. Mallomar loomed up in the orangey shadows. She pushed her humped back against the elevator door to hold it open and stood eye to eye with Pearl.

"I brought some books for Arak to use to teach the other neighborhood kits!" Pearl said.

Mrs. Mallomar shook her head.

"Nothing junky, not garbage or anything," Pearl rambled on. "These are some of the best Halloween books. They'll definitely make Rax Rex, and listen, the *Moon* is—"

The old raccoon went on shaking her head. Her eyes were sad, tired. Pearl stopped talking, realizing the basement was empty.

"They're gone?"

Mrs. Mallomar nodded and waved a weary paw at Pearl to indicate that she should go back upstairs.

"Mary Ann?" Things were awfully quiet around here. "And Arak?"

Another nod.

"But where?" Pearl asked again.

Mrs. Mallomar's paw waved again, a big circle that seemed to indicate the whole city.

"Out of town? Like where Eloise is? Or where Matilda went?"

Mrs. Mallomar sighed, as tired a sigh as Bruce ever sighed on his lowest day.

....

1 *Guess What?* by Mem Fox, illustrated by Vivienne Goodman (Australia: Omnibus, 1988/U.S.: Harcourt Brace Jovanovich, 1990).

2 *Heckedy Peg* by Audrey Wood, illustrated by Don Wood (Harcourt Brace Jovanovich, 1987).

Pearl felt her confusion and oldness. She knew how it felt to think a family member would act on her own and leave you wondering why, as if what you'd prefer didn't concern them.

The old raccoon pushed the door closed. But Pearl stuck her foot in the door and jammed the elevator. She stuck her head out. Mrs. Mallomar paused as she was walking away, and looked back over her shoulder at Pearl.

"I know you'd rather have Mary Ann, but she's taught me a lot. I'll help you," said Pearl. "I can write things now. And—" She hesitated, appalled at her own daring. Would she? Could she? "I have a really good idea."

Maybe Mrs. Mallomar smiled a raccoon smile, even though her teeth didn't show; Pearl couldn't be sure, but she felt hopeful. "Okay?" she added.

Mrs. Mallomar nodded a different, quicker, more accepting kind of nod. She waved Pearl back into the elevator.

Pearl tucked her feet in, let the door close, felt the elevator lift. She jumped out behind the circ counter. Mom and Bruce were standing there with their arms around each other. Good, but—

"I'm going to need the costume again, Bruce," Pearl said. "Somebody's going to have to stand in for Mary Ann."

Mom and Bruce turned and looked at Pearl.

How could Mary Ann be gone, after all that the Reading Raccoons had accomplished? What good was it that the library was saved if Mary Ann's family was pulled apart, if neither they nor Nichols had a nest? How could that be a good resolution?

So much had succeeded, but major things had failed. Pearl thought if she totaled up the damages, the result might be worse than she could stand. She collapsed at the waist, her head in her arms on the circ counter, distraught, her mind everywhere, her heart exhausted.

"Oh, Pearl!" said Mom. "Mary Ann knows what she's doing."

"You hope," Pearl heard Bruce murmur.

All of a sudden, there was a shout from the back door. It was Danesh.

"Hey, you guys! The baby is on the way!"

A Sidebar About Reproduction

That?

Yes, that. Grow up. Oh, wait. You might be as old as me, but you're not as mature.

You think I'm kidding?

Female raccoons can mate and have kits of their own at just one year old.

Male raccoons take a little longer to grow up (same with humans)—about two years instead of one for the females.

Raccoon pregnancies last 63–65 days. Like everything else about our lives, we squeeze more growth and development into less time.

But regardless of species, when a baby decides it's coming, there's no holding it back.

—M.A.M.

NEWSSTAND

48: THE NOON RACCOON

NOV 3-4 (THREE DAYS TO ELECTION DAY)

If Mrs. Mallomar knew where Mary Ann and Arak were, she wasn't saying. Pearl figured she couldn't know precisely, but she marched on, and she made sure Pearl did, too. She wrote daily statements about the fate of the library, incorporating statistics provided by Pearl about how many new library cards were issued and how many caps had been sold, while warning readers that these numbers—generated by kids, for the most part—might not be enough to sway the vote. Unfortunately, adult humans were the only ones who could vote.

Pearl thought it was impossible to tell, in the days after the Halloween Howl, how the vote would go down. November 1 felt like the real start of winter, a steel-gray sky making the early darkness feel even darker and unpromising. "Where are Mary Ann and Arak?" she persistently pestered Mrs. Mallomar. But the old raccoon shrugged as dramatically as Tallulah did when Pearl asked her, twice a day or more, if she'd seen Mr. Nichols. "They come, they go," said Tallulah, maddeningly. Mrs. Mallomar's grandchildren had never been anywhere but Lancaster Avenue; why did *she* have such a calm attitude?

In the end, her silence forced Pearl to shut up, too. If Mrs. Mallomar wasn't panicking, she must have faith in Mary Ann. That didn't stop Pearl from lying awake when she was supposed to be asleep, thinking about Mary Ann out there somewhere in the dark, trying—to do what? After school but before homework each day, Pearl climbed the straight stairs and made a serious attempt to select the very best books to recommend.

On the way to school in the morning, Pearl dropped her latest Rex in the little mail slot at 22½ Beep Street. When she came home in the evening, edited pages were neatly rolled and tucked into the big mail slot at 8 Beep Street.

Since the column was something that was going into print, it had to be just so in terms of writing, and Pearl saw that Mrs. M was doing a lot of tweaks and twists to pull her words up to the style of Mary Ann's. But as far as the books being recommended went, Pearl seemed to be doing fine. Mrs. M went so far as to write her a note about it:

Vincent would approve.

"What about Mary Ann?" asked Pearl, never willing to let a chance to ask slip by.

Mary Ann is working on a plan of her own, wrote Mrs. M. That's reality. So she doesn't get an opinion!

Pearl didn't need anyone spelling out reality for her anymore. She was well aware of everything that could happen, that could *still* happen, even after all that she and Mom and Mary Ann had done. She kept things pushed away as much as she could behind her mental wall, but her fear about the Election Day vote squeaked through like cold November wind blowing through the pine trees: Mary Ann was gone. Pearl and Mom would have to go somewhere else, too. Only Gully would be left to tell the story of the library that was once where the new apartments were, and who could guess what kind of story *he'd* tell? Pearl brought printouts of Rax Rex to school for Ms. Judge to distribute, complete with voting locations and hours, so kids could take them home. The books, and her words, were going to work, but Pearl was on the lookout for something—anything—more.

It was all well enough for Mary Ann to go off on a mission, well enough for Bruce to continually crunch numbers, well enough for Mrs. Mallomar to quietly use the midnight *Moon* to shine a light on good books.

Pearl felt a growing desire to get loud.

* * *

On the sunny Saturday morning after Halloween, Pearl put on Bruce's raccoon costume, gathered a sheaf of papers hot off the printer under her arm, and headed for Tallulah's newsstand.

"I have a message from Mrs. Mallomar about the special edition," said Tallulah, indicating a sign she'd hung outside.

SPECIAL EDITION OF
THE MIDNIGHT *MOON*

THE *NOON RACCOON*

SPECIAL LIBRARY VOTE EDITION
ON SALE FOR A LIMITED TIME ONLY

ON BEHALF OF
MRS. MALLOMAR

"Have a seat," said Tallulah. "I'll do the honors." Tallulah switched the Saturday morning *Moon* stack with the stack of *Noon Raccoon*s, and started clipping them up like they were real newspapers.

LIBRARY CLOSING!

A Sidebar About Suspension of Disbelief

Successful fantasy writing depends on a suspension of disbelief.

Readers are predisposed to accept reality. So how do you get them to accept unreality?

By making everything else except the unreality as believable as possible. It can't all be unicorns and rainbows. The darker, more fragrant, more real the woods are— the more you'd swear you've been in those woods before, the stranger the sudden appearance of a unicorn would be, and the more acceptable. The grayer the sky, the wetter the rain, the more clearly angled the sun is, the more acceptable the rainbow will be.

So here's the thing: Lancaster Avenue wasn't some kind of magical place. Gully's gate was still rusty, still squeaked when he cranked it up or down. Francine was still separated from her parents, and Oleg still got Cs. The library's spiral stairs were still decrepit. People still screamed about the rats, the jobs, the subway, the city, the kids . . .

"Tallulah, do you think this is going to work?"

"We'll soon find out," Tallulah said. Pearl could feel the vibrations from underground as a subway train entered the station, and waited for the rush of footsteps coming up the stairs.

Lucky she was loud, this librarian's child. Lucky she'd learned something about drama.

"Special edition!" Pearl called from inside the raccoon suit. "Check out the *Noon Raccoon*! Bad news in the light of day!" She took a breath and bellowed out the headline. "LIBRARY CLOSING!"

"What?" a young father said. He turned back, one kid in a frontpack, one held by the hand.

"Dad, look at that raccoon!"

"Library closing!" yelled Pearl. She pointed a paw up at the papers dangling from the newsstand's eave. "Take one."

He dropped a crumpled buck on the counter. Monkey see, monkey do: Everybody stopped because everybody else stopped. Everybody took one. And everybody had something to say:

368

"Why's the library closing?"

Pearl asked, "How would you feel if it did?" And when she saw the dismay in their eyes, she felt her heart lift in hope.

"Don't know when the last time I was there, but still—it's an institution, isn't it?" someone said.

"This damn city, going to the dogs!" another said. "Or should I say the raccoons?" (Laughing at Pearl's costume.)

"I heard the statue got its head back. Is that true?"

"I heard they're tearing the place down. Is that true?"

"Tearing it down to make affordable housing."

"But replacing a *library*?"

"Isn't there a new library up near—"

"I hear raccoons around here can actually read. Is *that* true?"

In between shouting out the headline and using her big paws to point to the papers, Pearl talked back:

"Closing because the city thinks nobody cares!"

"Closing because nobody believes in our neighborhood!"

"Losing our library unless it gets the vote!"

"Raccoons wrote this newspaper!"

What better place for the midnight *Moon*?

What better place for raccoons who could read?

What better place for a YES vote?

What better place for a single mom and her child, who couldn't keep quiet?

Believe it, or don't. But it's more fun if you do.

—M.A.M

To each person who picked up a paper, Tallulah said, "District voting place is the Lancaster Avenue Public School, neighbor!"

And as each neighbor walked away, Pearl yelled, "Don't forget to vote!"

Jonathan Yoiks arrived, his Reading Raccoon hat on his head. He stood panting before the newsstand, and said, "The head Reading Raccoon, I presume." Pearl made a little bow. "What are you up to this time?"

"Purposeful publishing to promote the library. We can only stay open if the library gets the votes!"

"Then why does this headline say the library is closing?" said Yoiks.

"To warn the neighbors what might happen if they don't vote!" said Pearl. "Haven't you ever heard of reverse psychology?"

"Then you believe they will approve it?"

"I believe they will, but I don't *know* they will," said Pearl. "The neighborhood still has to *prove* they're really Reading Raccoons."

"Uh, you mean—"

"I mean they have to put in their vote. It's a Reading Raccoon Referendum."

She explained what would happen if the library won the vote, the way Mom and Bruce had explained it to her: Bruce was going to City Wildlife. Ramón would take partial retirement, working part-time. Alice was going on maternity leave, and Simon would take up the slack—with help from Pearl and Francine—until she returned. "Reduced staff means reduced costs. And Mom would take over as library manager."

"She's going to be the fearless leader?" Yoiks said. "That would be so great." He stared up at the papers. "'Neighborhood

Lady Leads Library' . . . 'Reading Raccoon Roots, Library Wings' . . ."

Pearl added, "'Reading Raccoons Rise, Become Library's Leading Light.'"

"That's long," said Yoiks, "but it's great." Then he leaned closer to Pearl. "I'm going to see your mom right now." Then he looked at Tallulah, to make sure she was listening, before asking Pearl if she'd seen Christopher Nichols. "I've got an idea about security—and construction, too," he said. "Stay tuned."

He picked up a *Noon Raccoon*, then he took a photo of Pearl sitting in the raccoon suit, posing like she was casually making notes as if she was running the newsstand, to make it easy for anyone looking at the photo to suspend disbelief. When he was done, he snapped his fingers.

"What?" said Pearl.

"Done," said Yoiks.

"Done with what?" asked Pearl. But he was gone before he told her.

49: ELECTION DAY

NOV 7

All day Election Day, when school was closed to host the voting, Pearl stayed at the newsstand in the raccoon costume, handing out the *Noon Raccoon* from morning 'til evening.

That night, Mom invited Bruce, Ramón, and Simon over to eat big deli sandwiches, drink beer or root beer, and watch the votes come in. And, even though it was a school night, Oleg and Francine were allowed to come, too.

"What's this poster mean?" asked Oleg, pointing at the *In the Night Kitchen* poster, at the skyline in it made of bottles and cartons, the fat, mustachioed bakers, the naked little boy falling into the milk.

"It's about how the city never sleeps," said Bruce.

"Raccoons are awake all night," said Francine knowledgeably.

"Some people are, too," said Ramón. "Trying to get everything set for the daytime. Keeping things safe and making the bread."

"Or up worrying," said Mom, shaking her head. The circles under her eyes were so dark, she could have had raccoon blood herself.

"But that's not why you love this poster, Pearl." Simon's deep eyes invited her. "It's your favorite book."

"I used to pretend I was in it," said Pearl.

The buzzer buzzed. Who else could it be?

"It's Jonathan Yoiks!" came the voice through the intercom. Pearl buzzed him in and opened the door.

Yoiks was traveling light: in a hooded sweatshirt with just a camera around his neck, his beaming face as round as the full moon.

"Did you hear?" he asked. "It just came over the wire." He held up his cell phone so they could all read the text from his editor:

TOMORROW'S HEADLINE: BELOVED NEW YORK LIBRARY STAYS OPEN!

Hurrah!

Giant cheers, clapping, stomping, and the spilling of root beer.

"Mrs. Library Manager! Speech!" announced Ramón.

"My people," began Mom, joking, glancing from one face to the next—and then stopped on Pearl's. Pearl considered the secret Mom had kept to save the library. She didn't exactly shrug it off, but she knew what she had to do. Now, for a little while longer, Pearl would help her mother build and rebuild. Mom pulled herself together. "We have people to thank, plans to make, problems to solve. What a story!" She started giggling. "Where do I even begin?"

"Begin with Vincent," said Pearl. "If she wasn't here, the library wouldn't be half as beautiful."

"Begin with her head being stolen," said Bruce. "If that hadn't happened, the library wouldn't have gotten any publicity." He smiled at Mom.

"Begin with the Rock Lady," said Oleg. "If Francine hadn't come up with that, the kids wouldn't have started coming."

"Begin with the Reading Raccoons," said Francine. "That's what *kept* them coming."

"But now listen," Yoiks said to Mom. "The construction guys mentioned your staff had an unusual idea for what's next. Have you given it any thought? Have you put it to any discussion?"

"About Mr. Nichols," Mom said, nodding around the room to include them.

"We approve," said Bruce.

"It'll work," said Ramón.

Pearl's suspicion rose. *She* hadn't been included in any discussion.

"If it works out, you'll love it, Pearl. There's just one thing," said Mom. "Nobody knows where to find him."

"I do," said Pearl.

* * *

It was as she'd expected. The rubber-banded wad of papers in the shed-shaped box were enough to track down Nichols's lawyer—who conveyed the city's offer to Nichols. (If he was going to use his credit card, he was going to have a post office box where he could get his bill.) And now Nichols was going to be a consultant to Mr. Bull and Mr. Dozer.

That's right. The architect Christopher Nichols, his name now cleared, was back and hired to consult on the library renovation. Instead of new housing, Mr. Bull and Mr. Dozer had put in a bid to restore the old library. With Mom, Ramón, and Mr. Christopher Nichols, they pored over the plans. Francine and Pearl weaseled in around them—Francine, to see how people made things, and Pearl because she thought she owned the place. Mom put a finger on the sketch of the security officer's office that they were building in the basement, along with office space and conference rooms for tutoring.

"Look," said Mom, looking into Pearl's eyes, "a bedroom for our new security guard."

"Like Mike Mulligan living in the basement of the new town hall," said Francine.

"That's me, for a bit," said Nichols, bowing shyly.

But he hadn't been too shy to suggest something else for the library basement: a section of lockers where homeless people could keep their belongings safe so they wouldn't have to carry them everywhere they went—and maybe a public bathroom down there, too, that homeless people would be welcome to use. And the staff agreed—if homeless people were part of their neighborhood, then the neighborhood branch should have services for them, too. In the face of this, Pearl couldn't bear to ask where Mary Ann and Arak would live if they ever came back.

But what was that noise? Bruce was bellowing Pearl's name from the garden door. She skidded down the hall and stopped short at the door, squeaking her sneakers. At the foot of Vincent's statue . . . was a middle-sized raccoon.

Pearl ran into the garden. "You got bigger," she said, grinning.

Mary Ann put up a paw in greeting and smiled back.

Pearl pulled out a catalog card from the stack she always kept in her pocket now, because she never knew when an idea for a story might hit her. The raccoon grabbed the card.

Couldn't stay away. Too much to write.

"I get it," said Pearl. "You can take a raccoon out of the neighborhood, but you can't take the neighborhood out of the raccoon?"

Mary Ann shook her head.

We need writers in the city and the country.
I'm the new editor in chief. Grandmar will be
reporting from the field. She's ready for a
change of pace.

At first, Pearl just laughed a little *huh.* "Literally from the field," she said. It made her remember. "Did you find Eloise?"

Mary Ann nodded, and cocked her head, asking Pearl a question with her eyes. Pearl didn't ask how, but she could tell: Mary Ann had somehow gotten the truth out of her cousin about who had stolen Vincent's head. Pearl looked at her feet, at her hands, over her shoulder—anywhere but at Mary Ann. Then she felt her friend's paw on her toe.

Your Mom is the future of the library.
As for you?

Mary Ann did her raccoon smile, showing her little teeth.

Pearl understood: Who knew what she'd do? Maybe she'd be a librarian herself, or maybe she'd write, or maybe she'd be a professional master of ceremonies with a show of her own.

"You won't tell anyone who stole the head?" she asked the acting editor in chief. What a scoop that would be! But the raccoon was her friend first, reporter second, and Mary Ann shook her head.

"Thanks," whispered Pearl. "I'm glad you're back." And then she thought about what it meant, that Mary Ann would be here alone. "I'll be the best coauthor I can be," she said, thinking of Mary Ann having so much work to do, running the midnight *Moon* by herself. "And friend."

Just then, a kit peeked his head out from behind Vincent's feet, smiling with all his teeth showing.

"Hey! Look who showed up!" said Pearl.

The little raccoon grabbed the pen. He wrote:

Arak
I rit.

"Nice job!" said Pearl.

But where were the raccoons going to live? She ran to her nook and huddled there, considering. She barely looked up when Nichols settled beside her.

"Pearl," he said. "I'm the one that showed you those reading raccoons in the first place. Did you really think I wouldn't consider them in the plan?"

"But Mr. Bull and Mr. Dozer and the city and—"

"What they don't know won't hurt them," said Nichols. "They wouldn't believe it anyway, if I told them there was raccoon space built into this plan. And naturally the renovated basement wouldn't be up to code without a storage closet or two."

"Mary Ann has to live in a closet?" Pearl said, but she felt hopeful.

"A closet with a back a foot or two short of the wall behind it, with, say, a small door so the plumber can access the heat pipes. See what I mean?"

She saw. She smiled.

A Sidebar About Friendship

It takes plenty of worms to make a good bin of compost, that's what Grandmar says. That's her way of saying don't expect all your friends to be just like you in every way. Just hope they are in the ways that matter.

—M.A.M.

* * *

The very next day, Ramón splayed an open copy of the morning *Moon* across Pearl's lap. There Pearl was, photographed at last, although she was pretty well hidden by the raccoon costume, not to mention upstaged by Mary Ann, standing on the newsstand ledge at her shoulder.

UNIQUE NEW YORKERS: MARY ANN MALLOMAR AND PEARL MORAN

In "the city that never sleeps," one reason New Yorkers are so uniquely nocturnal is doubtless the midnight *Moon*. Not the one in the sky—the one on the newsstand. In a city that's a symphony of language and literature, it's little surprise that the brains behind this deep, dark edition is a raccoon with a command of both.

Among the midnight *Moon*'s recent headlines, courtesy of reporter Mary Ann Mallomar, were tales of a cooperative cleanup after a Halloween party, as local rodents pitched in to squirrel away leftover pumpkin rind; newcomer park ranger Bruce Chambers led a Central Park animal census, revealing 212 species; and a string report covered a reunion involving a raccoon relocated weeks ago by Havahart trap.

Go looking for Mary Ann Mallomar, and chances are slim that you'll find her. What you will find is her spokesperson, Pearl Moran. Pearl is the daughter of the librarian in charge of the Lancaster Avenue branch library, recently threatened by the swing of the wrecking ball. The *Unique New Yorkers* reporter caught up with Pearl, dressed in the striped furs of the *Moon* editor herself, as she notified the neighborhood "Reading Raccoons"—a brand-new city symbol to rival Lady Liberty, or at least Mr. Met—of the need to vote for the library's new budget. The fastest-growing crowd south of Times Square, Lancaster Avenue's Reading Raccoons rally around a good story—such as the recent weird overnight reappearance of the stolen head of a beloved statue.

Perhaps, our reporter asked Pearl, Mary Ann Mallomar could shed light on this mystery? Pearl said with a shrug, "The head is back where it belongs—that's the main thing. As the old saying goes, 'There is history. There is mystery! It's a local public library.'"[1] In other words: a treasure. You heard it here first—straight from the librarian's child herself.

* * *

"So it is," Pearl told Francine, finishing her story, "that Mr. Christopher Nichols comes to live in the library—after living with Mr. Gary Gulliver during construction."

"Gully *had* to let him," said Francine. "He's on the library's side, after all those baseball cap sales." Sales of the raccoon-mask baseball caps had gone through the roof since Yoiks's story in all the *Moon* editions about the Reading Raccoons. It seemed that Lancaster Avenue had somehow gotten popular.

"This neighborhood was always exceptional," said Mom. Now everyone wanted a hat to show they were part of it.

"In the spring," Pearl continued, "Mr. Nichols will become the man of all work—security guard, building inspector, furnace man, and the consultant for other improvements. . . ."

Francine interrupted: "Who lives along with editor, reader, and raccoon Mary Ann!"

Pearl finished: "In the basement of the new library!"

"What a ridiculous story," said Francine.

Mary Ann, at their side, scrawled a hasty note.

Do tell.

---

1 These lines are from a jingle advertising the New York Public Library that played on TV in the sixties.

50: THE CHILDREN'S LIBRARIAN'S CHILD

DEC 1

Flash forward to December 1, or, as Pearl had come to call it, Demolition Day. Nichols had told Pearl that everybody would understand if she stayed away. "But I can't," said Pearl. "I'll at least stay in the garden with Vincent. Otherwise, what will she think?"

But she was inside. Why? Because Alice and Danesh were bringing their baby, Rose, to the library for the very first time.

"Rose has to see the cast-iron and glass reading room," Alice said, "even if she doesn't remember it later." The new parents didn't plan to stay once the demolition began, what with all the noise and dust that would cause. So they came early, passing through the double doors, the baby in a little carrier on Alice's front, her eyelids heavy.

"Don't fall asleep yet, little girl!" said Danesh. "Come and see what there is to see!"

They skirted around the cracked spiral staircase, padded softly up the straight stairs to the doorway of the reading room, and peeked under the caution tape.

Baby Rose gazed up at the window light filtering through the cloudy glass floor.

Pearl put her finger on a rainbow refraction on the wall. "Look, Rose!" she said.

"Take her and show her," said Alice.

Pearl reached for the baby and held her against her own front the way Alice did. She tried to imagine herself as a soft-bodied little cuddle-muffin, being carried around this building in someone's arms, and surprised herself by remembering one or two things that definitely felt like nonfiction.

Pearl carried Rose to the wall with the rainbow and held her up closer, to see the shimmer of color. Then she walked the length of the stacks. "See?" she told the bright-eyed little baby. "Remember this. You've got to. You're going to be the next librarian's child."

After the little family left, there was only a short wait before the trucks arrived. The first thing they did when they came was put up scaffolding around Vincent, and protected her with one of those green net coverings you see on buildings under construction. Workers screened off the reading room from the main room of the library, and children's and nonfiction from the cast-iron mezzanine.

And at long last, the actual demolition began: the creak of crowbars, then the whirr of power screwdrivers and wrenches, and finally the thud of sledgehammers.

A Sidebar About Stories

A good story will always rise up and get noticed. And good stories come from the strangest places. Not that there's anything really strange—or even unique—about Lancaster Avenue. Oh, no—the places I'm talking about are the ones inside people. (Or raccoons.)

—M.A.M.

Pearl was huddled in the open doorway to the book elevator when Francine arrived. Though she knew she was getting too big to travel that way, she sat there with her legs hanging out.

"Come on, Pearl," Francine said. "Come and take a peek."

"I don't want to," Pearl said.

"Be brave. Be a witness."

"Forget it, Francine."

"It's what you fought for, Pearl! You owe it to yourself."

"It'll just make me sad."

"Better to see than not to see," said Francine. "Better to know than not to know."

So Pearl let her friend pull her up and walk her to the doorway. They pulled aside the screening so they could see inside.

Ugh. It was like a blow to the stomach.

The mullioned windows had been removed and the holes boarded over with plywood. Pearl knew they would be put back again at the end, but right now, the sight was gut-wrenching. One whole side of the cast-iron framework of the mezzanine and the stacks below had been removed as though they had never been there. The room looked huge, gaping, empty, devastated.

Pearl couldn't speak. She could barely breathe.

"Gutted," said Francine, behind her. Pearl knew she meant both the room and herself.

"Nobody would ever know what used to be here," said Pearl.

"That's how it will be for the next generation," said Francine.

"Nobody will ever know what we did," Pearl added. "Kids like Rose will come for story hour with their parents and then when they're in school, they'll get their own library cards and take out books, and they'll mess around in the garden and play Rock Lady games just because they learned them at school without knowing why."

Francine added, "They'll wear Reading Raccoon baseball caps and read the *Moon* and not know where it all came from. And that'll be okay. That's how it's supposed to be. Because we'll know."

"They'll know, too," Pearl said. "I'll make sure of it."

"How?" asked Francine.

"Same as always," said Pearl. "That's what stories are for."

"Oh, world, I cannot hold thee close enough!"

—"GOD'S WORLD"
BY EDNA ST. VINCENT MILLAY[1]

THE END

1 From the poem "God's World," from *Renascence and Other Poems* by Edna St. Vincent Millay (Harper, 1917).

A Small Selection of the Books Pearl Reads

Alice's Adventures in Wonderland by Lewis Carroll • *A Victorian Anthology*, edited by Edmund Clarence Stedman • *Bedtime for Frances* by Russell Hoban • *The Book of Three* by Lloyd Alexander • *Bud, Not Buddy* by Christopher Paul Curtis • *Charlotte's Web* by E. B. White, illustrated by Garth Williams • *The Crossover* by Kwame Alexander *El Deafo* by Cece Bell • *The Golden Compass* by Philip Pullman *Guess What?* by Mem Fox, illustrated by Vivienne Goodman • *The Harp-Weaver and Other Poems* by Edna St. Vincent Millay • *Harriet the Spy* by Louise Fitzhugh • *Harry Potter and the Philosopher's Stone* by J.K. Rowling • *Heckedy Peg* by Audrey Wood • *Historical Atlas of New York State* by William P. Munger • *The Hobbit* by J.R.R. Tolkien *Holes* by Louis Sachar • *If You Give a Mouse a Cookie* by Laura Numeroff • *In the Night Kitchen* by Maurice Sendak • *In Search of Sasquatch* by Kelly Milner Halls • *The Jumbies* by Tracey Baptiste *The Kissing Hand* by Audrey Penn, illustrated by Ruth E. Harper and Nancy M. Leak • *The Legend of Sleepy Hollow* by Washington Irving *The Little House* by Virginia Lee Burton • *Little Women* by Louisa May Alcott • *Madeline* by Ludwig Bemelmans • *Matilda* by Roald Dahl, illustrated by Quentin Blake • *Mike Mulligan and His Steam Shovel* by Virginia Lee Burton • *Mine the Harvest* by Edna St. Vincent Millay • *Nuts to You* by Lynne Rae Perkins • *Paul Bunyan: A Tall Tale Retold and Illustrated* by Steven Kellogg • *Pinky Pye* by Eleanor Estes, illustrated by Edward Ardizzone • *The Princess Marries the Page: A Play in One Act* by Edna St. Vincent Millay • *Raccoons: A Natural History* by Samuel I. Zeveloff • *Raccoons Are the Brightest People* by Sterling North • *Rascal* by Sterling North • *Renascence and Other Poems* by Edna St. Vincent Millay • *The Snowy Day* by Ezra Jack Keats • *Strega Nona* by Tomie DePaola • *Sylvester and the Magic Pebble* by William Steig • *Through the Looking-Glass, and What Alice Found There* by Lewis Carroll • *Treehouse Chronicles: One Man's Dream of Life Aloft* by S. Peter Lewis and T.B.R. Walsh • *When You Reach Me* by Rebecca Stead • *National Geographic* • *The New Yorker* *Time Magazine* • *U.S. News & World Report* • *Utne Reader* • *The Wall Street Journal*

ACKNOWLEDGMENTS

The setting for this book is composed of a combination of libraries:

Fairfield Public Library; and the Harlem, Ottendorfer, Tompkins Square, and Hudson Park branches of the New York Public Library

Thank you to the following for their inspiration:

Fairfield Public Library, Fairfield, Connecticut, where I grew up and worked:

Arne Bass, Peggy Abramo, Pearl Wiebe, and Karen Whitney

pages Carol Stierle, Adéle Brownfield, Paul Meijer, Marlene Standish, Lynn Cressia, and David Kelleher

Thank you to the following for their guidance:

at the New York Public Library:
Kristy Raffensberger and Stevie Feliciano

at Connecticut State Library:
Linda Williams

at Cragin Memorial Library:
Kate Byroade and her recommendees

Maryclaire Quine
Gail Carson Levine
Bethany Pinho
Emily Young

There are so many more libraries and librarians who have sheltered and inspired me, each one a shining gem. Thank you.

Hugs also to Taylor, Kayla, Jessixa, and Faye.